PRAISE FOR
NEUROLINK

"M. M. Buckner scores two major victories here. First, she proves that her remarkable debut novel, *Hyperthought*, was no fluke: The same brilliance is very much evident in *Neurolink*. And second, she ably demonstrates that cyberpunk is nowhere near dead. Buckner is the first clear-cut new star of twenty-first-century SF."
—Robert J. Sawyer, Hugo Award–winning author of *Hominids*

PRAISE FOR
HYPERTHOUGHT

"Quick as a cobra and just as wicked, *Hyperthought* is a smart, fast-paced SF thriller, and one of the best debut novels I've read in a long time. Don't miss it." —Allen Steele

"This is one successful adventure story and a neatly packed allegory on thought and future." —*Booklist*

"*Hyperthought* comes from out of nowhere to provide a much needed shake-up to the cyberpunk subgenre . . . what a debut this is! M. M. Buckner instantly vaults to the status of an author to keep an eye on and put at the top of the reading pile . . . a genuine, lived-in near future with enough political and philosophical chops to rattle anyone's brain stem . . . Buckner writes well . . . It is quite awhile since I have encountered such an appealing, self-deprecating main character . . . a great deal of page-turning fun . . . Buckner skillfully invents and imagines a fully realized world for us to live in via Jolie . . . few authors in any genre create a credible multicultural cast so effortlessly. Add to that *Hyperthought*'s theme of questioning the nature of reality, consciousness, and perception, and the result is unforgettable." —*SFRA Review*

"*Hyperthought* is a cutting-edge science fiction that will appeal to fans of plenty of action." —*Midwest Book Review*

WAR SURF

M. M. BUCKNER

F
Buckner, M. M. APR ✓ 2006
War surf

MID-CONTINENT PUBLIC LIBRARY
Parkville Branch
8815 N.W. 45 Highway
Parkville, MO 64152

PV

ACE BOOKS, NEW YORK

MID-CONTINENT PUBLIC LIBRARY - BTM

3 0003 00082613 9

THE BERKLEY PUBLISHING GROUP
Published by the Penguin Group
Penguin Group (USA) Inc.
375 Hudson Street, New York, New York 10014, USA
Penguin Group (Canada), 90 Eglinton Avenue East, Suite 700, Toronto, Ontario M4P 2Y3, Canada
(a division of Pearson Penguin Canada Inc.)
Penguin Books Ltd., 80 Strand, London WC2R 0RL, England
Penguin Group Ireland, 25 St. Stephen's Green, Dublin 2, Ireland (a division of Penguin Books Ltd.)
Penguin Group (Australia), 250 Camberwell Road, Camberwell, Victoria 3124, Australia
(a division of Pearson Australia Group Pty. Ltd.)
Penguin Books India Pvt. Ltd., 11 Community Centre, Panchsheel Park, New Delhi—110 017, India
Penguin Group (NZ), Cnr. Airborne and Rosedale Roads, Albany, Auckland 1310, New Zealand
(a division of Pearson New Zealand Ltd.)
Penguin Books (South Africa) (Pty.) Ltd., 24 Sturdee Avenue, Rosebank, Johannesburg 2196,
South Africa

Penguin Books Ltd., Registered Offices: 80 Strand, London WC2R 0RL, England

This is a work of fiction. Names, characters, places, and incidents either are the product of the author's imagination or are used fictitiously, and any resemblance to actual persons, living or dead, business establishments, events, or locales is entirely coincidental.

WAR SURF

An Ace Book / published by arrangement with the author

PRINTING HISTORY
Ace mass market edition / September 2005

Copyright © 2005 by M. M. Buckner.
Cover art by Christian McGrath.
Cover design by Annette Fiore.
Interior text design by Tiffany Estreicher.

All rights reserved.
No part of this book may be reproduced, scanned, or distributed in any printed or electronic form without permission. Please do not participate in or encourage piracy of copyrighted materials in violation of the author's rights. Purchase only authorized editions.
For information address: The Berkley Publishing Group,
a division of Penguin Group (USA) Inc.,
375 Hudson Street, New York, New York 10014.

ISBN: 0-441-01320-1

ACE
Ace Books are published by The Berkley Publishing Group,
a division of Penguin Group (USA) Inc.,
375 Hudson Street, New York, New York 10014.
ACE and the "A" design are trademarks belonging to Penguin Group (USA) Inc.

PRINTED IN THE UNITED STATES OF AMERICA

10 9 8 7 6 5 4 3 2 1

If you purchased this book without a cover, you should be aware that this book is stolen property. It was reported as "unsold and destroyed" to the publisher, and neither the author nor the publisher has received any payment for this "stripped book."

MID-CONTINENT PUBLIC LIBRARY
Parkville Branch
8815 N.W. 45 Highway
Parkville, MO 64152

PV

For William and Nathan

ACKNOWLEDGMENTS

Deepest gratitude goes to my life partner and spouse, Jack Lyle. Heartfelt thanks also go to the many friends and colleagues who have encouraged me and critiqued my work, including in alphabetical order: Mary Helen Clarke, Joe DeGross, Mary Bess Dunn, Steve Edwards, Laura Fowler, Phil Geusz, Fred Grim, Les Johnson, Jan Keeling, Cindy Kershner, Lucas Obringer, Bonnie Parker, Nathan Parker, William Parker, Brian Relleva, Martha Rider, Robert J. Sawyer, Allen Steele, Rachel Steele, Carole Stice and Ava Weiner. Warm thanks to my agent, Richard Curtis. And everlasting appreciation to my editor, John Morgan.

1

ASK YOUR SUIT
FOR HELP

"Rage, rage against the dying of the light.
Though wise men at their end know dark is right . . ."
—DYLAN THOMAS

Life is addictive. Too much just makes you want more—
though it never quite matches your hope. I know. I'm
248 years old. And Sheeba? She wasn't even twenty when
we met. Perhaps I craved her sparkle, her innocent faith in
tomorrow, her playfulness, her spicy thighs. Or perhaps it
was simply timing. We connected at the ragged end of my
life and the dewy beginning of hers. And now, because of
Sheeba, this is my final war surf. I'm waiting here in this
battle zone to die.

The gunfire has stopped. I'm shivering under a table in
a cold, deserted anteroom. Broken benches litter the floor,
and a scummy film of mold covers everything. Overhead,
one fluorescent light blinks off and on like alien code.
That's the worst, that light. It's unzipping my rationality. I
could get out of here. There's still time. But I stay and wait
(calmly?) for the end. I have four hours left. Four hours to
tell you about Sheeba.

Sheeba who fixes my pain.

• • •

Let's say this began six months ago, on a Tuesday afternoon,
early January 2253—the afternoon Sheeba first watched me

surf a war zone. We were surfing the Copia.Com drug factory in Thule that day, a small feisty worker rebellion, seventeen levels underground.

Our surf crew, we were the best. We held top rank in the northern hemisphere, and the five of us had been surfing wars together for decades—Verinne, Kat, Winston, Grunze and me. All beautiful people, strong and rich and well past our second century, all addicted to war surfing. We'd grown up together during the grisly twenty-first century, and we'd grown wealthy during the twenty-second. I'd had sex with every one of them. I'd lived off and on with Kat. And once I'd been in love with Verinne. Maybe we were friends. Maybe rivals. The fact is, I treasured what we were together.

We called our crew the Agonists—in the sense of contenders, pro and anti—though we liked the connotations of death struggle, too. Let's say we shared a disdain for the commonplace. Let's say we chose to defy the moribund limits of ordinary life. We were senior execs, semiretired, all taking telomerase treatments and recloning our organs and pumping our cells full of bioNEMs to extend our youth. Pain was easy to kill. Work we delegated to others. Feasting, free sex, flash drugs, everything grows tedious after a while. Except war surfing.

"Nasir, you're too bloody slow," Grunze yelled over the crack of exploding concrete. "You missed the window."

I counted explosions and smiled at him across a corridor filled with dust. The Copia factory guards were using pulse lasers, and their noisy beams ricocheted down the corridor walls, drilling craters and punishing my eardrums. Across from me, Grunze waited in the opposite doorway, shaking his head. I was supposed to cross the corridor without getting hit. Picture me squatting in the subterranean doorjamb, breathing concrete dust and massaging my inflamed right hip.

Grunze yelled, "What're you doing? Taking a piss?"

"I'm savoring the moment," I yelled back.

"No time-outs." Verinne's dry voice scratched through

my helmet earphone, as if she were coughing the words. "You have sixty seconds, Nasir. Otherwise, you forfeit."

Her camera buzzed in front of me, a thumb-sized blur of mechanical wings. While Grunze and I raced through this underground factory, Verinne watched everything from her car, parked on the surface. I checked my helmet camera. Grunze and I were documenting, too.

Grunzie smirked at me from the opposite doorway. He'd crossed earlier, before the lasers started firing. His white body armor accentuated his massive shoulders, and the tight-fitting sports helmet outlined his boulder head. Grunze believed I wouldn't do this because, compared to him, I'm a small man, thin and wiry, and Grunze equated that with weakness. He'd bet half a million deutsch that I would freeze up and fail to run through the line of fire.

The laser barrage grew sporadic, unpredictable. *Zzt-zzt. Bam!* Imagine a razor-sharp reek of sweat and burnt plastic. And let's assume I felt fear. Salty, tight, deep-muscle anguish. The taste of iron dissolving in my mouth. Delectable terror. Let's imagine how I sank into it and let the shivers ride up my neck. Let's suppose I fantasized searing agony.

When and if I ran through the laser beams, Verinne would upload the live video to Kat and Winston back in Nordvik. Through the earphone, I could hear their wisecracks. They were placing bets, how many steps I would take, how many seconds, whether I would make a noise. Later, we would drink tequila and settle our wagers, and that dickhead Grunze would pay me half a million deutsch. Because I would do this. There was no doubt. Moments like this were the reason I stayed alive.

"Be here now," I whispered under my breath. And I thought of Sheeba. The clean scent of her soap, the sweet flesh under her chin.

As the lasers hissed, concrete shards flew up and stung my jaw. The floor looked like a map of the moon. But my sleek new quantum dot body armor changed colors when I moved, and the user's guide claimed it would deflect laser fire. I was getting ready to test the money-back guarantee.

"C'mon. It's almost time for lunch." Grunze gave me that taunting smile, wide blunt jaw and white teeth, and he crooked his index finger, come hither. It was part of his game.

Well, I could play the game, too. I nonchalantly lifted off my helmet, drew out a travel mirror and checked my hair. Handsome young Euro features reflected back at me—surgically standardized. Gene therapy had lightened my complexion. Only the droopy, almond shape of my eyes betrayed Hindu ancestry. Poetic eyes, some women called them. Amorous eyes, the color of smoke. Over the years, my droopy Far-Eastern eyes had served me well.

Kat buzzed through my earphone with her hypertensive whine. "Nasir, you're grandstanding."

"Katherine, take a pill and settle down." I calmly zipped the mirror back inside my pocket and replaced my helmet.

"Nass is doing a Zen thing," Winston said. His words over the phone were so slurred, he seemed to be drowning—in tequila, most likely.

"Thirty seconds," said Verinne.

A sudden whiff of smoke made me gag. Somewhere, pharmaceuticals were burning. I would have worn a hazard suit, but Grunze said no, that was a pussy move. Breathe the local air, he said. Be one with the war zone.

I leaned against the doorjamb, coughing on the chemical smoke and recalling with grim humor that my pal Grunze owned those burning medicines. His family held a large stake in this drug company, and for a hundred years, they'd earned solid returns—until out of nowhere last month, their employees trashed the production line and sent tons of expensive pharmaceuticals up in flames. Small labor disputes like this were cropping up everywhere, like a fad on the Net. And the battle cry was always the same: "Gimme what you got."

At least, these new war zones made for variety—we surfers craved fresh playing fields. But this fight was already winding down. Grunze's security guards were encircling the last few agitators. This might be Copia's final battle. As the floor and walls erupted in shards, I caught my breath and let the fear build. My heart was hammering. My eyesight sharpened. My brain picked up speed.

"Ten seconds," Verinne rasped.

"Shit." I stood up and dove across the corridor.

The laser guns exploded. For an instant, I may or may not have seen a wall of light flying toward me. Perhaps this occurred in slow motion. Or perhaps the seconds compressed into a single flash. I landed just shy of the open door and rolled to cover, slamming my hip and laughing hysterically. Safe behind the wall, the tremendous shivering release hit me like an orgasm.

"Well done," Verinne said.

"About time," said Kat.

"Okay, enough clowning. Let's get out of here." Grunze was pissed. Though he outweighed me by a good twenty-five kilos, I'd proved once again he couldn't top me in sheer nerve.

Blood pulsed through my limbs like a drumbeat. I swept damp black curls out of my eyes and spoke to the Bumblebee camera. "Verinne, how many seconds?"

"Point-eight-nine," she announced with her gruff cough. "Grunze's time was point-nine-two."

"Hear that? I beat your time, burly boy." I punched his shoulder and dodged when he tried to hit back. "Sore loser, ha."

Then a concussion knocked us both to the floor. "PBW!" we both yelled.

The particle beam weapon incinerated the wall across the corridor—exactly where I'd been standing seconds ago. My lungs fluttered like a pair of mistimed rockets. Two beats later, Grunze and I rolled in unison away from the door, then belly-crawled toward the shelter of an overturned metal desk. Another walloping particle beam struck farther down the corridor, and we hunkered together, panting and rubbing our aches and grinning at each other.

As soon as Grunze caught his breath, he yelled, "Surf the moment!"

"Molto perilous!" I yelled back. We were both blissed to the max on battle stress.

"What's a PBW?" Winston said through the phone, but no one bothered to answer.

"You Freds act like you just cruised Heaven," said Kat.

Grunze laughed. "No, it's not *that* sweet."

Heaven, ha. Everybody kept yakking about Heaven, the so-called "holy grail of war surfs." It was just an old orbiting sugar factory nicknamed for its sweet smell, but ever since the war broke out there nine months ago, Heaven had grown freaking legendary. Circling Earth in high polar orbit, the place was so rigorously guarded that no crew had attempted it yet. A virgin zone. It had a difficulty rating of Class Ten—the highest.

"Katherine, you're jealous," I said, affectionately butting helmets with Grunze. "You could be here now if you hadn't wimped out."

"I had a heart attack yesterday, you bimbus." Kat was touchy about her health.

Too soon after the rush, we felt the letdown. My side started throbbing where the lasers hit, and fiery pain shot down my right leg. Grunze's muscles locked up so badly, he had trouble bending his knees. I tugged off my helmet, flipped out my travel mirror and checked my hair. Then I whispered a private code to speed-call Sheeba.

Sheeba Zee, my physical therapist. Barely past adolescence, Shee had the most miraculous healer's touch I'd ever known. Only Shee could work this kink out of my hip. Waiting for her answer, I massaged my hamstring. My artificial right hip joint never had performed to spec. But Sheeba would know what to do. Shee knew the brands and models of all my artificial parts. She even knew about my bioNEMs, though we didn't speak of them. Sheeba didn't approve of Nano-Electronic Machines inside the human body. She didn't believe they were "natural."

NEMs were mega cutting-edge, and I had a thousand different kinds of the tiny buggers crabwalking through my cells. Complex silicon molecules, they ran on blood sugar, moved like proteins, and performed all the specialized functions my 248-year-old body could no longer handle. They didn't itch or make a noise, but in an uncanny way, I could sense them moving, like an exotic hive entity buzzing inside my skin. Maybe Shee was right about NEMs.

In fact, a doctor once showed me an MRI of the scary living lattice the NEMs wove through my tissues—like a second Nasir Deepra made of glass dust. Can you visualize it, a Nasir-shaped crystal man? If all my flesh and gristle were stripped away, I had a whimsical notion that this glass man would get up and walk around and tell you the same lies I'm telling now.

What I knew for sure was, the bloody NEMs cost a fortune—only the very wealthiest execs could pay the price. The doctor-inventors guarded their medical patents with a vengeance, and if you were caught sharing a copyrighted NEM, they'd stick you with the big D. Yeah, the Death penalty. (The doctors claimed moral issues about longevity—dwindling resources, problems with over-crowding, rights of the next generation, etc. Fear-mongering greed if you ask me.)

In any case, I'd been collecting different kinds of NEMs since my two hundredth birthday, paying full retail because there wasn't any alternative, and each time the docs invented something new, I added that to my cocktail. My NEMs repaired the inconveniences of aging. They gave me smooth skin, tight buns, curly black hair and all the traits of a swaggering young stud. But sometimes they were damned slow to act, I thought, massaging my right hip.

Then we saw flames in the corridor.

"Fuck, they're using a thermal gun. I'll phone the squad leader." Grunze touched the microphone mounted on his throat collar.

"Pussy move." I laughed, stowing my mirror. "One million says you can't get out of here without help."

"You're on, sweetheart." He gripped my helmet chin strap and tried to kiss me on the mouth. There'd been a time when I used to like that, but Grunze knew I wasn't into guys anymore. I was into girls again. One girl.

"Nasir? Do you need me?"

Sheeba. That fresh, dewy voice in my earphone made me forget the flames. "Sheeba," I whispered, cinching my helmet tighter, "can you squeeze me in for a session this afternoon?"

"Nass, you sound stressed. Are you hurting?"

"Yes. I'm hurting all over." Hurting for you, dear Shee. I fantasized her slanting cheekbones and the large luscious pillows of her lips.

Her laughter sparkled through my earphone. "I keep telling you, beau. Your extra soul layers need sympathic care." Delightful girl, she was always bubbling over with mystical healing gibberish. I could see her rocking from side to side, tossing her head back and effervescing cheerful nonsense, like a shaken bottle of underaged champagne. "Nasir, it's true. Your spiritual multiplexity makes you tender."

"This way." Grunze's voice sounded muffled. He'd closed his helmet visor.

Flames were spreading toward us like an orange wind, cutting us off from the elevators, and the heat penetrated through my armor. The room was filling with smoke, so I closed my visor and activated metavision so I could see. I also brought my emergency air supply online. Nasir Deepra was nobody's fool—I'd stowed a pony-bottle of filtered air in my backpack. Grunzie had one, too. For all our bravado, we never completely trusted war zone air. Down the hall, we heard screaming.

"Get down!" Grunze yelled. A plume of thermal energy exploded toward us through the door, and I barely had time to duck behind the metal desk. People say I'm quick and lithe, but the truth is, I don't move as fast as I once did. One whole side of my body armor glistened like melting plastic.

"This way, Nass." Grunze waved his arm.

His hulking form disappeared through a rear door, so I

sprinted after him, favoring my right hip. The heat pushed against my back like a giant hand, but as soon as the door slammed behind us, the noise went mute. Our steps echoed. This room felt cavernous. The bare concrete ceiling must have been twenty meters high, and rows of metal shelves towered over us, stacked with white plastic crates. As we trotted down an aisle between two rows, I read the labels. Analgesics, antibiotics, psychotropics—all Copia.Com brand names. This was Copia's main warehouse.

Kat spoke in her taut soprano over the phone. "You don't have a clue where you're going. Absolutely no sense of style." I could picture her curled up tight on my sofa in Nordvik, biting a strand of red hair between her teeth, her nerves jangled with cardiac meds as she watched our live video.

And somewhere in the background, Winston would be mixing margaritas. "I forgot our last bet," he said in a thickening drawl.

"You'll find a freight chute four hundred meters north-northeast of your position. Two lefts. Then a right." Verinne's dry logical wheeze seemed to echo from a crypt.

"Hey, no fair giving directions," I said. "Grunzie has to escape without help. We've got an active wager."

Grunze flexed his stiff elbows. "I know this place inside out. Who says I need help?"

Winston said something in the background, and Kat laughed. They were making a new side bet.

A deep, waffling roar told us the fire was spreading into the warehouse. One stack of crates lit up like a wax candle, and the highest crate tumbled to the floor, spreading flames. A vibrant point of fear tickled my nerves.

Kat said, "Does Grunzie have a time limit?"

"Nothing specified," said Verinne, faithful to facts.

"Lame," said Kat. "I'll lay odds they run out of air in fifteen minutes. Who's in?"

"Me." Winston hiccuped.

"I'll take that," said Verinne.

At the far end of the warehouse, three men stepped into

our aisle, wearing employee uniforms and hefting lengths of pipe. I felt a charge of cold fright. They were agitators. Dangerous thugs. In every war, you would find them blogging their twisted truth on the Net, rousing the rabble and provoking even sensible workers to rise up and injure their own Coms. They incensed me. Verinne's camera flew in close and documented their faces. One of them swatted at the little drone and tried to catch it in his hand.

When they took a step toward us, I waved Grunze ahead. "They're your protes. You deal with 'em."

Protes, protected workers—ingrates is what they were. No generation of employees had ever received more generous protection from their Coms. We execs gave them subsidized food and housing, free uniforms, guaranteed lifetime labor contracts. We took care of their families. We shielded protes from every difficulty in life. It baffled me why they kept stirring up these endless little strikes.

"No prob," said Grunze. He amped up his stun gun and sprayed a few bolts of electricity down the aisle toward the agitators. A harmless light show, but it worked. The thugs hurled their pipes, missing us of course, then moved back and melted into the shadows.

"Plasmic." Winston dribbled his sluggish laugh. "Next time, fry the cheeky bastards."

"Follow them, Verinne. Show us where they're hiding," Kat ordered.

Verinne cleared her throat. "Switching to metavision."

Her Bumblebee camera buzzed away, chasing the agitators. Her Bee carried the same adaptive optics as our helmet visors to help see through the smoke. Unfortunately, the metavision made everything glow in livid purple and yellow, except the fire. That radiated neon orange.

Another stack of crates lit up, with a sound of shattering glass. Heat burned through my armor, and I felt a wave of animal fear. Zone rush.

I said, "You're sure the freight chute's this way?"

"Just keep moving," Grunze answered.

We loped in single file between the long rows of crates,

me limping, Grunzie waddling with leg cramps. The girth of his Herculean thighs made him shuffle from side to side. Through our metavisors, the white crates gleamed like giant ice cubes, and purple shadows played over the smudged saffron floor. As the harsh chemical smoke seeped around my visor and invaded my nostrils, I bit hard into the plastic mouthpiece and sucked the filtered air. Picture me snorting and gagging. I should have worn that hazard suit.

"Through here," Grunze said, and we squeezed between crates into the next aisle over.

As we approached the spot where the agitators had slipped away, he flicked his stun gun and zapped the metal shelving. We heard a gasp, and behind the stacked crates, something clattered on the floor. Grunze must have scorched one of the agitators. Score one for our side. Verinne's camera darted back and forth through the shelves.

"Do you want visuals?" she asked.

"No outside help!" I shouted.

Verinne could have fed her video to our helmet visor displays and shown us the injured worker writhing on the floor, but—I'll confess it now—the gory stuff sickened me. It reminded me of things from the past, dim ugly scenes and . . . faces.

But that's not the point. What I meant to say was, we had a bet. Grunze wasn't supposed to get help, so that's why I stopped Verinne from showing us visuals. Because I wanted to win the bet.

Behind us, flames ignited another stack of crates, and the metavision orange flared so bright, my eyes watered. Radiant yellow snakes of fire coiled across the ceiling over our heads, and when Grunze saw that, he turned and ran. Before I could follow, another thermal wave exploded behind us, and the blast threw me headlong into Grunze's body. Heat sliced into my back like a million razor blades, and I wailed like a fiend.

"Ha. You owe me fifty," Winston laughed in the earphone.

"That was a moan, not a scream," said Kat.

"You're splitting hairs. Double or nothing, he'll scream again. Hey, Nasir, you awright?"

I couldn't articulate an answer. My new body armor had heat-welded to my back, and every move ripped a patch of my skin. As Verinne's camera flitted around us, Grunze hauled me up and dragged me toward the far end of the warehouse. I couldn't stop moaning. The voices in my earphone kept placing new bets, but my entire world contracted to one sensation, that raw pain washing down my back like acid.

Naturally, my left thumb started vibrating. That was my IBiS, my "Implanted BioSensor," a medical microprocessor embedded under my thumbnail. It was clanging a health alarm, but the last thing I had time for was to take off my glove and read the tiny screen mounted in my thumbnail. Tears blurred my vision, and I wouldn't have known where to go if Grunze hadn't jerked me along.

Then one clear young voice cut through the chatter like a pealing bell. Soft, dewy, brimming with concern. Sheeba, my darling.

"Ask your suit for help, Nass."

Sheeba hadn't terminated our connection. The pesky child had been eavesdropping on our private Web site, lurking and watching our surf.

Her words reminded me what to do. "Norphine," I muttered, "triple dose." The smart system in my body armor heard my command and triggered the patch. My underarm felt a slight itch as the patch sank its tiny teeth through my skin, and seconds later, the drug took effect. Numb relief. "Dear Sheeba, thank you."

"What are doing in that place?" she said. "Are you seeking the dark?"

Grunze was banging on a rusted metal door, and when it wouldn't open, he fired his stun gun into the key pad.

"Did you forget the code?" I asked.

He growled at me. "It's been tampered." Then he started kicking the door, but that didn't help.

"There's another exit—" Verinne began.

"Don't say it," Grunze cut her off. "Nasir'll claim you gave me help. No way will I let this little pipsqueak one-up me."

"Grunzie, this other exit, do you know where it is?" I eyed the orange flames that now engulfed half the warehouse.

Grunze pointed at the ceiling with his gun. "There."

In a distant purple corner, I saw a golden catwalk leading to a ceiling hatch. The flames ebbed and flowed toward that corner like a neon tide, but they hadn't reached it yet.

"How do we get up?"

"Ladder," he said. "Help me look for one. Or will that be considered 'outside help'?"

"The word in the bet was 'help,' nonspecific," Verinne reported in her raspy monotone. "That implies help in any form. If you ask Nasir to find the ladder, ipso facto, you forfeit. I can play back the footage if you like."

"Then get the fuck out of my way." Grunze shoved me against a crate of AIDS vaccine and headed off.

My air gauge showed less than five minutes remaining. For a second, I switched off the lurid purple-and-gold metavision, but black smoke engulfed the warehouse so thickly, I had to turn it back on. That catwalk hung just under the ceiling, twenty meters overhead. I visually estimated the distance from the top of the nearest metal shelf.

Then I spoke a command to temporarily exclude Grunze from the conference call. "Verinne, our bet was whether Grunze could escape without help, right? That doesn't apply to me. I can get all the help I want."

"Slippery Nass. What're you plotting?" Winston said.

"Grunze is wasting time looking for a ladder. You have to unlock that freight chute," Verinne said.

"Give us a look at the key pad. We'll help." Winston let out a belch.

"Take my advice," said Kat. "You should bribe one of those agitators to guide you."

I ignored them and slipped off my backpack. "Verinne,

can you lend me your eyes? Send your Bumblebee up to check out that catwalk, and feed me the visuals."

The little camera zoomed up toward the ceiling, and while Verinne's video played in the lower right corner of my visor, I pulled out my climbing gear. Why didn't Grunze think of climbing up the shelves to the catwalk? It seemed obvious.

About then, a scream echoed through the warehouse, and a man lurched out from between two stacks of crates with his clothes on fire. As he ran toward me, the flames trailed behind him, and he yowled like a savage beast. Could that be Grunze? No, it was an agitator. As he came closer, I saw his blackened, eyeless face. Like the faces in Lahore, the ones that haunted my sleep. On instinct, I dug through my pack for something to wrap him and smother the flames.

As I flung a foil blanket over his shoulders, Win said, "Why're you helping a hostile?"

Kat said, "Get out of the way, Nass. You're blocking Verinne's camera."

In any case, I was too late. The man blundered straight on and ran his head against the wall. He was too blind to see. I turned away, fighting nausea.

"Verinne, did you get that? That was *Reel*." Kat sounded giggly and overexcited.

"Yes, *Reel*," Verinne agreed. "I'm uploading it to our site."

Reel was our surfer lingo for the visceral photogenic underseams of our sport. Real War. Of all the surfer Web pages, the Agonist site had the sleekest, savviest *Reel* on the Net. Our broadcasts were meta-vivid. And meta-private. We bounced our signal in untraceable reverb loops that not even the World Trade Org could crack, although millions of fans knew where to find us. They lurked every time we surfed a zone and usually gave our *Reel* five-star reviews. But I didn't care about that. The smell of the man's cooking flesh had leaked into my helmet.

Tune it out, Deepra. Ditch the sappy attitude. You're the ace of war surfers.

Ace. Right. I covered my mouth and swallowed. The Reel was the one part of our sport I dreaded. Of course, I pretended to be as blasé as everyone else. The betting helped.

My gauge showed three minutes of air left, so I voiced a command to bring Grunze back into the conference call. "Grunzie, you still alive?"

"Have you finished whispering behind my back? I'm already outside. How about that, nasty Nass? You lose."

"You're out? I'm still in here!" I ogled my air gauge. My voice may have registered panic.

"How about another little wager?" he asked. "One mil says you can't get out without *my* help."

"Grunze, you sodder. You tricked me."

His asinine giggle bleated through my earphone, but I concentrated on the ceiling hatch. The flimsy metal shelf stood about fifteen meters high, and the catwalk hung at least five meters above it. I checked my air gauge. Barely two minutes left. Verinne's camera buzzed around my head like a pest. My climbing cord lay tangled at my feet, neon flames wafted toward me, and the approaching heat was blistering my body armor. If not for the Norphine coursing through my veins, I would probably have wept.

"I'll come back for you, sweet-piss. All you have to do is beg."

Ah, Grunze, how skillfully you fanned my flame. Adrenaline shivered through my limbs, and I relished its copper taste. This was why I came to the zone. This delicious, galvanizing angst. Verging on the brink of chaos, grappling for control, feeling my fate in jeopardy. Moments like this revived my will to live. I thrust out my chest and whispered, "Be here now."

Aloud I said, "Behold the master at play."

Flames already lapped halfway up the shelf unit that would take me to the catwalk. I gathered my climbing cord and raced down the aisle toward it. As soon as I reached the lowest shelf, I pulled myself up, hand over hand, past the burning plastic crates, ignoring the flames. Wounds meant extra status points, and besides, I felt no pain. The Norphine was kicking into high gear, and the glass bioNEM man inside me would repair my damaged cells.

A new caller rang through. "Boss, I don't like to disturb you now, but your InterMerc stock is tanking. Should I sell short?"

It was Chad, my personal cyberassistant. What timing. "How much has it fallen?" I asked.

"Three-point-seven billion and change."

"Yes, sell." I dumped Chad's call and clambered up the shelf.

When I made it to the top, all I had to do was throw my rope, swing to the catwalk and climb through the hatch. Ye gilded gods, I felt alive. I could almost hear the Net audience cheering me on. Being light made me an agile climber, so I bounded upward, feeling young and strong and free from the laws of gravity. Almost in a dream, I sensed the shelf unit sway. Then it toppled backward.

"Fifty says he'll crack his skull on the floor."

"I want part of that."

"Nasir, throw your rope!" Sheeba cried. Dear Sheeba child.

2

I FEEL REVIVED ALREADY

"No one may have the guts to say this, but if we could
make better human beings by knowing how to add
genes, why shouldn't we?"
—DR. JAMES WATSON,
FOUNDING DIRECTOR OF THE HUMAN GENOME PROJECT

When a surf goes right, it's transcendent. You plan
ahead, prepare your gear. You anticipate every contingency. Then you enter the zone, all senses alert, adrenaline charging through your veins like speed. You smell a
whiff of smoke. You see flames, hear the rumbling growl
of a particle beam shearing steel. Deep inside, the drama
catches you, and for a while, your life accelerates. Taking
chances, teasing destiny, running the slalom gates of war,
you pull spiritual G-forces that press you hard against the
present moment, so hard you know in your gut it's the only
thing that's real. Be Here Now. You want to shout at the
stars. And that's when you stretch beyond the envelope of
your own puny life span. You spread out like fire and music, wider than thought, and for an instant, you brush
against eternity. Ye idols of gold, I love it.

Radiant Sheeba, what did she think that afternoon as
she secretly spied on our war surf? Her first vision of a
zone, was she frightened? Or fascinated? As I sit alone in
this anteroom, probing my past by the vile blink of fluorescence, I can only speculate. She'd never witnessed war. So

far, her short young life had played out in softly cushioned therapy chambers with aromatic candles, sizz music and scented oils. No violence had touched her. Oh, I may have told her about war surfing. During our long and frequent therapy sessions, I possibly mentioned my exploits, but that's not the same as seeing live action. Until that infamous afternoon when she lurked on our private Web site and watched me crash in flames, Sheeba didn't know.

Sheeba Zee was my own personal find. I discovered her five years ago, toiling in a discount health church in Kotzebue. No one goes there anymore since the hot Alaskan currents drove that sludge up the coastline. But back then, Kotzebue advertised the best health-care bargains on the Bering Strait. And I've always liked saving money.

Picture Sheeba striding out to meet me in the tacky health church lobby. I'd booked a session, expecting the usual muscular nurse in whites and thick shoes. Instead, I got Sheeba, tall, wide-shouldered, regal as a goddess, poured into a leotard and dipped head to toe in gold paint. The church was running some kind of promotion. She took my voice away.

"Mr. Deepra?" she cooed, accenting the wrong syllable.

"Call me Nasir," I finally managed to croak.

"Nasir. You look like you could use a good squeeze." When she saw my reaction, she tossed her head back and laughed like a minx, a trill of high bubbly notes spilling upward. That carefree laugh got to me—that and the way the gold paint rippled when she moved.

"I mean your latissimus dorsi, beau. Deep massage. We'll start with a shiatsu, then we'll do some chromatherapy. Cool calming colors to tune your energy field. Indigo and jade would be right."

Under the cheesy gold paint, Sheeba appeared like all young girls of the executive class, cheerful and vapid, with no distinguishing traits beyond loveliness. But oh how lovely she was. Just eighteen, fresh out of school, away from home for the first time, with nothing to hide and everything to learn. God, I wanted to trade places with her for just one day.

She had dimples in her cheeks, in her elbows, in the backs of her glittering gold hands. Wide mouth. Wide hips and shoulders. Long vigorous legs. Delectable breasts and a tight round belly. Not fashionable, that little belly, but arousing.

She also had preter-natural skills with her hands. Her first session took 150 years off my stress load, and when she put my right leg through a range-of-motion routine, she immediately diagnosed my hip joint malfunction and looked up the part number I needed. With charming naïveté, she explained how much commission she would earn if I took her advice. What I took was her email address.

I brought her to Nordvik, set her up in private practice and coaxed my friends into booking her sessions. For the last five years, I'd been imbibing her therapy, doting on her splendors and hauling my heart around like a thick clay begging bowl.

That fateful afternoon when Grunze pulled me from the wreckage of the Copia.Com factory, Sheeba was already plunging toward me in a rented aircar, bringing blood plasma, trauma meds and polarizing magnets. While Grunze broadblasted my photo around the Net with tags like NASIR EXTRA CRISPY and DEEPRA-FRIED, Shee cradled my head in her lap and stroked my temples with an ankh.

"It'll revive your life force, beau." As she rubbed the Egyptian talisman over my eyebrows, the ambulance lifted off, and I got a close-up view of her jiggling young bosom compressed in spandex.

"You're right. I feel revived already."

That day, she had lacquered her hair with midnight blue wax, lined her eyes to look oriental and covered her arms in temporary tattoos. Her contact lenses were yellow. Sheeba went in for strong fashion statements.

"Don't worry about your ear. The docs can grow you an-other one." She opened a small vial and tipped a drop of clear liquid onto my pillow. "Cypress oil. It heals psychic wounds."

My health church wanted to keep me for seven weeks, but when I agreed to pay the full fees, they let me go after two days. I spent the next month holed up in my condo, mostly dozing in anesthetic haze while my bioNEMs rebuilt my burnt flesh cell by cell. I loathe convalescence. Memories of that time drool together like marbling paints, and the first lucid impression I recall is Sheeba standing in my doorway, a potted hothouse orchid cradled against her hip and a tin of southern-hemisphere chocolates tucked under her arm.

Her complexion may have been chartreuse that day. She had a penchant for skin dyes—in fact, I'd never seen her natural skin tone. And her hair was a work of art. Waxed pale green to match her face, it was sculpted in a spiky crest, interspersed with something frilly and pink that might have been plastic bird feathers. She also wore contact lenses the color of tangerines. Now imagine her appetizing green body squeezed into a short, white, pearl-studded, faux-leather chemise.

"Showboat," I said. "Come here and kiss me."

She rewarded me with her lullaby of laughter, dropped her gifts on the floor—where the orchid pot cracked in two—then galloped across the room to jump on my bed. A bouncing rainbow of rouge and paint, her embrace set off my IBiS, and I bit my left thumb to stop the tingling.

"This is for you," I said, offering her a box wrapped in fragile pink papyrus. Chad had gotten it through the Net.

"You don't have to keep buying me things." Sheeba eagerly tore off the paper and opened the box like a five-year-old kid on her birthday. "Wow!"

"You like it?" The gift was an antique seashell, rough and chalky outside, but inside, as pearly pink and smooth as the inside of Sheeba's ear.

"I love it, beau." She cradled the shell in both hands and gazed at it exactly the way I longed for her to gaze at me.

Then she planted a wet, smacking kiss on my cheek. "You sweet man."

"I'm glad it pleases you," I said, quietly thrilled. While she played with the shell, I slipped out a small mirror and adjusted one dangling curl over my forehead.

"Nass, I have a million things to tell you. Scoot over so I can sit." Sheeba made herself comfortable on my bed. "Let me see the flecks in your irises."

For the next hour, she tuned my aura, ran kinesiology tests on my muscles and battened me on gossip, the choicest, most nourishing little slanders about everyone I knew. She made me laugh till my new skin prickled. Sheeba understood my appetites.

"What about the Agonists?" I finally asked. "Have they been surfing? I'm sans loop."

Shee hopped off my bed and started kicking the pieces of broken flowerpot. Her succulent lower lip protruded. "You guys are always so hush-hush about war stuff."

I knew what was coming. "Did Kat say something rude?"

"Katherine's mad at the world." Sheeba kicked the pot.

"Probably she's upset because you lurked on our broadcast. It's supposed to be private."

Sheeba lifted one shoulder in a half shrug.

"Forget her. You can watch us anytime. I'll give you the password, the dates, the places." (Plus my fortune, my life's blood, my layered soul, anything you ask, Sheeba—though this part I left unsaid.)

"Thanks, beau." She picked up the naked orchid by its stem. Live plants were outrageously expensive—her gift flattered me and fanned my hopes. But she jiggled its curly roots with a roughness that wasn't like my gentle darling. "They breed these things to live on pure air," she said, "or maybe it needs a little mist. Where did I put the user's guide?"

As she ripped angrily through her bag for the orchid's documentation, I wondered why she'd become so agitated. Was it because I mentioned war surfing?

My sport wasn't popular with junior execs. Call it a generational disconnect. Sheeba's age group had missed the grisly Crash of 2057. Junior execs had no conception how fast the climate changed or how disastrously the markets collapsed. They'd never witnessed crowds of storm refugees trying to sleep in noxious, waist-high water or clawing each other like animals for one can of sweetened milk. Sheeba's friends couldn't imagine how gruesomely people died—or how barbaric the survivors had to become. Kids like Shee grew up safe and secure, and their placid lives never drove them into frenzies of gut-wrenching boredom. So a lot of juniors just didn't *get* our need for the salty thrills of the war zone.

But Sheeba was different. I didn't see that at first. I assumed she disliked my sport as much as her friends did. So that night, I steered the discussion away from war surfing. While she gave me a deep-tissue massage that verged on sensual nirvana, I told wicked jokes about Kat that made her laugh till tears rolled down her cheeks. Then I coaxed her into helping me with my stretches. Sitting face-to-face with Shee in her workout shorts transformed the dull therapy routine into an act of libidinous pleasure. I drew the session out, asking for special guidance with the yoga moves and savoring the feel of her hands on my newly cloned skin.

As soon as she left, though, I linked into the Agonist Web site and browsed the latest video. Our crew had logged several fairly interesting surfs, and watching their archives made me antsy to get back in the action. I scanned their blogs all night.

Chad, my cyberassistant, called every few hours to go through my mail, doctors' appointments and day trades. When I missed board meetings, Chad voted my proxy. He was also remodeling several floors of my eighty-story condo, and he kept flashing me color swatches. Avocado, lime, mint green—Chad blissed on the cutting edge of style.

"Stick with white. It goes with anything," I said, which made Chad heave a quantum sigh.

One by one, the Agonists dropped in to see me. Verinne came first. Two meters tall, slender and cool, she stalked into my room like a frigid fashion model. Her pewter-colored hair lay flat to her skull like a pelt, and she'd plucked her widow's peak into a sharp point, dividing her high forehead into two pale half-moons. Her narrow gray eyes canted upward at a slight angle, hinting Siberian lineage. She glanced at me briefly and dabbed her lips with gloss.

Her voice crackled. "You look better than I expected, Nasir." Then she planted a dry kiss on my cheek.

Verinne's ghoulish beauty had once bewitched me. But now, her dead-white skin wrinkled like fine crepe. After exhausting cosmetic creams and surgeries, Verinne resorted to high collars and long sleeves. She suffered from Sjogren's Syndrome, a disease of desiccation that not even bioNEMs could heal. Her skin, eyes, mouth, even her internal organs were literally drying up.

Once you love a woman, you never stop caring. That's my belief. Verinne wasn't beautiful anymore, but she'd always been a true friend. Solid. No nonsense. The sound of her failing voice tore at my heart.

"Do me a favor, Verinne." I kicked restlessly at my bed covers. "Convince me why any sane person would choose to live this long."

She coughed into her fist. "No time for chitchat. I need your condo password. The crew wants to meet tonight."

"You're planning a surf?"

"I have to hurry. Watch the Web site. You'll see." Verinne was not the type to discuss personal issues.

Grunze visited the next morning. He brought me a gift, an ePage calendar he and some of his weight-lifter pals had self-published, with pictures of themselves in various brawny poses. Grunze was February. His pale blue spandex jumpsuit displayed every swell of his physique, knotted and overdeveloped to the point of grim vulgarity. All execs doped their genes to improve muscle mass, but Grunze went radical. A few decades ago, the docs diagnosed him with sarcopenia—age-related muscle weakness. Since then, he'd fixated on bodybuilding.

Grunzie's fondness for me sometimes came out in awkward ways. Attached to the calendar was a schmaltzy gift card, and while I read the poem inside, he paced and blushed and rubbed his boulder head. He'd eliminated the problem of hair by surgically cauterizing his follicles.

"Grunze, why do we keep doing this?" I was in a pensive mood. The tedium of convalescence gave me black thoughts. "Why do we keep putting our bodies through this recuperative torture?"

He grinned uncertainly and shook my foot with rough affection. When we first met, his blue eyes had been round and bright, but now they looked like raisins, lost in the heavy musculature of his face. "How's the new ear?" he said. "Should've grown yourself a new prick while you were at it."

I pounded the mattress. "I'm sick of getting well. Why don't we just say, 'Enough!' "

"You first, sweetheart." He blew me a kiss.

Later that afternoon, Winston brought a sultry brunette and a hamper of champagne, though two of the four bottles were already empty and the brunette fell asleep across my feet. Good old Win, what an elegant man. His mane of auburn hair made him look like a statesman, or an actor, or perhaps a celebrity spokesman for life insurance. Noble chin, azure eyes, chiseled patrician nose. The features of his memory were a little less clear-cut.

"Why are you in this stupido bed, Nass? We're having maximal fun war surfs. Kat's talking about Heaven again. You're missing everything."

"Win, I had a little accident, remember?"

"Oh, that's right. Yeah, I think I remember that."

"Who's talking about Heaven? That's a suicide zone," I said.

"Well you know, Kat always wanted to do it. Why shouldn't we? Just because it's in outer space. How hard can that be?"

"Polar orbit, Win. Not outer space. But it's totally off limits."

"Right. Yeah. But that's, like . . . But I bought this sleek new space suit."

Katherine the Grand presented herself a few days later. How had I endured living with Kat for so many years? Maybe because we were both short? Even with her empress heels and tall hairstyles, she never overtopped me. Yet despite her lofty hair weaves and numerous face-lifts, to me Kat still looked like an angry fox with large teeth. Strangers often remarked on her blushing beauty, but friends knew the cause of her blooming complexion: intractable high blood pressure. She'd already gone through four self-cloned hearts. Still, Kat had her charms.

"Katherine, do you remember how we used to wake up early and watch the dawn?"

"What are the servants feeding you, Nass? You look abysmal." She yanked the fork from my hand and started chopping the blueberry waffles on my tray table. "Don't tell me you eat this dreck. I'd rather starve."

"You have to quit picking on Sheeba," I said.

"That girl is laughing at you. She despises all of us." Kat dropped the fork in my ice cream. "She thinks we're dirty-minded old stiffs."

Jealousy. Poor Kat's irrational jealousy blinded her to Sheeba's goodness. I didn't respond to her ravings. "What's this nonsense about surfing Heaven? You know it's impossible."

"Don't be a total Fred. All we need is the right gear and—"

"Over my martyred body, Kat. The idea's loco. No sane person would even think of surfing Heaven."

Kat fanned her red cheeks. "You're such a weenie."

"And you're such a birdbrain."

"Candy pants."

"Nudnik."

She threw a waffle at me, and I spritzed her with syrup. Food fights were our favorite style of communication.

Sheeba visited most often. She played healing music disks, aligned my chakras, piqued my pressure points and fed me wonderful chocolate bars smuggled in from the southern pole. I didn't bring up war surfing, and neither did she—not until the last night before my so-called "surprise" party.

That evening, I'd bought her a new set of aromatic massage oils, and she stayed longer than usual trying each one to see how they affected our moods. I'd forgotten a war surf was scheduled. Chad had set my screen on auto. The Agonists planned to buzz a zone in the Manhattan Protectorate where a few thousand ship builders were striking, and the employer, Trandent.Com, had brought in heavy energy guns. That night represented a rare treat, a war zone on Earth's surface.

Not many worksites remained on Earth's surface anymore. I don't have to tell you how our planet's fierce heat and pollution have driven most of humanity underground. But Trandent.Com's shipyard operated under a sealed dome on the Atlantic seawall, which made for unique conditions. If those big e-guns blew out the dome, then everyone inside would be exposed to Earth's malevolent atmosphere. For the Agonists, that meant wearing full hermetic surface suits. Glossy black Kevlax, tailor-made and bristling with gadgets. Molto sexy.

When Chad pinged me a reminder and the virtual screen automatically rastered at the foot of my bed, it caught me off guard.

"Do you have a show coming on?" Sheeba bounded onto my bed, giggling. "I hope it's an old movie. Wanna snuggle and watch together?"

"Snuggle? Yes." I breathed heavily. I moved toward the bed, ignoring the screen. Sheeba sat lotus style on top of the covers, hugging a pillow to her belly. With solemn restraint, I stretched out beside her and rested my hand on her bare knee. Her workout shorts were wrinkled and sweaty. They smelled ambrosial. My breath caught in my throat.

Don't let me lead you astray. Sheeba and I were not lovers, but every day I continued to hope. As the screen image sharpened, she wiggled her hips to make a nest among my pillows, and my face flushed with heat. I sidled closer and rested my head against her hipbone. The angle felt awkward and voluptuous. We watched the Agonists suit up.

Grunze and Kat were coating their faces with wild streaks of camo paint—a ludicrous conceit since they'd be wearing full helmet visors.

"What is this show, Nass? A comedy?"

"It's—" I eased my hand around her thigh and braced for rejection. "My friends are surfing a war tonight."

Sheeba had been stuffing pillows behind her rump, but my words arrested her.

"Flip the channel," I said. "You don't like violence."

"No, I want to see," she said.

I fingered her warm inner thigh, smoother than natural silk. It seemed almost sacrilegious to touch that pure, swelling firmness. I buried my nose against her clothing and breathed nectar.

Meanwhile, she opened sidebars to browse everyone's point-of-view video. She made a little gasp when the Agonists came under fire, and I glanced at the screen irritably. Reconnaissance mini-bots swarmed among the shipyard derricks, and plumes of smoke rose from the wrecked barricades. Spotlights glared like false suns. For an instant, I imagined being there. The intensity. The gunfire. The teleconference banter. All these weeks, I hadn't even placed a bet.

"Are they in danger?" Shee asked.

"Not really." I watched my friends with one eye while my inflamed fingertips searched the delicate pocket behind Sheeba's knee.

Surfers use a danger scale of One to Ten, and as zones
go, the Trandent.Com shipyard would rank Class Six. Lots
of booming thermal blasts. I nuzzled higher against
Sheeba's torso, till my eyelid fluttered against her spandex-
covered breast. I struggled not to groan.

On screen, Verinne's camera went in for the usual Reel
close-ups in purple-and-gold metavision, bodies scattered
in skewed positions, mostly male, not always intact. If
Sheeba hadn't been there, I would have turned that part off.
Instead, I rolled sideways and burrowed under her armpit,
nibbling her hollowed flesh.

"Silly beau, that tickles." She pushed me away and continued watching with serious attention. The Reel seemed to
magnetize her. When she glanced at me, three tiny furrows
creased her perfect eyebrows.

Even with the audio muted, we could hear Kat cursing.
Her royal grandness had just noticed a rip in her surface
suit, and she wanted to quit playing. Verinne and Grunze
got into an argument then, and Winston tried in his oblivious way to mediate. Kat walked off the game field in disgust. Then we saw the whole crew exit the dome through
an airlock and climb into Verinne's van, where Winston
immediately uncorked the vodka. What a lame surf.

I killed the virtual screen and scowled. That zone had so
much potential. Our crew could have played it for hours.
Why did they pick tonight to go limp—just when Sheeba
was watching? I eased toward her to snuggle again, but she
moved away, bunching her luscious lips in a frown. I expected her to ask the usual newbie questions about gear
and transportation, maybe risk factors.

Finally, she blurted, "Doesn't it whiplash your mind?"

"Whiplash?"

She hugged her knees to her chest and pointed at the
foot of the bed as if the screen were still there. "I mean,
one minute you're skipping through this gruesome battle
where people are fighting for their lives. The next, you're
safe and cozy, drinking beverages. It's gotta gnarl your
psyche."

I held back the smart remark. Sheeba often spouted nonsense, and I'd learned not to argue. My fingers traced the elegant hard curve of her anklebone.

"Sometimes I feel so—dumb," she said. "I've never talked to an employee in my life. Why do they start these wars? They have guaranteed homes and incomes, right?"

As she pleated a crease in my blanket, I watched her hands move. Large soft knuckles, sparkling rings. If she'd been a little more mature and logical, I might have explained the numbers behind these employee rebellions. Twelve billion people on the planet, 2 percent annual population growth, 4 percent annual resource deficit. We senior execs did our level best to keep everyone employed. After the Crash, we rebuilt the economy brick by virtual brick, and we swore in blood never to let it fail again, but . . .

a. there were too many workers for our Coms to absorb, and
b. the WTO had outlawed compulsory birth control, and
c. we were beggaring ourselves trying to support all the employee dependents, so therefore
d. sometimes we were forced to make cutbacks.

Instead of going into these details, I smiled and said, "Darling, don't trouble your pretty head. It's just a few agitators. We'll weed 'em out."

She bit her lip. "I should just go."

When she bounced off the bed and gathered her things to leave, I felt bereft. "Stay tonight. Please."

"Aw, beau." She zipped up her jacket. Then her expression softened, and she came back and sat on the edge of my bed. "We've talked about this before. You're my best friend. We adore each other. We don't want to demean that with sex."

"But—"

She rubbed her nose against mine. "C'mon, don't act sad. Be my sweetie."

It was always this way. Sheeba's excuses wounded and mystified me. What didn't she like? Most women found me boyishly attractive. Have I mentioned my poetic eyes? Then, too, I had money. A recent spine extension was my latest bid to win Sheeba's love. I'd added eight excruciating centimeters to my height, but she still topped me by a head. Let me say it now: Sheeba had me *besotted*. I had not fallen this hard since my first youth.

"Stay just a little while. We'll watch Cary Grant movies, and we won't talk about war surfing. I know you hate it."

"That's not true. I want to understand, but you won't take me seriously."

"Of course I do."

She held my hand and played with my fingers, working them back and forth. "It rattles me, beau. There's so much I don't understand. Sometimes, I feel like I'm living in a cage. A nice, clean, well-padded, completely accessorized cage."

"But dear, I'll buy you whatever you—"

"A CAGE!" she shouted, cutting me off. This wasn't her normal cheery style at all. She'd worked herself into a temper. "Would you believe I've lived my whole life and never once been scared? Or dirty? Or hungry? I want to experience everything, Nass. I want to go outside. Into the dark."

The dark. That was her latest spiritual healing craze. "But sweetness—"

"Why do you surf those war zones?" she demanded. "I saw you turn away from those dead bodies, but you still go there. Nass, you have too many soul layers to do this sport without a good reason."

Her words caught me up short. She'd been observing more closely than I realized. Her contact lenses shimmered like painted porcelain saucers and made me wonder what lay behind them. I sat up straighter in the pillows. How painfully eager I was to impress her. "You really want to know about war surfing?"

Her eyes widened. "Yes."

"Well . . ." I paused, gathering my thoughts. "The zone

is unpredictable. So few things are. And when you're on the mark, doing everything right, it's like escape velocity." I waved my hands, fanning up phrases. Talking about my sport was almost as much fun as doing it. "You ride the contingencies, react, think, improvise. You blast straight out of the mundane. Danger gives you no choice but to live, right here, right now, in the present moment."

Sheeba winced. "Be here now. I've heard you say that."

"Exactly."

"Nass, you're like me. You're seeking the dark."

Mystical fizz. I nodded and squeezed her hands. Discussing things with Sheeba often proved difficult. Age difference had its drawbacks.

3

YOU WERE A JUVENILE
ONCE YOURSELF

**"Age does not protect you from love, but love to some
extent protects you from age."**
—JEANNE MOUREAU

The next day saw the beginning of my "surprise" party, staged in my condo, with wine from my cellar, food from my kitchen, and entertainment charged to my account—all arranged by my dear friends, the Agonists—with mucho assistance from Chad. Winston supplied the psychotropic drugs, though of course I paid for them. About five hundred people stopped by. Sheeba wore pink.

"To celebrate your recovery, beau." She lifted her wrist and shook the heavy new diamond bracelet I'd just bought her. "Sparkly," she said with a smile.

The bracelet didn't seem to please her as much as that antique seashell. I made a mental note: Sheeba likes pearly pink things best.

She was craning her neck, scanning the crowd. "Mega-sublime party."

"Buffet and drinks on even-numbered stories. Dancing on every terrace. Movies in the screening room. Foosball, minigolf, karaoke and gaming on floors thirty through fifty-five. And I think Chad hired a psychic. She's on the ground floor channeling dead people. There's a directory by the elevator. So what'll you have, Shee?"

Sheeba flashed her starry smile. "I'll have some of everything!"

She paraded among my guests in a cloud of wispy pink foam that parted like soap bubbles wherever anyone touched her. Beneath the cloud, her highly visible naked body gleamed a nonbiological shade of iridescent rose. She'd waxed her hair fuchsia—all of her hair—and her eyes were jet-black, which stirred me to speculate if that might be their natural color. Who exactly was this chameleon child, this Sheeba Zee?

Her nudity wasn't the issue. Lots of people came to my party nude. I knew Sheeba sprang from minor executive lineage in some small American Com, that she'd earned top grades at a mediocre school, and that in her short career, she'd jumped from one health church to another almost as often as she'd changed her hair. She hadn't lived long enough to have a *past*. But thanks to my recommendations, half the geezers in my condo now booked Sheeba's physical therapy sessions. Did she snuggle and flirt with everyone the way she did with old Nasir? That doubt made me watch her all evening.

"To your health." Verinne rested against a window wall, clutching one elbow and sipping an unctuous yellow cocktail. She was always sampling new vitamin drinks. Outside the window, a swarm of adversects bumped steadily against the glass like flies, unable to spray their promo jingles through my security field.

"I see we have the usual crowd." She motioned with her drink toward a group of guests, and to my surprise, there stood Robert Trencher, my former protégé from Provendia.Com. Who had invited that creep? Not me. Two days ago, I'd demoted him for incompetence. Yet here he stood in his glossy white, patent-leather codpiece (padded, I'm sure), with his ashy eye shadow and body rings, his hairless skin the color of bruised lilies.

Verinne wasn't pointing at Trencher, though. She meant the woman standing next to him, a buxom courtesan stud-

ded in light-emitting rhinestones. It was one of Winston's
ex-girlfriends, a notorious epicuress who surfed parties
they way we Agonists surfed war zones. When the woman
moved aside, I saw what she had in tow—a child!

I gasped and turned away. Flaunting her young in public. It was beneath contempt. Everyone knew children
should be kept decently out of sight, but some execs would
break any taboo for degenerate shock value. I stole another
look. The child's head seemed disproportionately large on
its short, chubby body. With its slick white skin, half-
formed features and popping eyes, it resembled a pale am-
phibious toad.

The woman didn't look rich enough to afford a child.
Private crèches charged molto deutsch to bring fetuses to
term, and private schools charged even more to bring
neonates to adulthood. Hardly anyone bothered cultivating
heirs these days. Most executive young were gengineered
by commercial DNA banks on spec, then saddled with nurture loans when they reached maturity. I had a feeling this
rhinestone woman had "borrowed" her shocking accessory
for the evening.

Verinne sipped her yellow cocktail. "Don't act so strait-
laced. You were a juvenile once yourself."

"Not for ages," I said, shuddering. "That time is deleted
from my memory."

"I doubt it." Verinne wheezed with laughter. Her canted
eyes, gray tights and pointy white collar made her look
oddly like a Russian nun. "Do you know what, Nasir? Today is my birthday."

"My dear Verinne, I'd forgotten. Let me order champagne. We'll have a toast."

"No." She grabbed my arm when I tried to signal a
waiter. "I don't celebrate anymore. Nasir, this will be the
last one."

The amusement had drained from her face. She gazed
out the window wall, where Nordvik's heavy evening traffic streamed in ragged air lanes among the towers. Reflec-

tions from their brake lights flickered against the underside of the white city dome.

I took her hand. "Cara mia, you're sad. Birthdays are difficult, but they always pass. Put down your drink, and we'll do a cha-cha, the way we used to."

When I tried to steer her toward the dance floor, she pushed me away and nearly overturned a nearby sculpture. Verinne didn't usually show so much emotion. But she was the oldest of our crew, over 270. No cosmetics could hide the tiny cracks stretching around her mouth.

"Nasir, I'm dying."

"What? That's nonsense, love. You need another treatment. Don't—"

"I'm dying," she said again.

Verinne was not one to exaggerate. Her dry eyes glittered huge in her sunken sockets.

"When?" I whispered.

She drained her glass. "Within a year. Don't tell the others. Nasir, there's one thing I want to do before I go."

"Yes, cara. Anything."

"I want to surf Heaven."

"Oh." I stepped back. "You don't know what you're saying. There are things about Heaven . . . things I can't tell you."

A group of drunken revelers stumbled against us and shoved us apart. "Think about it." Verinne raised her husky voice. "Heaven."

"But you don't understand—"

One of the guests caught me in a bear hug, separating me farther from Verinne. Next, the lot of them insisted on lifting me up on their shoulders and traipsing around the dance floor. I didn't see Verinne again for hours.

Winston had ensconced himself in my library with an entourage of females and a steamer trunk of psychotropic diversions. I found him enthroned in an armchair like a high church deacon, dispensing pills, powders and skin patches to a line of supplicants. His wavy auburn hair framed his head like a lion's mane. The sight struck me as hilarious because Winston had, in fact, once been a deacon in the Nordvik Church of Acute Oncology. During his long career as a physician, he'd racked up a fortune even larger than mine. But he lost most of his money somehow. Perhaps he forgot where he put it.

"Nasty Nass, name your poison. How would ya like to feel tonight?" Intoxication slurred his consonants and elongated his vowels.

I lifted my hands like a stagy tragedian. "I want to feel heroic."

Winston grinned. "Uh-huh, yeah. Slip that under your tongue." He handed me a glossy black capsule. "You'll think you're the risen Krishna."

Time swirled in euphoric friezes after that, and I seem to recall riding up and down the elevator for hours. At some point, I discovered Kat binge-eating in my private pantry. She wore black fur, red skin dye and diamonds, and among her glittery choker necklaces dangled a silver key on a chain. The sight of that key half-eradicated my drug high. It was Kat's heart key. Should she experience cardiac arrest, we were supposed to insert that key in her chest port, turn it three-quarters clockwise and stand back. Preter-creepy.

But Kat didn't seem in danger of heart attack at the moment. Her tall lacquered hairdo had slipped to one side, and her face was smeared with chocolate sauce. "Darling." She flung a frozen éclair at my head.

"Dearest, for me?" I snatched the pastry from the air and took a bite.

Kat hated to be caught in one of her secret feasting sessions. "These things are stale, Nass. You're such a tightwad. When things get old, you should throw them out."

"Katherine, I wouldn't know where to begin."

She saw I didn't intend to leave, so she tore open another box of frozen pastries and crammed her cheeks full. The sight reminded me of something dark and frightening, something from the distant past. Lychee nuts. Long ago in my youth, I remembered cramming my cheeks with handful after handful, until I nearly choked. For two months, I survived on nothing but lychee nuts canned in sweet juice. Quickly, I swallowed another mouthful of éclair to block the memory.

"We're going to Heaven," Kat said through the half-masticated food.

"No we're not." I finished off the gooey éclair and took another.

"Don't be a stupido. Of course we're going. You're a lot of things, Nass, but you're no lily-liver."

"Kat, don't push it. There's more to Heaven than you'll find on the Net."

She swallowed a gulp so large that it made her eyes water. "Tell me. Don't be so freaking mysterious."

I winked and drew a line across my lips, to rile her. Then I grabbed a couple more pastries and left her alone with her banquet.

"Where's Sheeba?" I asked Chad.

He'd been keeping tabs on her with the house security cameras. "She's in the thirty-third-floor library, boss. She's talking with some of your younger guests."

I decided to drop in. She and her friends had pushed my furniture aside to lounge on the floor, and for a while, I stood in the doorway, listening to their nonsense. Sheeba was giving them some kind of lesson about healing.

"The dark is barbarous. It's the source of birth, pain, passion. It's destructive and creative at the same time." She sat cross-legged on a cushion, jouncing and frisking like a hyperactive pup, shedding far too many pink bubbles.

"Yeah, cosmic," said one of her sophomoric disciples. "The primal wildness," said another fool. They'd formed a circle with Shee at their center. Were they ogling her charms, or were these young turks actually paying attention to what she said?

She rocked with excitement. "We've been estranged from the dark, and we miss it. We need its healing violence to rip us apart and remake us."

"So valid." "I hear that." They responded like a chorus.

"We have to find it again." Her voice rose with mystical ardor. "The dark canal is the path."

Juvenile fizz. One of her faith-healer gurus had probably cooked it up—that smarmy Father Daniel, for instance.

With a dramatic flair, Sheeba pulled an e-book from my library shelf and held it up: *Advanced Physiology*. Then she thumped it savagely against the floor. What the heck? My book!

"This is what scientists call enlightenment. Vicious trash. It's heinously askew." She cracked the book's electronic spine, and its indicator lights went dead. "These authors treat the human body like a machine. They totally miss the animating spirit."

"That's an expensive book," I said, but the cheers and clicking mini-lites from her audience drowned me out.

Then she dumped my valuable e-book in the waste can, threw her head back and sighed. "It doesn't matter what they record in their books. Light can never touch darkness. It can only pass through."

I decided to retire before I said something rude. After all, no one expects a delicious young girl to be rational.

Winston's copious stock of drugs kept the party going well into the third day. When the uppers ran out, my guests either had themselves driven home or collapsed in comatose mounds on my carpet. Shee fell asleep in the small bedroom—from exhaustion—she didn't like drugs. I knew she was sleeping alone because Chad kept the security cameras trained on her bed and streamed the real-time images to my wrist-watch. I stole frequent glimpses of her curled pink body via the tiny screen.

Grunze sneaked up behind me and goosed me in the ribs, then leaned over my shoulder and grunted at the screen. "What's with you and that cagey call girl?"

"Call girl? Sheeba's a highly skilled physical therapist."

"She's a hooker. She's tricking you, Nass. I see her better than you do."

"You're wrong. Try her therapy sometime if you don't believe me."

Grunze rolled his shoulders and scoffed. He wore a white thong and body oil, and his skin looked like brown film shrink-wrapped over bulging muscles. For him, girls were a sideshow, a brief diversion from the main event. In our long years of friendship, sexual orientation was one of the few areas where we diverged. I didn't take his words about Sheeba seriously.

"Have you heard Katherine's latest nonsense?" I said. "She wants to surf Heaven. If I didn't know better, I'd say she's premenstrual."

Grunzie's good mood returned. "Kat's a lunatic on the subject. Totally unzipped." He loved taking potshots at Kat.

"Verinne wants to go, too," I said sadly. "We have to talk them out of it."

"Why? It might be a sleek surf. I never knew you to duck a little scary fun."

I shook my head. "Help me, Grunze. We have to change their minds."

He moved closer and bumped me with his hip. "What are you hiding, sweet-piss? You own that sugar factory."

Grunze was right. I held a majority interest in Provendia.Com, the owner of the orbiting factory nicknamed Heaven. Not only did I sit on Provendia's board, but thanks to my whopping investment, they'd elected me chairman emeritus. I knew all about Heaven. If Class One was a lazy stroll, and Class Ten was a death trip through hell, then Heaven was Class Twenty. But the details were too private to explain, even to my bosom pal Grunze.

I said, "Nondisclosure, Grunzie boy. My lips are zipped. But take my word, Heaven is the last place you want to be."

He shrugged his massive shoulders and left to find the sauna.

Some uncounted hours later, only the Agonists stayed awake talking. Win had saved a private stash of Peps to

keep our brains at the appropriate altitude, and we retreated
to my observatory on the eightieth floor—the official Agonist clubhouse. The décor suggested a tree dwelling, a con-
struct dimly recalled from my childhood. Lots of bio
motifs, leaf patterns, green velvet and polished synthetic
wood. Chad had been wanting to update this tree-house
theme for years, but I didn't like to keep changing things—
it cost too much.

My condo tower stood near the northwest arch of Nordvik's city-spanning dome, and my observatory bubbled
outside the dome like a small blister. High-powered tele-
scopic equipment poked out through my window walls.
Some peered at the smoggy Norwegian sky while others
tilted inside the dome toward neighboring condos. On a
wide-screen Net node, Verinne showed us her latest
research—she was always scouting out new wars. I sat on a
moss green ottoman, half-crocked, swaying gently back
and forth and gazing sloe-eyed at my comrades.

Winston sprawled across my sofa with one bare leg
thrown over the armrest. He balanced a liter of frozen
daiquiri on his chest, and its dripping moisture ringed the
front of his orange robe. Now and then, he snored. Grunze
sat on the floor, playing with Kat's toes, trying to annoy
her. Kat had commandeered my floral chaise lounge,
where she sat lotus style with a notebook spread in her lap,
sawing a strand of scarlet hair between her large front
teeth. Verinne perched on the edge of my desk, working a
handheld remote to scroll her research data. I glanced casually at my wrist-watch to check on Sheeba—and had to
grip my wrist to hold the screen steady. One of my male
guests was entering her bedroom.

"We're going to Heaven?" Winston sat up with a jerk
and barely caught his tilting drink.

"Forget that," I mumbled, glowering at my wrist. Who
was that guy in Sheeba's room?

"Heaven's only the nickname because it smells so
sweet. It's a sugar factory." Kat flicked her stylus steadily
against her knee, hyper as usual.

"I hardly think it has a smell, Katherine." Verinne cleared her throat. "The satellite orbits in hard vacuum. Its official name is Provendia A13, and it produces protein-glucose base. Not sugar."

Kat flushed and glared. When Grunze tugged one of her toes too hard, she kicked him in the teeth.

"We're not going to Heaven." My words came out garbled.

"It's in outer space? Fan-fuckin-tastic." Winston slurped frozen daiquiri through a straw and accidentally snorted a little out his nose.

"Heaven's rated a solid Class Ten. Some of you guys may want to sit this one out," Kat said provocatively.

Everyone protested. "Fuck that." "No way." "I'm up for it."

Everyone except me. I sat grinding my teeth, staring at my wrist-watch, split between this aggravating conversation and the unknown male whose shadow fell across Sheeba's bed.

Grunze pointed at me. "Nasir knows all about Heaven. Tell us, sweet-pee."

Tell you what? I could barely pronounce my own name. The man on my wrist screen was touching Sheeba's knee.

"Artificial gravity," I mumbled.

"What the fuck is that?" Grunze crossed his legs and made his thigh muscle jerk at me.

"The factory spins," Verinne answered, "and centrifugal force creates an effect like gravity."

On my tiny screen, the intruder leaned over Sheeba's pink body and nudged her awake. "Beast," I snarled. Then I fell off the ottoman.

"Sweet-pee, you're the one who's spinning." Grunze kneed me in the ribs.

"Nassssty Nas, you slipped off your stool." Winston giggled like a half-wit.

Verinne logged a note in her laptop, while Kat inhaled another line of Peps and fastidiously cleaned her nose.

On my wrist-watch, the stranger was crawling into bed

with Sheeba. I staggered to my feet. "Excuse me. Something I have to . . . Downstairs . . . I'll be . . ."

Kat snarled. "The cultured Mr. Deepra can't admit when he needs to piss."

"Don't let the toilet lid fall on your wanker," Winston added. "I did that once."

Winston was describing this emotional incident as I stepped into my elevator. "Seventy-eight," I said. The small bedroom lay two floors below my observatory, and as the elevator dropped, I fought to keep from retching. After three days of partying, quite a few mood swingers bopped through my bloodstream. Quickly, I whipped out my mirror and adjusted my hair.

When the elevator opened, I rushed down the hall, burst into Sheeba's bedroom and found Robert Trencher massaging my love's rosy thighs. His jaded eyes swiveled. Picture me tottering in the doorway, red-faced, clutching the jamb, breathing in snorts.

"Nasir." Sheeba sat up in bed.

She hadn't been fully awake until that moment. I could sense this by the way she instantly jerked apart from Trencher and drew the covers up to her chest. Clearly, I'd rescued her just in time.

"Sheeba darling, we need you upstairs. I'm not interrupting, am I?" Though the words caught in my throat like clotted mud, I tried to sound urbane.

She pushed waxy fuchsia locks out of her eyes and sighed—with relief, I'm sure. "Give me a minute, Nass."

"Trencher." I nodded in sullen greeting.

"Deepra." He nodded back, equally grim.

When Sheeba and I were alone in the elevator, I ground my false dental implants and plotted revenge against Trencher. The worst of it was, I'd hired him. The guy had showed so much potential, I'd treated him as a friend. Now look, the dirtbag was sneaking around with my Shee—in my own condo.

Sheeba smoothed her waning pink foam to cover more of her body. "Who needs me upstairs?"

Frankly, I hadn't considered why anyone might need Sheeba upstairs, but necessity is the mother of lies. "We're planning a surf. You want to understand why we do it, so I thought you could listen in."

"Oh." She brightened and bounced on tiptoes, then stooped to kiss my cheek. "Thanks for remembering, Nass. You are totally sympathic."

I kissed back, but in my woozy state, my lips missed her and sucked empty air.

In my absence, Verinne had rastered a virtual screen across the domed observatory ceiling, and the Agonists lay supine on couches and floor mats, gazing upward and arguing. The screen displayed a schematic view of A13, the orbiting satellite we surfers called Heaven. Blood rushed to my cheeks. Why couldn't they forget that place? When Sheeba said, "Hello," they sat up and scowled.

"Private session," Kat said. "No outsiders allowed."

Sheeba glanced at me, and her disappointment twisted my musty old heart inside out. She said, "Pardon, I thought I was invited."

"Screw you, Kat." I drunkenly nudged Sheeba forward. "Shee's my guest."

"Sheeba's a-okay with me." Winston lifted his glass and sloshed daiquiri on my carpet.

"Too risky. This is a Class Ten surf, and she's a freakin' newbie." Grunze lay back and laced his fingers behind his head.

Kat nodded. "Don't take this to heart, Sheeba dear, but if you screw up, you'll put the entire crew in danger."

Sheeba lowered her voice. "I'm not your danger, Kat."

"Leave her alone. She'll do just fine," I said without thinking. Never had it occurred to me that Sheeba might join our war surf. I'd brought her here to listen—to get her away from that Trencher slime. But I'd had too much to drink, and when my friends started razzing her, of course I took her side. "Sheeba's *in*."

"Beau." She pushed my weaving hand away. "If they don't want me—"

"But I want you, dear. Please stay."

As she tilted her head back and studied the projection on the ceiling, her eyes got that twinkly transcendent gleam, and I knew more spiritual fizz was about to bubble forth. Sure enough, she breathed almost reverently and said, "This may be the dark canal."

I glared at the crew. "Sheeba's my guest. Any objections?"

My challenge was potent, because they were all my guests, eating my food, drinking my booze—not just at this party but at all the parties. I played host every time. My condo was the staging ground for all our surfs. Not only that, I underwrote our Web site and paid for our teleconference minutes. The others were cheapskates.

Kat flushed purple and lay back to study the ceiling screen. "It's a stupid idea, Nass. Whatever happens, it's on your head."

Grunze was already drawing laser highlights on the schematic, tracing our proposed route. In a sour tone, he said, "Just keep her outta my way, sweetheart."

Verinne said, "You'll have to outfit her. She doesn't have any gear."

Winston patted a spot on his sofa. "Lie here, Sheeba girl. This is nice and comfy."

"No." I steered her to my personal futon. "Sheeba stays with me."

4

WE HAVE RULES

"The rapid progress of the sciences makes me, at
times, sorry that I was born so soon . . . All diseases
will be cured, even old age."
—BENJAMIN FRANKLIN

Sheeba fell among us like a raindrop among hard crystals of salt. However each of the Agonists may have
felt about her, we all coveted her youth. I see it clearly now.
Waiting in this anteroom with its murky fluorescent light, I
see how we envied and desired her, how we competed for
and against her. We longed for her unblemished surfaces.
We craved her oblivious good cheer. In our separate ways,
we yearned to steal inside her and dissolve.

"Your hands look rough, dear. You mustn't be careless
with your skin." Verinne squeezed a drop of pearlescent lotion into Shee's palm. "I'll lend you my cream. It's made
from human milk."

"Wanna watch me bench-press?" Grunze flexed to show
her his muscles. "Fifty says you can't lift a tenth the weight
I can. Come on, Shee. I dare ya."

"Poor Sheeba, no wonder you're clumsy. Your feet are
huge." Kat made a sucking sound with her teeth. "Didn't
your mother tell you about hormone control?"

Winston took her in his arms. "Hiya, Shee. Let's do a
movie tonight."

Leave Sheeba alone, I wanted to roar at them. Shee's
my guest. I found her. I'm paying her way. But of course I
didn't say that. Instead, I complained about aches and

coaxed Sheeba into giving me extra massages. And I bought her things.

Right after the party when I finally sobered up, my first urge had been to kick myself in the head for inviting Shee to a war surf. The risk, ye gods! But my darling girl talked nonstop about surfing. She attached some kooky spiritual meaning to the zone, and her enthusiasm for my sport secretly thrilled me. She kept gazing at me with moony eyes, chattering about the dark canal, and asking when we could go. Her attitude caromed from breezy playfulness to grave fascination. I couldn't let her down. So I decided it would be okay to take her through an easy Class One zone. And I vowed fervently to watch over her and keep her safe.

Kat's space shuttle needed maintenance, so she had to go offworld for a while. And Grunze had to get his ailing quadriceps replaced with electroactive polymer, a grueling operation but worth every wrenching spasm, according to his doctors.

Consequently, I organized an easy Class One expedition with just Sheeba, Winston, Verinne and myself. We planned to cruise a little brouhaha raging between Gromic.Com and one of its seafarms. A place called MR407 in Bengal Bay.

"Don't forget to take off your signet," I warned Verinne on the morning of our trip.

She gave me her classic scowl—acerbic tight lips and one arched eyebrow. Then she removed her signet stud from her tongue.

I said, "You, too, Win. The cops watch this seafarm twenty-four/seven. If they read our IDs, we're scorched."

"Right, right." Winston gamely tugged off his signet ring.

My signet was permanently implanted in my earlobe, so I would have to cover it later with magnetic tape to block its beam. Cops patrolled the mutinous seafarm every hour, and if they picked up our signet readings, they would be able to identify us remotely and bring us up on charges of criminal trespass. The surfer's second universal law was to remain anonymous. (The first was to remain alive.)

My observatory windows looked out on 3:00 A.M. darkness as we sorted and packed our gear. Chad catered a trailer load of yummy snacks for breakfast. We intended to leave Nordvik before dawn, and for convenience, everyone had slept over at my place. Everyone except Sheeba. Sheeba had not yet arrived. She was late.

Winston halfheartedly picked through his first-aid kit. "Who's she screwing these days? I saw her with some new guy at the Tortoise Club."

"Impossible. She works practically around the clock." I tried not to sound as aggrieved as I felt. With her perfect skin and galloping stride and happy naive laughter, Sheeba had always impressed me as virginal. I pictured her sleeping in a simple teddy between white gingham sheets, as chaste as starlight. Shee was too young to be sleeping around.

Verinne checked her watch—again. "Bengal Bay's in the cyclone belt. We absolutely have to get there and back before the midday heat."

Winston winked at me and patted Verinne's arm, but she was right. Getting a late start was no joke.

First, you need a mental picture of this seafarm. Imagine a translucent balloon floating with the tide like a jellyfish, trailing long ribbon tentacles through the viscous brown ocean. That was MR407 from a distance.

Closer, the balloon resolved into a solar still, a giant floating tub of filtered sea fluid domed with an airtight collection membrane. The sun's heat evaporated the fluid, and the condensed water vapor dribbled down the dome's membrane into catch-basins, while the salts, metals, chemicals and solids were raked off for shipment to subsidiary markets. And that was just the beginning.

Laced around the balloon was a fluted collar of solar panels and oxygen mills. The mills filtered breathable air from the atmosphere, while the solar panels delivered electricity. Shielded under the balloon was a three-story sealed submarine habitat—the farmstead itself—where resident ag workers cultivated an assortment of bioproducts in hydroponic tanks. And trailing underneath the habitat were the osmotic tentacles that harvested carbon, nitrogen, phosphorous, potassium and other basic fertilizers directly from the polluted sea.

Nearly eighteen hundred workers lived aboard MR407, and they were striking over email access. Apparently they wanted to chat with off-site relatives. To make their point, they kidnapped their local exec manager, and in reply, Gromic.Com dumped thick black paint over their solar still so they couldn't make water. Now the farm lay under a quiet, insidious siege.

I wanted Sheeba's maiden run to be as soft as baby fuzz. We would approach by jet skis, land on the collar, climb up the dome and stick on a transponder patch to prove we'd been there, then get away fast before the noon heat triggered thunderstorms. Nothing gnarly. No thermal-energy waves to dodge. No hostile encounters. The hardest part would be finding footholds on the slippery plastic membrane.

"Why bother with a plan? This is a Valium surf." Winston squinted at my maps through glum, wet eyes. His energy tabs were fighting a war with the alcohol left in his system from the night before, and his head jerked with infinitesimal quavers. He scratched his sparse chin hairs— he'd forgotten his beard suppressor again. "What am I doing awake at this hour?"

Verinne tossed him a climbing harness. "You'd do well to practice your form."

She was swiftly coiling rope into a bag, counting the loops in silence. Verinne approached every surf with solemn precision. She'd rolled up her sleeves for the work, though, and I marveled at how coarse her skin had grown. Her arms looked like packed sand.

"Time to load up," she said.

"I'm on it," Chad announced through the house intercom.

Then he directed his team of dumb robots to carry the gear, while he remained aloof. Chad existed strictly as a virtual Net agent. He considered it demeaning to instill himself in hardware.

"We can't leave without Sheeba." I frowned at the expensive new surface suit I'd bought her. Pearly pink with silver lightning bolts down the pant legs and a matching helmet. It lay across my futon like a glittery shadow of the missing girl.

Winston, Verinne and Chad's troop of robots were packing the car outside on my rooftop landing pad when Sheeba's call came through. I cupped my hand over my wrist-watch so I could see her tiny image better. "Where are you? Were you in an accident?"

Her smile was all frisky innocence. "I'm on my way up now."

The small screen showed her bopping into my elevator. Midnight blue hair, lemon yellow skin, dangling jewelry. She wore a white workout leotard, and she'd tied her hair back. Her makeup looked smudged.

"I expected you last night. What happened?"

She beamed a smile of pure candor. "I didn't think last night was definite."

Not definite? For an instant, I wanted to shake her. The closer I squinted at the screen, the clearer I saw the mascara smudged around her eyes and the lip gloss smeared over her chin. She'd come here straight from some lover's bed.

But then she bounded out of the elevator, grabbed me in an armlock and lifted me off my feet. "Good morning, Nass. I have a blissed feeling about today. We're beginning an Ordic journey. What's this? My new surfsuit? I love the colors!" She twirled around, holding the pink suit to her chest and making it sparkle. "Nass, I feel my center moving. This may be the beginning of a spiritual metamorphosis."

Lovable child. I drew her close and buried my nose in the soft flesh under her chin. Of course, I forgave her for being late. "Dear Shee, don't ever change. You're perfect, here and now."

"I'm not kidding, Nass. We're headed into the dark."

"Right, right." I nuzzled under her chin and inhaled her herbal scent.

Verinne came through the door with a look of disapproval. Then Winston pushed past her and made straight for Sheeba. "Do I get a morning kiss?"

Sheeba was tugging the new pink surfsuit over her leotard, but the silky Kevlax material didn't want to slide over her round feminine bottom. She paused to give Winston a peck on the cheek, and from the way his hands were hovering, I saw he meant to help her squeeze in.

I'm the one who paid for the damned suit. Elbowing Win aside, I showed her how to zip the gaskets and seat the helmet, and I explained the life-and-death significance of an airtight seal. One whiff of Earth's polluted atmosphere meant certain death—the usual safety talk.

"Give me your signet," I told her. "We'll leave it here, just to be molto certain the cops can't read your ID."

The barest trace of irritation passed across her features, then vanished behind her cheerful smile. She slipped off her modest silver ring with its plain glass smart chip. The humbleness of her signet touched me. I locked it in my safe.

Winston and I jockeyed for a place next to Shee in the car, but to no avail. She bounced into the front seat beside Verinne. Luckily, the high-speed flight from Nordvik to Bengal Bay took only two hours. Crammed in back with Winston, I listened with half an ear while he brayed about his new quasi-organic wetware. Good old Win, did he suppose he could captivate Sheeba with his memory sticks? He even pulled back his hair to show us the new ports behind his ears. The scars were still puffy and red. Win claimed these new organic sticks operated more like native memory and that his Alzheimer's problems were a thing of the past. I still had the old silicon type, so I secretly made note of his brand.

Up front, Verinne was speaking to Sheeba sotto voce. I leaned forward to eavesdrop.

". . . and you must preserve your eyes, dear. Have an extra pair of corneas cloned now, while you're still young. You have such lovely clean tears." When Verinne patted Sheeba's cheek, I gawked. Verinne never displayed affection. Imagine my dismay as I watched her chalky old fingers dwell on Sheeba's lemon-colored eyelids.

We landed in Nepal, where, thanks to the rising sea levels, the coastal mountains cut straight down into the thick yellow waters of Bengal Bay. A vast mat of floating debris clogged the harbor near the airport. Empty cargo containers, rusting barrels, plastic. In the hazy morning sun, the trash glistened like beaded tapestry.

Verinne spent a long time helping Sheeba undo her seat belt, and then Winston lifted her out of the car with both arms. Sheeba giggled and made raucous jokes. No doubt, their excessive attentions embarrassed her. As soon as possible, I claimed her hand.

The tepid bay lapped under a veil of surly ochre smog. India brought back no memories. My childhood. My little brother Raju. Prashka, the first love of my youth. All buried. Calcutta lay under the swampy ocean now. Only a few of its old skyscrapers still protruded above the waves, rotted by sun and salt. I had trained myself to forget the mass evacuation. That was long ago, another lifetime—those recollections were edited, erased, shunted to deep storage. I stood gazing at the foam that sloshed around the pier and thought of nothing.

Winston asked the local guides for a weather forecast, and while I was distracted paying for the rented jet skis, Verinne pointed out the special features of Sheeba's new pink surfsuit.

"Satellite earphone. Metavision. And here's your water recycler." Verinne patted the device on Sheeba's breast. "It captures and purifies your waste body moisture. This tube connects to a nozzle in your helmet."

"Sleek. Do I suck it?" Sheeba twirled the helmet and giggled.

"Yes, but first you need to put moisture in. There's a gel

pad here." When Verinne touched the place between Sheeba's legs, I dropped my cash card. Her white hand lingered, cupping Sheeba's crotch. "You can urinate now if you like. The pad will soak up everything. Try it?"

Sheeba must have blushed. I could imagine her color rising under the lemon skin dye.

Get away from Shee, you dried-up old bat. That's what I wanted to shout at the tall willowy woman I had once adored. Instead, I cranked one of the jet skis. Its throaty roar startled Verinne and made her drop her hand. Then I revved it up to drown further conversation. Storm clouds gathered overhead. I felt a dark mood coming on.

As the temperature rose over Bengal Bay, we zeroed our clocks and began timing Sheeba's virgin surf. My mood improved as we glided out through the harbor flotsam. Good old Win couldn't remember the local forecast. So much for his new memory sticks. Win suffered from a mutated strain of Alzheimer's that failed to respond to traditional antibody therapies. No matter how often he upgraded his implants, synaptic plaques kept fouling his interface.

But we weren't concerned about a forecast. After our global climate reeled through those first cataclysmic years, things settled down—as they always do—in predictable routines. Since the early 2200s, Bengal Bay's weather had followed a clockwork pattern: Morning calm. Afternoon cyclones. Evening heat.

Soon we encountered open sea and chop. Winds were coming out of the south, shearing froth from the crests of the lathery waves, and a dense morning smog closed in. Chad called with news about my Trandent holdings, and we decided to vote out the current CEO. He also reminded me of a hair appointment.

Since I was wearing a surfsuit and gloves, I couldn't browse the IBiS screen, so I asked Chad to check it remotely. On his command, my implanted biosensor instantly pinged every NEM in my body, then beamed the data through the Net to my various doctors and monitoring agents, and finally relayed a status back to the processor in my thumb.

Chad read the message aloud. "All systems normal, boss." Those words always warmed my heart.

Reassured, I spoke to Sheeba through my helmet sat phone. "Switch on your metavision, dear. It'll help you see."

"Try this, Sheeba." Winston accelerated to top speed, then stood up in his stirrups and nonchalantly crossed his arms. Breezes whipped at his surfsuit as he skimmed over the waves, steering the jet ski with his thighs. I'd seen him do this trick before.

Immediately, Sheeba followed suit. "Weeee!" she squealed, cutting a wide figure eight. For a beginner, she caught on fast. "Para-physical!"

Naturally, I had to prove I could do the trick as well. Verinne deployed her Bumblebee to take pictures, and we started bouncing over each other's wakes and getting air, which is not as easy as it looks, standing up with your arms crossed.

"Ooh! I see it!" Sheeba pointed south.

We all slowed down and scanned the horizon. Metavision turned the muddy sea to iridescent purple, and the sky glowed gold. Yes, far to the south, there was one small speck of black.

"Right." "That's it." "I see it, too," we chorused. The seafarm.

The way Shee bounced in her saddle made us laugh. Surfing with an eager newbie gave our sport a fresh tang, and in high spirits, we raced each other across the dingy waves, then braked and coasted into the foamy lee of the giant seafarm. The solar still loomed much larger than the video had led me to expect, and the dome, coated in Gromic.Com's gooey black paint, towered half a kilometer above sea level. We were supposed to climb that?

"Hmm." Verinne pointed to a patchy area halfway up the dome. "Should've brought my cameras."

I cued my visor for zoom, and when the image magnified, I saw the moving figures. Agitators. Twenty at least. They'd rigged flimsy rope ladders, and they were clinging to the dome's exterior, scraping off a small swath of black paint.

"They're not wearing surfsuits," said Sheeba. "They're breathing atmosphere. Doesn't that mean they'll die?"

True enough, they wore only their faded gray Gromic.Com uniforms. A few sported makeshift hoods, and most wore strips of cloth tied over their faces. Thin protection against poisonous atmosphere.

"Surfsuits are not standard issue for workers." Verinne flipped open the saddlebag to get her climbing gear.

"Yeah, protes don't go outside much," said Winston.

"But they're just kids." Sheeba gazed at the workers for a long time.

I chewed my lip, wanting to advise her to look away. Negative images like that can stick in your mind for years. Like lychee nuts. Bright little red fruits. They get inside your dreams. Look away, Sheeba. I was on the verge of speaking, but Verinne beat me to it.

"Ignore them, dear. Protes never live long anyway."

Sheeba said nothing.

The choppy waves bounced us around, and the sea-farm's collar rose and fell with mountainous slapping quakes. I tried to lasso a cleat on the collar, but the swells kept throwing off my aim. Heat was building up inside my suit, so I checked my watch again. Almost 11:00 A.M., local time. We were behind schedule. I boosted my suit's coolants and studied that collar of machinery. Boarding in these heavy seas would not be simple.

"I wanna talk to those kids." Sheeba looped her tether line around her forearm and stood up in her saddle.

"Crazy girl, you'll overturn!" I shouted.

Before any of us could react, she made a dazzling leap onto the collar, grabbed one of the oxygen mills and tied off her line. "Throw me your ropes. I'll pull you in," she said.

"Hey, guys, I have an idea." Winston had been goofing around, turning his jet ski in lazy donuts among the waves.

Now he spurted twenty meters away from us, then did a tight U-turn, revved up and headed straight into the collar at ramming speed.

"What is he doing?" Verinne rose in her stirrups, one gloved fist pressed to her helmeted mouth. "He thinks he can jump his jet ski onto the collar."

"He'll kill himself," I murmured, disbelieving.

As he roared past, he yelled, "Watch this, Sheeba."

Winston impacted the collar just as it was rising on a massive wave. When the jet ski tumbled, Win flew over the handlebars. He whacked into the face of a solar collector, which luckily swiveled on its mount and spun with his weight. Win accelerated like a space probe looping around the sun, then rocketed off in a short parabolic arc, splashed down in the waves and sank.

Sheeba dove into the water. I was staring dumbfounded at the empty place in the waves when I heard Verinne scream. Curiously, my first thought was how rarely Verinne raised her voice.

"Stop her!" Verinne screamed again. "She'll drown. I didn't show her how to inflate her life vest."

Verinne's words incited me to inflate my own life vest. Then the adrenaline of battle kicked in for both of us, and we settled into calm, swift action. In seconds, we secured our jet skis to Sheeba's line, then plopped into the sea and began paddling around the surface like snorkelers, peering into the deeps. With metavision, we could see hundreds of meters down. And there was Sheeba, ten fathoms below, dodging among the clabbered spirals of sea trash, kicking her strong young legs toward the surface with Winston's inert body in tow.

When her helmet broke through the waves, Verinne grabbed her arm, and I yanked the ring to inflate her vest. She was safe. Then I felt for Win's vest ring. His helmet appeared intact, but his body moved with the slack deadweight of unconsciousness.

"Be gentle. His back is broken," Sheeba said. "We should call an ambulance."

Verinne held tight to Sheeba's arm. "This is a war zone. We're here illegally. We never call outsiders."

While they were talking, I speed-called Chad and reported our situation. "Chad will have an ambulance waiting for us at the pier," I told them.

"Not good enough. We need help now!" Sheeba yelled.

"We'll call Kat," I suggested.

"She's offworld test-driving her shuttle. And Grunze is having quadriceps surgery. He's probably still under sedation." Verinne struck the waves with her fist. "Damn. I'm not even uploading any video. Nobody watches a Class One surf."

I tried to think. "Who else could we trust to keep this quiet?"

Verinne wiped a spray of brown foam off her faceplate. "Maybe we could call someone from the Paladin crew."

"Those pinheads? They'll never let us live it down," I said.

"Guys, he has a broken back." Sheeba pushed away from us and hauled Winston toward her jet ski. "First, I'm going to stabilize him. Them I'm going to call an ambulance."

"No, Sheeba. We have rules. You can't—"

A shadow passed over us, and we looked up to see the gleaming white underbelly of a World Trade Organization police cruiser. The loudspeaker blared, "Nasir Deepra, you are under arrest."

What? They knew my name? I slapped the side of my helmet. My earlobe. I'd forgotten the magnetic tape to seal my signet implant. Brilliant. The cops had scanned my identity.

"Nass, you're on your own. Come with me, Sheeba. Hurry!" Verinne mounted her jet ski, whipped out her knife and cut the tether line. "Sheeba, they don't know who we are. We can still get away. What are you doing?"

Amid the rolling waves, Sheeba was lashing Win's broken body to the side of her jet ski. She'd improvised a neck brace out of the seat pad. Clever, I noted, even as a lump of bilious dread rotated in my gut. Me, Nasir Deepra, trillionaire, chairman emeritus, member of half a dozen Com boards, I was under arrest for trespassing! The war surfer's deepest humiliation. And on a freaking Class One surf! I called Chad to mobilize my lawyers.

"Sheeba. Come," Verinne commanded.

"I can't." Sheeba finished lashing Win's body. "Go on. Find Winny an orthopedic surgeon. And get an Isis amulet. The best ones are made of jasper."

Verinne hesitated only a second. When she revved up her jet ski and took off, her wake splashed in our faces. Steam was rising from the ocean now, and grayish white-caps churned around the seafarm, pitching us like corks. One huge crasher drove me against Winston's overturned jet ski. Something snapped in my shoulder, and my left thumb tingled with an IBiS alert. "Norphine!" I shouted to my suit. As the cop cruiser lowered its grappling hook, I watched Verinne disappear in the violent sea.

The WTO cops rescued us just before the afternoon twisters touched down. Climbing through the smog in their cruiser, we caught glimpses of monstrous waterspouts, and I visualized Verinne dodging through the gale. Strange providence. Our exit came just in time, but we could hardly view the World Trade Org as a savior.

The cops took the three of us to a detention center in Kobe, Japan, and by the time we got there, Chad had arranged a teleconference with my lawyers. I liked Kobe, nice restaurants, but we didn't see much of it on that trip. Nor did we see a doctor, not even a cyberdoc. Following my cue, Sheeba steadily refused to give her identity—she giggled and played coy with the cops, treating the whole experience like a game—but that didn't prevent them from sampling her DNA and tagging her with a trespass viola-tion. Poor Win logged an arrest record, too, though he didn't know it till later, when he woke up in a Nordvik health church with six spanking new artificial vertebrae.

Chad paid the fines, they let us go, and for nine days, I became the laughingstock of war surfers. Nasir Deepra jokes suffused the airwaves. Lame. Stupido. But much worse than that, the Agonist crew slipped into second place in the northern hemisphere—and that jerkwad Paladin crew took first rank!

Back home in the privacy of my condo, I tore out the signet with my fingernails. If I'd been flexible enough, I would have kicked myself in the skull. Instead, I called Shee for a therapy session. Deep-tissue massage, that's what I needed. As she straddled my back on the floor mat in my observatory, I whimpered softly.

"Surfing didn't used to be this hard. What's wrong with me? How could I go so limp on a freaking Class One?"

"It doesn't matter, beau. We saved Winston's life." Since our return, Sheeba had grown distracted and subdued, probably worried about the arrest.

"I'll clear your record, Shee, no matter what it costs."

She dug her thumbs into my trapezius muscles. "Do you think those kids knew they were going to die?"

"They think I'm an idiot," I mumbled into my pillow—meaning of course my fans and rivals, not the pathetic Gromic.Com kids. I felt too chagrined to meet Sheeba's eyes. After all the bragging I'd done about my surfer skills, what must she think of me? That arrest had wounded me in the tenderest part of my makeup.

"They were so *small*," Sheeba said. "I've heard employees tend to be stunted because of their diet, but why don't they eat better? Their food's free." She leaned on my back and crushed the air out of my lungs. My spine popped in three places. "And why did they go outside without gear? That was askew."

"We'll have to do a gnarly bold surf to get back into first place." I chewed my pillow and brooded. "Something huge and unexpected. Maybe the *Lorelei*."

Sheeba's fingers traced circles in my hair. "Kat mentioned a zone called Heaven."

"Kat should keep her mouth shut."

I twisted the pillow. Kat kept harping on the one zone we could never go near. Still, we needed to pull off a mega-mother of a war surf—and soon. What would Sheeba think if we settled for second place?

"Forget what's past. Focus on what's next," I muttered, my personal motto.

"Because the future is certain, but the past can change," Sheeba replied. Then she blew a raspberry against my neck. "It's true, Nass. We revise our memories all the time. It's how we stay happy. Like making up fairy tales."

More mystical effervescence. At least she sounded more cheerful. I rolled to face her. How bewitching she looked straddling me on the mat. "Well, our future certainly has to include one huge, hairy war surf to take back the top rank."

She grinned. "Heaven?"

"Not Heaven. You can be certain of that."

5

YOU CAN AFFORD IT

**"Is it not strange that desire should so many years
outlive performance?"**
—WILLIAM SHAKESPEARE

"Ne-ver. Do I have to spell it?"

"But your lamebrain arrest doesn't leave us any choice."

"Katherine, that's absurd."

Kat and I circled each other practically nose to nose in the center of my observatory. The key to her heart bounced on its silver chain and caught the light every time she moved.

"We have to surf Heaven," she ranted.

"No. We can surf the *Lorelei*. It's a major Class Nine, and it'll earn us more than enough points to take back first rank."

The others watched from the sidelines, probably hoping for action. In our long, eventful relationship, Kat and I had more than once come to blows.

"They're calling us dinosaurs." Kat's front teeth protruded dangerously over her lower lip. "They say we're obsolete. Nasir, they're *laughing* at us."

As I cower here in this airless fluorescent room waiting for my future to unreel, how well I recollect our grim mood after the seafarm fiasco. My ego was rubbed raw. When a surf goes right, it's transcendent, but if you get cocky and let details slide, you can make a royal botch of things. Kat swore we would not let that happen again. We would prepare with utmost exactitude. We would focus, pay attention, itemize.

"But that won't be enough to get us through Heaven!" I roared.

Kat and I had been wrangling for days. She called me a mouse. I called her a redheaded fascist. I spouted breathtaking lies to scare my friends away from Heaven. My excuses ranged from limp to fairly ingenious, but I never gave the real reason. That was too shady and convoluted to explain.

Just as I was about to sputter one more annihilating insult, Verinne interrupted. "Nasir, please. I need this."

Cara Verinne. Her chalky brows rose in two hopeful arcs toward her widow's peak, and her dry gray eyes urged me to yield. Verinne wanted Heaven to be her swan song, her grand finale. Quietly, she coughed into her handkerchief with a hacking sound that cut through my resolve. It killed me to disappoint Verinne.

"We'll vote," Kat said. "Verinne and me, that's two for Heaven. Who else?"

Grunze rubbed his bald head and gave me a sheepish grin. "I'm with the girls on this."

"Grunzie!" Betrayed by my best friend.

"Ha, three votes. Majority rules." Kat sashayed around my futon, gloating.

"Screw voting. We WILL NOT do this surf." I went bonzo and started throwing cheese snacks. I threatened to lock up the tequila and cancel the Web site. I was desperate. For a fleeting instant, I actually considered telling them the truth about Heaven.

Thank the idol gods, events tend to arrange themselves by laws other than human will. That very day, an enormous CME occurred. For the uninitiated, that's "Coronal Mass Ejection." Basically, it's an aneurysm on the sun. Picture shock waves of solar wind spewing out from the sun's corona and colliding with the Earth's magnetic field. Intense X rays blast the ionosphere, and gigatons of solar protons auger in to zap communications. Lethal radiation builds up, threatening even the most spaceworthy passenger cars and disturbing the peace of war-surfing parties. This timely CME put Heaven beyond the pale.

But the canceled trip left Verinne devastated. She tried not to show it, although even Winston noticed her long silences. By that time, Verinne was spending half her waking hours in acute bioNEM therapy, and she admitted to me privately one night that it wasn't helping. I was the only one who knew how fast her time was running out.

To comfort Verinne and placate my crew, I offered to underwrite the full cost of surfing the *Lorelei*, a mega-challenging Class Nine rain-harvesting ship owned by Greenland.Com. Like Heaven, the *Lorelei* would be a "first assault," meaning no other crew had tried it yet. If we performed well, the *Lorelei* would put us back on top.

Let me be frank though. My main objective was to restore Sheeba's faith in me. That seafarm episode had left her quiet and gloomy, but if anything, it deepened her interest in surfing. She still hoped to find her dark canal, or whatever the heck it was. And I needed her approval too much to tell her she couldn't come. I needed her to witness my boldness. And, well, if she wanted dark scenes, the *Lorelei* would fill the bill.

Bombed out, radioactive and presumed lifeless, the old rain ship drifted in the Arctic Ocean. Why, you may ask, was this disabled hulk rated Class Nine? Partly due to its high ambient radiation, but mainly because of its cargo. The *Lorelei* carried a cache of fetuses. They were frozen DNA duplicates of Greenland.Com's senior staff—a sort of key-man insurance policy. When the Greenland execs hid their crèche aboard the *Lorelei*, they didn't account for the whims of the ship's aging and poorly maintained nuclear reactor.

Its explosion gutted the ship and fried the workers en masse. Still, many experts believed the cryogenic tanks preserved the precious cargo—and talk about salvage value. If those embryos were still viable, their price on the hot market would be staggering. But no one could go aboard to check because the ship was tied up in a lawsuit, and the World Trade Org maintained a sensor-net blockade to keep everyone out. That WTO blockade pegged the *Lorelei* a Class Nine.

"Strictly speaking, it's not a war," Verinne pointed out. "There are no hostiles."

"What do you call a WTO lawsuit?" I argued. "Nothing's more hostile than that. Besides, the *Lorelei* has an official zone rating. All crews recognize it."

"But I don't have a rad-hardened surfsuit," said Winston.

"Quit grousing. You can afford it." Grunze scooped up a cracker full of cheese dip and swallowed it whole, then noisily licked his fingers.

Perched on my sofa, Shee watched our faces and listened. She wore a lavender sari and a frosting of peach skin dye. Her pinwheel, turquoise-and-white contact lenses spun disconcertingly every time she blinked, and her hair was stuffed under a white knit cap, which made her look younger than ever.

Kat fidgeted beside her, flushed and ruddy, in jet beads and formfitting black suede, wrapping a strand of red hair round and round her index finger. Verinne, in her usual dun unisuit, crouched on the floor and squeezed medicinal drops in her eyes. Winston, in elegant silks, roamed aimlessly in the background, playing with my telescopes. Grunzie and I sprawled on the futon in our terry robes, near the food. We were feasting on cheese snacks, popping them into our mouths by the handfuls. Of course we all wore stomach pacemakers to control our digestion and limit caloric intake.

"The hard part is getting through the sensor net. That's mega-sleek tech," said Kat.

"Right. We can't circumvent it, so we run straight through it," I said.

Verinne wiped the excess eyedrops from her cheeks. "Run a WTO blockade? It's never been done."

"The trick is speed," I said. "We'll be in and out so fast, they won't even notice."

"And how do we achieve this faster-than-light velocity?" Verinne asked.

"Yeah, sweet-pee?" Grunze engulfed another cracker. "Don't tell me you're thinking about the *Celerity*."

When I grinned and nodded, Grunzie flashed his teeth. Kat spat out her strand of hair and said, "Ooh." And Verinne popped open her notebook to run a search.

Winston said, "What's the *Celerity*?"

Win knew about the *Celerity*, but he'd forgotten. So I explained it again, partly for Sheeba's benefit. The *Celerity* was an experimental, high-speed, plasma-powered submersible. It had been developed in secret by Deuteronomy.Com, on whose board of directors I faithfully served. Taking the *Celerity* out for a recreational spin wasn't exactly orthodox, even for a board member. But we Agonists had our ways.

"Um, Nasir?" Sheeba actually raised her hand like a schoolgirl. Those pinwheel contact lenses made it impossible to guess what she was thinking. "This rain ship, are all the workers dead?"

"Scorched to cinders." Grunze flexed his triceps. "The nuclear blast went through that ship like a blowtorch."

"Hostiles won't be a problem," Verinne added as she browsed her search results, "although we may get some noteworthy Reel."

Sheeba kept gazing wide-eyed, evidently hoping for more explanation, and those three adorable little furrows creased her eyebrows. I squeezed her hand.

"The *Celerity*'s docked in Point Barrow," Verinne announced. For fast info retrieval, count on Verinne every time.

"Perfect," I said. "It'll be a short hop from there to the *Lorelei*, once we find her."

Once we find her, yes. The WTO's sensor net blocked the rain ship's location on satellite scans. Didn't I say this was a Class Nine surf?

But trust Verinne. In the next few days, she scanned the Arctic from coast to coast using magnetic resonance and

gamma-ray triangulation. Her scans turned up a gargan-
tuan list of submarine objects somewhat close in size to the
rain ship. Then, with sublime artistry, she programmed an
algorithm to sift the data based on the *Lorelei*'s technical
specifications. From the two hundred thousand possibles
her search yielded, we were able to pick out the *Lorelei* by
exact weight.

While everyone was toasting Verinne's success, Sheeba
pulled me aside. "Nass, this rain ship rattles me. My aura's
turning beige."

"Dear heart." I embraced her. Despite my spine extension, Shee still overtopped me, and when we cuddled, my
nose nestled sumptuously under her chin. From there, I
said, "Sheeba, everybody's spooked by a Class Nine. All
you need is confidence."

"Beau, that's not it."

"Kat's been needling you. Just tune her out, Shee. Confidence is a matter of acting. Strut onto the stage like you
own it, and—"

She pushed away and shook her head. "We'll find dead
bodies."

"Oh." I patted her hand. The Reel. The thought of the
rotting corpses aboard that ship gave me the willies, too.
"Don't worry, Shee. In time, you'll learn to disconnect. It
just takes practice."

"Disconnect." She said the word as if testing the way it
felt on her tongue. After a long silence, she said, "The dark
canal is meta-grievous, beau."

Her words chilled me. I stroked her silky arm, envi-
sioning grisly scenes. Putrid flesh, blistered bones, loose
hanks of hair. Memories swirled up from the boggy bottom of my past, images I tried every day to forget. Suddenly, the taste of lychee nuts filled my mouth, and I
swallowed hard.

"Darling, we can arrange not to see any dead bodies.
Will that suit you?"

She seemed preoccupied, and when I kissed her, she
barely kissed back.

That same hour, I rewrote our surf plan. Instead of boarding the *Lorelei*, we would plant a transponder on the exterior hull. That would verify our feat. Nothing fancy, no run-ins with scorched cadavers. No five-star Reel either, but since I was footing the bill, my crewmates had to agree. Of course, only a powerful hyperwave transponder could break through the WTO's sensor-net blockade, and that meant a severe price tag. I sent Chad to cash some bonds.

In the tense quiet of my observatory three nights before the surf, we delegated tasks. Verinne would track the rain ship's drifting course. Grunze and I would steal the *Celerity*. And Kat would stock our base camp—Winston's yacht. Win would sail the vessel up from Baffin Bay, anchor off the Alaskan coast and play bartender. Winny didn't like his role. He wanted to come on the surf. But his backbone was still healing, and besides, I didn't give him a choice. He might screw up again.

The worst problem was, the submersible would carry only four people. So someone else besides Winston had to stay behind. When I named Grunze, he spat out his mouthful of martini and almost choked.

"You can't pick Sheeba over me!" His meaty fist pounded the table and made our cocktail glasses jump. "You need me, Nass. Everything depends on speed, and a newbie'll slow you down."

"For once, I agree with Grunze," said Kat. "Sheeba's liable to panic. She's too green."

I tried to catch Sheeba's eye, hoping my choice pleased her, but she drew back into the sofa cushions and toyed with her navel ring.

"You should have seen her at the seafarm," I said. "She was terrific."

"Right, the seafarm. That stellar success." Kat flicked her nails.

Verinne remained stiffly mute.

"Grunze, it's a four-seater." I faked a clownish grin. "You want to sit in my lap?"

His facial musculature twisted as if he might cry. "Where are your loyalties?"

Where, indeed? Grunze and I had been friends for a hundred years. We'd shared secrets and stock tips and sexually transmitted diseases. I couldn't answer his question, then or now. As I wait in this anteroom to die, his crestfallen gaze still skewers me. I wronged you, Grunze.

"It's all right, beau." Sheeba bounded off her sofa and scrambled into the hammock beside Winston. "I'll wait behind and go next time."

Win fondled her waist, and his lewd expression drove Grunze off my mental scope. "Sheeba, you're coming with me."

We didn't draw straws or cast lots. As financier, I made the choice by fiat. Sheeba, my inexperienced newbie therapist, would take the place of our seasoned crewmate, Grunze. No one liked it. Yes, it made a rift in our group. A subtle fissure.

We left Nordvik at dawn—always dawn, that ominous hour. I checked at least twenty times that I'd locked my new emerald signet ring in my safe. I would not make that mistake again. Grunze, still grumpy and miffed, flew us straight across the pole and landed on Win's yacht, anchored in MacKenzie Bay. No one was surprised to find Win still snug asleep in his cabin. His bartending skills wouldn't be needed till later.

Filching the submersible from Deuteronomy.Com proved simple enough, once Chad negotiated the various bribes. As we drove back to the yacht, Grunze hardly spoke three words. But sunlight filtered through the Arctic smog like honey, and the sub's power hummed through the steering yoke. At the yacht, we zeroed our clocks, waved goodbye to Grunze and glided away in the sub. I used my travel mirror to check my hair. Zone rush was building around us like a static charge.

"So much for Class Nine. This surf'll be as treacherous as a bubble bath." Grunzie spoke to us over the sat phone. "My money says you ladies finish this gig in two hours."

"One hour or less," I countered.

"I want some of that," said Kat from the backseat.

We were all making an effort to regain our sense of camaraderie. Sitting inside the tiny sub, trying to figure out all the switches and screens, we kept up a forced banter. But Sheeba stayed silent, and I twisted around to see how she was faring. Her porcelain white skin dye made her look waifish. She gave me an elusive half smile.

"This'll be fun," I said, to calm her nerves.

Right then, I should have performed a ritual to mollify the gilded gods. Touched wood. Tossed salt. Sacrificed a body part. Something! Our plan started unraveling the minute we left Win's yacht.

First, the *Celerity* overheated and stalled. The Deuteronomy engineers had designed a new catalytic add-on to increase fuel efficiency, and it crashed. With molto smug teasing, Grunze towed us back to shore, and while Chad found a discreet IT guy to uninstall the add-on, Kat and Verinne argued whether to set our clocks back to zero or to count this delay as surf time.

Then I got a tingly alert from my IBiS. One of my doctors was authorizing a telomerase booster by remote Net link. (The boost was preprogrammed, of course. The actual doctor was probably playing foosball on the moon.) Sure, I needed the boost to lengthen my telomeres and tone up my complexion, but it created inconvenient side effects, like heart palpitations and sudden urges to urinate. Even with Chad to remind me, I could never keep track of all these freaking doctors' appointments.

Next it started raining.

You wouldn't think rain would interfere with a submersible, but you have to understand what global warming has done to the Arctic rain. It falls at times in great brown pellets the size of your fist, half ice, half muddy grit blown up by the storms that scrape the northern continents. This so-called rain perforates the Arctic like a million piledrivers, penetrating ten meters deep. To reach maximum speed, the *Celerity* needed to travel just under the surface, but at that shallow depth, its hull would take punishing hits from the rain.

And we couldn't just wait out the storm, either. Once an Arctic rain system moves in, the pattern can last for weeks. After extended debate, we decided to take the *Celerity* deeper—and slower—till we reached the outer limits of the WTO's sensor net. Then we would rocket up to the rain-whipped shallows, accelerate to top speed and do a drive-by shooting to plant the *Lorelei* transponder by compression gun. Hopefully, this quick turnaround would minimize damage to the "borrowed" sub.

We finally decided to re-zero our clocks when we launched a second time, and I recalled my impetuous side bet. One hour or less. Ha. What sum had I mentioned? Two million deutsch? Well, at least I would plant that transponder and salvage our crew's reputation. With a brave glance at Sheeba, I said, "*Lorelei*, prepare to meet your master."

"Don't presume too much. We're not there yet." Verinne sat beside me in the front passenger seat, reading documentation on her new radiation-hardened helmet.

Meanwhile, Kat shuffled around in the back, making exasperated sighs. "Sheeba, you're hopeless. You have your camera mounted upside down. Give it here. I'll fix it."

That couldn't be. I'd personally checked Sheeba's gear. I twisted to see, but Kat had already popped Sheeba's camera out of its slot.

"Show me your radiation badge," Kat said next. "Sheeba, do you remember what the colors mean? You'll have to pay attention. We can't baby-sit you every minute."

I said, "Stop picking at her, Kat," but Sheeba remained oddly silent.

As we neared the *Lorelei*, Grunze came online to remind us that the sensor net would break our connection. Good old Grunze, he still sounded peeved. "Start your ascent, sweet-pee. And keep those cameras rolling. I wanna see the replay when you get back."

Alarm sirens blared when we hurtled through the WTO blockade. Climbing toward the surface, our sub bucked and vibrated like the inside of a snare drum. Preter-vicious rain. Verinne fought to click her seatbelt, and her new helmet ricocheted off the ceiling.

Kat shook the back of my seat. "Kill that noise. It's making me loco."

"Slack off, Katherine." I shut down the alarm, but the rain still pinged our hull like cosmic static. I glanced at Sheeba and yelled over the noise. "We have two minutes before the cops arrive. Everybody ready?"

The forward viewing screen showed the gutted rain ship floundering in swells not far ahead. Verinne fumbled with her compression gun. She was trying to load the transponder in the chamber when the sub reeled sideways and flung her against the armrest. She said, "How many spare transponders did you bring?"

"Spares? None. Hyperwave transponders cost a bloody pile," I said.

She looked at me with startled eyes. "What if I miss?"

Suddenly our screen view of the *Lorelei* vanished behind a wave that rose like a lathery claw. Its foamy white fangs crashed on our hull and hammered us nose down. We rolled and cartwheeled in the depths, and I had to wrestle the steering yoke and restart the CPU to get us moving upward again. When we surfaced, our distance to the *Lorelei* had widened.

"Ninety-four seconds till the cops come," Sheeba said. She'd set a stopwatch.

"Open the cockpit, and I'll fire the transponder," Verinne shouted. Then another wave bashed us, the sub lurched, and Verinne dropped her gun. "Fuck all."

That's when the certainty hit me. Verinne *would* miss. In this churn, she couldn't possibly hold her aim steady enough. After all this effort and expense, we would blow the surf. Again.

Had we, the almighty Agonists, degenerated into a gang of bumbling old farts? How could that be? The idea almost panicked me. Then sheer determination and a reckless will to spend money kicked in, and I resolved to take back the lead.

"We'll board the *Lorelei*'s hull," I shouted over the muddy ringing rain. "We'll plant the transponder by hand!"

Verinne stated the obvious. "That means more surface time. Your sub will take major damage."

When I turned to check Sheeba's reaction, Kat grabbed my hair and wrenched me around to face her. "Deepra, what about the freakin' cops?"

"We'll be quick," I said. "Everybody suit up."

An electric charge of haste spiked through the cockpit as we scrambled to zip our rad-hardened suits, and I put the submersible in a fast sideways skid, keeping just below the surface to avoid the worst of the rain. When we thwacked hard against the rain ship's flank and bobbed to the surface, the savor of dry fear tingled the undersides of my tongue.

"Nasir, your helmet's loose."

Sheeba leaned over my seat, and Kat grumbled, "You're in my way." But dear Shee persevered and helped me lock my neck ring.

"Double-check your cameras. This is one surf for the record," I said with a shiver. My radiation gauge was already measuring a 40-mrem dose. Pretty hot. Sheeba's badge read the same. I squeezed her hand, then popped our cockpit cover.

Blinding waves sloshed into the cockpit and smeared my helmet visor. The muddy rain hurt, even through our surfsuits. I thought we'd reach out and slap the transponder on the hull in one second flat. But the swells were huge. They'd already separated us from the ship by a good ten meters.

"Thirty-five seconds," Sheeba said through the helmet sat phone.

Mud coated my visor, and the waves tossed us around like a circus ride. In the distance, we saw the strobing flash of an approaching WTO cutter. As the rain pelted us,

Verinne tried again to load the transponder into her compression gun, and Kat and I both reached to help. Then the ocean rose around us like a mountain range, and a wall of water knocked my head against the console.

Perhaps time flowed through a mobius loop. In those pendulous thirty-five seconds, events propagated in ever-widening spheres of probability. Was I the first to unbuckle my seat belt? Did Verinne throw the transponder into the ocean, or did she drop it by accident? What words did Kat scream, and who grabbed my arm? Did I dive for the transponder, or did I fall overboard?

The cops fished me out with a gaffer's hook and reeled me onto their cutter. They blared orders through a megaphone. Kat and Verinne were already onboard, handcuffed together, hanging on to some kind of aerial and trying to stand upright on the rolling deck. And Sheeba?

"Where's Sheeba?" I coughed up sea fluid, then gripped the rail and peered into the rain-whipped swells. Had the *Celerity* sunk? Was my darling girl lost beneath the waves? Can you conceive my white-hot fugue of fear and guilt?

"Don't say anybody's name," Kat warned over our sat-phone connection. "The cops have probably hacked our conference call."

"It'll take the cops two seconds to sample our DNA," I yelled back with the bleak voice of experience. One of the peace officers was trying to cuff my wrist, but I tore away and elbowed him in the groin. "What happened to Sheeba?"

"Shut it," Kat snarled.

"She's still on the sub," said Verinne.

The guard twisted my arm painfully behind my back and snapped on the bracelet. He was about to cuff me to the aerial when a mighty blur of light and spume burst from the sea and arced over our heads. The guard and I hit the deck in unison. Above us, the apparition sailed over the WTO cutter and splashed down on the other side like some mythical seagoing goliath.

"What the fuck is she doing?" said Kat. "She doesn't know how to drive the sub."

My guard forgot about cuffing me and rushed to the rail with his comrades to see where the bizarre phantom had gone down. Seizing the moment, I staggered to my knees and crawled across the pitching deck to where Kat and Verinne were jerking each other by their mutual chain.

"That was the *Celerity*?" I whispered.

"Stupido. They'll overhear you." Kat shook her fist in my face, yanking Verinne's handcuffed arm. "That neophyte threw off our timing. I've never been arrested in my life."

Verinne rubbed her bruised wrist. "Considering your age, Katherine, that's rather sad."

Before Kat could sputter a comeback, the *Celerity* arced out of the ocean again and spiraled in a high, dizzy parabola several meters off the port bow. When it plummeted into the swells, its wake of sea spray exploded across the deck and washed us against the base of a gun mount. Then the cutter's engines powered up, the deck heaved, and the cops gave chase.

The cutter swung to port and sent us rolling. They were probably tracking Sheeba on sonar. When the cutter swung again, Kat grabbed me to keep from bashing into a ladder. "I told you she'd panic."

The ship turned hard to starboard, and we tumbled back toward the gun mount. Verinne's words came out garbled. "She's too young for this level of intensity."

I said, "At least she's making evasive moves."

"She should dive," said Verinne.

"She's outta control," Kat muttered.

All at once, the sub leaped over the cutter's sharp pointed bow and grazed the hull. Sparks flew, and the friction burned off paint. Through veils of rain, blue smoke curled off the deep gash in the *Celerity*'s keel before she vanished into the ocean again.

Kat snickered. "Didn't I read somewhere that sub cost

14 billion deutsch? Hope your little tart gives you your money's worth."

"Shut up, Katherine."

"Admit it, she's making a dunce of you," Kat went on. "Nubile young flesh, ha. A woman's not worth two cents till she's past fifty."

Then Verinne pointed into a deep black wave trough. "The transponder. Look."

Kat and I jostled against each other just in time to see it sink under a monstrous brown wave. The spray knocked us backward.

As Verinne pushed up from the deck, a gust of wind plastered her suit against her skinny chest. She said, "The Paladin crew will keep the lead."

"They're already calling us has-beens." Kat hugged the gun mount. "They say our surfing style's outmoded."

Verinne bowed her helmeted head. "I never dreamed we'd end this way."

I reached for her ankle. "Cara mia, this is not your fault."

Picture us clinging to the rail, huddled miserably in the rain, waiting for the inevitable arrest, fines and public humiliation. Had we reached the final fade-out? Ye graven icons, I hated for Sheeba to witness our demise.

Nothing's more fragile than the conceit of an old man who believes he's young. Sheeba had once called me a seeker. We were seeking the dark, she said. Mystical fizz, but it sounded brave and heroic. Picture me slanting bravely against the winds of reason and sound judgment. Imagine me jutting out my chin, pounding my pectorals and declaiming that I, Nasir Deepra, would show these bums something to remember. Hear me shouting like a vain old cockatiel through the roaring storm.

"We're still the best, and we'll prove it. We'll surf Heaven!"

Verinne crawled toward me. Behind her faceplate, her eyes darkened with hope. "Nasir, do you mean it?"

"Look around you," Kat yelled. "We're finished. We'll never see Heav—"

A thunderous wave drowned Kat's last sentence as the *Celerity* surged up onto the deck right beside us. We stumbled backward as the sub skidded over the rail, drenched us in sea fluid and bumped sideways into the gun mount. While the sub was still sliding, the cockpit cover retracted, and Sheeba yelled, "Hurry! Jump in!"

At first, no one moved. Nanoseconds streamed like light-years as rain bounced against the dented, blackened hull of the most expensive submersible ever built.

"Come on!" Sheeba yelled

The cops raced toward us. Verinne got to the sub first and hauled Kat in by brute force while I made a running jump for the dorsal elevator. The instant Sheeba saw me take hold, she powered up, slued across the deck and crashed through the opposite rail. When we hit the waves, she let go of the steering yoke to pull me inside. It was Kat who climbed into the driver's seat, closed the cockpit and took us down.

"Shee-Shee-Sheeba," Kat stuttered, wrestling the yoke and trying to catch her breath. "You did—that was—well-done!"

6

DOES IT ALWAYS JERK LIKE THAT?

"It is easy to believe that life is long and one's gifts are vast—easy at the beginning, that is."
—ALFRED ADLER

Sheeba's stunts with the submersible saved us from mortifying public arrest and finally earned her full-fledged acceptance by the Agonists. But our *Lorelei* surf was still a debacle. This new failure cost us more precious status points—not to mention a tanker load of my hard cash. In fact, our crew slipped from second rank in the northern hemisphere to fourth. After that, we needed Heaven badly.

Heaven. The zone of zones. It was to be our proof of prowess, reprieve from shame, ticket back to glory. And it scared me to death.

"Don't tell Shee that I, uh . . . that I'm connected with Heaven," I discreetly asked my crewmates.

We'd just finished a cheesecake binge in my observatory, and Kat was downloading her cardio stats through her IBiS. "You mean Shee doesn't know the cultured Mr. Deepra's a warmonger?"

"Slippery Nass." Win sucked his fork. "You want her to think your hands are clean."

"I'm just saying"—I glanced in my travel mirror and flicked an errant crumb from my lip—"Sheeba has some dewy ideas about business. So keep it mute, okay?"

Grunze buckled electronic pec-flexers across his beefy chest. "We got it, sweet-piss. We'll give your tart the snow job."

Five days later, we met again in my condo to run our first virtual-reality scout. The orbiting factory called A13 was not a typical satellite. For one thing, it did not travel in the G Ring with other Com traffic. In that dense belt of geosynchronous satellites circling Earth's waist, not only factories but also broadcast stations, resorts, private homes and science labs vied with each other for trajectory slots. Everyone wanted a site in the G Ring. By contrast, Heaven took its own strangely perturbed polar orbit, steering high and clear of shuttle lanes and distancing itself from neighbors.

Under my observatory dome, Win mixed the margaritas while Chad projected holographic images of A13, deviously lifted from a secure Provendia server. One way my firm controlled costs was by building its factories from the remains of old spaceships. They'd fashioned Heaven from an enormous, bullet-shaped fuel tank. Dented, corroded and weakened by radiation, the old fossil must have been drifting for over two centuries when Provendia resurrected it.

The bullet-shaped tower housed a complete five-story production line with two hundred live-aboard workers. Four lower decks held living quarters and support equipment, while the cavernous fifth deck occupied the tank's upper height—all the way up to the tapering bullet point. This fifth deck housed the food-brewing vats.

Now picture the tank's bullet point linked by a long, flexing tether to a colossal counterweight made from a rough-cut ball of asteroid. Can you see the tank and counterweight whirling around each other in space like a pair of figure skaters? That's it. Three revolutions per minute created enough centrifugal force in the tank's base to approximate Earth-normal gravity.

Verinne emailed us long boring descriptions of A13's artificial gravity, including its weird Coriolis effects. Personally, I didn't browse her text messages because we weren't going to dock with Heaven. Our war zone would

be strictly outside the satellite. On no account would we go
aboard.

Why did this particular war break out? It had been running for nine months, but Verinne's research uncovered no
explanations. Provendia kept A13 confidential, and since I
owned a majority share of the company, Grunze badgered
me for inside dirt. I put him off, claiming the nondisclosure
clause. Finally, I hinted that the protes wanted more vacation time. Well, that was one way to express their griev-
ance. I couldn't tell Grunze the truth.

The first act of war had occurred when A13's resident
workers sabotaged their own docking port. Since then,
they'd been fighting off anyone who tried to board—a
rather self-destructive act because that meant they couldn't
take on supplies. Provendia's gunship was strafing the tank
with small mass-to-target noisemaker missiles—irksome
and debilitating but not powerful enough to rupture the
hull. A13 represented, after all, a valuable piece of real estate. Still, one of those noisemakers could frappe a human
body if it detonated close enough. That fire zone between
the gunship and the factory, that would be our war surf. We
planned to space-dive straight through the middle, wearing
nothing but armored EVA suits. Vicious bold.

"Tell me again, what's the weekly rental on an EVA
suit?" I asked. My crewmates were scarfing snacks, and I
was totaling expenses in my head. Lately, I'd been hus-
banding my pence and pesos with more care.

"Don't go cheap," Grunze said through a mouthful of
Cheez Whiz. "We need the high-performance thruster
packs and full armor."

"Besides, we have to look sexy on our video. This is our
big comeback, and we have the Agonist image to uphold."
Kat licked fudge icing from her arm.

"Then you cough up the change," I said.

"Play nice." Verinne wiped crumbs from her lips and
printed out the price sheet. Now that her dying wish was
about to come true, she made every move with edgy restraint, as if one wrong gesture might jinx the surf and

cause another delay. Delay was one thing Verinne could not afford.

Near the south window wall, Winston and Sheeba erupted with peals of laughter. They were goofing around with my telescopes, pretending to hunt for stars through the heavy Norwegian smog. We all heard Win stage-whisper in Sheeba's ear, "What does EVA stand for?"

Kat and Grunze rolled their eyes. I said, "Win, you need to check your plaque levels again. You're getting that dementia glaze."

Grunze added, "Yeah, Winny, your wetware needs a pressure wash."

"I meant to install another upgrade last week," Win said with a crooked grin.

"They're just peeved because you're so gorgeous." Sheeba wrapped her arms around Win. When she kissed him on the mouth, I crushed a shrimp canapé in my fist, and tiny bits of pseudo-seafood rained on the carpet.

Then Sheeba lowered her voice. "EVA stands for extra vehicular activity. That means spacewalking."

I ground my fake molar implants and watched her blow a raspberry in his hair. She pities the old bugger. She's always drawn to needy people, I rationalized. Way too tenderhearted, that girl. I joined them at the window and offered Shee a fried wonton.

"No thanks, beau. I'm not hungry."

"You've hardly eaten anything." I held her waist and pushed the snack playfully against her lips.

"But I don't—" She laughed and tried to brush my hand away, but when I insisted, she finally opened her mouth and took the food from my hand. Afterward, there was an awkward silence.

"We're leaving early tomorrow," Verinne finally said. "Let's go home and rest."

"Sleep here," I whispered to Shee, "in the small bedroom if you like."

Sheeba loosened my arm from around her waist. "No, I'm too rattled to sleep."

Her answer disappointed me, but I understood how she felt. Heaven rattled me, too, more than any of them could know. Nevertheless, I was committed. My surfer status was on the line.

Chad reserved suites for us at the Mira Club, an elegant resort hotel hovering in G-Ring orbit, thirty-six thousand kilometers above the Amazon delta. We checked into our rooms twenty hours before Mira's path crossed under A13's peculiar trajectory, and we used the hotel's powerful telescopes to watch the Provendia gunship firing on the factory. Did I mention that, in the entire nine months since this war began, no one had penetrated Heaven's zone? Did I mention why?

First, space-diving through hard vacuum is no evening at the opera. You need precise skills and very expensive equipment. Second, even the best pro-line body armor will not block a noisemaker missile. If anyone in our crew took a direct hit, no amount of nanocellular repair could reconstitute the gory chunks of flesh into a living person. But there was a third and more critical reason why this surf surpassed all other Class Tens ever recorded in surfdom archives.

Provendia's management (i.e., myself and my board) had spread a warning that this zone was forbidden to surfers. We announced that violators would be prosecuted, fined, disenfranchised and possibly fired from their jobs. For an exec, getting fired was a catastrophe too dire to speak aloud. It meant demotion to the level of a prote.

Provendia's warning was not an empty threat, either. I signed the order myself. All I could do was trust that my chairman emeritus position—and Chad's draconian bribes—would protect us. More important, our surf route would not take us inside the factory. We would remain outside at all times. I thought that would keep us safe.

On June 6, 2253, local Mira time, we piled into Kat's space shuttle and lifted off. I kept offering Shee little attentions to make her comfortable, and once when I was readjusting her thruster harness, she snapped at me. Pre-surf jitters. Everyone had them. Almost at once, her good humor returned, and she apologized. I gave her a special present I'd been saving, a gold wrist-watch with a pearly pink glow-screen, inscribed with her name, the date and the word "Heaven." She slipped it on with a melancholy smile, and I couldn't tell if she liked it or not. Choosing the right gift for Shee was always so difficult.

Despite our secrecy, news of our attempt had spread like a virus through the surfer underground, and some of our fans chartered a big Dolphin 88 to follow along and watch us dodge bare-assed through Provendia's missile fire in nothing but our flimsy EVA suits. Fame. Huah! We waved our fists and preened for the crowd.

Five of us were making the run. Me, of course. Grunze, Kat, Verinne—and Sheeba. We made Win stay behind to drive the shuttle.

Looking back, I ask myself many questions. Why did we violate common sense and bring a beginner to the riskiest Class Ten in the solar system? Well, it was Kat who stirred Sheeba up with wild rumors about the place, and Grunze who showed her the schematics, and Verinne who took her to practice space-diving in a simulation tank. Winston bought her a smartskin longjohn to keep her snuggly warm. And me, what can I say? I let her eagerness cloud my judgment.

In a matter of weeks, Sheeba had moved from outsider newbie to become the warm magnetic core of our crew. For so many years, it had been just us five. Then subtly, all our positions shifted to align with Sheeba's fresh new field of energy. At least, I think so. Nothing I remember is firm, except how lovely Shee looked in her new EVA suit. It was white with black piping, the same as mine.

"Nasir, thank you." That day, she was all peachy blond, and her nervous fidgeting made her seem more vulnerable than ever. "This is the darkest thing I've ever done."

She wasn't wearing contact lenses, and I remember falling under the spell of her naked eyes. Streaks of gray, green and gold rayed out from her pupils like reflections on water. Why did she ever cover those amazing eyes?

"You can still stay behind. It's not too late." I'd taken every precaution I could think of to keep her safe, yet my neck still knotted.

Sheeba leaned against me and let me feel the weight of her robust young body. "Beau, there's a force building around this trip. We're meant to be here now."

How strangely her words ring in my memory as I wait through this acid fluorescent flicker. The four steel walls of this anteroom are not thick enough to hold my contrition. My remorse leaks through the vents and filters into the corridor. But the end hasn't come. I have still more time to wait, and to remember.

I want to tell you about Sheeba. I want to stick her to this page with words as sharp as diamonds. But every time I try, she vaporizes into waves of frothy, unfixed conjecture. I can't even describe the shade of her skin. I used to believe she was too young to be anyone in particular. All that wide-eyed bliss about seeking the dark—just a Net fad. Junior execs blogged "endarkment" the same way my friends and I used to blog transhumanism when we were kids. Sheeba was still growing. She hadn't finished becoming herself.

Or maybe it was me. Maybe I just couldn't see her.

At the time, I saw only that she needed looking after. There she was, virgin spacer, circling way outside the G Ring toward a mega-serious, legally proscribed war zone, thousands of kilometers from easy rescue, because of me. For the fortieth time, I rechecked her settings, really just an excuse to touch her.

"We'll dive through the fire zone, but you'll lurk at the edge, Shee. Understand? No one expects you to take the hero route."

"Yeah, I got it the first time." The briefest hint of annoyance twisted her lips. Then she beamed like the sun. "Silly beau, you stress too much." She grabbed my trembling hands and stooped to kiss me. Right then, I promised myself that after this surf was over, I would get another spine extension.

The gawky Dolphin 88 slowed us down—we felt obliged to wait for our fans—so it was past midnight, local Mira, when we intercepted Heaven's orbit. At first, we watched the action from about five hundred kilometers. While the fans in the Dolphin tried repeatedly to hack our conference call, I chugged cola through a low-gravity straw and squinted through the shuttle's small round window. Chad kept breaking my train of thought with last-minute questions about stock trades and wall-fabric choices. Grunze hovered weightless beside me, clinging to a grab-loop. His purple EVA suit scintillated with the silver and red paisleys. He looked like a carnival performer.

A13 and its rock chunk spun around each other like two balls on a chain, whirligigging their way across the familiar smoggy wad we called Mother Earth. Though the schematics showed A13 as a bullet-shaped tower, it actually lay parallel to Earth's surface, so that one side always faced "down" toward the planet while the other faced "up" toward the sun. And since the factory's strange polar orbit kept it in sunlight most of the time, the "up" side blazed almost constantly white while the "down" side hung in near perpetual shade. For only three hours in every twenty-four did Heaven dip through Earth's shadow and lose the light.

Provendia's gunship moved in unison with A13, keeping station half a kilometer off the tank's base and closely tracking its spin. A thin glossy ovoid, the ship looked like a drop of oil that had leaked from the bottom of the tank. Tracers of missile fire arced from the gunship to a cluster of solar panels mounted on the tank's sunny side, near the base. That was our war zone. We followed and waited. When Heaven moved out of the light, behind Earth's protective shield, then we would go.

"How the hell do we dock? It's spinning too fast," Grunze said.

Verinne arched one eyebrow and spoke like a schoolteacher. "If we wanted to dock, we'd match A13's spin and use a soft umbilical collar. But since we're doing a flyby, we don't need to dock."

"What was that?" Grunze poked his finger at the thick window glass. "Did you see that?"

"I caught it on video." For once, Verinne sounded excited. "Do you want a replay?"

In the tiny cabin, we pushed off from the window, sailed toward Verinne's workstation, and bumped into various pieces of equipment before coming to rest. Kat was buckled into the pilot's seat, while Sheeba floated directly above, turning slow playful somersaults to get a feel for weightlessness. Win lay Velcroed in the passenger bunk, lightly snoring. Everyone else gathered around Verinne's monitor to watch the replay. For an instant, tiny blue flames flashed along the side of the tank.

"Guidance rockets." Kat elbowed Verinne aside. "They're adjusting A13's orbit."

The tank jerked at its tether. Then a ripple ran visibly down the length of the flexing cable toward the asteroid chunk. We knocked our heads together, watching that ripple move. When it reached the end, the rock jerked, too, and that set up a reflex wave that rippled back toward the factory. For about two minutes, an interference pattern of waves propagated back and forth along the tether, and Heaven shuddered.

Verinne checked her notes. "The factory's guided by an Earth-based signal. That's a scheduled orbit correction."

Kat said, "Does it always jerk like that?"

Verinne cleared her throat. "The guidance rockets on the factory and counterweight should fire together. A synchronizer must have failed."

Grunze bumped me and messed with my hair. "You'd think those Provendia dickheads could do a smoother job."

"Factory owners should replace worn-out parts." Kat looked pointedly at me. "People can't expect things to last forever."

"Yes, well, maybe that would cost too much." I checked Sheeba's reaction. She still didn't know my role on Provendia's board.

As the last of the waves rippled back and forth along the

tether, I wondered what that adjustment must feel like inside the tank. Heaven quakes? Gradually, the ripples lost head, and the factory settled into stasis.

"How often do they make those adjustments?" Sheeba asked. Her loose blond hair drifted around her peachy face like seaweed.

Verinne let Sheeba's hair stream through her fingers. "Every 216 hours, dear. The schedule's regular as clockwork. I've checked data going back three months."

"That's every nine days," Sheeba said, almost to herself.

Kat broke open her compression gun and loaded a transponder in the chamber. "Those solar panels are taking the fire. One thousand says my flag lands there first."

Verinne dabbed moisturizer on her lips. "Eat my fumes, Katherine."

"Yeah, two to one says I plant my transponder *by hand* square in the middle of the panel array." Only Grunze would make a bet like that.

Win was still out cold. My turn. To preserve my status, I had to top Grunzie's wager.

Usually, this was the point at which I began to feel the old charge of anticipation. Raw hormonal heat would spread through my loins, and I would experience a primal urge to swagger. Then I would spout some insane bet, for instance, that I would reach the zone ahead of everyone and sit smack on top of a solar panel, as still as a smiling Buddha, for a full sixty seconds.

In fact, that is the insane bet I did spout. But not with zest. Sheeba threw off my focus. There, I admit it. I was worried about her, so I kept watching her expressions, glancing aside at critical moments. Sheeba's presence was the cause of everything that happened. She wanted to come. But still, I won't say it was her fault.

"I've been timing the volleys," Verinne said. "My calculations put them roughly 6.45 minutes apart. That's our window."

"Right. We go after the next round of strafing." Kat edged her shuttle a few kilometers closer to the action, as

close as she dared with that Provendia gunship standing
guard. Only my stupendous bribes kept us from immediate
arrest and prosecution, and we knew better than to push our
luck.

Kat said, "Somebody wake up Winston."

Sheeba kicked off the ceiling, floated down to Win's
couch, and gently shook his shoulder. "Winny, we're about
to exit. We need you to drive the shuttle."

Win sat up and blinked. "Sheeba."

The way he murmured her name. The way they touched
foreheads. That intimate exchange. A crunching noise
growled inside my head, which turned out to be my porcelain dental implants grinding together. Had Winston slept
with Sheeba? When he sat up in the couch and pinched her
bottom, I wanted to knock his bloody teeth in.

"Here's how we'll exit." Verinne called out our names
according to a random computer generation, our standard
ritual.

"Huah!" Grunze and Kat answered in zone-blissed hi-
larity, but my mouth had gone dry. Sheeba would be exiting second, after Grunze. I was going last. While everyone
ran final suit checks, I watched Win take the pilot's chair,
and the palms of my hands started aching. Had that old sod
screwed my virgin Shee?

"Bring me a souvenir," Winston joked. Lecherous bastard.

Outside the window, the factory and gunship whirled in
unison across Earth's bleary belly, and the silent tracers of
gunfire looked like fairy beams. Then, in the blink of an
eye, Heaven slipped into darkness, and the firing halted.

"That's our cue." Grunze raised his fist, and we shouted
together, "WAR SURF!"

In a rush, we crowded into the airlock, and Sheeba gave
me a tender, hurried hug. "Take care of yourself, beau. I
slipped an ankh in your pocket for good luck."

"You did?"

She pecked her helmet playfully against mine and made
kissing sounds. Why had I doubted her? She couldn't have

slept with Winny. Stress was warping my imagination. My gloved fingers closed on the dear little talisman she'd dropped in my pocket, and my heart eased.

"Fly around the fire zone, Shee. Not through it. Promise."

"God, how many times do I have to promise?" She made funny faces at me through her visor.

"On your mark." Kat opened the outer hatch.

Then I forgot about Winston. All I could see was infinity. Cold boundless space yawned around us. At a distance beyond comprehension, Earth's nighttime face loomed like a huge smoldering coal dotted with a billion flecks of firelight. Its eastern rim glowed amber with the setting sun, and that thin arc of light blotted out the stars. Together, we climbed out onto the hull and clung to the handgrips. Since our craft was tracking Heaven's rapid circular whirl, the angular momentum slung me out and almost dislocated my shoulder. My mind stopped working. I think I was holding my breath.

Kat said, "Now."

And then I was streaking full speed, pushing my thruster to the limit, over the limit, crazy to get there, make my touchdown, count sixty, then get the hell out.

Our fans in the Dolphin had succeeded in hacking our conference call, and they were critiquing our moves, but I barely heard them. All four of my thruster nozzles screamed full bore. Verinne estimated six-plus minutes between rounds of fire, but that was just an average. I wanted to make it out and back in under three.

It takes longer than you think to cover twenty kilometers in a thruster-powered space suit. Far behind, Sheeba was doing her first EVA, and I glanced over my shoulder to keep her in sight. I was still a klick away when the gunship opened fire again. So much for averages. Missiles the size of my forearm streaked around me, and as their silent glittery tracers crisscrossed my view, I imagined one of them slicing through my EVA suit and blasting me to bloody crumbs.

I might have veered off, but Verinne was right behind me. Ye golden gods, that woman had grit. Seeing her there gave me a lift, so I kept heading in, tracking through the fire zone, dodging, diving, pirouetting like a fiend to avoid those pretty beams. What a rip!

"Hey, sweet-piss, I'm winning," Grunzie taunted over the phone.

"It ain't over, burly boy."

Grunze was way ahead, but I didn't care. He might beat me to the objective, but he would never sit still under fire for sixty seconds.

Ahead, the tank swung toward me, looking older, shabbier and more dilapidated the closer we came. The gunship kept pace like a magnet, strafing the solar panels. Square and red, the panels clustered along the tank's sunward face like a patch of poppies. One of them took a hit, and shards of plastic went spinning into space. Explosion without noise, way weird. I dodged through the debris field.

Most of the missiles detonated against the tank's base, leaving dents and scars. I couldn't hear them, but anyone in that satellite would certainly feel their thunderous compression waves. The gunship was laying down nuisance fire, pummeling the protes with noise. Provendia didn't intend to do real damage to this high-ticket asset.

All at once, the strafing stopped. Did my bribes do that? Verinne shot her transponder toward the panels, then saluted me, swerved away and rocketed out of the zone. As I watched her go, the old love welled up inside and made my eyes water. Her last war surf. Good for you, Verinne. You did it.

Kat had fallen way back. Too slow, she'd missed the whole firefight. Grunze was already through. And Sheeba? I went inverted and looked around, but I couldn't see her. She must have circled wide.

Since the fairy beams were on pause, I took my time steering down toward the center panel, pinging the hull with a locator fix, and setting my thruster navigation to synchronize with Heaven's spin. Once my trajectory stabilized, I arranged myself in a slightly unhinged lotus position just above the center panel and set my stopwatch for sixty. Still no sign of Shee. Dear child, she'd kept her promise and steered clear of the zone.

Forty-nine, forty-eight, forty-seven . . . easy as falling off a log-on queue. I placed my magnetized transponder and made sure it stuck fast to the panel frame. Score! Then I shook my fist in the air for the fans' benefit. Next, I considered what gift to buy for Sheeba with my winnings.

No way could she have slept with that old puttybrain Winston. She was mothering him. A nurturer, that was my Shee. Once, believe it or not, she confided to me that her ovaries were still fertile. Does that appall you? When I asked why she hadn't suppressed her hormones like any normal executive girl, she said she was keeping her options open. She actually considered live mammalian birth an *option*. I knew Shee went in for fringe theories, but that was molto screwy.

Thirty-five. Thirty-four. Thirty-three.

Her flaky ideas had made her a target for sexual predators before. Father Daniel, for one. That smarmy con artist, with his yoga chants and chest hair. Of course, I'd hired investigators and brought his devilish tricks to light. The dear girl needed a guardian. When we got back from this surf, I would invite her to live in my condo. She'd be safe there, and I would—

Noisemakers fractured my thoughts. They rained down on the panels where I sat and shook me like tactile megaton thunder. The compression waves vibrated through my spine. Missiles peppered the butt end of the tank, and I could hear in my bones how the factory rang beneath me like a xylophone. Nearby, a solar panel took a solid impact, and jagged pieces flew in all directions. Something heavy walloped my thigh.

Pain fell like an axe blow. My IBiS started vibrating, but I couldn't look at my thumbscreen. Then a wild keening noise shrilled inside my suit. Escaping air. That shard had ripped my Kevlax. Ye graven gold, I was losing compression! The jet of escaping air whipped me around like a toy, and I had just enough wits to grab the solar panel so it didn't spin me out of control. Missiles continued to pound the panel array, and my thigh throbbed with anguishing pulses, as if someone were amputating my leg with a nail file.

"Nasir's hit. He's bleeding." Winston was monitoring everyone's biosensors from the shuttle. At least, the old fart was still awake.

"Fifty thou says he blacks out, and we have to send a robot," said Kat.

"It's a bet," Verinne said.

"Better deploy it now," said Grunze. "Sweety-pee faints at the sight of his own blood."

"Nasir?" That soft, dewy voice.

"Sheeba," I wheezed. In my compromised suit, drawing breath took hard labor. After seconds that felt like eons, my suit finally self-sealed, and the shrill noise faded. "Norphine," I croaked, hooking my good leg around the collector panel to hold my position. The satellite's powerful angular momentum pulled against me like gravity. Those noisemakers must have knocked out my thruster's synchronization with Heaven's spin. As the array vibrated under the flogging of Provendia's guns, I struggled to hold on. Then the Norphine kicked in, and my leg felt numb relief. Twenty-seven, twenty-six, twenty-five . . .

"Deepra! Deepra! Deepra!" the fans were chanting over the phone. Verinne would be uploading the Reel to millions. And Sheeba? Where was she? Bright missile tracers blocked my view, but I imagined her drifting just out of sight, watching.

Yes, I could do this. Be here now. The sharp copper tang of the zone curled my tongue, and I grinned. I no longer felt pain. Numbness crept up my chest and made me shiver. "Heat," I told my suit. Only a few more seconds. Wedging my good leg under the solar panel, I resumed my Buddha lotus, and the fans erupted in cheers. I gripped the bouncing panel frame and gazed defiantly up at the light-streaked blackness. "Sixteen, fifteen, fourteen," the fans counted down.

Then I caught something in peripheral vision. Movement. A shadow. I turned and saw figures crawling up between the panels. They wore faded gray space suits with old-fashioned, collapsible helmets and clunky external air hoses. And they were carrying something heavy and menacing that looked like—chains?

"Protes!" Kat shouted.

"Fuckin' agitators," Grunze said at the same time. "Get out of there."

"Ten, nine, eight," the fans counted.

Two agitators, one tall, the other short, they circled and flanked me. When the short one swung his chain, the heavy metal links lashed across my helmet and hurled me backward. Stunned, I gazed at the villain through a burst of sparks. At first, I thought his chain had damaged my visor, but the light trick was inside my head. Another chain whacked across my armored ribs and knocked the wind out of my lungs, but my boot stayed wedged under the solar panel. Then the short agitator tried to shake my boot free and drive me off.

At that moment, the gunship sent a targeted burst of missile fire in our direction, and the hostiles disappeared under the panels. Cowards.

"Three, two, one, zero!" The fans screamed applause.

"Fuckin' A, you did it!" Grunzie shouted, proud of me despite the fact that he'd just lost two mil.

"Margarita, martini, Manhattan, what'll you have?" Winston asked.

Sixty seconds in Heaven. That record would stand for decades. I did it. I, Nasir Deepra. Laughing aloud, I unwedged my boot and spoke a quick command to activate my thruster and get the hell out of the zone. But my thruster didn't respond.

"Nasty Nass, quit clowning," said Winston.

Kat laughed. "Double or nothing, he's got a malfunction."

Quickly, I grabbed the solar panel to keep from flying

off on a tangent, and I voiced commands to launch a backup navigation routine. Noisemakers zipped around me in bright streams, but the thruster showed no sign of life. Worse, the hostiles reappeared with their chains.

"On!" I shouted at my thruster. "Come ON, you bloody machine!"

But even the backup system was dead. If I let go of Heaven, my forward inertia would hurl me into the night, and who knows how long before my friends would find me? So I gripped the panel and waited. Caught between two devils—my company and my employees—I couldn't guess who would kill me first. In total unabashed panic, I wailed for help.

Then out of the inky black, Kat's robot zoomed to my rescue. Like a white blur, it soared full throttle toward me, rocketing undaunted through the hail of missile fire. On it came, straight as an arrow into the zone. In no time, it would be here to whisk me away.

"Martini. And make it a double," I said, mentally counting the seconds as a heavy chain looped toward my feet. On came the robot, faster and faster, streaking like a comet. Wasn't it going to brake? It seemed to be accelerating.

Then I saw the helmet, the EVA suit, the screaming thruster on her back. Just before she slammed into my chest at top speed, I saw the black piping on her shoulders. Sheeba.

7

ARTIFICIAL GRAVITY

"The older I grow, the more I distrust the familiar
doctrine that age brings wisdom."
—H. L. MENCKEN

Sheeba and I plowed into Heaven at Mach 10. Actually,
I exaggerate. We weren't going quite that fast, and the
solar panel absorbed a lot of our momentum when it collapsed beneath us. On cue, our expensive pro-line body armor deployed, enveloping each of us in full bubble-cluster
body shields. These bouncy wrappers kept us from squash-
ing each other to bloody gore. My IBiS set off pyrotech-
nics in my thumb, and as the bubble wrappers deflated, I
expected to lose consciousness—but I wasn't that lucky.

"Beau, your leg."

Sheeba tried to press her hands over the rip in my space
suit, although it had already self-sealed. My right thigh felt
as if someone had twisted it in two.

I said, "Turn off your thrusters, dear!"

Sheeba's thruster pack was still blasting away, pinning
us against the hull—pressing my back uncomfortably
against a broken support strut. I grasped her controls and
shut off the ignition. Then Provendia's spotlight silhouetted a pair of dark figures moving toward us, one tall and
one short—the agitators. Their chains unreeled like snake
heads. Then I did faint.

I awoke in semidarkness, and details took shape slowly.
A ringing vibration. Cold, stale air. One stripe of pale gray
light spilled through a partly open doorway, and moldy

stains bloomed across a metal ceiling. I lay rigid, afraid to move, afraid to find myself paralyzed from the neck down. Cold seeped up from the floor.

"Sheeba?"

"I'm here, beau."

She crouched in the oval-shaped doorway, listening. The air smelled like a stale refrigerator.

"Are you all right?" I asked.

"I'm fine. You should rest."

The room was barely larger than a closet, and its ceiling hung low enough to induce claustrophobia. A scummy fungal growth coated the welded steel walls and floor, and there was something peculiar about the room's shape. After staring for a long time, I realized it wasn't square. It was shaped like a stumpy triangle. The oval door cut across its sharpest corner, and the wall opposite the door was curved.

"Sheeba?"

"Do you need something, beau?"

I was trying very hard to figure out where we were. Someone had painted a large E on one of the straight walls, and a W on the other. East and West? I studied the curved wall, but instead of an N or S, there was a hand-scrawled A. Another A marked the door. What bizarre place had we landed in?

The ice-cold floor chilled my bones, and the scratchy blanket offered little warmth. Scratchy, yes. I moved my fingertips over its rough weave, delighted to find that my hands still functioned. But what had happened to my gloves? And my EVA suit?

Sheeba crawled toward me. She wasn't wearing her suit, either, only her white smartskin longjohn and socks. "Nass, we're inside the ship. Do you want some water?"

"The gunship?" Ye gods, we'd been arrested by my own company. Maximally embarrassing moment. This was going to cost me a bundle.

"No, I mean we're in Heaven," Sheeba said. "Those

workers tried to shove us off into space. They don't want us here, Nass."

When Sheeba's words finally soaked through to my brain, I sat bolt upright—and discovered that I was not paralyzed, only bruised and battered from head to toe. My right leg felt bludgeoned, and my left thumb was practically playing a symphony. "We can't be here!"

"Why did they want us to leave? We wouldn't hurt anybody." Sheeba squeezed water into my mouth from a plastic sack, then wiped my chin with her sleeve and made me lie back down. "Take it easy, beau. Your leg's broken in two places."

When I tried to sit up again, she laughed gently and cradled my head in her lap. Her fingers made soft round circles over my temples, across my forehead and down the bridge of my nose. "I keep thinking and thinking about these wars, Nass. The employees have everything they need. Why do they get so angry?"

I shivered with cold—my smartskin longjohn was supposed to deliver better insulation than this. My thumb-screen kept up a steady tremor, but I didn't want to check it while Sheeba was watching. Sheeba disapproved of implanted biosensors. Skin dye, contact lenses, tattoos—that cosmetic stuff was fine, but Shee thought health care should "harmonize with nature," whatever the heck that meant.

"Maybe if the whole world did a group meditation, then people wouldn't feel so aggressive." She smoothed my eyebrows. "You know, we could pick one day and do a unified chant, like a global tantric purification."

I chewed my vibrating thumb. "We're inside A13?"

"Liam promised to send a doctor," she said. "Are you hungry. They left us these hard crackers. Not bad if you don't mind the carbs."

"Where's my suit? Sheeba, we have to get away from this place."

"Well, that's the thing." She raked her fingernails

through my hair the way I loved, and tingles of pleasure washed down my spine. She continued in a soft murmur, kneading the cords in the back of my neck. "When I talked Liam into letting us come inside, he took our space suits."

"You talked to who? Liam?" I felt faint again. "You asked the agitators to bring us inside? Sheeba, we can't stay here!"

"Beau, your leg needs attention. Besides, this is what we came for. To seek the dark canal."

"No! We have to LEAVE!"

"But why, Nass? I have so many questions, and there's magna cum energy in this place."

"The agitators will kill us and eat us."

Sheeba's mouth dropped open.

Of course I was making that up. I couldn't tell her the real truth about Heaven, not then, not my delicate Sheeba. Scenarios played in my mind. If the agitators held us for ransom, Chad would need time to raise the cash. How long would that take? With my bioNEMs, a short-term exposure might not hurt me. But Sheeba had no NEMs to protect her. The dear child was completely exposed.

This was no time for surfer scruples. I would hail the gunship. Provendia would arrest us, my fellow directors would sue my ass to kingdom come, and the World Trade Org would ream us for who knows what arcane human resource infractions. I could visualize the hourly news, Nasir Deepra's fifteen seconds of fame. But with Shee's life at stake, a little public humiliation wouldn't bother me at all.

I searched for my helmet-mounted sat phone, but the room was bare. The agitators had taken it. They had taken everything. Without my phone, we were disconnected from the known world. They had even taken my travel mirror. Phew, Heaven smelled old and rancid, not sugary sweet. I took shallow breaths in case the air was infected. The field reports about the disease had been woefully nonspecific.

Sheeba was still chattering away, unsuspecting, "He carried you down here in his arms, beau. You wouldn't believe how considerate he was."

Sheeba, how green can you be? I counted ten to stop hyperventilating. "Did you see where they put my sat phone? Tell me everything that happened."

While I wrapped myself in the blanket, Sheeba told me about this agitator thug called Liam, the factory foreman who had been "kaleidoscopically polite." Outside on the hull, when this "mega-kind man" tried to shove us off into space, she touched helmets with him so her voice would carry to his ears. Clever girl to think of that. I could only guess what charms she used to persuade this rogue to abduct us.

She said Liam and his sidekick brought us into Heaven through an airlock, and she described their ancient twentieth-century EVA suits, worn bald and patched with duct tape. Once inside, she said the agitators stripped us to our smartskin longjohns and blindfolded both of us.

"That was certainly polite," I said. The idea of that thug ogling my Shee in her underwear made me seethe.

"Don't worry, beau. I counted the steps to this room and memorized the Ordic emanations. I can feel my way back to that airlock—no prob."

"Can you feel your way to our EVA suits?"

"Well . . ."

"We need the sat phone in my helmet to call Grunze." I tried to get up, but when I rolled onto one knee, blood rushed away from my brain. An icon blinked on my left thumbnail, and I hid it behind my back.

"Don't stand up. You'll get dizzy. Watch." Sheeba grinned and used the wall to push herself up to her feet. "Something weird's going on with the floor."

She widened her stance as if she were balancing on a moving conveyor belt, then took a few steps toward the wall marked W, weaving like a drunk. "Preter-sleek," she said, giggling. Then she did a quick pirouette, toppled and caught herself against the wall. She threw her head back and shrieked with laughter. "Too fun!" After steadying herself again, she stepped toward the E wall, holding her hands out like a tightrope walker. "Wee! Look at me! It feels different going this way."

I realized what was happening. "Sheeba, it's the artificial gravity."

"When I move this way, I feel a teensy bit heavier." She pivoted on her heel, then ran toward the W again. "Ooh, this way feels light!"

"It's centrifugal force," I said.

"Yeah, like the factory's spinning really fast, you know? Like a giant bucket swinging in a circle, and we're pinned to the bottom." She spoke breathlessly, balancing on tiptoes. Then she sat down, peeled off one of her socks and rolled it into a ball.

"What are you doing?" I leaned back on my elbows, perplexed.

"Watch this." She tossed her balled-up sock in the air, and then the most uncanny thing happened. Instead of rising and falling back into her hand, the sock flew in a funny loop and fell in a curve toward the wall marked W.

"Whoa," I said.

"Psychedesque!" Sheeba went to get her sock. "It's the Coriolis effect. Verinne's handouts told all about this stuff."

"You read them?"

"Sure. Artificial gravity's beyond spiritual. It's a physiocosmic law." She sat cross-legged on the floor, tossing her sock at different angles and clapping her hands at the screwy magic that kept curving its path toward the W.

"W, that's West," she pointed. "That means retrograde. And East means prograde, the direction of our spin."

"And A?" I asked.

She stretched both arms out full length and pointed at the pair of A's on the curved wall and the door. "That's axial, in line with the axis of the spin. That's like neutral. You feel less effect when you move that way."

She tossed her sock ball at the door, but it still veered slightly West and missed the mark.

I prodded my broken right leg. Above the knee, my flesh felt swollen and tender and hot to the touch, so I focused on the Nasir-shaped glass man coexisting inside my skin. Right now, the bioNEMs would be scurrying around like busy clerks, moving calcium molecules to mend my fractures.

"Did you notice the creepy shape of this room?" I asked.

She munched a cracker and studied the walls. "Heaven's a cylinder, and the decks are round, so I guess all the rooms are shaped like pizza wedges."

"Of course they are." Her power of deduction surprised me. I helped myself to a cracker. It tasted of yeast and sugar, remarkably satisfying, so I took a second and a third.

Then a shadow blocked the light falling through our open door. Sheeba moved out of the way, and a tall angular man with a hawk nose and tangled blond hair ducked through the low opening. An agitator. I drew back against the wall and searched around me for some means of defense. Could I strangle him with the blanket?

"Liam." Sheeba dropped her sock and blushed. Then she turned to me. "This is Liam, the foreman."

So this was the mighty chief of thugs. He looked like a common criminal. Thin and washed-out, in threadbare coveralls and frayed sneakers, he duplicated every factory worker I'd ever seen. A nasty blond braid swung down to the middle of his back, and his height and wide lean shoulders made him awkward in the narrow room. He seemed uncertain where to stand. His blue eyes darted nervously. Why, he was just a juvenile, not even thirty years old. This was the war leader? Contempt replaced my fear.

"I demand to speak with my people. Return my sat phone at once," I said.

Sheeba touched my arm. "Nasir, he saved your life."

"Shhh," I whispered, warning her off. "Don't give our names. Don't give any information he might use against us."

The juvenile chieftain grunted. I have a distinct recollection of his lip curling.

"But Nass—"

I clenched Sheeba's wrist to quiet her, and the chieftain's pale blue eyes rested on my hand. They were deep-set, hooded and gloomy. His eyebrows, mustache and beard bristled like copper filaments, several shades darker than his yellow hair. But it was his nose that impressed me, long and narrow, curved like a beak. I tried to stand and face him, but the pain in my leg, plus the weird Coriolis effect, made me stumble and fall. When I turned my head too fast, disturbing events transpired in my ear canals.

"Lean on me, Nass." Sheeba hooked her elbow under my armpit.

I waved her away and held myself up on my one good knee by deliberately leaning toward the E, the direction of our spin. Sneering at the boy-chief, I marshaled my most authoritative tone. "State your intentions."

The juve quirked his lips and didn't answer. Ill-mannered brute. I suppose, kneeling in my underwear, disabled and disconnected from my crewmates, I must have cut a poor figure. Still, I held myself as erect as possible and stared him down.

But he was no longer looking at me. The cur was ogling Sheeba. Devouring her, you might say, with his miserable, ice-blue eyes. As Shee knelt to examine my broken leg, his gaze stole along the lines of her waist and hips with a kind of forlorn awe. The punk infuriated me.

I shook my fist. "Give me back my phone."

At last, he said—in a surprisingly resonant baritone— "The Net don't work here."

"What? That's absurd. The Net reaches everywhere in the inhabited solar system. Don't try to hoodwink me."

Again, he refused to answer—insolent lout. For a juvenile, he wore an uncommonly dark expression. Shadowed cheek. Grim, hard-set mouth. His lips curved almost too gracefully for a man, but they were camouflaged by his tawny mustache. When Sheeba smiled, he blushed and didn't seem to know where to put his hands. What a kid. This thug was way too immature to be a factory foreman. No one with less than three decades should be in charge of anything!

Behind him, a stumpy female hopped through our oval

door carrying a hammer. Her patched gray EVA suit was literally falling off in shreds, and a collapsible helmet dangled from her belt. So this was Liam's chain-wielding henchman. Dark brown skin, grimy fingernails. A scar stretched across her left temple and disfigured her otherwise handsome face. Both of the juves wore the typical sullen expressions of factory protes. It wasn't necessary to read their uniform labels to know they were my employees.

"Is this the doctor?" Sheeba asked. "Nasir needs analgesic vibra-therapy. Do you have a stim gun?"

"Don't know what that is." Liam's voice rose with a rich timbre. If he'd been an exec, he might have trained as a vocalist.

By contrast, his stocky woman friend spoke in grating soprano. "I ain't no doc, babe. I your guard. You treat me right, I treat you right." Then she made an obscene gesture with her hammer.

Sheeba shot to her feet. "But Liam, you promised a doctor." The Coriolis effect made her falter sideways, and the punk caught her in his arms.

Did I mark that moment as a pivot around which my life would bend and warp out of all recognition? No, I was too distracted. But here and now, I can't forget how he looked at her. How the tendons moved in his forearm, how he reeked of sweat, and how their faces nearly touched.

"Doc busy," he said, and his splendid baritone jarred with his mongrel worker accent. Then he set Sheeba on her feet—gently, I realize now, though at the time, everything he did seemed coarse. "Careful how you move. Takes a while to get your balance here."

He nodded at me, and without another word, he left us. The great chieftain. What a tongue-tied whelp. Then I collapsed on the floor.

After he'd gone, Sheeba wrapped me in the thin scratchy blanket and eased my swollen leg into a position that didn't hurt. The scar-faced girl stayed by the door, hefting her hammer in menacing ways. Except for the pale wound on her temple, her skin was smooth and glossy, as dark as burnt caffeine. Thick black lashes fringed her green eyes, and a ferocious grin twisted her shapely features. She'd wound her black hair in a large, heavy bun that was coming loose. When I curled in my blanket, she stepped closer and rubbed her knee against Sheeba's cheek.

"How ya like your visit so far, babe? Remember you asked to come in. We didn't invite you."

Sheeba kept silent, but I shook with suppressed rage. "Let's make this easy. Return my sat phone, and I'll call my bank."

"Ho. You gonna buy your way out? Guess that's how you 'xecutives do."

The girl spoke in a such a thick worker accent, it was difficult to understand her. She leaned over my supine body and balanced her hammer on one finger directly above me. I wanted to bash her smirking face, except she might have dropped the hammer.

But she was just a child. Her vulgar behavior made her seem older, yet there was no mistaking the soft, smooth roundness under her chin. She was twenty at most.

"How much money you got in that 'xecutive bank?" she said in her high-pitched voice.

"I'll pay any reasonable figure. Just return my sat phone."

"However much, it ain't enough." She made as if to let the hammer go, then caught it quickly. "Oops." With one parting sneer, she stepped outside and shut the door. We heard her stout body settle to the deck just outside.

With the door closed, no light leaked in from the corridor, and pitch-blackness surrounded us. The air seemed even colder. But there were sounds I hadn't noticed before. In the quiet, engines thrummed, air whuffed through ducts, and liquid sluiced down pipes. Faint voices echoed through the steel walls like tones in a tuning fork. Our prison enveloped us in aural vibrations. Peculiar place, this Heaven.

"Sheeba," I whispered.

Her only response was an inarticulate grumble. Dear

girl, she was probably terrified. Nothing had prepared her for this savage place. She'd never seen anything worse than an X-rated movie.

Or possibly a few segments of the Reel.

Resolutely, I dragged myself across the steel floor, sliding the blanket under me to avoid jerking my swollen leg. In the darkness, I found her by touch. She was sitting with her back against the wall.

"Sweetness, don't be frightened." I stroked her arm. "I'll think of something. I always do."

"He hardly said a word to me."

I took her hand. It was warmer than mine. "We'll make it through this. I'm sure Chad's got our lawyers online. As soon as we locate my sat phone, I'll call Grunze."

"Why didn't he stay and talk? You'd think he'd be interested to know who we are."

"Chad will pay whatever ransom they ask. Our friends will get us out." I positioned my leg so it throbbed less viciously.

"How many visitors does he get on your average weekend, I'd like to know. We might have news. He should interrogate us." In the darkness, she rocked back and forth. "It's creepy in here."

"Well, Shee"—I let out a wry chuckle—"didn't you come seeking the dark?"

"It's not supposed to be like this. How can we understand the zone if they keep us locked up? I want to look around. And talk to them." She scrambled to the door and beat the steel panels with her fists. "Come back! I have another question."

Poor Shee. Her fizzy quest for the dark was already vaporizing. The steel door opened a crack, and Scar-Face poked her nose inside. "Hi, babe. You need somethin'?"

Sheeba seemed disappointed. "Where's Liam?"

"Light is what we need," I called over her shoulder. "And more blankets. And my sat phone."

"And a doctor," Sheeba added. "Tell Liam we don't like promise breakers."

The girl laughed. "Okay, babe, I tell him."

She started closing the heavy steel door, but Sheeba caught hold of it. I cringed at the thought of her crushed fingers, but she managed to hold it open. "Wait. What's your name? I'm Sheeba Zee from Nordvik."

Oh fine. Sheeba was making friends with this prote cub. I couldn't see the smile she gave the kid, but I knew well enough the power of her charm. The kid's green eyes reflected points of light as she let the door fall a little wider open. "Name's Geraldine. If you're nice, you can call me Gee."

Sheeba curled her body toward Geraldine like a blossom turning to the sun, and this produced a noticeable effect on the kid. I'd seen Sheeba do this move before. When she talked to people, she devoted her entire physical attention. Youthful exuberance, I thought. But now I noticed the sly way she nudged one shoulder through the door so Geraldine couldn't close it.

"Gee, are you like second-in-command?"

The kid sat on the floor just outside and rested her hammer across her knees. Silhouetted against the corridor light, her heavy bundle of hair adorned her like a black corona. "You could say that. I work the power plant. My turbines make all the power and heat. This place be stone cold without my handiwork."

Stupid brat, it *is* stone cold. What have you done with the adults? I wanted to growl. Pain and exhaustion were taking their toll on my 248-year-old body. Those bioNEMs drew their power from my blood sugar, and since they had a lot of breakage to repair, they were seriously sapping my energy. While the girls chatted, I finished off the crackers. Then, despite my best efforts to follow their talk, I rolled up in the blanket and dozed.

But one exchange startled me awake. It rang as clear as breaking crystal. Sheeba asked if Liam had a girlfriend.

"His aura looks like smoke. I think he needs someone to—to—"

"To screw his brains out?" Geraldine yipped and chortled.

No doubt, Sheeba found the girl's crude talk repugnant. No doubt, she joined in the laughter just to be friendly. Shee was friendly to everyone. Her trilling laugh echoed through the steel room, and she rocked back and forth. "Oops, almost wet my panties." She pressed her belly and shook with giggles. "Oh wow, I've got a vicious need to pee."

At those words, my own overfull bladder did a vague lurch, but fatigue was carrying me off into dreamland. The last thing I remember, Sheeba slipped out through the door with her new pal.

8

YOU'LL FEEL A LOT
BETTER NOW

**"Overall deterioration of the body that comes with
growing old is not inevitable."**
—DR. DANIEL RUDMAN

S urf the moment. Ride the contingencies. Improvise. I
woke to pitch-darkness, interrupting a nightmare about
frigid, mind-numbing thunder. But it was no dream. The
icy floor rang beneath me like a gong. That gunship was
firing again.

Sheeba! In panic, I thrust out both hands—and Shee
was there, curled next to me in the thin blanket. How could
she sleep through this dreadful booming? The steel deck
transmitted subzero cold, so I eased my broken leg aside
and pressed myself full length to Sheeba's warm body.

With no NEMs to clean her skin, she smelled pungent,
and her aroma stirred me. Her firm round belly swelled
against my abdomen, and the sweet flesh under her chin
molded to my mouth. Her skin tasted of spice and salt. She
didn't wake when I licked her ear, so I sucked her throat,
and my hands wandered lower, along the curve of her hip
and down between her legs. My fingers fumbled with
snaps, then slid into the damp sweet warmth of her crotch.
Velvet wetness. My organ throbbed against her thigh, and I
shifted carefully, easing closer, hoping the gunship's barrage would drown my groans.

But Shee was not asleep. "It's the war, Nass. Listen."

"Yes." I froze in midbreath. My fingers stopped moving.

"That isn't real gunfire, just noisemakers, right?" She rolled away, and the cold air hit me like a shower.

"Right," I said, wilting.

Letting Sheeba go felt like dying. As I curled in the blanket, each move brought new aches. My chest felt bruised, my broken leg screamed. Every part of my body had stiffened while I slept on this freezing deck. Cold and pain annihilated my lust.

Pow! Pow! The noisemakers thudded at migraine decibels. Provendia obviously didn't know their chairman emeritus was onboard. Maybe my friends had concealed my identity.

When the guns stopped booming, uneasy silence followed. Sheeba sat up and yawned, and I could tell from the sounds she made in the darkness that she was doing yoga stretches.

"Dearest, we have to find my sat phone."

She yawned again. "Liam said the Net doesn't work here."

"Nonsense. My phone's hyperwave. It works anywhere."

As she moved through the Child's Pose, her thigh pressed my shoulder, and her warm, spicy smell made me want to pull her under the blanket again. Her smartskin underwear popped with sparks.

I said, "Where did the prote girl take you?"

"Well, the toilet's like teensy, and it's four doors down. I told her you couldn't walk that far, so she gave me this cup."

"What?"

Sheeba shoved a plastic cup in my hand, and I was too shocked to speak. She continued stretching and chatting in a breezy tone. "I'm getting used to the artificial gravity. They've painted E's and W's everywhere to help you stay oriented."

"Did you find the airlock? Were our EVA suits still there?"

"Geraldine stayed with me the whole time, so I couldn't look around. It felt really good to pee though."

I squeezed the cup in my fist and calculated. Searching for our suits with this broken leg wouldn't be easy. But sending Sheeba alone might be worse. She was so green and gullible. I tugged at my longjohn, considered alternatives and, finally, caved to the inevitable.

"Sheeba, you'll have to find my sat phone. I'm too banged up to walk."

"No prob. I can hardly wait to get out and look around." Her laughter rippled through the dark. "Can you believe it? We're inside Heaven. Maybe I can coax Gee into giving me a tour. She's right outside."

"Well, you could ask her."

She did another stretch.

"Shee?"

"Yes, beau?"

"Go ahead and ask her now." Those sparks from her underwear were driving me nuts.

"Okay, sure. I just always like to start my mornings with yoga. To find my psychic center."

"How do you know it's morning? They took our watches."

Sheeba got up, padded barefoot across the frigid steel and rapped with her knuckles. "Gee? Are you awake?"

The door opened, and Geraldine stuck her head inside. "I'm here, babe. You want the light on?"

"Yes, please."

A few seconds later, a single incandescent bulb glowed from its recessed niche in the ceiling. I blinked at its weak radiance. Why hadn't I noticed that before? Its gloomy light seemed to hang like fog, barely illuminating the walls. Long ago, perhaps this room had been painted factory beige, but now the chips, stains and black fungus made a collage of dinginess. On the floor lay the remains of our meal, empty water sacks and a bag of cracker crumbs.

"Megalicious crackers," Sheeba said to her new friend. "Can we have some more?"

Geraldine leered. "Sure, doll-face. I got something to make your mouth water."

Sheeba let out a side-splitting laugh. I'm sure she was only pretending. That vulgar girl couldn't possibly amuse her. She said, "Stay and talk, Gee."

"Can't. Got stuff to do. You want anything, ring the bell."

Of course there was no bell. When Geraldine closed the door, Sheeba slapped the wall. "Damn. She left too soon."

"Revolting wench." I upended the cracker bag and swallowed the last crumbs. My teeth felt sticky—for some reason, my dental NEMs hadn't cleaned them. Thank goodness my beard was suppressed.

Sheeba pointed to a small object mounted to the ceiling in one corner. A surveillance camera. "I wonder who's watching us?"

"It's not active," I said without thinking. Oops. Provendia had shut down surveillance a couple of months ago, but I wasn't supposed to know that. "No indicator lights, see, and the camera doesn't swivel. If it was working, it would sweep back and forth. . . ."

Sheeba wasn't listening. "Chilly in here." She tugged her socks on and knelt to check my fracture. Her powerful fingers probed my thigh. "The swelling's gone down. This cold floor probably helped. You need a cast, beau."

I didn't mention my bioNEMs. Waiting for breakfast, we huddled in the center of our frigid closet, and Sheeba let me have most of the blanket. As she massaged away my aches, I snuck a peek at my IBiS. The blinking icon wasn't the health alert I'd expected. There was some kind of system error. I tapped the thumbscreen with my pinky stylus and read the holographic pop-up: "Net not responding."

That was odd. Usually, my IBiS stayed in constant dialog with the Net, reporting to the cyberagents of my various doctors and downloading new medical orders. In fact, my NEMs needed regular orders to perform their most basic routines. Without fresh doctors' orders, the NEMs would lock down and go into idle mode.

The docs claimed this authorization process was a safety precaution, but I felt sure their real motive was to

protect their damned copyrights and preserve their
monthly fees. After all, the whole process was automated.
Preprogrammed cyberagents routed all the data. The doctors probably never even checked the readouts. I shook my
thumb and stuck it in my mouth, but my IBiS still couldn't
find the Net.

"Does your hand hurt, beau?"

I hid my thumbscreen and smiled. "Just a cramp."

Sheeba swayed back and forth, grinning like a dirty-
faced angel. When we began this surf, she'd been wearing
peach skin dye, but now it was rubbing off. Under the pale
peach, her skin looked dusky olive—not what I'd expected.

"Hold still, dear. You're a mess," I said.

Shee closed her eyes and waited obediently while I
cleaned her face with my sleeve. The more I wiped, the
more of her lustrous olive skin emerged. Burnished bronze
with golden highlights. She was darker than any of my
Euro friends. Like me, Sheeba came of mixed blood, but
unlike me, she hadn't suppressed her skin pigment. My ancestors emigrated from the Asian subcontinent, but her
complexion spoke of a different origin.

"All clean," I said.

"Um, that feels nice." She opened her glorious hazel
eyes, and my breath caught. Then she bent and shook her
long blond hair forward over her face. It spilled like a
golden waterfall, and she combed it with her fingers.

"Sheeba, what's your lineage? I'm curious."

She kept working at her hair. "I don't know. American?"

"That's not a lineage, that's a stew," I said. "What are
you doing?"

She was pulling long strands of hair loose from her
scalp and piling them on the floor between her knees.

"Sheeba, your hair."

She laughed at my reaction. "It's an artificial weave.
I'm tired of having it fall in my eyes."

Dumbfounded, I watched the lovely silken tresses accu-
mulate on the floor, and when she finished, her natural hair
stuck out in short nappy tufts all around her scalp, barely a

few centimeters long. Her real hair was bleached to match the false strands, but dark roots showed near her scalp. Despite this change, Sheeba was gorgeous. Her close-cropped hair merely set off the regal shape of her head.

When the door opened, I hoped to see Geraldine bearing a fragrant tray of breakfast, but instead, a man stood in profile. Right. Liam again.

"Have you come to return our property? It's about time," I said.

Only after my eyes adjusted did I notice the man's wavy, shoulder-length hair. Not Liam. This agitator was smiling. He wore a stained blue lab coat over his uniform, and he carried a first-aid kit.

"Are you the doctor?" Sheeba, the innocent dear, hopped up and offered her hand in greeting. This time, she moved with balance. She'd been practicing.

The man shrugged pleasantly and clasped her hand, palm to palm in the prote style. He had quick brown eyes and a slight build. "I'm Vladimir, the medic. We got no doctor."

"But Liam said—"

"Liam, he call me doc. He embellish. I just a medic." All these agitators spoke in the same broken drawl, but this man's tone was jovial, not curt or vulgar. He turned my way. "Is this the 'xecutive with the broken leg?"

"This is Nasir," Shee said.

"Hello, Nasir." When the medic knelt beside me, a couple of objects tumbled out of his bulging pockets, and he scooped them up, embarrassed. A pair of tweezers and a magnifying glass. After stuffing them back in his pockets, he gently drew my smartskin longjohn up over my knee. He had the first clean hands I'd seen in this factory, but there was something lopsided about his face, as if his jaw had once been fractured. His right cheek sagged, and one eye drooped slightly. It gave him a cockeyed look. With a friendly nod, he poked at my leg.

"Ow. Give me some Norphine before you do that."

"Sorry, no Norphine." He kept prodding, and his brown

eyes gleamed with friendliness. "I go examine your bones, see how to set them properly."

"How old are you? Twenty-five?" When I asked that, Sheeba gave the medic a wink. Maybe she thought I wouldn't notice.

"Old enough." He grinned, probing my thigh with his fingertips. He had a complexion as smooth as baby cheeks, and a patchy stubble covered his chin, too sparse to be called a beard. Where were all the adults? I hadn't seen so many underagers in decades.

"You got a clean double break," he said, "but the bones go slip outta place. I gotta pull them back."

Sheeba bounced on her knees, frisky and breathless. "I'm a physical therapist. Can I help?"

"You 'xecutive. I should assist you." A homely dimple creased his misshapen cheek.

Sheeba rocked back and forth and beamed, as if she'd just been turned loose in a gaming arcade. "I've never set a broken bone before."

"Well, I have," he said. "We see plenty accidents around Justment—"

"Both of you, put it on pause." I glared at the lop-jawed medic. "No untrained boy is going to screw with my leg. Give me some painkillers, and I'll get treatment when you return me to my people."

Vladimir gave me a thoughtful smile, deepening the dimple in his cheek. "Who your people, may I ask?"

"You may not ask. You may give me back my phone, and I'll call them."

Vlad's sagging eye narrowed. "The chief saw that gunship fire at you. Why they do that? You take our side?"

His question caught me unprepared. I would have shifted away, but I was already pressed hard against the wall. Sheeba looked embarrassed.

"I don't have your phone," the boy medic continued, "but you go find it don't work. That gunship scrambling our signal."

Sheeba clutched the medic's sleeve, fixing him with the

full power of her gaze. "Vlad, your aura's deep blue, so I totally trust you for the truth. Please tell us why you started this war."

He looked down at her hand on his sleeve, then back up into her eyes. I knew what he was seeing, those dazzling rays of green, gray and gold. "We trying to survive," he said.

She tugged at his sleeve again. "Is vacation time worth dying for?"

"Vacation time? I don't know what that is."

"Sir, I have the splints."

We all turned to see who had spoken. There in the doorway stood a bud of a girl, eighteen if I had to guess, another urchin. But she was thin and undersized for her age. Her Asiatic eyes were too small and too widely spaced for beauty. A cord cinched her uniform at her narrow waist, and the long sleeves hung over her hands. A faded yellow cloth hid her hair.

Vlad sprang up to take the heavy tray from her hands. "Thank you, Kaioko. I didn't mean for you to carry all this."

The girl stepped quietly into the room. She was barefoot, and she'd rolled up her pantlegs, but the cuffs whisked across the dirty floor as she moved. Vlad set the tray down, and she knelt beside it. When their fingers touched, the young medic edged closer, but the girl drew back.

"This my assistant, Kaioko," said Vlad, inclining his head toward the girl with an air of gentle pride. "And these our guests, Nasir and Sheeba Zee."

Kaioko nodded at each of us with a nearsighted squint. I found her plain in the extreme, so the medic's affectionate attitude baffled me. Her tray held a roll of nylon netting, some wire and several scraps of flat hard plastic. Very peculiar medical equipment.

About then, our floor started booming again—another volley of Provendia's noisemakers. Kaioko cringed and covered her ears, and her face mottled as if she meant to cry. The medic rushed to hold her, but she struck out hysterically, batting him away. When Sheeba offered her a water sack, she knocked it to the floor. What melodrama! She made an unnatural peeping chirp, and she groped the floor with splayed hands. Vlad endured her slaps and held her.

Sheeba turned to me with that ardent expression—as if she expected me to *do* something. But what the heck could I do? Eventually, the gunfire stopped, and the thrumming, whuffing and sluicing sounds vibrated through the steel walls again.

Vlad sighed. "That one didn't last so long. You did fine, Kaioko. Next time, it be easier."

The girl gazed straight ahead with unfocused eyes. At least, she'd stopped chirping.

"Kai-Kai," the medic said softly, "tell me how many splints you brought."

"I don't know," the girl murmured almost too low to hear.

"Count them." Vlad tapped the tray to get her attention.

Kaioko glanced around the room, seemingly lost, till she noticed the tray on the floor beside her. Slowly, she picked through the items, reciting numbers aloud like a preschooler. I began to think she was addled.

Then the door banged on its hinges, and Geraldine rushed in. "Kai-Kai, you all right? You shouldn't be down here when the guns go off. Vlad shouldn't bring you here."

The medic slid away from Kaioko with an uncomfortable shrug. "She handled it fine."

Geraldine flared her nostrils at him, then shouldered between them and elbowed the medic away. She squared her jaw with a kind of fierce nobility. But when she turned to Kaioko, the lines of her face softened. Tenderly, she adjusted the folds of Kaioko's head cloth. "Come with me, babe. You don't have to nurse this commie."

"Commie!" I bristled at the slur. Protes used that term to insult Com executives.

But Shee put a restraining hand on my arm and shushed me.

"How your head feel?" Geraldine whispered in a gentle hush. Like night and day, she'd changed from bruiser to turtledove.

"I well, Gee. Please don't worry." Kaioko drew close to Geraldine, and her dainty white hand glided along the dark girl's muscular arm.

I hadn't lived 248 years without learning to recognize that kind of touch. The quickening glance between them, the unspoken communication, I knew at once they were lovers. But what a pair. Geraldine—brawny, brown and rude, yet despite the scar, I admit she had a striking face. Kaioko—just the opposite, small, pale, graceful, and ugly. And both just children.

"I gotta get back to the plant," Geraldine said. "Come with me."

Vlad spoke up. "I need her here." There was no trace of a dimple now. He'd withdrawn to the foot of my blanket, doing his best to hide his raw, juvenile jealousy.

"She ain't no servant."

"Please, Gee, I want to stay." Kaioko leaned against Geraldine's chest and brushed some dirt from the front of her uniform. "You go to your work. I fine."

"Don't let these 'xecs boss you. Liam said not to talk to 'em." Geraldine planted a showy kiss on Kaioko's lips.

As they hugged, Sheeba elbowed me in the ribs. Evidently, Shee found this soap opera as droll as I did. Geraldine shot one last menacing frown at Vlad, then stomped out.

Poor Vlad. Misery painted his sagging features. He took a folding ruler out of his pocket, fumbled with it, then put it back. "Kaioko, I set this patient's leg. You hold him steady?"

"Yes sir." As the girl moved briskly around to the head of my pallet, Vlad followed her with his eyes. She moved as gracefully as a ballet dancer. Maybe that's what attracted him.

Sheeba said, "How do you move like that, Kai-Kai? The spinning doesn't bother you at all."

"Spinning?" The girl ducked her head.

"Kaioko born here." Vlad gazed at her admiringly. "She move like a sunbeam. Down on your Earth, maybe she have a hard time. Maybe her bones break."

Three creases formed between Sheeba's eyebrows. "Do you mean Kaioko has never been to Earth?"

"None of us. We all born here." He tapped his wrist joint with his fingers. "Our bones too thin to go groundside."

Sheeba gave me that ardent look again. I opened my hands, pretending ignorance. As far as she knew, I had no connection with Provendia.

This news affected her badly though. She hugged her knees and studied Kaioko's tiny feet. The girl's weak bones were part of the Reel, and my solution was never to think about the Reel. Getting too involved in local scenarios hampered my reaction time. But Shee was a newbie. She hadn't developed a surfer's emotional blocks. All the more reason to get her out of this place as soon as possible.

"Gee told us you come from Nordvik," Vlad was saying as he fiddled with the gear on the tray. "Have you seen mountains—"

"Skip the travelogue. Vladimir, you seem to be a steady young man. We don't belong here. If you return our EVA suits, we'll leave in peace. I'm perfectly willing to pay."

Vlad shrugged. "It not up to me. Liam decide."

"Liam! That punk? He's barely past adolescence. Who elected him god?"

"Liam is oldest," said Vladimir.

Sheeba said, "Nasir, they have a right to choose their own foreman."

I ignored her naive remark. "Let me talk to some of the adults. They'll see reason."

Vlad said, "Please, I just here to set your broken leg."

At the mention of setting my leg, the little girl grasped me under the armpits as if she meant to hold me till the end of days.

"Let go, you devil."

I made a grab for her hands but succeeded only in wrenching off her head scarf. Underneath the cloth, her bald scalp was hideously blistered. The sight gave me such a shock that when the girl seized her scarf, I didn't let go at first, and it ripped in two.

"Oh Nass." Sheeba picked up the shredded cloth.

Then the girl's ugly face mottled and creased. Molto pathetic.

"Hell, I didn't mean to tear your scarf. Stop moaning. I'll get you a new one."

"And where you get a new scarf?" Vlad glowered at me.

He caressed the weepy girl and shielded her head with his hand. His level glance seemed far too acute for a mere prote. It smacked of impertinence.

"It was an accident. I didn't mean to embarrass her." The girl's livid burns made me wince.

"How about this smartskin?" Sheeba tugged the pant leg of her longjohn. "Maybe I could cut it and make a scarf."

"No, don't do that." Vlad took off his lab coat and ripped it at the seam. The frayed synthetic came apart easily in his hands, and he tore out a neat white square of fabric. Sheeba helped Kaioko tie it to cover her unsightly head.

"Prettier than ever," said Vlad.

"It makes you look like a nurse," Sheeba added.

The girl nodded at their pack of lies. Without looking at me, she got up and solemnly left the room.

"So much for my assistant." Vlad's homely cheek dimpled. "Sheeba Zee, will you go hold the patient while I align these bones?"

"How many times do I have to say it? You're not touching my leg."

"Nass, listen." Sheeba's fingertips drew slow, soothing circles over my forehead and down the bridge of my nose. "We may be here a while. Better to have your leg set and splinted. You'll be in less pain."

"But he's a juve."

"You can have it redone later," she wisely noted.

Sheeba took her place at my head and grasped under my armpits as the little bald girl had done, while Vlad positioned himself at my feet and gripped my right ankle.

"Are you ready, Sheeba Zee?"

"Yes, Vladimir. And just call me Sheeba."

"Then please, call me Vlad."

"Will you two stop flirting and do this?" I said.

Provendia chose that moment to launch another volley of noisemakers. This was a heavier round. The deck shook beneath me like a drumhead.

"That sounds close," said Shee.

Vlad pointed at the floor. "It right outside the hull."

I jerked free of Sheeba's hold and sat straight up. "You quartered us where the gunship's firing? There must be some law in the Geneva Convention about that."

"Liam say the gravitation on One feel more like Earth. He say you be more comfortable here." Vlad gently forced me back down.

"Liam says," I grumbled.

Vlad and Sheeba held me stretched out between them like a piece of meat, waiting for the barrage to end. Sheeba raised her voice just enough to make herself heard. "How did Kai-Kai get those burns?"

Vlad frowned. "Justment. Hot soup flying around."

Hot soup did that? My scalp prickled at the thought. Sheeba had no time to follow up because two seconds after the barrage ended, Vlad gave my ankle a terrific yank. There was a loud pop, a louder scream—from me—and my artificial hip wrenched out of its plastic socket. Oh, fine.

"Recite your mantra, beau." Shee kissed my eyelids and acupressed my pain points.

For the next several minutes, until Sheeba and Vlad snapped my plastic hip joint back together, the agony in my ligaments was so intense that I could only blather. The IBiS vibrated my thumb like a jackhammer.

"You're going to be fine," Sheeba cooed in my ear, while the juvenile medic tortured me with his fingertips.

"Almost," he kept saying, half closing his eyes and setting my broken bones by feel.

Sheeba stroked my forehead. "No painkillers, huh?"

"Nada." Vlad pressed down hard, and I almost bit through my tongue.

A pause full of rough breathing and strain. Then Sheeba asked, "Are you the only medic?"

Vlad nodded. "I training Kaioko."

Another labored pause, then Sheeba continued, "Do you need another assistant? I know first aid."

What a bright girl, I thought between bouts of agony. She was devising a scheme to get out of this closet and find my sat phone.

"You know biology." Vlad thumped my kneecap. "Maybe you teach me some things."

"But you've had more field experience." Shee racked my shoulder joints.

"Oh no, my skills puny. You be a tremendous help." What gush. They sounded like schoolchildren.

"We'd better ask Liam, since he's foreman," said Shee.

Vlad nodded. "We should."

Liam, that infernal clod. Did he arbitrate every decision in this orbiting purgatory?

"Do you know where he is? We could go ask him together," Shee said.

While the boy medic played havoc with my bones, my left thumb shivered with endless IBiS alerts. Finally, I lost patience. "Young man, take Sheeba with you. She's the most gifted physical therapist I've ever known."

Vlad grinned and launched into a new, more ingenious cruelty. Using the stiff nylon netting, he bound my leg and interlaced the flat hard scraps of plastic between the layers. Pressing it down with one hand, he pulled the nylon tight with the other.

Sheeba said, "Maybe if we talk to Liam together, he'll say yes."

"All done," said the medic, as he bound the bizarre dressing in wire.

All done indeed. My leg shouted pain with every bursting pulse of blood.

"Good job." Sheeba sprang to her feet, and when her

socks slipped on the steel deck, she caught herself against the wall. "So . . . we'll go see Liam?"

Vlad was gathering his leftover materials. "Okay, we go."

"Transcendenzic!" Shee stooped and peeled off her socks for better traction. Then she gave me a hasty kiss and skipped toward the door. "You'll feel a lot better now."

Who in hell was she talking to? Not me.

9

MAN, DON'T TURN YOUR HEAD SO MUCH

"To sleep: perchance to dream: aye, there's the rub;
For in that sleep of death what dreams may come."
—WILLIAM SHAKESPEARE

Since the Crash of '57—and the unspeakable months that followed—I have never enjoyed peaceful sleep. Especially in these last few years, the sense of missing time makes me nervous, although I sometimes nod off without meaning to. Then I doze through fitful nightmares and wake with an urge to urinate and hawk phlegm—reassuring signs of liquidity, I suppose.

After dropping off a second time in Heaven's dark cell, I woke to the sound of a drumming so powerful, it rattled my spine. Was the gunfire getting closer? Was that sinister lightbulb dying? Was my tightly bound leg going to explode? I sat up with a chill sense that something disastrous had happened. Sheeba was gone.

She should have been back by now. Callow child, she had no instinct for the zone. I should never have let her out of my sight. Worse, she'd gone off to find that punk, Liam. The brute who grabbed her in his arms. I could still see the greedy lust in his eyes. Rapist eyes.

In haste, I pushed myself up to one knee, caught a glimpse of the W painted in the corner, and immediately smashed my chin on the floor. With a groan, I rolled over and straightened out my injured leg. Then I took inventory of the E, the W, the pair of A's. The rough brown blanket. The plastic cup. I seized the cup, sat up and relieved myself.

A tray by the door held a fresh water sack and a bowl of oily gruel. I recognized the mess—Provendia's protein-stew. The stuff was barely palatable, but I was so hungry, I ate it all, and I gulped the water to wash away the taste. Those busy NEMs were chewing through a lot of blood sugar, repairing my injuries, and they needed sustenance.

My IBiS still showed the NET NOT RESPONDING message, and other memos as well. I'd missed a telomerase infusion, a dental cleaning and a pedicure. It irked me how thoroughly the medical profession hamstrung my NEMs. Safety precaution, ha. I rubbed my teeth with my index finger and grumbled.

At least the nanomachines had begun to heal my fractures. At length, I struggled to my feet. Sheeba had been right about my leg. With the fractures tightly bound, my leg didn't hurt as much. I leaned against the wall and kept my weight on my good left leg.

But acclimating to artificial gravity wasn't so simple. Between the bizarre effects of centrifugal force and Coriolis, even turning my head threw me off balance. It was like standing at the bottom of an enormous bucket that was swinging around in a fast, tight circle. Three times per minute, Verinne had said.

Oh Verinne, if you could see me now. Only a few hours ago, I'd been winging across the firmament, cutting sleek pirouettes through a hail of missiles. Now I couldn't even take a step without toppling over. But the glass man inside me was alive and kicking. Slowly, that Nasir-shaped lattice of silicon was mending my carbon-based flesh. I intended to master this artificial gravity shtick and find my Sheeba.

So I hopped on one foot toward the nearest hand-painted W, toppled against the wall, caught myself, toppled again. It felt like riding a Tilt-A-Whirl. Now for the E. East meant prograde. The tank was spinning in that direction. Theoretically, when I moved that way, I would spin faster, and the increased centrifugal force would make me heavier.

Picture me sweeping my arms out, lifting my right foot and squatting on my good left leg to spring. That's how the guard found me when he pushed open the door. I gasped and tumbled.

"Man, you gonna hurt yourself doing that," said the imbecile guard.

I bared my teeth at this new agitator, another juve of course. This boy had a round baby face the color of caramel and a pair of huge brown eyes. His thick lips were wreathed in coarse black facial hair, and his wide, pimply nose wrinkled when he grinned. Plus, his eyebrows ran together in the middle. What a beauty.

All the other protes wore standard-issue Provendia uniforms, but not this boy. He'd turned his gray coverall inside out so the fuzzy seams showed, then he'd hacked off the sleeves and rolled up the pant legs to show his thick hairy legs. He leaned against the oval doorjamb, scratching his elbow and watching me.

"Give me your hand," I ordered.

The boy flexed his unibrow in surprise.

"Didn't you hear what I said?"

He shrugged and pulled me to my feet. When the room whirled, I grabbed his shoulder. He was a few centimeters shorter than me, and that put his shoulder at a convenient level. Like his blond chieftain, this boy wore a braid down his back, but his hair was dark, and he'd woven colorful strands of plastic-coated wire among his plaits. Green. White. Red. Yellow. Very ornamental.

"What's your name?" I demanded.

"I'm Juani." The boy started guiding me back toward the blanket.

"No, not that way. The door," I said.

"You need the toilet?"

"That's it. Yes, the toilet. How old are you?" I wanted to keep him in a subservient mindset.

"I not supposed to tell you anything."

"That's ridiculous. Who am I going to talk to?"

The oval door had a raised sill, maybe ten centimeters

above the floor. Anyone with two good legs could easily step over it, but for me, hopping on one foot, it was like an Olympic hurdle.

"Jump. You can do it," said Juani.

He grasped me around my middle and lifted me. By leaning heavily against him, I managed to bound sideways through the door and land outside in the corridor. Liberty at last.

But the corridor felt even more claustrophobic. Provendia's engineers had wasted no space in A13's floorplan. The corridor was so narrow, I had to turn sideways to avoid brushing against the walls. And it didn't run straight—it curved.

"That way." The boy pointed clockwise. "Four doors on the left."

"You wait here." I pushed him aside and bobbed down the narrow corridor, staggering against one wall, then the other. Dead surveillance cameras drooped from the ceiling. Several meters down, I nearly tripped over a gaggle of children who had chosen that spot to congregate. Can you imagine, they were running up and down the public hall.

"Whoa!" My crash sent them squealing in every direction.

"Man, don't turn your head so much. You go get dizzy." Juani pulled me up and offered his shoulder again. "See that E? Lean into it. Yeah, there you go. You getting the idea."

My breath came in gasps as I hopped down the corridor, clutching Juani's arm. We passed more prepubescent types, leaping about like popeyed toads. Some of them crawled on all fours, too young to walk. Soft little arms and feet, squeaky voices, oversized heads and noses like buds, such half-formed grotesqueries should be kept out of sight until they reached normal size.

As we passed one oval door after another, I noticed scribbles and childish drawings scratched into the wall just at knee level. One of the toads must have run amuck with a penknife. Was there no discipline in this place? More and more, I leaned on Juani's shoulder.

"This the toilet." He wrenched open an oval-shaped metal door and switched on the light. Yes, you could call the tiny cupboard a toilet. It had the correct gear, but it was microsized. Smaller than the lavatory on a jump-jet. Juani wrinkled his pug nose at me.

"Very well, you can return to your post," I said.

I tried shooing him away, but he held the door and waited. I had no choice but to accept his assistance to hop inside, where I promptly banged my good knee on the metal toilet lid. Juani winced and made a comical face, then eased the door shut.

Take it from me, using a prote toilet in an orbiting satellite factory qualifies as Reel. The flush made an eerie grating noise, the sink lacked a mirror, the tap yielded only a fine mist of disinfectant, and there were no wipes. The defunct surveillance camera grazed my temple. I growled at the roll of rough synthetic paper. Liam and his thugs must have commandeered the executive lavatory. Still, I scrubbed my hands and used some of the paper to clean my teeth.

When I opened the door, Juani offered his elbow like an usher.

"I'm going for a walk," I said, trying and failing to navigate the raised doorsill on my own.

Juani grabbed my waist and lifted me over the sill. "You can't go past here. This the outside limit."

"I need exercise," I said.

"Uh-uh," said Juani.

I shoved him away and took a few hops down the hall. What could he do, shoot me? He had no weapons. He was barefoot. And, ye gilders, he was a teenager.

"Stop, man. Don't make me come after you," he said.

I laughed and kept hurtling along, sliding my hands against both walls, ignoring the dizziness and the rude little toads who got in my way and tried to trip me. Freedom went to my head like wine, and I seized one of the door levers. It was unlocked, and when the door fell open, I saw more youngsters and blankets on the floor. Before I could observe anything else, Juani's bare foot landed a kick at the back of my good knee, and I went down hard.

"By all the freaking gold-plated gods." I cradled my throbbing broken leg.

Juani grabbed the back of my longjohn and started dragging me along the floor. He hauled me back toward my prison, knocking my head against one wall and my injured leg against the other. The prepubescents scattered and giggled.

I said, "Let go, zit-face. You're killing me."

"Man, you a real sharp blade."

"I'll pay money. I'll get you a transfer, a better job, shorter hours, more perks. I'll tell Provendia you helped me, and they'll give you a pardon."

The boy didn't slow down.

"What do you want? I'll get it for you. Please let me go."

He said, "Be calm, blade. You too sharp for me."

He dragged me back to my den, slammed the door, and in cruel retribution, turned off my incandescent lightbulb. My first attempt at freedom—nipped in the bud.

Basking in cold dark misery, I pressed my ear to the fungus-covered door—hoping, I suppose, to hear Sheeba coming back. Why did Shee leave me alone to go traipsing after that twentysomething foreman? Would she massage his shoulders and tell him his aura "looks like smoke"? The possibility made me quiver.

What I heard instead was Juani singing. Something about wagons and stars—his voice broke on the high notes.

Molto frustration. How could I get that imbecile kid to let me go? Well, if a newbie surfer like Sheeba could beguile agitators, certainly I, with my centuries of worldly experience, could do it better.

"Juani!" I yelled through the door. "Open up and let's talk."

He opened the door a crack and poked his shiny nose through. "What does zit-face mean?"

I sighed. "Use your brain. I'm a rich man. Treat me well, and I can do good things for you."

The boy's single eyebrow knotted like a fuzzy worm. "You mean, like magic wishes?"

"I can buy you things, okay? New clothes. Music discs. Air scooter. Just name it."

Juani glanced down the hall in both directions. His lean, muscled shoulders rolled up and down in the ridiculous inside-out coverall. Then he moved closer, and I noticed the startling clarity of his dark brown eyes. "Will you go tell me about Earth?"

"Sure." I nudged my shoulder into the door the way Sheeba had done, so Juani couldn't close it. "What do you want to know?"

"Anything. Tell me what she look like."

"Haven't you browsed the Net?"

"I mostly been in the factory." He wiggled into a more comfortable position. "Once I went spacewalking. Yeah, I see Earth very completely then."

"You've been EVA only once?"

He reddened and scrubbed his neck with his stubby fingers. "Sooner later, I go again. Tell me what she look like under the clouds."

The kid had a thirst for details. He knew almost nothing. What the hell, I told him how Earth's sky was yellow instead of black and how all the people lived near the poles where the weather was mild. He asked ridiculous questions, like could we walk on the clouds. I told him the clouds held lots of useful chemicals that we harvested. He moved his mouth as if savoring the taste of my words. Ignorant cub, he amused me.

So I kept going. I told him how everyone on Earth lived underground or under sealed domes, and how the best shops were always high in the towers, while the best music clubs were deep down where the protes lived. Juani needed

to know what a shop was, and a tower and a music club. He
wanted to know how many people lived on Earth, and
when I told him 12 billion, he gave me a skeptical grin.
That's when I noticed his front tooth was missing. He kept
rubbing his hairy legs and asking more questions.

"Twelve billion people? Blade, you lie. How they remember each other's names?" He sprawled on his belly in
the corridor, leaned on his elbows and gazed up at me as if
I held the light of the world. The soles of his feet were
crusted soot-black. Soon, a few of the tiny toads joined
him. They clustered around my door.

I said, "Believe me, most people are not worth remembering. That's why wars are so handy. Natural population
control."

Juani said, "What does 'natural' mean?"

"It means free. You don't have to pay for it."

"I thought free had a big price," he said.

"Now you're getting into semantics."

Playing guru was fun, but after a while, I'd had enough.
"I told you about Earth. Now make yourself useful, and get
my sat phone."

"What's a sat phone?"

I forced myself not to growl. Talking to this juve felt
like biting through concrete. "Help me get out of here, and
I'll buy you a cybrary."

"What's a—"

I held up both hands. "Put it on pause. A cybrary is an
earring that tells you the meaning of words. Game session
over, okay?"

Juani had a way of crinkling his eyes to slits as if he half
suspected I was making everything up. He poked his
tongue through the gap in his teeth and made a fluttering
sound.

I tried pleading. "Kid, I'm going nuts in here. I need exercise. A change of scene. A window for godsakes. Please
let me out."

"What's a window?"

"Grrrr. Let me out, kid, or I'll do something harsh."

Juani kicked his dirty toes against the wall. "Liam'll bust me."

The infernal Liam. "What does your foreman think I'll do, blow up the factory? Look at me. I'm utterly harmless."

"It's because . . ." Juani chewed the corner of his mouth. "Gee say you come from that gunship."

"Not true. I have nothing to do with that gunship." When I shook my head, the Coriolis made me dizzy.

"Then why you here?" He and the toads watched me closely. My audience had grown. A little girl scooted close and touched my longjohn. A bright red amoeba-shaped birthmark stained half her face, and when she grinned, it bunched like a flower.

Juani drew the girl into his lap. "You come to help us, blade?"

I blurted the first thing that came to mind. "Sheeba and I were sightseeing."

Of course, Juani had to ask, "What's sightseeing?"

"Ye gilded gods. It's something you do to pick up anecdotes for parties."

The little girl blinked as if I were speaking Martian, and Juani crinkled his eyes to slits. "Blade, you seriously unlinked. You want sights? I show you sights."

He waved the kids aside and helped me over the doorsill. Again he let me lean on his shoulder. Juani, the human crutch. His musky teenage smell was growing familiar, and I was even getting used to the Coriolis. He told me again the trick was to stay oriented, lean into the spin, and don't turn my head too fast.

This time out, he steered me counterclockwise around the curving corridor, and a whole troop of toads followed at our heels. The little birthmark girl skipped ahead, glancing back every second, till Juani said, "Keesha, you got chores?" She stopped in her tracks, scrunched up her tiny nose and nodded. Then she and the others drifted back the way they'd come.

Oval bulkheads faced each other at regular intervals, all painted the same dingy beige and all coated with the same oily film of fungus, except where the graffiti artist had carved his drawings. Provendia must not have cleaned this place in ages. What musty air.

To keep Juani's favor, I didn't risk trying another door lever, but I counted the doors for future reference. We had just passed the fourth pair when another corridor slanted to the left. Narrow and unlighted, it evidently led inward toward the tank's core.

"What's that way?"

"Ladder," said the witless juve.

"And where does the ladder go?"

"Two," he said. "We on One now. This deck have crew quarters and cargo bay. Ladder take us to Two."

For a kid who wasn't supposed to talk to me, Juani had a loose lip. I knew A13 housed five decks, but I hadn't studied the schematics all that closely. Our surf was supposed to be strictly EVA. So I kept Juani talking. "What's on Two?"

"I'll show you," he said, "if you can handle the ladder."

The ladder. Yes. As we approached the tank's core, the dark corridor narrowed until my elbows rubbed against both scummy walls. Fungus blossomed along the welded-steel seams, and I couldn't avoid touching it. Mega-distasteful. Space fungus was an eternal nuisance. It grew in every satellite, and no one knew how to get rid of it. Early astronauts brought it from Earth, then it mutated to adapt to its new environment. Its smudgy black film proliferated in every orbiting station.

The corridor terminated at a thick bulkhead door, which opened into a spooky round room. "This the ladder well," said Juani.

It smelled of stale musk overlaid with a very slight trace of sugar. Compared to the spaces I'd seen so far, this cylindrical well was a bit larger, probably three meters wide, but its ceiling hung low, and the inevitable surveillance camera dangled like a dead bat. A row of bare bulbs cast a dim glow, and the ladder stood out from the wall at a right angle, with one side rail bolted in. It took me a while to notice the small, round hatch above.

Directly across from us lay another bulkhead door, marked with a large angular U drawn in reflective silver tape.

"That the Up door. This Down." Juani pointed behind us with his thumb. A shiny silver D was taped to the door we'd just stepped through.

"Every deck have a Up and Down," Juani explained.

This, of course, made no sense. The Up and Down doors lay directly across from each other on the same level. Left and right would have been better nomenclature. The doors were also marked with A's, so that meant they were in line with Heaven's axis of spin. Aha. I deduced a theory. "Juani, which way is the sun?"

He grinned and pointed to the U door. "That brightside, man. That Up."

Exactly what I thought. Up meant the side of the tank that faced the sun. Down meant the side facing Earth.

But when Juani began to mount the ladder in a direction perpendicular to the Up and Down doors, my brain fuzzed. Logically, I understood he was moving sideways in relation to Earth's surface, yet every one of my senses shouted that he was climbing "up" that ladder.

In fact, he scampered up the half dozen rungs like a circus performer, leaving me stranded at the base. I studied the ceiling just above my head. With a good strong jump, I could have touched it. When Juani saw me balancing on one foot, struggling to chin myself up to the first rung, he laughed and returned to help. The ladder terminated at a small, sliding hatch near the wall, but most of the ceiling was taken up by a second, larger hatch, with overlapping spiral leaves like the irising aperture of an old-fashioned camera.

"What's that for?" I asked, pointing to the irising hatch.

"That the cargo door, for bringing down the bales."

"Bales?"

"Bales of that pro-glue, that trash they eat on Earth."

Protein-glucose base, he meant. "Do you eat something different in Heaven?"

"Haven?" He mispronounced the word. "What's haven?"

"This satellite," I said, gesturing to the walls. "What do you call it?"

Juani reflected, curling his tongue through the gap in his teeth. Then he rolled his teenaged shoulders. "We just call it . . . here."

With Juani pushing my butt from below, I was able to heave my good leg up the ladder, one rung at a time, while my broken leg dangled and throbbed like an overfull water balloon. That wasn't the worst though. Much more evil was the ladder's tendency to bend. Despite the evidence of my eyes that it was made of solid steel, my body told me it was bending.

"Move around to the other side," Juani said. "Might be easier."

The lurching in my stomach made me willing to try anything, but when I twisted around to the other side, the unruly ladder wanted to tumble over on top of me. Solid steel, mind you. I could feel the rigid metal with my hands. Yet I swear it writhed beneath me like a living creature. More Coriolis effect.

A couple of meters overhead, the ladder intercepted the ceiling, and Juani opened the hatch.

"This the safety lock," he said. "Double doors between the decks, just in case."

We climbed up through the hatch into a space so tiny and black that even squatting, our heads bumped the ceiling. After Juani closed and sealed the hatch beneath us, he opened an identical one above, and as I wrestled my way up through the opening, I remembered Verinne's schematic. These locks segmented A13's ladder well at every level. What a hassle.

Then I noticed another peculiar sensation. I didn't have to grunt so hard to move. My body was getting lighter. No, I should say the artificial gravity was getting weaker. By the time I'd climbed all the way out of the lock, I felt almost springy. Juani closed the floor hatch, and we found ourselves in another identical segment of the ladder well—with another hatch overhead.

"This Two," said Juani.

On Deck Two, another pair of oval-shaped doors faced each other across the well, marked with the same reflective U and D. Juani leaned his weight to twist the Up door's wheel, and it opened onto scintillating whiteness. I'd been living in semidark so long, the brilliance dazzled me. Haloed figures moved toward us. One short. One tall. With Juani's support, I took a tentative hop forward, and what happened next will forever remain unclear.

Did Juani and I both scream at once? We stared at each other and winced as, around and through us, terrible harmonies swelled. Imagine high-pitched sirens oscillating your skull. In unison, Juani and I sank to the floor and pressed our hands to our ears, while across the bright room, the other two figures staggered and fell. Agonizing strains of sound convulsed my vital organs. I curled like a fetus and covered my head. Yet the piercing torment went on and on.

I don't know how long it lasted. I came to my senses, wrapped in an awful ringing silence. My jaw ached. In the blinding light, Juani rolled on his side and shook. I crawled toward him. His eyes were clenched shut.

"Juani?" My voice sounded cottony and distant even to me. "Juani, it's over."

I couldn't mistake what had happened. Provendia had just used its sonic lathe. I'd seen the dog-and-pony presentation at a recent board meeting and voted to approve the funds. The sonic lathe was supposed to be a nonlethal crowd-control device. Visualize a diamond drill the size of a flagpole, rifling around at thirty thousand revolutions per minute. Now watch Provendia's gunship glide in close enough to touch Heaven's hull with this drill. Earsplitting sound waves were supposed to propagate at ludicrous frequencies, immobilizing agitators and quelling resistance.

The lathe was meant to stop riots, but I had never imagined how it would feel. Juani's glazed eyes beseeched me, and across the shining room, someone rose from the floor. A tall angular shadow with a hawk nose.

Liam.

10

THIS IS A DISASTER

"The dead might as well try to speak to the living as the old to the young."
—WILLA CATHER

Wait. Slow down. Things are getting out of order. My recollections dissolve the instant I try to clarify them, and I begin to suspect the protein code in my brain is passing beyond its half-life of nuclear decay. But the last hour hasn't come yet. Pacing here in this anxious fluorescent fog, I notice how time moves in compression waves like sound. Neuroscientists say each perceptual moment lasts one hundred milliseconds in the brain, but sometimes I believe the ticks of the clock are separated by wide troughs of infinity. Sheeba, where are you?

Have you gone dashing after another needy soul? Another seductive hero of a desperate cause? But those romances never last, Shee. Have you forgotten Father Daniel?

Daniel Monnahan. The thought of that smarmy young faith healer made me want to retch. Sheeba's Father Daniel phase had ended three years ago, but I could still see him kneeling on his yoga mat, his robe parted to reveal his shaggy chest. In the basement clinic, he would hum a single note while his devotees poked little seeds down into a communal pot of fake loam—and dropped deutsch in his collection plate. The seeds were plastic. When I bit mine to make sure, Sheeba took offense. She said it was the sym-

bolism that mattered. When I hired detectives to turn up
the rascal's string of legal problems, ex-girlfriends and
chemical dependencies, Sheeba wept.

"I wanted to show you the light," I said.

"Sometimes the light hurts," she answered.

But she never grew wise, never let go of her dreamy
trust in Father Daniel. Long after I'd exposed that fraud
and had him arrested, she still showed up at our therapy
sessions with fake black loam under her fingernails.

And here on A13, as Provendia's sonic lathe jarred our
ears, the lean, lanky shadow of her next hopeless hero staggered up from the floor. Liam. Chieftain of lost juves.
When his dark silhouette reeled, I knew at once that Sheeba
would rush to his aid. Ah, passionate child. She wanted to
believe a mystical force had appointed her path to this
satellite and that some brave destiny awaited her. I won't
try to measure her passage through Heaven. She soared like
a golden comet. And like a comet's tail, I followed.

• • •

"Where is she?" I shouted through the tintinnabulations of
the sonic lathe.

When the noise stopped, a startling quiet fell. White
light shimmered across the floor where I lay blinking and
rubbing my ears. Liam stumbled against some pipes. His
stiff braid swung down his back like a rope, and his figure
cut a silhouette against a light so blinding sharp, I had to
look away at once. Was Sheeba with him? I shaded my
eyes to see, but the light's radiation eclipsed the room more
thoroughly than darkness. I glimpsed its source and turned
away quickly, a small globe half recessed in the wall.

Juani sat up and said something I couldn't hear. My
skull still echoed, and my eyes ached. A new IBiS alert vibrated my left thumbnail, but I couldn't read it. Probably a
bruised eardrum. A new set of tympanums waited for me
back in Kat's shuttle. I was thinking about that when a
short chunky figure jerked my arm.

"What're you doin' here, commie? You come to spy on us?" Ah, the delightful Geraldine.

She yanked me to my feet—or foot rather, and when she backed away, I swung my arms urgently for support. But I could barely see. The wall was too far, and Juani was still sitting on the floor. So I bumped against a cylinder and squinted painfully at its label. Nitrogen.

Every noise sounded muffled and flat, but as my pupils contracted, details began to emerge from the light. Machinery. Coiling tubes. Wires. The ever-present E, W and A's. Then someone covered the light with an old rag.

Auburn brilliance boiled through the folds of the rag and gleamed on the clutter of machinery that was now much easier to see. Turbines, condensers and pumps crowded the small room. Some were torn apart, and their insides glistened like metallic viscera. Others rumbled and shuddered. A bank of storage batteries filled one concave wall, and though the room was larger than my cell on Deck One, the ceiling hung just as low. This had to be the solar plant. The panels where I'd perched like a Buddha were probably mounted right outside the hull. The airlock might be nearby, too. I sharpened my survey.

This was an old-style hybrid plant that used both photovoltaic panels and solar-heated steam pipes lacing through the hull. The steam was used to drive three small turbines, which occupied most of the plant's floor. The equipment looked battered and worn. Cracks in the metal housings had been patched with glue and solder, and the mountings that bolted the turbines to the floor were scarred and broken, as if the machines had been repeatedly ripped off their moorings. One turbine was out of service, and there was a smell of ozone mixed with machine oil.

In all my vacations at orbiting resorts, never once had I wondered where the power came from. I took for granted the elegant service, the views, the gourmet food. Now, gazing at this rickety old equipment that circulated Heaven's air, water and heat, it struck me how tenuous life on a satellite could be.

I made a mental note: Upgrade the power equipment. It should have been replaced years ago. And why had the engineers set that blinding light at eye level in the wall? Even covered with the rag, it gave me a headache.

"What drives that freaking light globe?" I asked.

Juani got up off the floor. "That a porthole, man. Sunlight coming through."

I lurched backward. "Pure sunlight? That's lethal!"

Juani patted my back. "Be calm. It's filtered."

I turned away from the globe, pulled my longjohn collar up around my ears and hid my bare hands in my armpits. On Earth, people fled from sunlight. It burned worse than acid rain. Here in space, it had to be worse.

I kept looking for the airlock. The usual letters marked the four cardinal directions, and more of that childish graffiti marred the walls. There was no airlock in sight.

"Liam, he a spy," said Geraldine. "You want me to blindfold him?"

The chief of thugs moved away from the light, and I saw his face. Same surly expression. Hooded blue eyes. Sunken cheek. Graceful hard-set mouth. Copper beard. And despite the worried creases in his forehead, his skin had the undeniable smoothness of youth. "We got no secrets, Gee."

His rich baritone carried an edginess. Whimsical young girls might find that attractive, but to me, he sounded brutish. I drew myself up with dignity.

"You feeling better?" He nodded at my broken leg.

"Where've you taken Sheeba?" I said.

Liam circled around me. At first, I thought he was trying to intimidate me, but then I realized he was just reaching for his toolbox. He and Geraldine had torn down one of their cumbersome machines for repair.

"Where are you holding her?" I repeated. The artificial gravity felt weaker on Deck Two, and it was easier to put weight on my injured leg. But the Coriolis still made me dizzy.

He knelt beside his oily apparatus and started prying a bolt loose. "She helping Doc in sick-ward."

"Sick-ward. You've exposed her to the disease!"

Liam stopped what he was doing. "What do you know about our disease?"

Too late, I tried to cover my tracks. "Well, influenza, fungal itch. Whatever filthy ailments you people have."

The word "disease" didn't begin to describe the obscure constellation of forces affecting Heaven. I feared some airborne chemical, but Provendia's scientists had ruled that out. It wasn't infectious or viral. They hadn't found contaminants in the air, food or water. No one knew what caused Heaven's malady, but I couldn't get over my dread that it might be contagious. And Sheeba had gone to sick-ward, the very epicenter of pestilence.

Liam was still drilling me with his ice-blue eyes. I watched the tendons moving in his forearms.

"She has no resistance," I said. "You're putting her in harm's way."

"What are you, her nursemaid?" Geraldine's sneer wrinkled the scar on her temple. Her heavy bun had come loose in a black halo of corkscrew curls. "Doll-face asked to go help. She always inviting herself into places."

Sweat trickled down my chest inside my longjohn. I kept watching Liam's forearms, hoping Shee hadn't fallen into his clutches again. "Take me to Sheeba at once."

Geraldine cackled. "If doll-face wanted to stay with you, she woulda stayed."

Gullible Shee held extreme ideas about healing. It was easy to imagine her rushing into Heaven's sick-ward. Hideous combination of words. Sick—a churlish sound. And ward—a caution against evil. I pictured a catacomb of foul, dying bodies.

Let me confess, pangs of guilt shivered through me. I should have warned Shee about Heaven's affliction. I only meant to shelter her from the Reel. No, that wasn't all. I was afraid to tell her the truth—afraid of how she might judge me. But my concealment had put her at risk. I had to find her.

Juani idly knocked some fungus loose from a switch-box. "He ask for a tour, chief. I thought it be okay."

Liam nodded and went back to tinkering with his machine. Geraldine handed him a different wrench, and Juani simply waited, balancing first on one foot, then the other. The arrogance of this twentysomething foreman incensed me. Who was he to keep me waiting? I hadn't had to deal with such a swellheaded junior in over a hundred years.

"Blade didn't come from that gunship," Juani said. "He don't have anything to do with them."

"Bloody liar," said Geraldine.

Juani scratched his neck. "He sightseeing."

Liam shot me a glance, and Geraldine said, "What's that?"

"It antidotes for parties"—Juani rubbed his pimply nose—"something they do on Earth."

"We oughtta chain him up and throw him out the air-lock," Geraldine said.

Evil-eyed wench. I fantasized grabbing handfuls of her wiry black hair. But that would gain me nothing. Dealing with these juves required diplomacy. "My people will pay. Return my sat phone, and let me call them."

Liam slotted a new bolt and tightened it. I thought he smiled, but I may have been mistaken.

Juani said, "We can't call the Net from here. We might try flashing our signal mirrors again."

Geraldine rummaged through her toolbox. "Waste of time. They never answer."

I said, "Then give us our EVA suits, and let us leave. We'll carry whatever message you want to send." Brazen lies. Geraldine was correct about that much. "We appreciate the first aid, but we're not part of this war. You have no legitimate reason to hold us."

Liam's blue eyes darted my way, but he continued working at his infernal bolt.

That white-hot globe was making me sweat like a foun-

tain. I slapped the top of Liam's machine. "She's innocent. Anyone can see that. You're taking advantage of her
kindness."

The punk's jaw quivered, but he still wouldn't answer.

Furious, I limped toward the door. "Juani, take me to
Sheeba."

Juani said, "Wanna see our veggies first? They beautiful, man."

Geraldine's snicker grated my nerves. "The commie's
too bothered about his wandering girlfriend to look at
cabbages."

Blood rushed to my head, and I yelled, "Sheeba's too
good for you vermin."

A heavy iron tool clattered to the floor behind me. I
turned to see Liam standing in the midst of his broken-
down machinery, clenching his fists at his sides. "It was her
that offered to help. Her. She said. And then you—you—"
The brute couldn't form a complete sentence.

"You've exposed her to the malady!" I railed.

Liam's face turned a dull brick color, and I bit my
tongue. I'd said too much.

"Why you come?" he said. "The 'xecs don't need a spy.
They could watch us if they cared to, but they cut off their
cameras."

"I don't know anything about that," I lied.

Geraldine snorted. "Chief, he a commie 'xec same as
them others."

"We're tourists. We got lost," I said.

Geraldine gave me a shove that sent me staggering.

"Gee," said Liam.

That one word, murmured softly under his breath,
snapped her to a standstill. Just as quietly, Liam spoke to
me. "Have you come to euth' us?"

"What a question," I said. "No."

He looked me square in the eye. "Save yourself the trouble. We won't last much longer."

"Then why make Sheeba die with you?"

His expression changed. I won't say his eyes softened,

but his scowl grew less severe. "Sheeba Zee not afraid of our trouble. She crave to help. I never heard anyone talk like her—" He made a fist in front of his chest, then opened his hand as if the right word might fly out.

I knew what he meant. Sheeba had that effect on people. "She's impulsive. You can see she's had very little experience of the world."

His expression hinted the possibility of agreement, so I continued, "Let me take her back home where she'll be safe."

He tugged at his copper beard, and with unexpected mildness, he asked, "Is she your wife?"

Wife. What an old-fashioned word. No one married anymore—except for protes. With their short, miserable lives, they could afford to. The quaint nostalgia of that word "wife" temporarily derailed my anger. I pictured peaceful domestic evenings, slippers by the fire, quiet dinners, images of a custom long erased from the executive scene. With our ever-increasing life spans, who in his right mind would promise "till death do us part"? Perhaps, though, I would promise that to Sheeba. What a sweet thought.

"Nobody forced her," Liam was saying. "She wanted to help Doc in sick-ward."

His words brought me back to the present, Sheeba in that hellish pit, exposed far too long to Heaven's terrible malady. I snapped my fingers. "Give me my sat phone. I can solve this problem in one minute."

"Bloody hell." He wiped his wet lips and stamped across to a workstation littered with metal parts. There in plain sight lay my satellite phone. Funny I hadn't spotted it before. When he flung it at me, its trajectory veered off toward the W, and I had to lunge sideways to catch it. "Call," he said.

I flipped open the cover and ran diagnostics. It was still in working order, and as far as I could tell, none of my files had been accessed. Maybe these idiots didn't know how. With tremendous relief, I spoke a command to call Grunze.

"No service," the message came back.

I tried calling Chad. "No service."

Maybe the voice-command memory was fried. I activated the virtual key pad, and a grid of holographic numbers spread through the air like a small shimmering checkerboard. "Hoo, look at that," Juani said in the background. Rapidly, I tapped out Chad's ID code by hand.

"No service."

"We told ya they blocking our signal." Geraldine jostled me with her elbow. "You think everybody lies the way you do."

"But this is hyperwave." I ran diagnostics again. Provendia had to keep A13 under wraps to prevent a financial panic, but I didn't know our gunship could scramble a hyperwave signal. I stared at the tiny screen. My sat phone was fully functional—and perfectly useless. "This is a disaster."

Geraldine exploded with high-pitched giggles, and Liam nodded, vindicated. I would have said he was gloating, but his expression was too morose. Juani peeked over my shoulder at the sat phone. "Can I see it?" he asked.

Geraldine batted her eyelashes, mocking me. "You stuck here like the rest of us, and you lucky we let you breathe. It's not like the air's free."

"Return our EVA suits, and we'll go," I said.

She ripped the sat phone from my hand and gave it to Juani, who cheerfully started punching buttons at random. "We need your fancy space suits to fix our life support. Ours too leaky. So get your skinny 'xec ass back down to One, and be grateful."

"Juani, take him to sick-ward," said the chieftain. "Help him find his lady."

"Liam, no." Geraldine flared her shapely nostrils.

But the chieftain didn't react. I glared at his knife-edged profile. He was working at his machine again and wouldn't look at me. How incredibly reckless. He was giving me free run of the factory? On second thought, his casual treatment felt like an insult. It seemed the mighty Liam had no fear of me.

Fuming, I gripped Juani's shoulder. "Let's go."

Juani stuck my useless sat phone in his waistband and beamed. "Sick-ward up on Four. We go look at the veggies on our way."

As we left the solar plant, I glanced back and caught Liam watching me. He turned away and pretended to be absorbed by his repair project. Then he slowly raised his cold blue eyes again. No mistaking the challenge in his look. I hadn't answered his question—hadn't claimed Sheeba as my wife.

11

VEGGIES

"Every old man complains of the growing depravity of
the world, of the petulance and insolence of the
rising generation."
—DR. JOHNSON

Two's corridors were just as narrow and scummy as
One's had been. The ceilings were just as claustropho-
bically low, the surveillance cameras dangled just as
inertly, and there were no windows anywhere. It amazed
me that the engineers hadn't provided a way to see out.
More squealing toads milled around, playing their silly
games and blocking our way. My left thumb had been vibrating constantly since the episode with the sonic lathe, so
as Juani marched ahead, I covertly tapped my thumbscreen
with my pinky stylus. A menu popped up with a ton of
messages.

"Net not responding" topped the list, and I finally realized why. Provendia's Net blockade was scrambling my
IBiS signal as well as my sat phone. Sure enough, the processor in my thumb had logged a dozen missed
appointments—scheduled maintenance on my thymus, for
one. That device controlled my T-cells. I'd also missed another telomerase infusion. If I skipped too many of those,
the telomeres in my cells would shrivel, and my skin would
sag. Not good.

Ahead in the corridor, Juani was singing mindless sentimental lyrics of love and heartbreak, as if a boy his age
would know anything about that.

"Where did you learn that stupid song?" I asked.

Juani grinned and came back to offer me his elbow. "Sing me some Earth songs, blade."

"I don't sing." I rubbed my jaw and brooded over my shriveling telomeres. But my skin still felt smooth and tight. As we passed bulkhead doors, more and more useless little employee dependents wandered underfoot. Sometimes I had to knee them out of my way. No wonder A13's overhead costs had gotten so seriously out of line.

Juani guided me around Deck Two, narrating like a tour guide. "Over there, ops bay. Here, circulator pumps push the air and water."

He stopped in front of an oval door, grabbed its wheel with both hands and mysteriously wiggled his eyebrow up and down. "Veggies."

"Listen, kid, I just want to find Sheeba."

Juani ignored me. When the door swung open, light blazed through, and a wet gurgling sound echoed. More powerful than light or sound was the mesmerizing fragrance. How can I describe the amazing perfume that wafted through this door?

Fresh, that was the main impression. Sweet, but also sour, sharp, tangy. The smell appealed to me on a primitive level. My mouth actually watered. I stepped farther in and felt a breeze, the first positive airflow I'd experienced in Heaven. A low rhythmic purr hinted some kind of mechanical rotor fans. And there was dripping, like the tinkle of small bells. The humidity settled on my skin.

Set into the outer curving wall were a score of blinding light-globes like the one in the solar plant. Their beams sparkled through the mist. The inner wall curved, too, giving the room a half-torus shape, like the inside of one half of a hollow donut. The dazzling white beams ricocheted across ranks and ranks of tables. I cupped my hands around my eyes and peered. The tables were covered with leaves.

Hundreds—no, thousands of green leaves fluttered in the breeze of the fans. The room held actual living plants.

Scores of them. A veritable treasure trove of greenware. I bent over a table and gawked. The plants were growing in long thick bars of solid plastic.

Juani stepped aside and grinned as he watched my reaction. "Watch this." He jammed his stubby finger under one of the plastic bars, and its top flipped up like a lid. So the bar was not solid plastic. It was a long, slender lidded tray with holes in the top for the plants to grow through. Juani opened the lid only a few centimeters, careful not to disturb the plants. I stooped to peek inside, where plant roots coiled like white threads, soaking up a cloudy yellowish liquid. Yes, I recognized this technology. Hydroponics. I'd browsed video about it.

"The cover keeps the juice from sloshing out during Justment," Juani said, "but we still get a little splatter sometimes."

Justment? Peculiar word. On the floor, furry tufts of black space fungus outlined the strokes where someone had mopped up repeated spills. I wondered what caused the liquid nutrient to splash so much. As I studied the open tray, a new stream of liquid surged through, washing the roots gently back and forth. Then ceiling-mounted misters erupted and shot a fine spray over the leaves for about five seconds. When the misters subsided, the damp leaves trembled and shed heavy, glittering droplets. A sheen of moisture covered every verdant surface. Juani snapped the tray's lid back into place.

I'd seen so few real plants in my life. Hothouse orchids brought in for parties. Astronomically expensive endive salad to celebrate a birthday. Even wealthy execs relied on synthesized foods, textiles and medicines most of the time. When greenhouse gases thickened our skies and poisoned our rain, plants had to be moved indoors. On a mass scale, that absorbed way too many resources, and the results were too chancy, too subject to terrorist attack and genetic mutation. Farming had never been a good investment. Synthetics, on the other hand, paid back in spades. Synthetics could be standardized, patented and kept secure. After years of Provendia board meetings, I knew more about food processing than I cared to admit.

"What are these plants, Juani?"

"This ruffled one, this kale." He ran his open palm along the tops of the leaves, smiling with gap-toothed affection. "Those over there, they look like heads. They cabbages."

Nearby stood a tray of deep green foliage. I parted the dark leaves and discovered, to my delight, a small pulpy floret the color of emeralds. It sparkled with droplets of mist.

Juani said, "That broccoli, man. Pinch off a piece. It's okay."

I snapped off a floret, sniffed it, then tested it with the tip of my tongue.

"It's good." Juani broke off a larger stalk and chomped, smiling as he chewed.

I took a tiny bite, then another. Bittersweet, crunchy. The texture alone was a marvel. And the flavor, transcendental. I snapped another floret and devoured it. Nothing in my experience had prepared me for this exotic taste.

"This Primo," said Juani, gesturing at the crescent-shaped room. Half a dozen prepubescent kids were moving among the tables, doing things to the plants. Juani kept talking. "Dr. Bashevitz, he built this. This our first hydro-pod. This where we start our seedlings."

Without thinking, I rested my weight on my injured leg, but in Two's reduced gravity, the pain jarred me with less force. When I moved toward the cabbages, a brilliant beam spotlighted me, and that's when I noticed the light beams were moving—slowly roving over the leaves like searchlights.

"Just babies here. Little shoots. Our main garden up on Five," Juani said.

"Deck Five is the factory floor," I mused absently, studying the light beams.

"Up there, man, we got fruit. Melons." Juani followed at my heels, speaking rapidly. "Dr. Bashevitz, he brought the seeds here. He a botanist. He built this Primo, and we copied his plans up on Five."

I squinted to see what made the light beams move. On the ceiling, rows of small round mirrors hung on mounts that swiveled like searching eyes.

Juani kept chattering away. His thick eyebrow fringe rose and fell as he talked, and a happy grin wrinkled his pug nose. "Primo supposed to breed psuedoplankton to make oxygen. Green stinky mess. I used to go rake it. But Dr. Bashevitz, he snuck in veggie seeds. They say he plant seeds in a thousand factories before he got busted. For a while, his veggies growin' all over the G Ring. Then the 'xecutives go burn 'em out."

The ceiling mirrors were reflecting the light beams from the globes and sweeping them evenly across the growing plants. Clever design, I thought.

"'Xecutives say the gardens not clean enough. Harbor germs. Say we gotta sterilize."

Juani bent over another tray, pulled off a dead leaf and rolled it between his palms. He raised the lid and crumbled the leaf into the pale liquid sluicing through the channels, feeding the threadlike roots.

I watched the fluid waves in fascination. "What's in that liquid?"

"Everything good goes into the garden." Juani's large brown eyes gleamed with mystery and mischief. "We recycle."

"Oh." I plucked another bit of—what did he call it, broccoli? The taste aroused deep feelings of satisfaction, as if I remembered its essence from a former life. What would Sheeba say about that? She loved the concept of reincarnation.

"Sooner later, I show you the garden on Five. That one beautiful sight."

"Has Sheeba seen this?" I asked. This was definitely her kind of place. She would imagine all sorts of mystical forces among the seedlings. I could almost hear her joyful gibberish. "Let's go find Sheeba."

"Yeah, man." Juani escorted me through the curving torus room, proudly explaining as we went how the mirrors bent the sunlight around to reach all the tables. He recited plant names. Clearly, he loved having an audience. I knew he was taking unnecessary detours to show off his seedlings, and I had to keep urging him forward. Still, he amused me. He revered those plants.

"Juani, I've lost all sense of direction. Which way is Sheeba from here?"

He leaned against the curved outer wall and scoured away the film of black fungus with his thumb to reveal a stenciled X. More wall alphabet. I'd noticed a few X's earlier, intermingled with the A's, E's, W's, U's and D's.

"X mean exterior," he said. "This the hull. Nothing beyond this wall but vacuum, and it sucks." His eyes closed to merry slits, enjoying the stale joke. "If you get lost, follow a X wall till you come to something familiar."

My leg was aching, and I tried to shove a hydroponic tray aside so I could sit on the table to rest. But since the trays were welded in place, I could only lean my butt against the table edge. "Juani, try to grasp this. Nothing here is familiar to me."

The comical way his nose wrinkled almost made me laugh. He didn't have an inkling what I meant. Every centimeter of this hellish satellite must have been engraved in his brain like tribal memory.

"Enough X-wall lessons. Let's just find Sheeba."

He rubbed the stenciled X, and his caramel face gleamed with the damp. Fungus blackened his stubby, boyish hands. The fungus was everywhere. Here in the hydroponic section, rings of it bloomed along the walls in a morbid floral pattern, following the arcs of a scrub brush where someone had tried to clean. With disgust, I noted my own blackened hands and sock feet.

"You don't have X walls on Earth?" Juani said. "You gotta have something to hold in the air."

I sighed, because he was right. Even on Earth, breathable air had to be contained within sealed habitats. Beyond our terrestrial walls lay not the airless void but something

just as lethal—toxic pollution. "We don't stencil X's everywhere," I said. "On Earth, we use street signs."

Juani gave me that googly expression kids get when
they're curious. His liquid brown eyes widened. How do
you deal with a look like that?

Some of the urchins drew closer, and Juani lifted a toddler in his arms. I scooted farther back against the welded
tray and rested my sore leg across my knee. It crossed my
mind to abandon Juani and go looking for Sheeba on my
own, but more toads gathered at my feet, hemming me in.
They gripped their knobby knees and looked up at me with
big, popping eyes. Among them sat the little girl with the
red birthmark. She scratched my foot to get my attention.
"What color is Earth?"

That started a deluge. The little beasties had more questions than a Com has vice presidents. They wanted to know
what held the oceans down, and why mountains changed
into sand. These infants knew so little, only myths and
half-truths gleaned from storytelling.

"Don't you ever browse the Net?" I asked.

The toads looked at Juani, who merely shrugged and
jostled the toddler he was holding in his arms. Then I remembered that employees weren't given Net access unless
their jobs required it. I glanced at the dingy surface of the
X wall, decorated with graffiti. "How do you stand this
place without windows? You can't see *anything*."

Juani puffed out his chest like a strutting young bird.
"Some day I go spacewalking again."

The birthmark girl scratched my foot again. "What's a
window?"

Juani tousled her hair. "Keesha, you a smart aleck."

Then he got up, lowered the child he was holding into
Keesha's lap, and started picking veggies to feed the kids.
As the wee ones crunched and nibbled, Juani kept interro-
gating me, and each time I answered, he would lean toward
me and wiggle his fingers as if he could pluck learning
from the air. He made me feel like a sage.

"The oceans stay put because the land is above sea level. . . . No no no, you don't get lighter when you climb a mountain. Gravity's the same everywhere." I answered whether I knew the facts or not. No one had ever hung on my words the way Juani and these toads did.

I sat munching handfuls of what they called "cherry tomatoes," and while I gushed erudition, the juice ran down my chin. Ye gilders, I hadn't met so many inquisitive minds in decades. The younger kids must have lived all their short lives in this rusty spinning bucket, and these wedge-shaped steel rooms comprised their entire universe. As I watched Juani dawdle over his greenery, I tried to imagine what that would be like.

Ditch the sentiment. You're going sappy, Deepra.

The edge of the table was eating into my butt, and the little red fruits began to upset my stomach. They looked too much like lychee nuts. Nearby, another broccoli flower glistened, so I broke off the entire stalk and took big bites to wash the bitter taste away. "Juani, let's get going. We've wasted enough time."

He was examining another withered leaf, smoothing it with his blunt boyish fingertips. "Strange. Live all your life on Earth, and never see broccoli."

The younger kids laughed at that.

"There's some kind of disease in this place," I said abruptly. "Tell me about it."

Juani flinched. My change of subject must have shocked him. His face closed up, and he turned away to adjust a mister nozzle, while the kids glanced back and forth between the two of us with worried frowns.

"What about you, Juani? Do you have any symptoms?"

He found a tool under the table and began to scrape a whitish crust off the nozzle jet. "Dr. Bashevitz say the plants on Earth all gone. Why you go let them die, blade?"

"What?"

"Why you make such a wreckage?" he asked.

"I didn't do it!"

I bit down hard on the broccoli stalk but found it diffi-

cult to chew. Wreckage, he called it. Earth's Big D—
Defloration—began in the twentieth century, long before I
was born. And this illiterate child was accusing *me*? What
did he know, stupid kid. I crunched another bite. He talked
as if I were personally responsible for the climate change.

Juani gave me a stern look and put his tool away. Keesha
whispered something, and the other kids drifted back to their
chores, while I sat chomping and scowling and ruminating.

Earth's plants died because of chemical alterations in
the atmosphere that heated the oceans and drove our
weather patterns into cosmic freak-out. When the last tun-
dras burned off, I was building my first Com, working
night and day, recruiting coders to patch the sub-Asian Internet back together. Meeting payroll took my entire focus.
I didn't have time to spare for moss and lichen.

"You're too young to understand."

"I old, blade."

"Ridiculous. You can't be more than sixteen."

"I been living fast."

Juani stripped the leaves from a broccoli stem and used
it to clean his teeth, all the while studying me with his clear
brown eyes. They made me nervous, those eyes. If I didn't
know better, I'd have said he felt sorry for me.

"Are you going to take me to Sheeba or not?"

"What happened to Earth?" he said. "For real."

I propped up my splinted leg and picked at my sock.
Earth's past was not a subject I liked to remember, any
more than my own, but the distress in Juani's eye touched
me. Maybe he deserved an answer.

"Rainfall. That's what we noticed first. It fell too hard in
the wrong places, gorging out gullies and washing away
the soil. In other places, there were droughts and dust
storms."

The kids scrambled closer again, all ears. Juani wrung
out a wet rag and wiped veggie juice from their faces. They
probably expected an adventure tale. Ha, they had no idea.
Nothing I could say about our magnificent home planet
would make sense to them.

"The floods blew out landfills and waste sites. There were toxic spills and leakages. Bad things started washing into the oceans, which were heating up faster than we knew." I rambled on, knowing the kids wouldn't understand. "The polar ice melted so slowly, we didn't notice at first how the ocean currents were shifting. The Ag Coms kept gengineering their major crops to survive the hotter climate. And who cared about a few wild species going extinct?"

Juani sat down with the kids and waited for me to go on, but I couldn't meet his eyes. I picked at the fungus matted to my sock.

"The big changes came gradually. Wind storms carried poisonous dust as high as the stratosphere. The cyclones got worse, and the tides—"

I scraped at my socks, remembering the filthy floodwaters overtaking my parents' home. "People had to move inland. There were mass evacuations."

Who can see the future? I had gone to Delhi for a conference. I wasn't there when the storm tides hit the coast, higher than any on record. Prashka's voice lilted over the phone like birdsong. "Don't worry, my love. We'll meet in Lahore." But when the floods took Calcutta, she couldn't get out. Airline employees seized the airport and auctioned off tickets to the highest bidder. They laughed at her worthless rupees. . . .

Keesha reached up and patted my hand. Her little round eyes held such compassion—ye gilded effigies, I jerked away. I didn't need sympathy from a prote child.

"Show's over." I stood and gruffly waved the toads away. "No more fucking nursery school. Take me to Sheeba now."

Keesha drew back as if I'd slapped her, and the kids scattered. Juani folded his wet rag and laid it on a bench. Then he knelt beside the table where I'd been sitting and clamped down the tray lid I'd knocked askew. For a moment, I regretted my rudeness. He was brainier than I'd expected. Curious, enthusiastic and fairly polite. Not a bad sort. But I was getting sappy again.

"Sheeba may be lost," I said.

"Lost here? It just one old tank, man. How she go get lost?"

Juani instructed the kids to finish picking tomatoes. Then he led me back to the ladder well, and he sealed the door behind us. Straight across the well, the reflective silver U glinted from the Up door. We'd entered the solar plant that way, but we were coming out through the Down door. Juani had led me halfway around Deck Two.

"Sick-ward on Four. We go climb." He helped me hop up the first rung.

The ladder well seemed darker and smellier after the bright hydroponic rooms. Struggling upward, I felt the short ladder slope away again, and no matter how rigid it appeared to my eye, I had to cling with both hands to keep from flying off. The Coriolis effect unzipped my equilibrium. Yet with each step upward, the artificial gravity grew very slightly weaker. At the ceiling hatch, I felt light and nimble enough to pull myself up with my hands. But in this crazy place, "up" didn't mean what it did on Earth. Climbing the ladder meant moving closer toward the tether that spun Heaven around its counterweight.

"Why won't you talk about the sickness?" I asked when we reached the low ceiling.

Juani opened the hatch, which led to another tiny black enclosure—the safety lock between Two and Three. The engineers should have built some lighting in these double-door coffins between the decks. I made a mental note: Heaven's lighting needed a thorough upgrade.

"What about it, Juani? Why won't you tell me?"

He'd turned sullen. Not good. I needed Juani on my side. "Okay, forgive me for prying."

"Blade, you too keen."

"My intentions are good, I swear." We squeezed into the tiny lock, and just as Juani finished sealing us in, a jolt knocked us against the upper hatch. "What was that?" I said.

"Dunno."

Juani pressed his hand to the enclosure's floor, apparently feeling for vibrations. I could feel them, too, through the soles of my sock feet. The gunship was firing again.

He said, "We better move outta here."

He locked the hatch beneath us, then opened the one above, and we hustled up into the next ladder well segment. On Deck Three, the false gravity was noticeably weaker, and I could walk on my injured leg without pain. Juani sealed the floor hatch, then opened the bulkhead door marked D for Down. As soon as the door swung open, a new aroma hit me like a warm bath. I knew that smell. Sweet syrupy protein-glucose base, the smell that gave Heaven its name. I held my nose to keep from gagging, and Juani said, "This the drying room."

Almost at once, we heard a clanging in the ladder well behind us, and I turned just in time to see the floor hatch open again. Liam popped out and raced past us in a dead run. He moved in long, loping strides into the drying room, and his blond braid streamed out behind. He didn't so much as acknowledge our presence. Next, Geraldine's brown face poked up through the hatch.

"What happened?" Juani asked.

"Hull breach on Two." She elbowed her way up. "Damn commies splintered our X wall. Chief gone to get the welder."

"My seedlings okay?" Juani's adolescent voice cracked on the last syllable.

Geraldine shook her head. "Help the Chief get that welder. And bring the houseguest. Maybe we can use him for glue."

12

KIDS DON'T THINK

"We are always the same age inside."
—GERTRUDE STEIN

Have I mentioned Sheeba's arms? Round and long, with fine downy hair. Her young muscles burgeoned gently under taut smooth skin, and how those swelling shapes bewitched me. How I loved to watch her arms move. Especially when she lifted heavy objects like her weight bench or the massage chair.

Sheeba's vigorous arms filled my thoughts as I pushed and pulled myself awkwardly through the drying room in Three's light gravity. The ovens stood in rows like battered sarcophagi. They were used to bake raw food product into hard dry bales for easier transport to Earth. But they weren't operating. The room felt stone cold, and the sight of these nonproducing assets irked me. I visualized the red ink bleeding across Provendia's balance sheet.

Protein-glucose slaked the world's hunger—as much of the world's hunger as could ever be slaked by market forces. Of course, there would always be pockets of mismanagement and famine. That bearded prophet was right twenty-three centuries ago when he said the poor would always be with us. Still, "pro-glu" was a miracle of chemistry. With appropriate additives and processing, it could be made to resemble any menu item, from petit fours to pepper steak. The original inventors sold their patent to Provendia.Com for 60 billion deutsch.

As Juani hurried me ahead, I held my nose to block the

saccharine reek. I'd seen plenty of oven rooms like this—
on video at our board meetings. They all looked the same.
Three decades ago, a Provendia scientist discovered that
pro-glu congealed faster in low gravity, and since then,
we'd sited all our bulk brewing factories in orbit. We
bought cast-off fuel tanks at bargain rates, then rehabbed
them as multilevel vat farms. Space garbage made excellent counterweights, and we got our tethers, guidance rockets and radiation shielding from contractor surplus.

None of our other satellites had developed Heaven's
malady though, not so far. To date, our other properties still
cycled around the G Ring, functioning at optimum
throughput. Who knows why this one unit, A13, was
stricken? The situation baffled our analysts—and scared us
board members to death. None of us wanted to contemplate another financial panic like the Crash of '57. So we
altered Heaven's course to a high polar orbit, locked down
communications and laid plans for damage control.

Far ahead, Liam loped in high-arcing strides among the
drying ovens, then disappeared around a corner. We found
him wrestling with a portable welding rig that was cabled
to the floor. Impatiently, he flung his yellow braid over his
shoulder and unclipped the last cable. Then he and Juani
grabbed its handles and slid the thing across the deck toward the ladder well. I brought up the rear, asking myself
why I'd been in such a hurry to follow.

Back at the ladder, Liam punched a switch that irised
the huge cargo door open, the door they used to move bales
of product down the well. Together, Liam and Juani
hoisted the welder onto a suspended freight platform, then
used a pulley system to lower it to Deck Two. Geraldine
shoved me down through the cargo door, and when I
landed on my injured leg, it was all I could do to choke
back a curse. The others jumped down after me, and as
soon as Juani closed the cargo door, Liam pried open the
door to the veggie room.

The bulkhead seal popped open with a sucking hiss, and
the door swung inward and banged on its hinges. Wind

whistled past my ears, and a herd of little toads burst out. I recognized some of their faces. Keesha for one. Quickly, Juani herded them into the solar plant and sealed the door behind them, while Liam tilted the welder into the veggie room. As we entered behind him, a sudden gust plastered my curls flat.

"Help me shut this door," Geraldine demanded.

She leaned her short burly body against the door we'd just come through, trying to push it closed against the air rushing in from the ladder well. Her shank muscles popped with strain. Reluctantly, I wedged my back against the door and helped her force it closed. Only after the fourth turn of the wheel did the air stop shrieking through the door's gasket.

Geraldine gave the wheel one final twist. "We got a bad leak."

Finding the hull breach wasn't difficult. We followed the flying bits of green leaves. The seedlings lay flat in their trays, pummeled by the rushing air. I nearly slipped on a wet cabbage leaf stuck to the floor.

Liam and Juani were kneeling at the X wall, working with the welder. A hairline crack ran from floor to ceiling. Liam knelt and pressed the lower part together with his palms, while Juani operated the welding torch. Geraldine pulled a white squeeze tube from her pocket and started extruding thick brown gunk along the crack near the ceiling. Though the crack was barely visible, air escaped through with an ominous squeal.

"Juani, help me hold this," Liam grunted.

The boy immediately dropped his welding torch and sprang to help press the seam closed, but in the light gravity, they both kept slipping out of position.

"Man, my broccoli," Juani said panting.

This was taking too long. I grabbed Juani's welding torch and started working at the bottom of the crack again, while Geraldine made her way down from the ceiling with her brown gunk. As the rupture closed, air shrieked through in a high-pitched scream. Amazing that such a tiny leak could cause so loud a roar. Geraldine and I gradually overwhelmed the crack with our patch-weld and sealer glue. When we met in the middle, the whistling faded.

"Bless a sweet Jeez." Juani rushed to examine the trays of ravaged foliage. "They down, but they strong. Sooner later, they stand back up." He sounded as if he needed to convince himself.

Geraldine wiped sweat from her face. "This patch won't hold long, chief. We gotta fix the outer hull."

"I'll suit up. You stay here just in case it breaks loose." Liam in profile looked more than ever like a predatory hawk. He turned hastily and almost bowled me over.

"Who go help you with the welder?" said Geraldine. "Juani can't do it."

Liam was already loping away. "I'll get Vlad."

"Vlad supposed to be playing doctor!" she yelled at his retreating back.

Liam halted and half turned. He moistened his lips, thinking. Then Juani leaped out. "I can do it, chief. I won't faint this time, I swear."

Liam shook his head, and his face creased like that of a weather-beaten old man. Then his blue eyes glittered at me. I was shielding myself under a tray table in case the crack opened again, which of course was pointless. If the hull blew, we'd all be swept into space.

Liam lunged toward me and thrust out his hand. "Let me feel your grip."

What kind of challenge was this? I grasped his hand in a manly squeeze.

"Fair enough. You'll do." He yanked me out from under the tray table and steered me toward the ladder well.

"Do for what?" I said, sailing through the light gravity. As if I couldn't guess. "Call your other crewmates. What do I know about hull repair? You said I could go find Sheeba."

Liam ignored me. "Juani, clear this section. Make sure the people safe. And Gee, you suit up and lock the bulk-heads. Just in case."

"In case of what?" I said. "Please let me find Sheeba."

My complaints failed to arouse any response from the chieftain, except another shove toward the ladder. He intended to press me into service as his welding assistant, but why? He should rely on his experienced fellow employees, not me. But who could fathom the mind of an immature prote?

In the ladder well, Liam bullied me across to the Up door and twisted the wheel to open it. When I demanded again why he was forcing an unskilled stranger to help make a critical repair, he took his sweet time to answer.

"Juani get spacesick. Geraldine and Vlad busy. So that leave you." Behind the bristly mustache, his lip curled very slightly. "Or your lady."

"Screw you," I said.

But I was bewildered. A couple of months ago, this factory still had sixty active employees. That's when we killed the surveillance cameras and stopped tracking the death rate, but surely not that many people could have fallen sick in two months.

"I can't believe there's no one else. What about some of those little kids?"

The chieftain gave me a look so full of seething insolence that I'm ashamed to admit, I cringed. Then he shoved me through the Up door, and I stumbled through the solar plant, trying to make sense of this crazy scenario. Liam, Geraldine, Juani, Vlad, were they the only healthy adults left on A13? Hell, they weren't adults—they hadn't even broken thirty.

I had to jog to keep pace with Liam. In the operations bay, we found the herd of toads. Twenty or thirty of the little beggars huddled together on the floor looking frightened. Don't get me wrong, I recognize the necessity of children. Haven't I donated my reproductive fluids to EuroBank? But underagers hadn't played any part in my life for molto decades, and I'd never seen so many squirmy toads gathered in one place. It was like some misbegotten human rookery. In my ideal world, there would be no need for replacement offspring because we would live forever.

I looked over the children's heads and examined the ops bay. Heaven's nerve center. Our site manager had worked there, tracking product volume, value and cost every second to the centime. Inventories, purchase orders, shipping transmittals, profit and loss, every vital statistic was documented here. But the Net nodes were gone. Our manager must have absconded with the hardware when he fled.

The ops bay held only a few useless dumb terminals, overturned wastebaskets and broken lamps. Empty desks lay tumbled on their sides, drawers flung helter-skelter. Office supplies strewed the floor, some shattered to bits. I saw one stylus impaled in a terminal screen. Watching the children's anxious faces, I found it slightly pathetic that the protes had taken their revenge on this furniture.

In one shadowy corner, something odd spiraled across the wall like a woolly vine. Had one of Juani's hydropods grown out of control? On closer inspection, it turned out to be a swirl of furry black space fungus following the outlines of the factory's blossoming corrosion.

We hadn't gone far when Liam yanked open a service closet and drew out two space suits. Mine and Sheeba's. Crisp white, with attractive military-style black piping, they looked only slightly the worse for their one brief flight to Heaven. I could see where the torn right leg of my suit had self-sealed. The patch looked solid. A sparkling point of bliss tickled my nerves. These suits would get us home.

"Pick one and put it on," said Liam.

Never had I expected to see our suits again, and this inept war leader was simply handing them over. My confidence swelled. This was going to be easy. Soon, I thought, Sheeba and I would be drinking toasts back in Nordvik, telling tales and celebrating our escapade. I hefted one of the thruster packs. Sheeba's had performed just fine, but mine had malfunctioned. Now I saw why. One of Provendia's noisemakers had ruptured the fuel reservoir. That blackened gash made my neck prickle. Only pure chance had kept my thruster from detonating like a bomb and cutting me in two.

"Leave that," he said.

No prob. I set the damaged thruster next to the good one and made careful note of the surroundings so I could find the closet later. I took Sheeba's suit. Then Liam showed me the way to the airlock. No blindfold. No circuitous route. Can you imagine? He led me straight to it. How easy could he make this?

I tried not to grin as I slithered into Sheeba's suit and inhaled her soapy herbal aroma. When the suit snagged on my cast of plastic and wire, I ripped the blasted contraption to pieces. My fracture didn't hurt as much as before. Soon, I reflected, Sheeba and I would be snuggling together in a nice hot bubble bath, telling each other jokes.

Then a wrenching shudder spiked through my left thumb. As Liam stuffed his long braid into his helmet, I took a quick peek at my IBiS. I'd missed an appointment to have my false eyes recalibrated. More worrisome, my dental NEMs had gone totally dormant. That scared me. Without Net access, how many other classes of NEMs would shut down? My heart NEMs? The buggers in my brain? I had to get back to the Net.

Right. I would signal the gunship the minute we exited. Surely they would notice my blinking helmet lights, and surely their onboard AI would recognize my face. The Provendia chairman emeritus—they were bound to have my facial pattern on file. Right?

If only I still wore my signet. I pinched my earlobe with a groan. One scan from the gunship would have revealed my full profile: "Nasir Deepra, trillionaire, majority stock holder, molto senior exec. Handle with awe."

Inside the suit, I sniffed the pungency of Sheeba's soap and let luxurious memories drift through my head—of Shee reposing in bubbles. Yes, we had bathed together. That herbal scent brought back a deluge of warm sensations. Shee lived at peace with her body and went nude as often as not, for which I lit incense of gratitude to the gilded gods. I, though, had grown to manhood in a different time, and public disrobing gave me goosebumps. You'd think the millions I'd invested in manly beauty would make me bold, but on the four occasions when Sheeba and I shared a bath—yes, I count them on my fingers and salivate—still I was always glad of the bubbles.

• • •

"What's gnarling you, beau? Your neck's got heinous knots." Shee sat behind me in the tub, wrapping her soap-slick legs around my waist and massaging my back with her foamy fingertips. She'd scented the water with essential flower oils—artificial esters mixed by hand, paradise in a bottle.

"Is it some of those boards?" she asked. Sheeba knew I served on the boards of a dozen commercial enterprises. She knew I sat for hours in uncomfortable chairs, sipping tepid brandy and listening to memoranda. She understood how I loathed Robert's Rules of Order. Grueling work. But that wasn't what knotted my shoulders. It was Sheeba.

"You've taken on some new clients," I said.

"Um-hum, my practice is going supernova." She sucked my ear and closed her teeth just enough to let me feel the sharp pressure. Hot shivers rode up my spine, and I sank deeper in the bubbles. "It's because of you, Nass. You told your friends how I balanced your soul's primal energy, and how it cleared up your backache."

Rubbish. My friends were letches and slimes. They didn't want Shee to balance their souls. "Dear heart, not everyone's as pure-minded as you are."

"Oh, I'm not especially virtuous."

"You're generous and trusting and very inexperienced," I said. "How old are you now? Nineteen?"

"Twenty-three!" She laughed and roughed up my scalp with her plastic loofa. "You never notice time passing, beau. You live the same year over and over."

• • •

"Need help with that?" Liam's words jolted me back to the present. He was pointing at the helmet clipped to my belt.

We had already entered the airlock, and Liam had wrestled the cumbersome welding rig in between us. Chagrined, I clapped the helmet on my head and sealed the neck ring.

"Ready to go?" he asked.

I nodded curtly. His baritone sounded muffled, and I realized the satellite phones in our helmets weren't working. They needed the Net to relay their signals back and forth. "How're we supposed to communicate?" I shouted.

"Hand signals," he shouted back, though his hands remained motionless.

While we waited, I casually chinned on my helmet's heads-up display and checked the time. And the date! Ye golden statuettes. Over sixty hours had passed since Sheeba and I crashed into Heaven. By Earth measure, we'd spent more than two days in this pestilence-ridden satellite. Breathing this air, imbibing these molecules, suffering the onslaughts of Heaven's mysterious influence. We had to get out of here.

With a barely audible thump, the airlock's outer door slid open. Our home planet swelled below us like a fat yellow belly, blanketed in woolly whorls of smog, and its glow blotted out the stars. I couldn't see the gunship. The sun was not in sight. We had exited on the wrong side of Heaven.

The instant I stepped out, my body careened away from the hull. I'd forgotten how fast Heaven rocketed around its counterweight. There was no friction, nothing like wind resistance to indicate our speed, but the very blood in my veins felt the momentum. And I had no computerized thruster navigation to hold me in track with the spin.

In panic, I clutched the safety line clipped to my belt. The line jolted me to a stop, then hauled me along like the tail of a kite as Heaven raced around its tight circular path. Grunting with effort, I pulled myself hand over hand back toward the hull—and felt like a dunce for drifting loose, like any green kid on his first space walk.

Liam was already heaving the welder along a line of handholds fastened to the hull. I got myself oriented and realized Liam had brought us out on Heaven's shady side, where the ship couldn't see us. I would have to crawl around to the sunny face where the solar panels were mounted—straight into the fire zone.

You may think Nasir Deepra, surfer ace, was thrilled to the ends of his hair follicles by the magnificent danger surrounding him. This had to be the most exhilarating war zone I'd ever surfed. Oh yes, I would have been blissed to the max—with a working sat phone in my pocket and my friends standing by with rescue robots. But Heaven was proving too actual and acute for entertainment value. Surfs were not supposed to last this long.

The almighty chief of thugs was watching me, so I had no choice but to haul myself along the safety line and scramble after him. Still I glanced around, trying to devise a plan.

One end of the dented tank terminated in a blunt base, while the other tapered to a vanishing point, beyond which, far in the distance, the white chunk of asteroid gleamed. The counterweight looked small from my perspective, and the tether stretched toward it like a shining ribbon. I couldn't see how the tether attached, but I remembered a schematic of massive cables and bolts affixed to the tank's bullet point.

The chieftain shook my shoulder. Well, of course I was distracted by all these sights. I didn't go spacewalking every day, certainly not on a crazy whirling satellite. Liam grabbed my arm and towed me like deadweight toward the welder, which he had clamped into place with magnetic lock-downs. He grasped my helmet and shook it to make sure he had my attention. I batted his hand away.

Very conspicuously, he pointed to a valve mechanism attached to the welder's gas cylinder. It apparently controlled the regulator, which released compressed gas through the hose to power his welding torch. He mimed twisting the valve clockwise, then made a thumbs-up signal. Next he mimed reversing it counterclockwise, and that came with a thumbs-down. I nodded to show I understood.

Before he left me, he pressed my fingers around a hand-hold. Insolent pup. As if he expected me to drift away again. Next, incredibly, he unclipped himself from the safety line. Spacewalking without a safety line! On a hull spinning this fast!

You know, kids don't think. They're dumb as rocks. I would've lectured him about the risks, but we hadn't worked out the hand signals for scolding.

Without looking my way, he gathered up the coiled hose and slid along the hull. Not only did the punk dispense with his safety line. He also moved away from the row of handholds. He flattened himself to the pitted hull, wedged his boots against small bolts and forced his gloved fingers into tiny crevices. Obviously, he'd pulled this prank before. He moved with extreme deliberation, like a mountain climber scaling a sheer face. At times he seemed to cling by willpower alone. I had to admire his agility. It crossed my mind that my surfer friends would pay serious deutsch to learn those skills.

With a tense grace I envied, he passed around the curve of the hull deeper into the shade of Heaven's underbelly, until all I could see was the top of his helmet. Could I do that—crawl around the hull in the other direction, with no safety line, no handholds, hoping the gunship's cameras would spot me? Well, Liam did it. I examined the section of hull nearest me. It looked ancient, the seams ridged and knotty, the metal pockmarked by space debris and de-graded by radiation. But the dents looked too shallow to provide a decent hold. It was a dicey plan.

Still, the gunship had to be right there, just above the tank's horizon. If I could free-climb a few meters into the sunlight, I would see it. This might be the best opportunity I would ever get. Surf the moment.

I eased away from the handhold and grasped a cooling vane. The hull's powerful momentum strained my shoulder ligaments as I pulled up around the curve as far as my safety line would extend. From there, I could see the tops of the solar panels glittering in the sunlight. Many were

twisted and shattered. I saw only two panels left standing.
The gunship's noisemakers weren't supposed to damage
them like that. Someone was going to be held accountable.

Liam's welder hose looped like a bowel, silhouetted
against Earth's albedo, but Liam had disappeared. A chill
solitude overtook me. Distances in space are so incompre-
hensibly vast, they play with your mind. Why didn't my
friends circle around and see me? But they wouldn't be
looking here in the shadows. No one would look for me
here.

Briefly, I imagined yanking free of the safety line and
kicking off into space, flying out into view of Provendia's
gunship. I pictured the troops recognizing me as their pa-
tron, drawing me into their hold and paying homage.
Huah! What a surf! Only the ace Nasir Deepra could have
pulled it off. Yes, we'll go back at once and rescue your
mistress.

Conceive the reinforcements I would call in, the spaceships, the hordes of special assault troops, the lawyers and
bankers. Visualize the relief on Sheeba's face when I
swooped down and lifted her to safety. Her head thrown
back. Her lips moist and parted. Her bosoms gently rising
toward my mouth. Oh.

But what if the gunship didn't spot me? Streaking off at
a tangent to Heaven's spin, hardly a speck in this great
black void—I might fly away too quickly, beyond the range
of the Net, beyond health churches and bioNEMs, beyond
the glow of the known world.

"Into the dark," Sheeba whispered with breathless enthusiasm. And I slipped back to my handhold and gave the
safety line a tug. Still secure, yes.

Then the hull exploded. A gaping rent flapped open in
Heaven's underbelly, and pressurized air rushed from the
interior outward toward the vacuum, carrying twisted steel
tables, water vapor and a supernova of green foliage.
Among the debris, I saw a strange white shape whirling
above me. It was Liam tumbling head over heels.

13

I LOVE MY LIFE

**"Men are wise in proportion, not to their experience,
but to their capacity for experience."**
—GEORGE BERNARD SHAW

Like an idiot, I kicked off from the hull and hurled myself toward Liam. Why did I risk my life for this twentysomething boy? Even now, I can't tell you. I reached the end of my line in seconds, grappled for his outstretched hand, caught hold—then lost him. Like a snapping whip, I recoiled back toward the factory. Yet our brief connection had changed Liam's trajectory. Instead of flying away, he was now revolving toward me—but not fast enough to keep up with Heaven.

When the seam in the tank ripped wider, one of the hydroponic tables broke loose, and for a teetering instant, it plugged the breach. Then the table burst out, the hull splayed apart, and in the jet of escaping air, every class of object came tumbling after it. Leaves and roots. Shreds of partition wall. A bucket and mop sloshing great globules of dirty ice. These items flew around me like missiles.

With adrenaline speed, I seized a long remnant of welding hose as it sailed past, then unclipped my safety line from my belt and lashed it to the hose with a single hasty knot. I looped the end of the hose tight around my forearm, and with this improvised extension, I kicked off from the flapping hull again.

The escaping air burble had shunted Liam sideways,

and the welding hose gave me just enough extra length to clutch the sole of his boot. For a few brief seconds, I dragged him along in Heaven's wake. Then he slipped from my grasp. But not far. I stretched my gloved fingers and clawed at the empty space between us.

With no conscious decision, I unwound the loops of hose from my arm and let the momentum sling me farther out. As the hose slid through my glove, I stretched my good left leg for Liam to grab. Picture me straightening every joint, elongating every muscle to fullest extension. Only at the last moment did I grip the hose's ragged end and hold firm. Then with a startling jolt, another section of the hull blew. The panel that anchored my safety line came loose at one corner and buckled outward, sailing me another meter toward Liam. He spun, I stretched, and he caught my leg.

See us spinning together like a pair of skaters, eyeing that precarious hull. Feel my fist tightening on the frazzled end of that hose. The panel kept tearing, and the hose oscillated back and forth, jerking my half-hitch knot looser from the safety line with every tug. Liam pulled himself along my body till we were both clinging to the hose. Only much later did I comprehend—I could have been rid of him.

Long seconds passed before Two emptied itself of air and the blowout subsided. By a miracle, the panel anchoring our safety line held firm, and the welding rig remained anchored to its magnets. With only Earth-glow and our helmet lights to guide us, Liam and I gingerly hauled ourselves in and climbed through Heaven's gaping side, where we found scenes of madness.

Torn walls, floors warped into towering sculptures, cabinets ruptured, every surface scarred and blackened by the friction of escaping objects, which in some places had literally burned away the paint. No loose items remained. Most of the hydroponic tables had been ripped off their bolts and flung into space, but a few still tilted and spun like sad skeletons. No trace of the seedlings remained.

"Geraldine and Juani must have made it out," I said, trying to sound sure.

But in our EVA suits with the nonfunctioning sat phones, Liam still couldn't hear me. Our helmet lights flickered silently over the wreckage, and we picked our way to the ladder well. We found the door wrenched open, but the ladder was gone. The blowout had ripped it from the wall, and the remaining bolts jutted out like a row of broken teeth.

Liam sprang lightly across the well and checked the door to the solar plant. He gave the wheel a firm yank, but it wouldn't move. Ye graven gold, what if that door had burst open, too? Without electrical power, Heaven's life support would wink out like an expiring star. Not a bulb in the ladder well glimmered.

I pressed my helmet to Liam's so the sound of my voice would carry. "Did we lose power?"

"People in there." Liam banged the door with his fist.

Right, youngsters were hiding in ops bay. "What about the solar plant?"

He leaned his helmet against mine. "This door sealed tight. They probably still have air pressure. We gotta close off this well and repressurize. Then we can open the door."

The punk's words made sense. Only half of Deck Two had voided its air. The half with the solar plant and ops bay remained intact, and the pressure behind that door was holding it shut.

Liam touched his helmet to mine again, and his breath fogged his faceplate. "I going below to see about the people on One. You wait."

"There are people on Deck One?" I asked, but he'd already moved away.

While he hustled down through the lock, I made another desperate call on my helmet sat phone, with no luck, of course. My EVA glove covered the IBiS, but from the way my thumb tingled, I knew it still wasn't connecting, either. I paced and waited, working myself into a gloomy funk. A dead surveillance camera gave me a blank stare.

As a distraction, I started scraping fungus off the wall with my boot to see the graffiti better. The childish drawings had been scratched into the metal, then colored with crayon. There were lines and ranks of portraits, mostly grouped in family units, mothers and fathers with strings of neonates holding hands. It suggested some kind of genealogy record. Many portraits were stick figures, while others had been more fully drawn, either by multiple artists or by a single creator whose craft had evolved.

Liam emerged from the floor hatch and gave me a thumbs-up. "People on One okay for now," he shouted, pressing his helmet to mine.

Then he pulled himself up the side of the well along the row of broken bolts. When he reached the ceiling and opened the safety hatch leading to Three, he offered me a hand. Once we were inside the tiny lock, he sealed the hatch and punched a button, which started a noisy machine. A compressor. It was filling the lock with air. I offered silent thanks to the brilliant engineers who had installed these safety airlocks between the decks. They had contained the blowout and saved my Sheeba!

Liam and I squatted shoulder to shoulder for some eternity of minutes while the compressor chugged, and I began to feel the familiar letdown after a surf. My adrenaline plummeted, my brain went dull. I wanted a margarita and some nice snacks. Maybe some of my NEMs had shut down, but the others were still guzzling blood sugar. My empty bowel rumbled.

Only after we'd climbed out of the airlock and latched it securely beneath us did Liam signal to remove our helmets. Darkness drenched Three's ladder well, just like Two. Not a promising sign. We clipped our helmets to our belts, and the lights shot off in crazy angles, dancing across the walls.

"That hull breach was a mistake." I wiped sweaty curls off my forehead, glad for once that I had no mirror. "Provendia wouldn't damage its own factory."

"Mistake?" Liam spoke as if he begrudged the very shape of the word. In the dimness, I could barely make out his bearded face.

"That hull breach wasn't anywhere near where the gunship was firing," I said.

"You think we stupid enough to blow our home?"

"You were stupid enough to start this war."

He almost answered, then gritted his teeth and slung his braid behind his shoulder.

"Look where you are," I went on. "You live on a freaking satellite. Totally dependent on artificial life support. Even your orbit has to be controlled from Earth. You have absolutely no chance in hell. What were you thinking?"

His eyes glittered in the uneasy light, and he scraped fungus off the bulkhead hinges with his glove. Dumb brute. I was just about convinced of his utter disability with language when his baritone resonated through the well. "Nasir, why you save my life?"

"I don't know," I said, thrown off balance.

He touched my arm. "Thank you." The next instant, he unclipped my helmet and shut off its lights.

"Give that back!" I shouted.

"Save the batteries." He shut off his own lights and sank us both into pitch-darkness.

I stood frozen with rage. Were batteries so scarce? If another hull breach occurred, I would need that helmet. I heard him clipping my helmet to his belt. Next he opened the door into Three, and I heard his boots leap over the sill and run down an unlighted corridor. I couldn't see a thing.

"Come back here."

I'd risked my life for that punk. My very toes curled with rage. I wanted to annihilate the stupid lout. Then I remembered Sheeba, so I hurried after him into Three.

• • •

"Dark is evil. It's ignorance and depravity. Everything wicked."

"Yes, that's part of it," Sheeba admitted.

She and I were lounging in my bed, with an old movie muted and forgotten on the screen. She was waxing ecstatic about her usual theme, the dark, and I was baiting her, for the fun of it.

"In the dark, we find rest and healing." She hugged a cushion to her chest and rocked. Her eyes got that dreamy sparkle. "Life quickens in the dark. Stars are born there. Dark laces the universe together."

"It's also the underworld where nasty things slither and rot," I teased.

"Well, Nass, you're as slithery as they come." She tickled the back of my arm. "And don't we tunnel in the Earth for shelter?"

"I see. You're calling me a worm."

"I'm saying the dark leads us home."

"Gilty gods, you mean the grave. Do you want me to die?"

She laughed. "You're the one who wants that."

I kicked off the covers and sat up. "Just because my sport's a little dangerous, don't assume I have a death wish. I'm very cautious, darling. I love my life."

"Liar. You hate it as much as I do. Everything's too cozy. It's not supposed to be like this."

"You'd rather live in poverty, I suppose."

She squeezed the cushion tighter. "Maybe."

Scatterbrain. You don't know what the hell you're talking about, I almost yelled. Our discussion was getting edgy. Shee and I had never argued, and I didn't want to begin, but her tomfool remarks upset me. Too cozy? My friends and I practically sacrificed our souls to give her this comfort. I tried to laugh it off.

"Be serious, Nass. You're hurting all over. I feel your muscles every day." To prove her point, she started kneading my tense shoulders. "It's our nature to scream and fight and tear things. We need the dark."

"But Shee—do you seriously want evil in your life?"

Her eyes sparkled. "I want some of everything."

• • •

Simple child. As I felt my way along Heaven's pitch-black corridor, her words resonated. You might say, they *haunted* me. Sheeba had no idea how ugly and dangerous the dark could become. My shoulder brushed an unseen wall. The air tasted of long stale enclosure, and I couldn't see three centimeters in front of my nose. Somewhere ahead, Liam twisted another creaking wheel. Despite the fact that I loathed him, his nearness reassured me, so I hurried to catch up.

A flash of light showed a door opening, and his silhouette darted through. Then the door slammed, and darkness engulfed me again.

Punk. He could have left the door open. The very thought of the risks I'd taken for that twentysomething thug made me want to bash his teeth in. I should have used the blowout to make my escape. With that extra length of hose, I should have sailed out and signaled the gunship. Instead, I helped that—that agitator.

At that very moment, he was racing ahead to meet Sheeba, with who knows what ulterior purposes. No way would I let him get there first. I slid my glove along the wall, grumbling under my breath and searching for the door. By feel alone, I located the wheel and fumbled to open it.

"Catch."

Geraldine hurled a bulky object toward me the instant the door fell open, and I caught it by reflex. It was a heavy, ten-liter can of stew. I glanced around and recognized the same drying room I'd visited earlier, only now the rows of ovens stood open. Emergency fluorescent tubes buzzed from the ceiling, and Geraldine stuck her head in one of the oven doors. All the lids had been folded back, so I peeked inside. Each oven contained a hoard of food cans marked with Provendia's logo. Standard employee provisions. They must have been stockpiling their rations for months.

Geraldine and Juani were transferring the ovens' contents into a handcart. I read the label on the can Geraldine had tossed to me: CHILI DIABLO. It was some kind of spicy protein mixture, and the description on the label made me salivate.

"We're taking everything up to Four, just in case." Geraldine hurled another steel can in my direction. Behind her, Juani sang a song about moonlight.

Just in case. I didn't like that phrase. As I ducked to let the next can fly over my shoulder, Juani gestured for me to help him push his cart. It was severely overloaded, and apparently, he wanted to move it to the ladder well.

I said, "Where's Sheeba?"

"Nasir, I'm here."

In the breathless moment that followed, I turned and saw her framed in a nearby doorway, lighted in the jittery halo of fluorescent green. She'd changed. Her appearance shocked me. Only after my eyes adjusted to the light did I understand. Her pale skin dye had faded even further, revealing more of her complexion's true olive tone. She gleamed a deep burnished bronze. And those eyes, sparkling with all the shades of a northern lake stirred by rain. It made a jarring combination.

"We're moving these supplies up to sick-ward," she said.

I ran across the room and seized her in my arms, but at first I couldn't speak.

Gently, she released herself from my grip. "We're going to seal ourselves in and make a stand."

"Make a stand? Sheeba, listen to yourself. You sound as if you're siding with these protes."

"Of course I am, Nass." She checked out the EVA suit I still wore.

"Dearest." I pressed my mouth to her ear and whispered, "We have to leave. This place might blow any second."

"I know," she whispered back, "but first, we have to help these people. Their situation's heinous." Then she hurried to help Juani push his cart.

By accident, the cart tipped over, and when Sheeba

launched herself bodily to catch the spilling cans, I recognized what had happened. She was caught up in the thrill of war surfing. The ardor shining in her eyes told the story. The chemicals of fear, the need for fast action, the deep salty urge to fight, these instincts had overwhelmed her reason. Zone bliss had so completely captivated her that she'd forgotten which team she belonged to.

"Darling," I pleaded.

"Help us, beau." She dashed to an oven and started scooping up cans of food with both hands. Her chaste white longjohn had turned filthy gray, and there was a rip across her belly where something had snagged the smartskin. Her lovely dimpled hands were bleeding.

Geraldine squeezed past me toward the ladder, then paused to bump me with her hip. Her rank smell almost made me cough. "Lover, you haul the freight hoist. I show you what to do."

"Go with her, Nass. We don't have time to discuss things now. We'll talk soon." Sheeba's gray-green-blue eyes shone out of her dark golden face like beacons.

It was useless to argue. Sheeba moved in hasty jerks, totally absorbed in her task. Geraldine handed me a water sack, and as I sucked it down, the wench patted my butt. "This way, sugar buns."

A large pile of food cans had accumulated in Three's ladder well, and my task, as Geraldine explained, was to convey them onto the freight hoist—the platform that moved up and down through the cargo door by a hand-operated pulley. Above, a flock of little toads was unloading and stacking the cans.

Imagine how my gut knotted with hunger pangs as I handled that Chili Diablo. After an hour of lifting and twisting, my broken leg throbbed, not to mention my shoulders. The designer additives in my blood gave me extra stamina though, and in Three's reduced gravity, the cans weighed half what they usually would given their mass. Since the little toads bore up without complaint, I kept my grievances quiet.

After we moved the canned food, Juani and Sheeba started carting out glossy plastic sacks of water, but the sacks were slick and floppy, and they kept sliding off the hoist. In a rush of impatience, Sheeba tore off her longjohn and improvised a cargo net to hold the slippery sacks on the platform. Juani and Geraldine both gawked when she stripped naked, but Sheeba didn't seem to notice. She was plasmically focused on the moment.

I tried not to see her nude body. Without the skin dye, her nakedness seemed more intimate and personal. When we met in the corridor, I edged past without touching her. Shee's unwashed skin radiated a compelling pungency, yet for the first time, her nakedness embarrassed me. I wanted to cover her up. She seemed exposed, yes, but not vulnerable. Nothing about Sheeba seemed vulnerable.

Shee squeezed my arm and grinned. "Ordic emanations, can you feel them? I knew you'd want to help." Then she hurried off on some new errand.

Far below, the hull rumbled as Provendia's gunship resumed fire. Deck One was taking most of the hits, but occasionally a stray noisemaker would ricochet across the flank, and its impact would vibrate in the walls.

Juani shouted for me to come help him siphon the last of the water from their collector cistern, but I felt ravenous. I searched the gaping ovens for food—cracker crumbs, moldy powdered soup, anything to stuff in my mouth. Nothing. They'd moved it all. Juani had disappeared beyond the rows of ovens, so I marched along, irritably calling his name.

"Man, don't yell so loud. I'm in here."

He was kneeling in a nearby utility closet, shining a flashlight at a bank of old-fashioned analog dials and shaking his head. Some of the ornamental wire in his braid had come loose, and the sharp copper points stuck out like a frayed connection. "Cistern pressure too low to use the pumps anymore. We gotta suck out the rest by mouth."

"You're joking."

He got up off the floor and wrinkled his nose. "How strong your lungs, blade?"

"Is this necessary? We've transported a megaton of water already. Why can't you just turn on your recycler and make more water?"

As we wound through the drying room with his flashlight, he explained how they'd "rehabbed" a food vat to make their cistern. He was talking again as freely as ever.

"Through here," he said. "Watch the overhang."

I ducked under some pipes, and Juani's unraveling braid almost hit me in the eye. "Wait, wait, your hair's a menace. Let me fix it." I caught hold of his braid, and he stopped and let me twist the sharp ends of the wires back into his plaits. "What caused that hull breach anyway?" I asked. "The gunship wasn't targeting that area. I suspect sabotage."

"Sabo-what?" Juani felt his braid to see what I'd done.

"Your treacherous chief did it to gain publicity. That's what I think."

"Blade, you so sharp you cut yourself."

When he tried to take off, I caught his shoulder. "Provendia's gunfire didn't cause that breach. How do you explain it?"

"Plain old stress." Juani grinned and thumped his fist softly against the steel wall. "This tank, he ancient. All that gunfire, he tremble."

Well, that gave me something to chew on.

Juani led me to their makeshift cistern, a spherical steel food vat anchored to the floor with bolts, patch-welds and also magnets. Quite a lot of redundancy, I thought. Still, the mounts had obviously bumped around a few times. I wondered what force could have moved this heavy cistern.

We had to crabwalk around the vat to locate the small pump valve, and the floor was wet where they'd been filling water sacks. When Juani twisted the valve full open, only a hollow whuffing sound came through. He insisted the tank held more water, though, and he jammed a short section of plastic tube inside the faucet to siphon it out. While I held the tube in place with both hands, he tried his manful best to suck the water out, but there was no result. He sank back on the floor, red-faced from the strain.

"We already have enough water," I said.

"For how long?" His words struck me as ominous.

How long indeed? And how many people would have to share it? I envisioned the sick-ward crowded with thirsty, dying workers. All the adults must be there.

"Where's the recycler?" I said. "Ye gods, was it damaged in the blowout?" From my decades of board meetings, I knew just enough about life-support recyclers to spout a little jargon. "If the main lagoons are intact, maybe we can repair the machinery. We still have power, right?"

Juani leaned back on his hands and gazed at the underside of the cistern, humming softly. "The recycler safe on Five, man, but it may as well be on the other side of the moon. The pumps down in Two, and I can't get there to restart 'em."

I sat beside him, careful to avoid the puddles. My muscles were so fatigued that the steel deck actually felt comfortable. Silently, I worked out the ramifications of not having water pumps. "But we still have power, right? Those fluorescent lights were working."

"We running off sick-ward's emergency generator."

Then another thought hit me. "What about air?"

Juani fingered his woven wire braid. "All the pumps down on Two."

"Great golden gilders, we're trapped with no air." I thought fast. "Take my EVA suit. You can exit through the hull breach and get to the pumps through Two's airlock."

When Juani's mouth shut in a flat line, I remembered the earlier discussion about his spacesickness. Fainting on a space walk was no joke. It could mean asphyxiation. But so could no air pumps.

"All right, if you can't go, someone else can," I said. "Surely you're not the only one who knows the recycler machinery."

"Not machinery. It's the garden." Juani ground his knuckles in his eye sockets. "The garden, she breathe and drink. She give us air and water and food."

At first, I couldn't take this in. "You don't have recycling machinery? But every Provendia satellite comes equipped with a standard recycling plant."

"We rehabbed it," he said.

"What do you mean, rehabbed it? Did you have proper authorization?"

"We cut up the parts to build our garden." Juani jammed the plastic tube back into the cistern faucet. "We fine, blade. The garden keep us alive. It's the people on One and Two, they trapped."

"Where's Liam?"

"The chief down there trying to fix the cracks so we can repress'."

I got up and started crabwalking toward the exit.

"Hey, man, we gotta get this water," he said.

In my weariness, I didn't notice the overhead strut till it banged my forehead and knocked me dizzy. I got back up, rubbed my head and staggered on. I had to find Sheeba. She and I were spinning through space in an ancient, decomposing fuel tank run by a covey of little hellions who had destroyed their recycling plant. And any second, the whole decrepit place might tremble to bits.

14

TIME AND SPACE

**"No one is so old as to think he cannot live one
more year."**
—CICERO

" This place is a freaking death chamber." I charged
along the corridor, ignoring hunger and fatigue,
searching for Sheeba. Surf the moment. Ride the contingencies. We had to get out of this leaky spinning tank before it self-destructed.

But how? Liam had stolen my helmet. I had to find the
wordless brute and get it back. Juani followed at my heels.
Maybe he thought I had a plan to save everyone.

"Where did Liam put my helmet?"

"He gave it to Geraldine." Juani patted my shoulder.
"Be calm, man. You gonna bust a vein."

I wheeled open a bulkhead door and collided head-on
with Geraldine.

"Strip, lover. I need your trousseau," she said.

Before I could react, she unzipped my EVA suit, and
Juani slid past me, whispering under his breath, "I go
check the generator, just in case."

Ha. There lay my helmet at Geraldine's feet. But when I
bent to reach it, she jerked my EVA suit off my shoulders.
I grabbed the folds of silky Kevlax and tried to fling her
off, but the wench clung to me like Velcro.

"Nass, give her the suit," Sheeba said. Out of nowhere,
Shee was standing behind me, whispering in my ear and
tracing tiny circles up and down my neck. Gently, she

tugged the suit loose from my fingers. "Gee needs it. Her suit's leaky. She has to help Liam restore our life support."

Sheeba's words sounded reasonable. Life support, yes. Restoring it had to be a positive step.

"Nass, let go of the suit," she whispered, caressing me from behind.

As her breath warmed my ear, my grip on the Kevlax loosened. Geraldine tugged the suit down around my ankles, and the two of them helped me step out of it like a docile old geezer. Then I just stood there in my longjohn.

Sheeba helped Geraldine suit up. "Nass, this place is mesmic. Do you sense the dark energy? It's got my aura streaming, like, ultraviolet." Shee wasn't naked anymore. She'd dressed in a gray prote uniform, cut off at the elbows and knees.

Only when Geraldine stretched out her short brawny arms to admire the black piping on my suit did I realize how they had violated me. Hot blood rose to my cheeks. "Sheeba," I sputtered, misting her face with saliva, "this satellite's about to rupture. We'll be killed."

Sheeba whistled through her teeth. "Be here now, Nass." Then she waved a cheery good-bye and galloped after Geraldine toward the ladder well.

"Wait. I've come to save you. Don't leave me." In my eagerness, I momentarily forgot about the Coriolis effect, leaned in the wrong direction and smacked against the wall. "You said we would talk."

But she didn't hear me. Her bare, sooty feet disappeared down the corridor. I remembered kissing each one of those dimpled toes.

"Sir, would you like something to eat?" said a soft girlish voice.

I barely heard. I was watching the corridor where Sheeba had vanished. A strange new Sheeba. Transfigured by the zone.

"I cooking a meal, sir. Will you come?"

Kaioko waited some distance away, and her Asian eyes rested on me with a look of profound distrust. She'd arranged her white head rag in a more becoming fashion, and she touched it self-consciously. For the first time, I noticed her delicate nub of a nose and her small lips. The pointed chin shaped her face like a heart. Too bad her eyes were so small and squinty. She got to her feet and moved down the hall, glancing over her shoulder to see that I was following.

"Are we going to sick-ward?" I asked.

"To the galley," she said.

"Is that where Sheeba went?" I asked hopefully. The last place I wanted to see was sick-ward. Lurid video of Heaven's afflicted workers flashed across my mental screen. I really did not want to see those faces.

Kaioko tiptoed close to the wall, bending forward at the waist to see around the curve. She seemed fearful of running into some obstacle. No little toads blocked our way, and this gave Deck Three an air of vacancy. "Where are all the brats?" I asked.

She didn't answer. At the galley door, she motioned for me to pass ahead, and as I came near, she flattened herself against the wall. Did she think I would bite?

My injured leg still ached, but I could tell from the way it moved that my bones had healed. Amazingly, my orthopedic NEMs had not waited for doctors' orders. The smart little buggers had figured a way to act on their own. If I'd had Net access, the NEMs would have mended the fractures in an hour. But I couldn't complain. The glass man had finally done his job. I stomped past the stiff-lipped Kaioko, entered the galley and found it empty. No Sheeba. I flopped down in a chair.

A chair. An actual piece of furniture designed to hold the human form. This was the first comfortable seat Heaven had offered me. The galley turned out to be yet another miniscule wedge-shaped closet. Besides the delightful molded plastic chair, it held a tiny stainless-steel table, a small work counter, two cabinets, an infinitesimal sink and a stack of microwave ovens. Like everything in Heaven, these items were heavily bolted and secured to the floor. On the wall hung an old-fashioned clock. It had the face of a large-eared cartoon bunny with whiskers for clock hands.

"So where's Sheeba?" I asked.

Kaioko rolled up her long sleeves, climbed onto a step-stool and began struggling over a huge can of Chili Diablo that was set out on the counter. She used a hand-operated opener with a crank turn that seemed to require all her strength. What a production she made of it, bending her small body over that ten-liter can.

I relinquished my cozy chair with a sigh. "All right, give it here."

When I took the can, she jerked backward and rolled down her sleeves to cover her hands. Then she explained the complicated can opener. It had a coin-sized wheel that fit down over the can's rim, and when applied with a clamp, it sliced into the steel lid and cut neatly all the way around by the force of the hand-turned crank.

I was just remarking on its clever design when, without warning, Provendia's noisemakers drummed the hull, and Kaioko threw herself against me. Her frail arms clutched my waist like pliers, and she buried her head against my ribs. I'd never had such intimate contact with an employee before. Hesitantly, I patted her shoulder. The walls groaned and popped, and I held my breath, waiting for the next hull breach. But the barrage didn't last long. When it ended, Kaioko jerked away as if my touch burned her. Then with a show of mutual nonchalance, we finished opening the can.

You may find it odd that I would calmly help Kaioko heat stew when Sheeba had gone missing again and at any moment the satellite's creaky old hull might blow to pieces. If so, you have forgotten the violence of human hunger. Too many hours had passed since my last meal, and my NEMs had devoured my blood sugar. "Chili Dia-blo." Those words set off my taste receptors like a call from the gods, and though the cartoon bunny face said four o'clock, my biorhythms roared, "Dinnertime!"

Four o'clock. I gazed at the bunny face while Kaioko

put away her utensils, locked the drawers and bins and waited for the microwave to beep. Exactly how many hours had passed since I checked the time and date in my helmet display? That was just before the blowout. "What day is this, Kaioko?"

"What day?" She stopped scrubbing the counter and screwed up her wide-set little eyes.

"Sunday, Monday, Tuesday? You know, what day?"

Slowly, her fingertips searched the folds of her head scarf. "Sun day?"

"Okay, what day of the month? Surely you have months. The moon's right outside."

She continued to fondle her head scarf, squinching up her eyes. Then her fingers closed on something tucked in one of the folds. A small dried flower. "I've heard of the moon. When it come close, it pull our blood."

What gibberish. "Forget the moon. I just want to know how long I've been here."

She resumed her scrubbing with a look of satisfaction. "You want to know how many orbits."

"That's a start," I said. "How many?"

"I don't know. We lost our senses."

She said this with such deadpan sincerity that for a moment I simply gawped. Then she blinked her beady eyes and gave me that resentful look.

Laboring to keep a straight face, I said, "Explain that again."

She pursed her lips and scoured the cabinet doors. "The commies took our senses."

Sensors, she meant. I couldn't help but chuckle as she flayed a layer of plastic off the countertop. Then I went and tapped the bunny face clock with my fingernail. "What about this?"

Impudent child, she refused to look my way—until I started moving the bunny's second-hand whisker. That caught her interest, and she watched in silence. Next, I touched the hour-hand whisker. "Since I came here, how many times has this short whisker gone around?"

Very hesitantly, she stepped closer, stood on tiptoes and pushed the minute-hand whisker. When it budged a centimeter clockwise, she said, "Ah." Then she screwed up her little eyes and pushed the hour hand from four to five. Her long sleeve fell back, revealing her dainty white forearm crosshatched with fresh knife wounds. The sight stunned me, but Kaioko didn't realize I'd seen it. She spoke with gentle eagerness. "I didn't know his nose hairs would move."

"You've never seen them move?"

"No one touched them before."

In other words, the clock was dead. I dropped back into my chair and slumped over the table. The microwave was taking an eon, and the girl's wounded arm lingered unpleasantly in my memory. "Kaioko, do you understand the concept of time?"

"What is time?" she said with forced politeness.

"Time? Well, it's the past, present and future. Every event happens in time."

She polished the sink, and her sleeves trailed in the soap lather. "You asked how many orbits. Orbits happen in space."

"No, no, time is different from space."

I glanced around the galley, searching for some way to make myself understood. My head buzzed from hunger and lack of sleep. And Kaioko was just an illiterate child. Why was I wasting my—ha—time? Probably, my ego was involved. The microwave buzzed, and Kaioko lifted out two bowls of steaming protein stew, using her long sleeves as mitts. When she placed them on the table, I studied the anonymous brown chunks floating in red sauce.

"Okay, here's a concrete example. This stew was cold when you set it in the oven. Then a period of waiting passed, and voilà! Now it's hot. That period of waiting was time."

"Time is heat." Her black eyes gleamed.

"No, not heat." I tugged at my hair, but by now, I was determined to prove how coherent I could be. Kaioko sat down and blew softly on a spoonful of stew, reminding me of my own ravening hunger. I gulped a scalding mouthful and wiped the juice from my chin. Spicy. What a sting!

"Think of a lifetime," I said, chewing. "You've heard that word, lifetime?"

Her eyebrows rose, watching me eat. Perhaps I slurped.

"You're born. You grow old. Then you die," I said. "The length of your life is measured in years. That's time."

"What's a year?" She sipped delicately from her spoon.

Easy question. I tilted my bowl to drink the red sauce, then said, "A year's how long it takes the Earth to make one revolution around the sun."

"So it's space." She stuck out her pointed chin and smiled, awfully pleased with herself.

What could I do but laugh and surrender? "Is there any more stew?"

We fixed a tray for the others, and as she was setting out bowls, she said, "May I go ask a question?"

I was beginning to realize her stiff courtesy arose from shyness. She wasn't used to strangers. I sloshed hot stew into the row of bowls and said, "Fire away."

She wiped up my spills and squeezed out her rag. "Liam told us about the people here before we came. He said they old. What is old? Is that like time?"

"You mean the adult workers. I can't believe they're all sick."

"I didn't know them. They gone before I remember."

"Nonsense. Two months ago, this factory still had sixty productive workers."

"Sixty?"

"Surely you know how to count," I said.

"I'm learning. Vlad teaching me."

Great gobs of gilders, this child couldn't count? No wonder time confused her. Kaioko had to be in her late teens, and she seemed intelligent enough. Had she never entered a classroom? Well no, she hadn't. Factory profits were too low to cover dependent education. She gazed at my gleaming false fingernails. Her nails were chewed to the quick.

Suddenly, the galley felt too small and crowded. I lifted the tray of bloodred stew and lurched into the corridor.

"Please," she said, following, "tell me what old means."

"It means learning not to ask foolish questions."

At least the Coriolis effect no longer plagued me. With a certain gratification, I adjusted my lean and reeled down the corridor with almost all the dinner tray intact.

"You know about old," Kaioko persisted. "They say Earth has many such types. How they different from us?"

I was pleased that she included me in the set of youth. One or two wisecracks popped into my mind, but the child's eyebrows rose so earnestly that I held them back. After a few more steps, I set down the heavy tray to rest. Now that my stomach was full, my body cried out for sleep.

"In the pictures, their skin wrinkles." She pointed at the crayon drawings along the baseboard. The scribbles were everywhere in Heaven, along the bottoms of all the walls. I'd almost stopped seeing them.

"My brother Nobi draw these." She knelt and pointed to a couple of human figures, white-haired and stooped with age. "See, they puckered like melons falling off the vine."

This vivid description made me grin, and Kaioko giggled, covering her mouth with both hands. Her laughter startled me. Could it be she was warming up to me a little? As she studied the crayon man, I noticed her dried flower coming loose from her scarf, so I tucked it back in.

"You've never seen an old person in this factory?" I asked.

"No one. But Liam and Vlad told us stories. And Nobi put them in his pictures."

"Nobi, your brother?" Exhaustion fuzzed my faculties, but her words posed a riddle. If Heaven's oldest workers died before Kaioko could remember, that was nearly eighteen years ago. Had the malady been active that long? If so, our site manager had covered it up with elaborate cunning. Well, that's what we paid him for. But all those years, how had he kept the product flowing? He must have put more juveniles to work than we realized.

"I not asking about the puckers." Kaioko touched the crayon man's face, then she touched her head scarf. "Outside doesn't matter. How are old people different inside?"

"What a question." Visions of clogged arteries and diseased livers waltzed through my drowsy mind, but Kaioko didn't mean that. Her question upset me. I'd spent so many years and deutsch trying to prove there was no difference at all. As long as you kept healthy, it was the same as being young. At 248, I felt as fresh and energetic as ever. Right, fresh and energetic. See me slumped in the corridor, ready to nod off. An icon blinked on my thumbnail, but I was too tired to read it. Hell, what did I care if this impertinent prote girl warmed up to me?

"Maybe . . ." the girl timidly began.

"Maybe what?" The kid needled me.

"Maybe since old people make more orbits, they think longer, and so . . ."

"Please tell me your brilliant theory on aging," I said.

"So they less afraid to die?"

"Not bloody likely."

Less afraid of oblivion? Less afraid to have your name dropped from invitation lists, your stocks redistributed, and your gear auctioned on the Net? Ye gilded icons, age only increased the dread. Didn't I tell you before, life is an addiction. The more you get, the more you want . . . though the pleasure dwindles.

I pushed back my mop of curls—curls I had suffered acute pain to have embedded in my scalp. Every passing year felt like a page ripped savagely from my diary, and every time the docs diagnosed me with a new ailment, I donated more funds to medical science and sent Chad to search the Net for new bioNEMs. At 248, I had every right to expect another fifty years of life, but what then? The idea that age would make a person less afraid of death—why, it was ludicrous. Then Sheeba's words wafted through my memory.

. . .

"What are you looking for in those war zones?"

Death. That's what Shee thought. I closed my eyes, and there was my mother standing in our living room in a blue sari. I hadn't thought about my mother in decades. She died nearly two centuries ago, but I could still smell the perfume caught in the folds of her dress. "Nasir, come practice your verbs." My mother's voice no longer echoed anywhere on Earth, and the grief caught me again, as fresh as a new wound.

And there stood Prashka, my first true love, waving from the porch of our summerhouse in the Andaman Islands. And shimmering in the background, our sailboat, the *Durga*. Gone now, house and boat, along with Prashka's beautiful body, crushed and drowned in the horrific storm of 2057, when the entire population of Calcutta tried to evacuate in one day.

Loss. Depletion. Holes torn in my life that no NEMs would heal. I couldn't reach Prashka in time. I was trapped in Lahore that day. How cruelly fresh the memories keep. Those first savage months barricaded in the warehouse, the faces pressing through barred windows, the inhuman voices. And the taste of lychee juice. No, forget that. What was I saying? Let me rephrase.

I remember Sayeed, my first business partner. We met in '62, after the worst was over. What days and nights we shared, scavenging the wasteland for technicians. We traveled by sea kayak and bicycle, evangelists of the new economy, and we rebuilt the Asian Internet. Sayeed drafted anyone with a metric screwdriver and a head for code, and I made payroll with stock options printed on old beer boxes.

Ha, I remembered Mustafa's Bar, where Sayeed and I hatched our best ideas. There was a green couch and an espresso machine that made too much noise. Gone now. All gone. Sayeed died in a car crash—ironic after all we survived.

And Nasir Deepra? A few days earlier, I would have called my life rich and satisfying. Yet here in Heaven, facing this inquisitive girl, my existence seemed to fray like a tissue of gaping voids, held together by nothing more solid than a latticework of glass.

"What are you looking for in those war zones?" Sheeba kept asking. "Nasir, you're seeking the dark."

• • •

Kaioko watched me from a distance, as if my expression alarmed her. I felt weary beyond measure, but I straightened up and tried to speak in a normal voice. "Everyone's afraid of death." Then I picked up my tray, leaned into the spin and tilted down the corridor.

We found Sheeba at last, sitting with Juani on the floor of a machinery closet—no comfortable chairs in sight. I staggered to Sheeba's side, nearly upsetting the bowls on my tray.

"Have some food, dear. You must be famished," I said.

She glanced up with the same overexcited expression as before—a mixture of sleep deprivation, tense muscles and pure hyper adrenaline. War surfer's bliss. She was deep in the moment. "Look at me! I'm helping Juani fix the generator!"

I placed the tray beside her on the floor and nearly toppled over. Juani was glad to lay down his tools and dig into the gory stew, but Sheeba hopped up and dusted off her bum.

"Rest your leg, Nass. I'll take this food up to Vlad in sick-ward." She balanced the tray on her fingertips and started to leave.

"Sick-ward? Sheeba, don't go there. Stay with me."

She made a funny face and stuck out her tongue. "You baby me too much. I'm a big girl."

I stumbled against her and made her spill the stew. "Please don't go there."

"Take a breath, beau. You're dead on your feet. Sit down and recite your mantra. I'll be back in a minute."

Before I could respond, she skipped down the corridor, weaving and balancing the tray like an exuberant juggler.

I dogged after her, trying to think of something to say that would stop her. But I hadn't concocted a plausible lie, and my mind reeled with fatigue. Zealous girl, if only she weren't so damned compassionate.

"Sheeba, wait. Let me go instead."

"You've been up too long," she said as she climbed into the safety lock leading to Four. "Take a nap."

I should have followed her. I even put my hand on the ladder. Then I halted in a stupor and watched her close the hatch in my face. The malady was everywhere, not just in sick-ward. Sheeba had a strong constitution. She couldn't catch a prote ailment. Ye idols of gold, who was I fooling? I was afraid to go to sick-ward. That was the simple truth.

I slunk back to the machinery closet and sank to the floor. While Juani guzzled the last of his stew, I squeezed my eyes shut and tried to remember that silly meditation mantra Shee taught me. Was it "baksheesh"? That didn't sound right. As I breathed the word in and out, I thought of those bowls on her tray. "Baksheesh. Baksheesh." Three white bowls. One for Shee. One for Vlad. One for Liam?

Something fell. It sounded distant, like tinkling porcelain. My eyes opened slowly, and I sat up with a grunt. My hand lay in something cold and repulsive. Ugh. Congealed stew. I jerked my fingers out of the bowl. I'd fallen asleep.

Juani sat nearby tinkering with the generator, and Kaioko handed him tools. I watched for a while, trying to remember the horrible dream I'd been having. The bowl reminded me of something.

"Where's Liam?"

Juani pointed down. "The chief sealing cracks in Two so we can repress."

My tongue tasted rancid, and I tried to clean it against the roof of my mouth. My dental NEMs had totally failed. Juani kept chattering away. He said Liam and Geraldine were repairing the blown-out door in Two's segment of the ladder well. As soon as they made the well airtight, they would "repressed it," by which he meant "repressurize."

"People trapped on One and Two," he said. "We gotta repress and get 'em out."

"What people?" I said.

"The people you saw."

Oh. Not people. He meant the children.

He explained that Liam's welding rig would soon need its batteries recharged, and he wanted to be ready. While he tapped away at an old keyboard balanced across his lap, he tried to teach me about his so-called thermionic generator. This was my payback for telling him about Earth. Juani said the thermionic device was mounted outside the hull to catch sunlight. He described it as a layer cake of semiconductors that transformed solar heat directly into electricity. It was an old model though, not very efficient, and Juani was trying to tweak its performance.

"How can I help?" I said. By that point, I'd put aside class differences. I was willing to lend a hand with anything that might ensure our survival.

Juani's stubby fingers clicked rapidly over the keyboard, and he hunched forward to read the tiny screen. "What I wanna do, I wanna shut everything down for a little while and run all the power into my CAES."

"Your case?"

"Those bottles you leaning against, they my CAES. Stands for compressed air 'lectricity storage."

I glanced at the row of squat titanium cylinders behind me. Although lashed to the wall with heavy steel cable, they bore the scars and dents of violent tumbling. "Is this our air supply?"

"No, blade, that where I store my 'lectricity. See my compressor? He mash the air down inside the bottles. Then when I need the 'lectricity back, the air spring out and spin my compressor backward, make it a turbine."

If he thought this explanation made any kind of sense, he was mistaken. I glanced at the small compressor welded to the floor and didn't ask for details. "What can I do?"

"You and Kai-Kai go around, turn off all the switches. When I power back up, I gonna do a black start, and I don't wanna fry none of the devices."

Black start. That sounded scary. I stood up and stretched. "You heard the man, Kai-Kai. Where do we find all the switches?"

The girl seemed eager to get going. "This way. We start here on Three."

But at the entrance to the ladder well, she knelt and pressed her hand against the floor. Juani had done that earlier, feeling for vibrations. Then I remembered Kaioko's lover, Geraldine, was down below in the airless ladder well, helping Liam seal the cracks. I said, "You're worried about your friend?"

Kaioko hid her hands in her sleeves and blushed. She got up and hurried along the corridor, keeping close to the wall as usual. At the first door, she stopped and tried to twist the wheel. But she weighed no more than a doll, so I eased her aside and took charge.

"Kaioko, your friend will be fine," I said, turning the wheel. "She's wearing a high-performance EVA suit. Molto expensive."

Kaioko said nothing. We passed through the drying room, where the empty ovens gaped open, and she found the first bank of switches inside a recessed box in the wall. They were large and heavy, and when she showed me how to flip them, darkness closed around us like thick black ink. I heard clicks and fading drones as unseen motors cycled off.

Kaioko seized my shirttail. "I don't like the dark," she said.

"Me, neither. Let's go back."

"We can't, sir. There more switchboxes ahead."

Her little fist gripped my shirt, and she literally nestled against me. She hadn't wanted to stand anywhere near me before, but now I could hear her panting softly in the darkness, just at my elbow. She was almost hyperventilating. Maybe I was, too. I flipped the switches back on.

When the lights came up and the motors whirred back to life, I said, "Let's save these switches for last. How many other boxes?"

Kaioko's relieved little eyes peered up at me with such gratitude, I felt embarrassed. She glanced around and counted on her fingers. And without warning, the noisemakers exploded again. They sounded close this time. A stray scatter must have ricocheted right outside our X wall. Kaioko and I clung together, and I shut my eyes, certain that this time, the ancient, eroded hull would shatter like a rusted can. The floor shook. The walls growled with stress. While the barrage lasted, Heaven vibrated like a broken bell.

When it was over, we drew apart slowly and caught our breaths. Our glances met, and a silent understanding passed between us. Kaioko's face looked damp and gray. I knew now why those noisemakers upset her so much.

"Where are the other switches?" I said to break the spell.

She gripped my undershirt with both hands. "Gee down there."

Gee, her lover. A pair of glistening tears streaked her ashen face. I didn't know how to respond. The best I could do was to pat her bony shoulder and pull her head scarf back into place. Finally, she released her death grip on my shirt, turned away and wiped her nose.

"We have to go finish these switches." She pointed toward the ceiling. "Then sick-ward."

15

OPEN YOUR MOUTH

"The older you get, the stronger the wind gets—and it's
always in your face."
—JACK NICKLAUS

One switchbox after another, Kaioko and I shut off the
circuit breakers, spreading a wake of silent darkness.
We'd left Juani tweaking his generator with only a flashlight. Soon we would finish Deck Three, then we'd have to
climb the ladder to sick-ward.

Sheeba had gone there to deliver the food tray. A
strange new Sheeba, a woman I barely recognized. But the
difference was only cosmetic, I told myself. Her skin dye
had faded, but Shee was still my golden beloved. At least,
without a space suit, she couldn't follow Liam into the un-
pressurized ladder well. So for the moment, she was safe.

Safe? Sheeba was in sick-ward!

And where else would she be? My darling lived to suc-
cor the needy. She thrived on it. Sheeba shared the same
mission as my NEMs—a single-minded drive to heal.
Can't you see her chatting with the patients, recolorizing
their auras, tuning their energy fields, rubbing their feet? I
almost envied those stricken protes, feeling the touch of
her potent hands. But I did not want to see their faces.

Ah, Sheeba had a million theories about healing. She
jumped from one medical creed to another, always seeking
the next big therapy. By contrast, I put my faith in one
mainstream church—the Mayo Clinic. Mayo was the best.
Why change? Hadn't I spent months and years laid up in

its hallowed halls, recovering from my self-cloned organ transplants, skin grafts, joint replacements, hair-growth procedures? Why, my medical records alone took a gigabyte of ROM. I hated clinics and doctors.

But the Mayo was Shangri-La compared to Heaven's sick-ward. That surveillance video stayed with me. Malady, malaise, malignant despair—whatever name you might choose, Heaven's affliction unmanned me. Those vacant eyes staring at the ceiling. Listless hands. Thin gray bodies too debilitated to eat or drink. How many ways had I tried to delete that video from my memory. But there it was, stuck in my head like a repeating loop of Reel.

As we climbed up the ladder to Four, dread of that place almost overwhelmed my compulsion to find Sheeba. What arrogant folly had led me to bring her here? The Reel didn't repel her, it drew her like a pole star.

•   •   •

"You can't resist the force of the dark canal," she told me once. We'd gone to her apartment in Nordvik, a tiny place downtown near the airport—she refused to let me pay her rent. The walls were draped in cheap faux silk and tissue paper, turquoise, azure, veridian. She'd painted the ceiling black, and she'd disabled the lighting fixtures. The only piece of furniture in her living room was a holographic projection of a waterfall reflecting dappled fake sunlight.

"The dark canal is always there," she went on, offering me a cup of instant tea. Dim watery flickers swam across the tissue walls. Aquamarine shadows danced. She placed a sugar bowl in the middle of the floor and gestured with her plastic spoon. "It's like an urge, deep in your body. Like when things build up and make you want to scream. But you hold it in because you have to, and the feeling just ripples inside."

"You mean orgasm," I teased, feeling my way toward her through the dizzy light. "Your dark canal is your vagina, dear heart."

When she sat on the floor, blue dust bunnies wafted up around her like froth. Did the child not own a cleaning bot?

"I'm trying to be honest, Nass. Don't laugh at me. You of all people."

Glittery blues and greens played over her splendid shoulders and legs. I lowered myself to her floor. "Why me of all people?"

"Because you have a multiplex soul," she said.

"Like a cinema?"

"Exactly," she said, leaving me without a clue. Hell's bells, I adored her. Yes, I would brave Heaven's sick-ward to find her.

• • •

"You don't have to push, Kaioko."

"Please hurry, sir."

As I stumbled up the ladder, trying to stay focused on Sheeba, Heaven's malady loomed above like a poison smog. This war began nine months ago, but the strange affliction had started earlier—two years earlier, so our site manager said. Now I suspected he had deceived us for years. Maybe the disorder infiltrated Heaven from the beginning, when the factory first came online three decades ago.

Our site manager was my own protégé, Robert Trencher. Just two years back, his field reports showed nothing more than a few unexplained fatalities. A minor curiosity. He assured us there were no radiation leaks, diseases or toxins. Just people dying. At first, we took it as good news. A13's population had grown bloated with dependent offspring, and costs were out of balance. This small death spike fell in our laps like a gift. It opened up new jobs for the older juves and helped lower our costs.

Kaioko bumped against me on the ladder, but all I could think about was how Trencher must have cynically falsified the numbers. Feeding us crap by the spoonful. Us. The directors. Only last year, when production plummeted, did he admit the truth—a major outbreak.

On that news, the markets might have come apart at the seams if we hadn't reacted fast. What if this malady spread to other satellites? An epidemic like that could tear our patched-up economy to shreds. So with all due prudence, we locked down the satellite's communications, sent it into high polar orbit and issued press releases full of smoke and mirrors—and warnings to keep off.

Then we started to look for the cause. And that's precisely when Trencher turned tail and fled. Gutless liar, not a single one of his staff showed symptoms—our doctors swore their bioNEMs gave them immunity. But Trencher and his entourage evacuated en masse. What really chapped me was, I'd given Trencher his start. I'd trained him. Who knew he would be such a noodge? To save face, I personally had to demote him to junior management.

After Trencher abandoned his post, we were forced to send cyberdocs and robotic probes to study A13 remotely. The new surveillance equipment chewed up a lot of cash, and some of our directors grumbled. But I kept hoping for a solution, and despite a bad case of queasiness, I spent hours poring over the surveillance video. All the employees showed the typical consequences of living for years on a satellite. Weight loss, sleeplessness, chronic depression. But where were the warning signs of imminent death? I couldn't see any. Not till they took to their beds did they begin to show symptoms.

Our remote probes crawled all over Heaven, scraping up dust and analyzing electromagnetic fields. For a while, Heaven's production line limped along at 50 percent output, while we kept seeking the triggering agent. But after months of sampling and testing, our robots failed to find any hint of a cause for Heaven's malady. And worse, our futile investigations were costing a freightload of deutsch.

How long could we keep tossing good money after bad? I held out the longest, believing our scientists needed more time for research, but in the end, I yielded. It wasn't worth the expense. So nine months ago, we voted to shut down operations, euthanize the workers and reclaim the real estate. That's what started the war.

That's what I couldn't admit to Grunze—how much money we'd wasted for nothing. We'd bollixed the whole situation. We probably should have dumped A13 on the World Health Org and let them figure it out. Provendia's balance sheet would have read a damn sight better if we had, but then the news might have leaked out and wrecked investor confidence. None of us was willing to risk a market meltdown. Another Crash was unthinkable. But still, the episode made us look like saps.

Somewhere, the hull creaked with a loud echo of warping steel. Kaioko grabbed my shirttail and bit down on the cloth. We halted together on the ladder till the noise died.

"Tell me about the sick people," I said, closing my hand over the little fist that still gripped my shirt. When facing danger, I'd found that it helped to visualize what was coming. "How many are up there now?"

Kaioko aimed her flashlight at the hatch just above my head. "Please climb, sir."

"Are they very sick?" The surveillance video kept running instant replays through my head, but the images were only bit-map recollections of pixels rastered on a screen.

"Yes," she said after a pause.

I loosened her fist from my undershirt and swung to the side of the ladder. "You go on. I'll be there in a while." Memories of that video were blunting my surfer's edge. I had to forget that stuff and clear my mind. "Be here now," I whispered.

"Please, sir." Pitiful squeaky girl. She pawed at me with her puny hand, and her long sleeve accidentally fell back, revealing the cut marks on her arm. Were those cuts a sign of the malady? Was she beginning to die?

"You don't look well. Maybe you're dehydrated. Let's go back to the galley and get some water." I tried to pull her down the ladder.

But Kaioko wrapped her arms around the rungs and

wouldn't budge. "Sir, we have to shut off those switches. Juani's waiting."

I took a long breath and let it out slowly. It was their eyes I dreaded most, wide-open but not looking at anything, not accusing anyone. Like the faces in Lahore.

No, delete that last part. Disconnect. Focus on the moment. I gripped the ladder in both hands. This used to be easier. What was happening to Nasir Deepra, the war surfer ace?

"Tell me about those cuts on your arm, Kaioko."

The girl reddened and tugged at her sleeves.

"You did that to yourself, didn't you?"

She turned away and murmured so softly, I had to lean forward.

Then Provendia launched another barrage, and Kaioko nearly slipped off the ladder. When I caught her, she buried her head against my chest. Loud booms shuddered through the walls, and Kaioko's keening wail seemed to leak out of her mouth like steam from a pressure vent. Finally, I understood what she was saying. "Geeeeee."

"Geraldine will be fine. Let's go back and check on her," I said, grateful for any delay.

"Geeeee," she kept whining.

I caught her wrists, and her sleeves fell back, revealing more scars. "Oh, child. Why would you cut yourself like that?"

She bit her trembling lower lip. Then she whispered, "It something Gee and I do. To let the hurting out."

"She's your girlfriend, right?"

"My husband," Kaioko chirruped, biting my shirt. "Gee and I married. I'm her wife."

"Wife." That word again. At any time, it would have sounded alien, but the incongruities in this context left me speechless. Geraldine and Kaioko were barely out of diapers, yet already they'd promised each other their lives? In dismay, I stroked Kaioko's narrow shoulders and listened to the groaning walls. When the noisemakers grew louder, she gripped my torso and trembled. Then something Juani said came back to me. He said he was living fast.

As the noisemakers boomed and the ladder shook, I thought about employee life spans. Sixty, seventy, eighty years at most. Without NEM-inspired longevity, workers had to cram all their living into a few short decades. Maybe that's why they could afford to promise each other eternity. These unfamiliar and strangely conflicting notions assaulted me as we mounted up the ladder.

At last, the volley of gunfire ended with Heaven still intact. Cycling through the lock took far too little time, and when Kaioko opened the hatch to sick-ward, a vein in my neck started throbbing.

Four's segment of the ladder well did not reek of medicinal disinfectant. It smelled—unearthly. With infinite slowness, I emerged from the lock and cast my flashlight around the cylindrical walls. The well dripped with space fungus.

Black mounds covered the floor like a sooty carpet and gave the walls a dark velvet sheen. Smoky ruffles festooned the ceiling, and dark, fluted sprays clustered around the ladder leading up to Five. Where the ladder met the hatch above, fibrous black stalactites swelled downward. Deck Five held the factory. Perhaps some of Heaven's sugar had seeped down through the hatch to feed this fungal growth. In my flashlight beam, the fibers glittered like onyx.

And that scent! How can I describe the rainbow of deep, lusty aromas? Acrid, bittersweet and briny, too, like sea salt. It reminded me of Juani's veggies, but more musky and concentrated, full of buttery nut-like essence. In an uncanny way, the smell attracted me.

On Four, the artificial gravity felt weaker still, and we bounced over the fungus with springy, muted steps. The silver D and U glimmered weakly in the flashlight beam. "Which way?" I asked.

"Up lead to the 'pactor room. Switches already off in there." She pointed to the D. "We go sick-ward."

She pushed back her sleeves and struggled to open the Down door. Less gravity made it difficult for her to gain leverage on the wheel, but I held back and didn't help. The door opened sluggishly. Then a stark greenish light flashed through the open door. With prickling neck hairs, I leaned to look inside.

The walls and surfaces strobed bright, then dark, then bright. A dying fluorescent tube buzzed off and on as if possessed by devils. But where were the rows of beds? I saw no moaning victims, only a small room, wedge-shaped like the others. The lime-green light intermittently revealed cabinets, work counter, a tiny sink. Plastic benches filled one corner, suggesting a waiting area. This wasn't sickward. This was just a check-in station—an anteroom.

Four light-globes winked from recesses in the low ceiling, but they were as dark as the bulbs in the ladder well. A dead surveillance camera tilted off center. Only the fluorescent tube seemed to be wired to Juani's emergency generator. I stepped inside and inspected the anteroom more carefully.

A film of fungus covered everything, but there were indications that someone had tried to scrub it away. And unlike the galley where every loose item was stored in a bin, this room held a chaos of junk. Antique medical apparatus, glass jars, spoons and plastic tubing were flung about, as if recently engaged in some urgent experiment.

Supine on the steel table under the blinking light lay a partially dismantled cyberdoc. Evidently, someone had cannibalized its inner workings for lab equipment. A rack of specimen vials occupied one end of the table, filled with various shades of pinkish fluid. There were also a nanoscope and something that looked obscurely like a centrifuge. More parts cluttered the work counter, and after a puzzled examination, I recognized the remains of one of my robotic probes.

These kids had taken apart my scientific equipment? Did they think we sent the probes as toys? That gear cost us mega-deutsch, and look at it. A pile of rubbish.

Kaioko motioned me toward another door at the back, an ordinary oval bulkhead with a raised sill like the others in Heaven. "That sick-ward," she said and pointed.

And then, oh gilty gods, I did hear moaning. The door stood open a crack, and a pale yellow light flickered on the other side. Vague shadows moved on the wall, and the moaning started again, very faint and hoarse. I did not want to pass through that door.

Can you feel how I dreaded it? The idea of people waiting to die—it swamped my imagination. After spending so much money, time and—let me say it—*passion,* on keeping myself well, I simply could not find a way to understand.

Kaioko gave me a weak little shove, but I resisted. "You know where the switch boxes are. You go."

"Nobi, please take another drink." That was Sheeba's voice. She was in there, inside sick-ward with those victims. I should have rushed in to rescue her, no matter what septic corruption awaited me. Instead I stood petrified— and I eavesdropped.

"Please, just one tiny sip." The sorrow in her voice made me shiver.

Then Vlad spoke. "Please take some water, Nobi."

"Save it," said a feeble voice. "They'll need it later."

"Please, Nobi, try," said Sheeba.

With a whimper, Kaioko hurried through the door into sick-ward and left me standing alone in the anteroom. Mortified by my own cowardice, I pushed the sick-ward door closed so they wouldn't see me skulking outside. Nobi, that was Kaioko's brother, the graffiti artist. Through the almost-closed door, I heard Kaioko's piping wail. I stood as if anchored by magnets.

Near the door, Vlad whispered something rapidly to Sheeba. I didn't catch all of it. Something about mixing blood serum to make a cure. Sheeba's blood. Was he using Sheeba's blood? No, Shee wouldn't let him do that. I moved a little closer, listening. Yes, he said it again. He had mixed some kind of potion from Sheeba's healthy blood, but it didn't work.

In shock, I picked up one of the vials from the table and held it to the light. Inside the plastic vial, scarlet threads of liquid rose and spun in a thick yellow oil, then settled gently back to a pool at the bottom. Gilty gods. That untrained kid had taken Sheeba's blood? I pictured a bristling wad of dirty needles. To what had Shee exposed herself? That juvenile thought he could cure an unknown pathology when Provendia's brightest scientists had failed? Of course his snake oil didn't work.

But Vlad was coming through the door. ". . . I can't save him. I can't do anything." When his hand touched the jamb, I stepped quickly behind a cabinet.

"It was worth a try. Don't blame yourself," said Shee.

The door opened wider. I couldn't let Sheeba find me trembling in the shadows like this. As Vlad stepped over the sill, I streaked for the ladder well and fled.

16

A NOWER

**"Youth is a blunder, manhood is a struggle and old
age a regret."**
—BENJAMIN DISRAELI

I hadn't seen anyone die since my youth. No, let me qual-
ify that. Of course I'd seen casualties of war zones, but
that was just the Reel. Luminous pixels in purple-and-gold
metavision. When we browsed Verinne's playbacks of agitators burning, bleeding, breaking apart and flying to
pieces, we coded in frames and special effects and descrip-
tive captions, and the dying workers shrank to bit-maps of
data. To us seasoned surfers, war dead counted no more
than bets placed, time elapsed and winnings paid.

Okay, that's not true, either. The Reel bothered me.
Lately, I'd been feeling more uneasy than ever, and sometimes when we watched the playbacks, the taste of lychee
juice would well up at the back of my throat. Then I'd have
to rush out of the screening room and throw up. I used to be
able to hide it better, and for the sake of the Agonists, I still
tried to keep up the bravado.

But not here in Heaven. That feeble voice from sick-
ward harrowed me. The boy was suffering. All these protes
should have been decently euthanized weeks ago.

Right, I know what you're thinking. But before you ac-
cuse me of cold-blooded murder, try living through a market collapse. Witness the sea rise over your native
coastline, and watch your national government expire in a
matter of days. Root frantically through your basement for

an antique radio because angry mobs have ripped down all the Net links. Burn your last tank of petrol driving the back roads to Lahore, praying your wife is still alive. Then lie alone on a warehouse roof, feeding old batteries through your radio, and listen while your whole family dies in a traffic jam. After that, call me a murderer.

I couldn't get back to Calcutta that day. I couldn't stop the panicked drivers from crushing each other's vehicles against the bases of buildings. I couldn't get there in time to unlock the broken doors. I couldn't . . .

Euthanasia is humane. It's painless and quick, and there are many things worse than death. Many things . . . You wonder how I could still think that way after meeting Heaven's juveniles face-to-face, sharing their food and listening to their dreams. True, I'd grown fond of them—some of them. But you still couldn't convince me that their handful of short, dreary lives would ever be more important than a stable world.

Yes, I fled from the voice in sick-ward, across the anteroom and down the evil ladder to Three. I ran through the dark corridors, following the beam of my flashlight, till I found Juani lying unconscious on the floor of his generator closet. Graven gods. Had he died, too?

"Breathe, Juani. Breathe." My beam danced over his sprawling body and stopped at his gap-toothed grin.

"Man, you so slow, I take a siesta."

Freaking hell. I had to rest against the wall to compose myself. Why did the sight of this teenager's acne-pocked face bring me such relief?

"All switches off. You can mash your CAES anytime you like," I lied. Deck Four's switches were still on, but I rationalized that it probably wouldn't make a difference.

"Hey, blade, you slow but sure. Where's Kai-Kai?"

"She's with Nobi," I said.

In the near darkness, I heard the boy sigh. Then he jabbed his old keyboard as if he wanted to punish it. This time, he didn't explain what he was doing, but I could hear the compressor firing up and forcing air into the rank of titanium bottles lined against the wall. He was storing potential energy in his CAES.

But the compressor was a fossil. It sputtered and complained, and the tanks filled slowly. Minutes dragged by until a reading finally appeared on Juani's gauge. I asked, "How long will this take?"

"Till the blue light come on."

"Well, make a rough guess. Half an hour? Less? More?"

"Half a what? A Nower?"

He wasn't wearing a watch. Evidently, timekeeping eluded the precocious young minds of Heaven. Okay, I could go with that. I crouched and watched the screen till the blue light came on.

"Now what?" I said.

"We do a black start. Make a plus sign for me."

"Plus sign?"

Juani angled the flashlight beam to show me his crossed fingers. The screen glow lighted his huge grin. "It means hoping for good news."

With fingers still crimped together, he punched a rapid series of keys. Then he cocked his head sideways, listening. I didn't hear a sound. No woofing, sluicing or whirring in the walls. No creaking hull. Nothing.

"Hm." Juani tapped one key several times in a row and watched the screen. Then he scrolled and tapped another rapid string of code. The lights blinked once, and a sound reared up like a wild animal roaring through its death throes. Then nothing. Darkness and silence.

"Man, don't let go that plus sign. I'm gonna try one more thing."

Before he could touch a key, a different noise started up, a thumping rattle in the ladder well. Someone was pounding on the hatch from below. Juani shot to his feet. "The chief. He want in, but I can't juice the airlock yet. Man, I hope he's not in trouble." The boy looked back and forth from the thumping noise to his dim little screen.

"Does the hatch have a manual override?" I asked.

"You mean hand-operated? Yeah. It's this red lever, and

a bellows pops out of the floor. Then you go pump air with your foot."

I was already halfway to the well, casting my flashlight beam toward the red lever. I didn't ask what a bellows was. "I'll find it. You do your black start."

"Keep that plus sign tight, blade. Tight!" he called after me.

I did, too. I curled my two fingers together so firmly that my knuckles cracked. Apparently it worked, because just as I reached for the red lever, the well's incandescent lights blinked on, and the lock started running through its cycle, filling with compressed air. Juani's black start had succeeded. Thank the golden gods, I didn't have to pump air with my foot.

Moments later, the hatch slid open, and Liam and Geraldine climbed out. Liam was carrying the welder's battery on one shoulder like Mr. Universe, and Geraldine snarled, "Move outta the way, commie."

This irked me in the extreme, considering my only purpose had been to help them. I ground my teeth and let the evil wench pass. Liam gave me a civil nod.

"Have you got it sealed off?" I asked. "How long till we can repressurize?"

"I seal your runny mouth," said Geraldine.

Her high-pitched gibe pushed me over the edge, and I tossed out a nasty wisecrack. "While you were screwing around, Nobi was dying."

At that, they both halted, and Geraldine's emerald eyes went wide. Liam set his welder down and thoughtfully rubbed his hands, but Geraldine yelled, "You lie."

My remark was unbelievably crass, I know. You have to understand how angry that girl made me. She exercised zero control of her emotions. Liam touched her arm, but that didn't stop Geraldine. She slapped my chest with her open hand, knocking me backward.

"Your 'xec friends split our hull. Now they coming aboard to euth' us." She walloped my chest again and forced me farther back. "Stupid 'xecs, all they gotta do is go wait. Sooner later, we all be dead."

"Gee." One cautionary word from Liam shut her up. He raked a strand of yellow hair out of his eyes. "Truly, Nobi is gone?"

"I'm not sure," I answered, shamefaced. "He sounded bad when I left."

Liam motioned with his head, and Geraldine reluctantly moved off toward the generator closet. Then the chief nodded at me. "Will you help carry this battery?"

He lifted one end and waited for me to lift the other. He'd scuffed my white space suit pretty badly, but what caught my eye was the thruster harnessed to his back—the good one that hadn't been damaged. I also took note of the helmet clipped to his belt. When he took off that gear, maybe I could lay hands on it and slip outside. If Provendia's troops really were attempting to board, I wouldn't have far to go.

With a shrug, I gripped the other end of the battery, and we lifted together. The thing weighed only a few kilos in Three's reduced gravity—Liam didn't need my assistance. At the time, I thought he was hassling me, but looking back, I believe he was trying in his mute, primitive way to soothe my feelings.

He and I carried the battery into the generator closet, where Juani was waiting with his recharger cables. While Geraldine helped hook up the connections, Liam said, "Be calm, Nasir. You safe here." It seemed as if he wanted to add something. His lips opened. The straw-colored braid had fallen forward across his chest, and with an unconscious gesture, he flung it behind his back. Then he closed his mouth and returned to the ladder well.

I followed and spied while he stowed my thruster behind the ladder and climbed up toward sick-ward. As soon as he closed himself into the safety hatch, I grabbed the thruster and checked its diagnostics. Good. All systems functional. But I needed the helmet and EVA suit as well.

So I pursued him up to Four. I tiptoed into the anteroom just in time to see him disappear into sick-ward, and I caught the door to keep it from closing all the way.

"Liam." The warmth of Sheeba's voice made me knot my fists. I hid behind the door to listen.

Liam said, "How's he doing, Doc?"

If Vlad spoke, I didn't hear it. Nobi's hoarse voice answered instead. "Chief, you don't have to whisper. I going into the garden."

Kaioko moaned, "Not yet, Nobi."

"But I want to," her brother said.

Kaioko started chirruping again, and Sheeba murmured consoling phrases. "There, now. It's okay. He's just resting."

I tried to feel scorn for all this sentimental crap, to pretend the black sorrow opening in my chest was only a stomach cramp from the awful chili. But I'd had a brother once.

Raju. Without warning, a pocket of suppressed memories opened up inside me like a gaseous burble erupting from a buried landfill. I hadn't thought of my brother in decades. Raju died that day in Calcutta. My parents died then, too. Sometimes I forgot their names. Sanjay and Gaeti. They were trampled two blocks from their front door. My father used to cook chicken tandoori.

Vlad said, "Nobi, won't you try one sip of water?"

Sheeba whispered in a singsong chant, "It's okay. Your brother's going to be fine."

My brother didn't exist any longer, not anywhere. His memory lay deep under the rising waters of Bengal Bay. Time had moved on.

"Hold on to him, sir!" shrieked Kaioko.

And Sheeba cried, "He's gone."

At the sound of Shee's voice, I crammed a knuckle in my mouth. The pain in my chest was not grief. That boy meant nothing to me. I'd never seen him. I barely knew Kaioko. Poor, innocent Shee shouldn't have to witness this kind of thing. It was the Reel. Only the Reel.

When Kaioko burst into sobs, I felt ashamed of eavesdropping and moved away from the door. My face burned. So the boy was dead. Score one for whose side now? I tried to summon up the war surfer's emotional armor, but there was no purple-and-gold metavision to give me perspective. I spread my hands and stared at my glossy fake fingernails. This—whatever this emotion was—it felt too actual. I turned to flee—and ran straight into Geraldine.

"Chief, the commies invaded. They inside Two." Geraldine elbowed past me, but she came to an abrupt halt halfway through the sick-ward door. "Oh gosh."

She stepped inside. They were all together now, while I waited in the anteroom, gnawing at my artificial nails. No one spoke, and even Kaioko's sobs were muffled. I imagined her biting into Geraldine's shirt the way she had bitten into mine.

Liam was the first to appear through the doorway, followed by Sheeba, then Vlad. I shrank against the wall. Sounds filtered from sick-ward, Kaioko and Geraldine sobbing quietly at Nobi's beside.

In the anteroom, Vlad slumped against the steel table and closed his eyes. A pair of forceps tumbled from one of his bulging pockets and jangled on the floor, and Liam picked them up with a distracted air.

Sheeba's eyelids were swollen, and sweat mashed her hair flat on one side. Her shoulders slumped forward, and her arms did not swing when she moved. At first, she didn't notice me standing in the shadows. She raised her hand as if to touch Liam's shoulder, but at the last minute, she hesitated and shied away. At the little sink, she stood vacantly, staring at the drain.

Liam rapped the blinking fluorescent tube with his fist. "Jeez. This light!" When he hit it again, the greenish tube stopped flashing and gave a steady glow.

Vlad pinched the bridge of his nose. His crooked face looked gray, and when Kaioko's sobs momentarily rose in sick-ward, he swung his arm angrily at the rack of pinkish vials. "All my stupid mixes. They garbage."

The tubes would have fallen to the floor if Liam hadn't

caught them. "Be calm, Doc." He restored the rack to the table, then rested a hand on Vlad's shoulder and examined one of the vials. "Sooner later, these mixes go work."

Sheeba washed her face and hands at the sink, then wiped them on the front of her uniform and wrapped her arms around Vlad. Funny, she wasn't the least bit shy with the medic. A trace of her former zeal returned when she said, "We need you, Vlad. You're our best hope."

Who did she mean by "we"? Sheeba and I didn't have their filthy disease. We were execs. They were agitators. I tried to catch her eye, but she was too intent on comforting the sorry medic.

Liam arched his spine with a popping sound, and I noticed he was taller than Shee. For some reason, this trivial detail affected me beyond proportion. It didn't seem fair. I'd gone through so much effort to be tall, and he hadn't done anything.

In hindsight, many facts become clearer. Sheeba's empathy with these dying juves was inevitable. She'd chosen a career of caregiving, and here were the archetypal suffering victims in need of her skill. Then, too, they were all so young. I didn't want to believe that made a difference, but it did.

Liam crossed the tiny room and pressed his ear to the steel wall. "Gee say 'xecs coming aboard. And we got people trapped on One and Two." His baritone stayed low and steady, though his quivering jaw betrayed the strain he was under.

Vlad folded his arms. "Do we have a plan?"

"First, we get the people. Then we push out the 'xecs. Gee and Kai-Kai gotta take Nobi to the garden. So I need every one of you." Liam looked pointedly at me. I didn't realize he'd seen me till then.

"Do we have weapons?" Sheeba asked. My peace-loving Sheeba wanted weapons?

"We got the welding rig." Liam rubbed his chin. "Go see if you can find Juani."

Unbelievably, Sheeba snapped to attention and dashed away like a gung-ho trooper.

A short while later, the five of us descended into the thin frigid air of Two's ladder well—Juani, Sheeba, Vlad, Liam and me. Do you wonder why I allowed Liam to draft me into combat? We were going EVA, the chance I'd been waiting for.

"Stay quiet," Liam whispered.

The commies were just on the other side of Two's Down door. (The commies—listen to me. I'm starting to talk like Geraldine.)

Liam had sealed the blown-out door and reinforced it with heavy sheet metal, but Two's ladder well was still re-pressurizing. My ears crackled and ached as denser air escaped through my eustachian tubes. The ladder felt ice-cold through my gloves. Liam warned us not to touch anything with our bare hands. Our breath made clouds.

Geraldine had given me her leaky space suit, but I delayed putting on the collapsible helmet. The nasty thing looked like a wad of duct tape dangling from my belt. Worse, the scary old suit had no self-sealing capability. One rip would mean total death.

Liam and Vlad wore the new white suits, and Sheeba wore a gray one only marginally more functional than mine. Juani shivered bravely in nothing but his inside-out uniform, work boots and gardening gloves. Apparently, these four suits represented A13's entire inventory of EVA gear. Ye gilt, were we really planning to brave hard vacuum in these getups? Yes, for a little while, we would have to.

Liam's plan was simple and hopeless. After we rescued the kiddies, we would exit through Deck Two's airlock, then circle around to where Provendia's well-armed troops were entering through the ruptured hull. The plan was to ambush the troops with chains, boots and one welding torch. Yeah, that's right.

My plan, of course, was different. Once outside, I would

grab Shee and surrender to the Provendia troops. What could be easier?

Juani tried to open the door leading into the pressurized section of Two. He looked chilled and vulnerable without a space suit, but since he suffered from spacesickness, he couldn't go EVA. When the door's wheel refused to budge, Liam and Vlad added their strength. Still, the wheel wouldn't turn. Apparently, the blowout had damaged its gasket.

Sheeba joined in. They made quite a sight, four people trying to turn a one-half-meter wheel. Finally, I scrambled up on Juani's shoulders and kicked the top of the wheel with my boot. When the door let go, the pressurized air inside nearly broke its hinges. The gust threw us across the ladder well like a heap of crash dummies.

Imagine the bright light exploding from the solar plant. Feel how we squinted and covered our faces. After our long semidarkness, I felt as if my eyes were bleeding. My false optics usually adjusted for glare, but not this time—maybe because I'd missed that eye recalibration. Juani peeked through his fingers, and Vlad slowly uncovered his face. Liam unfolded two long scraps of gauze from his pocket. He tied one over his eyes and gave the other to Sheeba. Curse the graven gods, I wish I'd thought of that.

The bevy of little trapped toads came pouring out through the bulkhead, cheering like foosball fans, and soon, everyone was hugging and laughing—molto syrupy moment. Slowly, the ambient temperature rose in the ladder well. Sheeba started handing the children up the ladder to Vlad, who cycled them in quiet groups through the safety lock. As she tickled their bellies and rubbed noses, I watched with relief. She was acting like her cheerful self again. Meanwhile, Juani hurried inside to restart the circulator pumps, and Liam cycled down to One to rescue the kids trapped there. I leaned against the wall and felt for the reassuring vibrations of whooshing and sluicing.

Eventually, we got used to the light, and Sheeba tugged her improvised mask down around her throat so she could work more easily. As she lifted the children, her slender muscles popped, and the white gauze danced around her throat like an air pilot's rakish silk scarf. I couldn't take my eyes off her. Never had I felt such excruciating love.

After the kids were safely stowed on the deck above, Liam led us into the ops bay, where the light was less severe. The overturned desks and office supplies sprawled in massive chaos, and we picked our way through with care.

"First, Vlad and I go outside, see what the 'xecs up to," Liam said. He nodded at Sheeba and me. "You wait here."

"But we can help," I said, eager to get out.

"Right, Liam. We're not babies." Sheeba zipped up her suit and pulled on her gloves.

He shook his head. "Too dangerous."

"But—"

"No." He gave Sheeba a look that made her draw an exasperated breath. Then she sat on the floor to wait, and her luscious lips showed only a trace of a pout.

By now, I'd learned there was no point in arguing with Liam, so I sat on the floor beside her. Inept as Liam might be with language, the punk knew how to get his way. So while Sheeba and I sweated in the overheated ops bay, Liam and Vlad slipped outside to run reconnaissance. Vlad would circle the tank prograde. Liam, retro. They would spy on the invading troops from opposite sides of the hull.

Juani joined us with a grin and a thumbs-up. His pimply, optimistic face reassured me. He said the circulator pumps were working just fine, and the air and water were flowing freely again. Even though spacewalking gave him vertigo, he still wanted to help with our mission, so while we waited, he layered more duct tape around our crumbling air hoses and entertained us with a stupid song about yellow bricks. By chance, I found a row of punctures in Sheeba's sleeve, and he helped me plug them with sealer glue. After that, I examined every square centimeter of her suit while Juani did the same for mine.

Damn these old suits. The manufacturer should have been sued for not installing a self-repair function. I slathered glue over every suspicious scuff mark. Sheeba remained quiet and still, which was not at all her usual style. The three adorable creases between her eyebrows deepened to grooves. Surf the moment, I kept telling myself, but these leaky suits unzipped my peace.

Vlad was the first to return. He said Provendia had a small troop carrier hovering outside, and he'd counted eight commies entering through the blown-out hull. He didn't get close, but from the rumbling noises in the walls, he thought they were trying to drill through Liam's patch into the ladder well. I asked why they didn't simply enter through the airlock, and Juani said the commies were too gutless to try that. Airlocks could be rigged with gas, he said, like euthanasia chambers.

"Would you do that?" Sheeba asked.

"We already did," Vlad said bitterly, and Sheeba whistled through her teeth.

Recalling my own passage through the airlock, I studied Vlad's lopsided face with new respect. Sheeba asked if the troops might come through the docking port on Deck One, but Juani said he and Geraldine had jammed the doors. I knew they'd sabotaged the dock, but I wanted details, and as usual, it wasn't hard to coax Juani into talking. He said they'd dumped five tons of fully loaded shipping pallets on top of the cargo doors so they wouldn't slide open.

"Sleek." Sheeba did the palm-to-palm prote handshake with Juani.

"Fully loaded with what?" I asked.

"Product, man. That pro-glu crap they eat on Earth."

Product? Heaven still had five tons of pro-glu? That much product translated into nontrivial cash value. I made a mental note to inform the staff as soon as I escaped. If we could relabel that product with new expiration dates, we might be able to recoup some of our war expense.

Liam kept us waiting a long time. Juani said he probably went inside Two for a closer look, and Vlad said maybe the troops spotted him. I could feel Shee's jumpiness. I rubbed her arm to comfort her, all the while knowing how little I succeeded. She didn't want me. She wanted that agitator. She was infatuated with his—what? Good looks? No, I was more handsome. Not to boast, but any jury would choose my superbly crafted features over his gauntness.

Was it his courage then? But hadn't I proved my mettle time after time in the zones? He had no assets, no accomplishments, no eighty-story condo. All that punk could offer was the brevity of his life. He was a short-timer, a neophyte, a young man. Was that supposed to be some kind of achievement?

Youth is for sophomores. It's stupid and embarrassing, a time to be endured and forgotten as soon as possible. When I think back—oh yes, I can still recall those queasy, hormone-drunken days. That was long before the Crash. Yes, I remember fumbling in the dark for girls' clothing and overturned bottles and questions I couldn't begin to articulate. The futile rage and confusion, the teapot tempests, wrecked cars, theatrics in restaurant doorways, desperate emails, lost hearts. Now as I wait through these last moments of my life, I want to fling out my arms and rage tempestuously, "Sheeba, you can't be in love with that juvenile!"

"Relax, beau." She squeezed my fingers. "He'll be back soon with good news. I feel it."

"Um-hm." In the sweltering ops bay, I leaned my head on her shoulder.

No sooner had my nose settled under her chin than the mighty chief's shadow fell across us. He took off his helmet and spoke rapidly in his subdued bad grammar. He'd been all through the blown-out section of Two. The Provendia troops were trying to drill into the ladder well, just as Vlad guessed.

Vlad said, "Juani's seedlings already ruined. We could set a plasma fire."

"I'm thinking explosion," Liam muttered. "Blow the hydroponic tables around. Knock a few heads."

The groves reappeared between Shee's eyebrows. "Will people die?"

Vlad nodded fiercely. "We hope."

But Liam chewed the ends of his mustache, ruminating. "Trick is to set off a little pop without rippin' the X wall."

"This is so lame." I couldn't refrain any longer from speaking. "Why do you even bother? Look at the trouble you're causing your employers. They built this satellite, and they subsidize all your costs of living. You owe them your loyalty. How long have you been holding back those pallets of product?"

"Nass." Sheeba edged away from me.

"Well, Shee, dammit, be fair. Who started this war?"

Liam caught hold of my collar and pulled me closer. He kneaded the smartskin fabric between his fingers as if testing its quality. His blue eyes glittered like cut glass.

"Gee say you a commie spy. Is she right?"

"That's nonsense. I'm a tourist, the same as Sheeba. You trust Sheeba, don't you?" Why had I opened my mouth? Now, he might not let me go EVA.

Sheeba wriggled her shoulders and tried to signal me, but I couldn't read her meaning. She looked angry.

"Are you with us or against us?" Liam said.

I swallowed. "I'm with you."

He released my collar but continued to hold me with his eyes. Quite a commanding power the kid had. "Prove it, Nasir. I want to believe you."

Liam moved toward the door, and Sheeba followed, glancing doubtfully over her shoulder to see what I would do. Of course, I hustled along with the others. My entire escape plan depended on going EVA.

Inside the ladder well, the drilling noise echoed almost as fiercely as the sonic lathe. I pressed my hands over my ears and thought of the fresh pair of disposable eardrums waiting for me in Kat's shuttle. When we cycled down to Deck One, I found myself back in full Earth-normal gravity, back at the bottom of the spinning bucket where I'd first awakened with a broken leg—how long ago? Four days?

Liam led us through the Up door this time, into the

cargo bay. When we stepped over the sill, the first thing I saw were the bales of dried pro-glu stacked all the way to the low ceiling. The shipping pallets rested squarely on top of the huge sliding doors where Provendia's freighters were supposed to dock. Five tons, Juani had said. It was hard to imagine anyone pushing through that much weight. Still, Provendia's troops were notoriously resourceful. I was trying to estimate the number of bales when Liam's low voice caught my attention.

"Sheeba, you want too much from me. I said no."

Strange words. The sound drew me closer. In a closet-sized work area just off the main cargo bay, Liam and Shee were standing face-to-face, and he was running his finger gently across a gob of sealant crusted on her space suit, just at her collarbone. The sight stopped me cold.

Sheeba caught his hand and pressed it to her lips. "You need me, beau."

Beau. That was my name. Sheeba child, what were you thinking? I found it very hard right then, very hard to forgive her for that. No doubt, brutal emotions played across my face, but no one was looking at me. Juani and Vlad were busy with some nitrogen cylinders.

Liam murmured so softly, I almost missed what he said. "Your suit's not safe. Wait here, and if the commies break through, you get your chance to help."

"I want to come with you," she said.

Then he kissed her. "No."

He glanced around and saw me watching. When he moved away to help Vlad lift the cylinders, I got a clear view of Sheeba's dark golden face. She was glowing.

17

DISTANCES CAN FOOL YOU

> "It was one of the deadliest and heaviest feelings of
> my life to feel that I was no longer a boy. From that
> moment I began to grow old in my own esteem—and
> in my esteem, age is not estimable."
> —LORD BYRON

A death sentence is never definitive. The judge may schedule your execution, set the date and name the hour with a ponderous knock of the gavel, but it's guesswork. First there are appeals, stays, reprieves. Then abject pleadings for pardon. Of course, you're not innocent, but you probably know someone in office. You write letters, call friends. As you run out of options, you pray the killing apparatus will break down. You look for hiding places in your cell, under the cot, for instance, or up behind the ceiling fan. You make lists of promises. You dream of your past. Perhaps a time comes when you grow tired of waiting and yearn for death—but I doubt it.

Life is a lie we make up to hide in. I didn't see Liam kissing Shee. I imagined it. Where's my memory delete key? I want to punch the damn thing and forget. As I sit here waiting in the anteroom, my body feels vigorous and lucid, yet in a finite number of minutes, Heaven will pass beyond Earth's shadow, and I will die. Can that be possible? Look at these hands, the fingers still work beautifully. Look at my strong, pearly nails. These hands are too good to throw away. Perhaps I can dig a hole through this steel deck with my fingernails. Perhaps I can cry out again for Sheeba.

Sheeba who glows in the dark.

In the cargo bay, she leaned against the wall, listening to the steel with her eyes shut, while Liam and Vlad went spacewalking to set their explosion. In the dimness, her olive skin merged with the shadows, and her fingertips drew circles in the oily black fungus, unconsciously revealing the graffiti underneath. Her lips parted. Perspiration darkened her uniform. She was mesmerized by the zone.

I wanted to grip her shoulders and shake her awake. This thrill won't last, dearest. As soon as you get back to civilization, you'll come down off your surfer high and see that juve for what he is—a prote agitator. The zone is a fantastical outland. It's not our reality. It's the Reel.

But Shee was in no mood to hear my warnings. The zone's electric bliss held her fast in its grip. Eyes clenched tight, she pressed closer to the steel wall, intent on every faint vibration. Under the gray suit, her long, lovely muscles tensed and quivered. I knew how she felt—waiting for action, elevated on stress and adrenaline. Hadn't I experienced that sweet high? Zone addiction. I had no choice but to save her—if necessary, against her will.

To do that, I needed to get outside the hull and signal Provendia. But Liam wouldn't let me go EVA. He said Geraldine almost died the last time she used this old space suit. The punk was concerned about my well-being, can you believe it? He made Sheeba and me wear the suits just in case something unfortunate happened during the explosion. Just in case. Ye glittering gods, how that phrase ticked me.

"We gotta reinforce the hatches," said Juani. "When that explosion come, this old tank gonna shiver. Will you help me carry the welder?"

"In a minute." I needed to think.

For some time, my IBiS had been tingling an alert, so I

slipped off my glove to check it. Oh, great news. My dental NEMs had developed a work-around for their program error. They'd given up waiting for doctors' orders through the Net, and the little bootstrappers were going ahead with my dental hygiene all on their own. I rolled my tongue around my newly sanitized mouth. Hurrah. Minty fresh.

One more time, I tugged at the glue crusting my derelict space suit and assured myself it would hold. Juani was trying to walk the heavy welder onto a dolly so he could move it to the ladder well. He wanted me to help, but when his back was turned, I tugged Geraldine's mildewed helmet over my head. Shee was too immersed to see what I was doing. She splayed her body against the wall as if she were begging for sounds. Dear deluded child, she didn't open her eyes when I slipped out of sight around the curving corridor.

Finding the airlock was easy—Liam had showed me the way earlier. I cycled through, opened the hatch and felt the cold at once. That was not a good sign. Geraldine's old suit must have lost some of its insulating capacity. The satellite's angular momentum didn't catch me by surprise this time. I hung on tight and took shallow breaths through the musty old-style mouthpiece in the helmet. Then I reached back to check the air-hose connections again.

A row of handholds glinted softly around Heaven's waist. I gripped the first one and pulled myself toward the Up side. When I emerged from the shade, solar radiation blazed around me like a nuclear burn. Sunset. A13 was just passing behind the Earth. As the sun's fireball sank behind Earth's gilded horizon, I quickly turned away to save my eyesight. Geraldine's visor lacked basic photochromic darkening.

I hadn't expected to reach Heaven's sunward face so quickly. In the sun's dying rays, my suit was heating up, and the hull was too silvery bright to look at. Head down, I swung back into the shadow side, where the temperature inside my suit instantly dropped to the shivering range. From this position, I had a satellite's eye view of twilight

Earth blanketed in steamy clouds. Whorls of gray and rich rusty brown marbled the ochre smog in fanciful patterns. Those whorls must have been the size of Sweden for me to see them this far away.

Beyond Heaven's bullet point, the asteroid counterweight glowed like a yin-yang symbol, half in sunlight, half in black shade. Briefly, I paused to listen for hisses inside my suit, but so far, the glue was holding. I double-checked my safety line, then started crawling again.

Heaven's hull seemed more pitted than ever, pocked with rust and dents. The tank had hauled fuel all through the solar system before we bought it secondhand. Had anyone checked its rated lifetime?

I noticed something peculiar. The tank appeared longer than it should have. I'd visited four levels so far, and each was three meters high at most. The fifth deck held the main factory, so it would naturally be larger. I mentally added the numbers, but the tank was triple the length I expected. Optical illusion? Distances can fool you when you're under severe stress. Either that or the fifth deck was enormous.

Heaven raced around its track like a roulette ball. I clutched the handholds and moved deeper into the shade. Surf it. Ride it. Savor the thrill. How many seconds do any of us glide on the keen thin edge of life? War surfers do it more than ordinary people, but the experience remains rare. I drank in the scenery. One rim of Earth's black orb still glowed where the sun had set, and beyond that, the ether of space glimmered with spectral agitation. Brain chemicals sharpened my senses to an extraordinary pitch. I thought: This will make a molto vivid blog for the Web site.

A seam ran down the full length of A13's underbelly, and the rivets stuck out five centimeters. It was almost as good as a ladder. I could follow this seam down to the tank's base and signal the gunship. The only problem was, halfway down the ladder of rivets, I reached the end of my safety line.

What the heck. I had made it this far without slipping.

Besides, Liam did it. So I unclipped. Imagine me slithering along, clinging to those rivets for dear life, braving the deeps of space. Ye graven gold, how I wished Verinne had her cameras trained on me.

The closer I moved toward the tank's butt end, the stronger grew the angular momentum. By the time I gripped the lowest rim of the tank, my legs were flying out from the hull, and it was all I could do to hold on. I peeked over the rim at the blunt, flat bottom of the tank.

Picture the brouhaha that awaited. A few meters away, Vlad and Liam hung by their feet from Heaven's bottom, wearing their (my) shining white suits, and surrounded by blue-clad mercenaries. No, not Provendia troops. These were hired commandos. I recognized their logo, IVet.Com. Why was Provendia hiring mercenaries? We maintained a small army of our own security guards.

In any case, it was obvious that Liam's plan had crashed on takeoff. He and Vlad had been spotted and attacked before they could detonate their ill-conceived explosion. To have their hands free, they'd jammed their boots into the overlapping seam of the cargo doors, and now they were stuck there, unable to maneuver. So they hung from Heaven's butt, swinging their chains and trying to fight their way backward, sliding their boots along the seam in precisely my direction.

Visualize their chains impacting those blue IVet helmets in eerie quiet. See the sparks fly, and watch the chains bounce in loose spiraling curls. Take my word, it was fascinating. When one of the mercs spotted me and fired a fléchette, I almost lost my grip trying to duck.

Vlad struggled awkwardly. He meant well, but he wasn't a fighter. When a merc grabbed his legs, he tried to wrench free, and his boots lifted out of the seam. After that, it was child's play for the mercs to seize him.

Next, Liam ignited his (my) thruster and astounded everyone by zooming straight out into space. He tried to circle around, flailing his chain. No doubt his intention was to rescue his friend, but he wasn't very experienced at steering. Four of the mercs zoomed up to surround him, and they were just about to close in when he abruptly spurted away like a meteor. Probably his accelerator hung up. He might have hit the lock button by accident. In seconds, he dwindled to a distant white speck in the sky, and the four mercs called off their chase.

They massed around Vlad like viruses, and the whole squirming clump of them drifted in my direction. The young medic writhed in feral panic, but the men in blue held him tight, and I felt an insane compulsion to try and free him. Without thinking, I rose up over the rim in plain sight.

Vlad recognized me. We were almost near enough to touch, and I could see his mouth moving. In a desperate lunge, he tossed his chain toward me. The chain swung erratically, and in reflex, I freed one hand to grasp it. Then the nearest merc spotted me.

"I surrender!" I shouted uselessly inside my helmet. Quickly, I lowered the chain and bowed to show total submission. But the damned chain kept undulating with waves of inertia. The more I fought it, the more it whipped around. So I wedged my boot in the seam and grabbed the wicked thing with both hands.

Then Vlad gave me a look I'll never forget, and he mouthed two words through his visor: "Help me."

I hesitated. This was my chance to escape. Here were my rescuers. All I had to do was let them take me, and this nightmare surf would come to an end. But I stared at Vlad's desperate expression and—ye gods—I wavered. When the merc zoomed toward me aiming his handgun, I had no choice but to bash him with the chain.

Out of nowhere, reinforcements converged. But these new troops weren't wearing IVet's mercenary blue. One of them wore a purple suit with silver and red paisleys, exactly like my old friend Grunze. Hell, it was Grunze. I knew that helmet. And that tall skinny person beside him in black, that was Verinne. No mistaking her willowy shape. Several meters off, Kat was hovering. The Agonists had come to save me!

Imagine my bliss. My dear beloved friends. I waved to them in wild delight. Winston was probably back in the shuttle mixing margaritas. Lime juice and salt, good old Win, he knew my favorite poison. I waved frantically with the chain to get their attention and nearly tugged my boot loose from the seam, but they didn't see me. All their attention was focused on Vlad, who strained less and less in the iron grip of the mercenaries.

A swarm of space-hardened cameras buzzed around—Verinne was documenting the scuffle, probably uploading it to the Net. When the merc I'd assaulted started peppering me with fléchettes, my friends not only failed to intervene, they didn't send one solitary camera to take my picture. The brawl with Vlad absorbed them. Ye images of gold, that white EVA suit. They thought Vlad was me!

I abandoned the chain and flattened myself to the hull to escape the fléchettes. This old gray suit made me look like an agitator. I clawed at the globby glue and hated my life. I would have ripped the suit off there and then to reveal my true face—except that wasn't feasible. Steady, I told myself. Improvise.

So I kicked off from the hull and let the momentum carry me toward Verinne. Close up, she would surely recognize my face through the visor. My aim was good. I sailed straight for her. No way could I miss. Any second, she would see my helmeted face and open her arms to catch me. Cara mia. I waved and smiled. She would probably win some bet at my expense, but I didn't mind.

When she noticed me coming, she moved aside. Not far. Just enough to avoid me. Ten centimeters beyond my outstretched hand, she let me streak past without so much as a sideways glance. In this prote getup, I held no interest for her. She could at least have shoved me back toward the satellite. But she was too busy recording her Reel.

So there I was, racing into the night in my leaky gray, glue-crusted agitator suit, running out of air and losing way too much heat, while Heaven and the gunship and everyone I cared for in the world wheeled inexorably away be-

hind me in total mind-fucking indifference. Times like
these give a man food for thought.

I torqued my body around to avoid the sunset in my
eyes—and managed to throw myself into a slow, rifling
spin. Every few seconds, Earth rose and set around me like
a fast-forward moon. Shivering with cold, I threw my head
back to get a better look at A13, but the helmet limited my
view. For several long minutes, I drifted, intermittently
holding my breath to preserve my air supply, then hyperventilating in nervous agitation. Does that work? And one
thought orbited through my skull: What would Sheeba do?

Sooner or later, she would discover me missing. I fantasized how she would search through the factory, calling my
name. How forlorn she would sound. Perhaps her voice
would break and a tear would drip down her bronze cheek.
Too late, she would sense the void I left in her life, and a
moan would burst softly from her lips. Then she would
beat her breasts, violently, wishing we'd made love. Ah
Shee, we should have shared that intimacy.

Picture me gliding through the void, stately and sad. All
the while, one image enwraps my shivering body like a
warm pink nimbus of soap bubbles. Myself and Sheeba
making love. Feel the erotic dream, replete with sounds
and pinpricks of sweat running up and down my groin.
Sense the rapid rhythm of my hands. See my body hump-
ing the darkness. Taste the heat.

Now envision that voluptuous fantasy whirling away
down a black vortex.

Somehow, I had cranked myself into a faster spin, and
Earth was circling me every second. I closed my eyes to
keep from throwing up in my helmet. And I knew Sheeba
would not be calling my name. She'd be playing tongue-tie
with that agitator.

"She's mine!" I shouted inside my helmet. "Let go of
her!"

Then he hit me.

Out of the clear black sky, he hit me full force and
stopped my spin. Before I could react, his helmet punched

me in the stomach. Then he caught me in his outstretched arms and shoved me ahead like a forklift loading a pallet. My ribs impacted his chest with crushing violence, and in absolute terror, I threw my arms around his neck.

Eventually, when I gathered my wits and took note of what had happened, Liam and I were streaking back toward Heaven at an ever-increasing rate of speed, building up toward a molto vicious crash straight into the cargo doors. His thruster accelerator was still locked, although he seemed to have discovered how to steer.

Hastily, I reached for his controls and flipped off the lock, but though we stopped accelerating, our speed did not diminish. No friction, you see.

He touched his helmet to mine and asked, "Did Sheeba come outside?"

I wanted to spit in his face. Instead I pressed my visor against his and grunted, "Aren't you interested in the braking jets?"

I showed him how to operate the controls to kill off our speed. By the time we settled back to Heaven, no one was there. No mercs, no Agonists, no Vlad. "Shit," I heard the punk say when our helmets bumped. For once, I agreed.

In taut silence, he steered us back to Two's airlock, and together we climbed inside and cycled through. We had nothing to say to each other. Sheeba was waiting.

Ha. She hugged me first. Her long arms clamped around me like a vise. "You risked your life defending us. Dear Nass, your karma's totally primeval. You've got old, old spiritual layers going back to Genesis."

While I ruminated on this strange praise, Sheeba hugged the chief of thugs. Of course, I counted the seconds to see which embrace would last longer. They broke apart almost immediately, blushing and lowering their eyes. A less experienced rival might have been pleased by their awkwardness, but I knew what it meant. Ye deities, budding lust. I wadded my gloves in my pocket, longing to stuff my fist down Liam's throat.

"Where's Vlad?" Sheeba peered into the airlock.

"They took him," I said.

Liam, with his usual linguistic eloquence, merely slammed his (my) helmet to the deck, where it bounced hard and rolled.

"They got Vlad?" Sheeba searched the airlock, as if the medic would magically reappear.

I picked up my helmet and took note of the unsightly new scuff mark. Then, biting my lip till it bled, I watched Sheeba stroke Liam's back. "Calm down. It wasn't your fault." Her large, dimpled hands moved along the gaunt lines of his shoulderblades, and she whispered in his ear, "Tell me what happened."

"They all slipping away. I can't protect them," said the punk.

"We're still here, beau. We believe in you."

As her hands massaged his back, brutal hatred washed through me, sharper and more potent than any war-zone rush. It boiled in my stomach like acid and threatened to lift off the top of my skull. She called him her "beau" again. Watching Shee comfort that snot-nosed thug right in front of me, without any attempt to conceal her conduct, why, it made me quiver. My fists clenched, and my toes curled in my boots. I felt capable of bloody acts.

Then a new inspiration struck me. Like a bolt of genius, the idea materialized in my head—a clean, simple way to get rid of the punk forever.

"We have to board that gunship and rescue Vlad," I said. "You and me, Liam. Let's go now."

Naturally, I didn't mention that the Agonists had taken Vlad away, not the gunship troops. All I wanted was to see Liam captured. If I could persuade him to go aboard Provendia's gunship—my gunship—then I would take command, and oh what vengeance I would wreak. I sucked my minty teeth and visualized Liam slumped in the euthanasia chamber.

"Nass, you'd go there to free Vlad? You have a deeper spirit than I ever knew." Sheeba danced across, holding her arms out toward me. She gave me another hug and a big wet kiss on the ear that rang through my head like a tympani drum.

I grinned at Liam. "We should hurry."

Shee bobbed up on her tiptoes. "Nasir's right. There's not a minute to lose."

Juani had been waiting to speak. Now he came forward, grinned and punched me gently in the arm. "You amaze me, blade. You righteous."

Surf it. Ride it. Improvise. This was developing much better than I could have planned. As we waited to hear Liam's response, Sheeba beamed and fidgeted, while Juani nodded proudly and waited with a knowing smile. But Liam clenched his mouth in a tight line and studied the fungal rings on the floor.

I'd spiked him on the horns of a no-win dilemma. Either he would accept my generous help and set off on an impossible mission to board a fully armed Com gunship—during which he would be captured and euthanized while I would surely escape. Or he would reject my brave-hearted suggestion and lose major status points with Shee, not to mention his leadership credibility. I sidled a little closer to my beloved and watched the punk's face.

"All right, Nasir, we go," he said at last.

"Parabolic!" Sheeba jumped up and down like a kid. "You guys are rip!"

"But I need time to work it out in my head," Liam added.

Molto slippery tactic, I had to give him credit. But this was excellent. Better and better. As Shee waltzed off with the punk, I watched them hold hands with a smidgen less than my usual bitter despair. In a little while, he and I would find ourselves on my gunship, surrounded by my executives. Then I would deal with the juvenile chief of thugs.

Suddenly, we heard pounding, and everyone halted and turned. Was the hull trembling apart. Was this the end?

"The hatch." Liam pointed toward the ladder well. "It's Geraldine."

As a safety precaution, Juani had welded the safety hatch shut, just in case Liam's explosion caused another blowout. Now Geraldine was pounding the hatch with her hammer and shouting.

Liam and I raced for the well and got stuck pushing simultaneously through the bulkhead door. Together we rushed up the ladder and started tugging at the welded lever, while Juani went to find a crowbar. We could hear Geraldine yelling down from Deck Three, but nobody could make out what she was trying to say.

18

UNIVERSAL DONOR

> **"In the name of Hypocrites, doctors have invented
> the most exquisite form of torture ever known to
> man: survival."**
> —LUIS BUÑUEL

"**K**aioko!" Geraldine bellowed, when we finally got the hatch open. "She—she—she—"

"Be calm." Liam guided the overwrought girl down the ladder a few rungs. "What about Kaioko?"

Geraldine's face streamed with tears, and her heavy hair rayed around her head in tight damp coils. "Kaioko want to go into the garden."

Why this should excite so much alarm, I couldn't say, but Geraldine's words detonated an uproar. The juves raced up the ladder like a band of wild children pursuing a pied piper. Liam squeezed into the safety lock with Geraldine— he didn't even stop to take off the thruster. Meanwhile, Juani and Sheeba hung on the ladder, waiting their turn. All this pandemonium erupted because Kaioko wanted to pick veggies? Ye golden idols—what had happened to our plan to board the gunship?

"What about Vlad?" I very reasonably asked from halfway down the ladder. "Who cares why one little girl gets a yen for broccoli? Our friend Vlad's been arrested."

But Juani was already climbing into the safety lock, and Sheeba merely shrugged and followed him in.

Left alone, I sat on the ladder and stared at my scuffed white helmet. The gray suit I wore was too antiquated to mate with this helmet's newer design. True, the old suit functioned well enough, and I still had Geraldine's helmet clipped to my belt. I could slip outside again. No one was there to stop me. But what would I do, space-dive to the gunship with no thruster? I'd already experimented with that little ploy. The distance was too far, Heaven was spinning too fast, and if my aim was off by just a fraction of a degree, I would miss the ship and drift into eternity.

I spun the helmet idly around and around, recalling the way Sheeba's eyes softened when she looked at Liam. When he talked, she leaned toward him as if his baritone voice created a freaking gravitational pull. My strong vibrant Shee, how could she trail after that punk like some moony satellite. She was obsessed with the Reel, that's all. But if I told her, she wouldn't believe me.

Maybe she would believe the other Agonists, though. With their help, surely I could break her free of this zone trance. Grunzie, Verinne, Kat, Win, the thought of their affectionate faces turned me sappy and foolish. Stress, I told myself, batting the tears away. Lack of sleep. Molto freaking hunger. I could deal with another ten-liter can of Chili Diablo.

By now, my friends would have discovered their mistake in capturing the medic. Naturally they would interrogate him with psychotropics, but some employees resisted that kind of therapy. Even under chemicals, Vlad might not tell them anything.

So what would the Agonists do next? They would line up another surf, of course, but first they would have to send out their gear for maintenance and cleaning. Then they'd argue about strategy, place new wagers, and generally fart around getting ready. Two hours minimum. After that, they'd come back. Wouldn't they? I kept spinning the white helmet between my hands, trying to think of a way to reach them.

One more time, I dropped the white helmet over my head, chinned the sat phone and called Grunze. "No service," the mechanical voice reminded me. Provendia was still scrambling my signal.

The disconnect infuriated me. Sure, I'd signed the order to jam Heaven's Net link, but who decided to kill the ship-to-ship channel? It must have been the gunship captain. What if the Heavenians wanted to give themselves up? They couldn't surrender if they couldn't hail the gunship. It was inexcusable arrogance on the part of the gunship captain. Not to mention the inconvenience to me.

And then I screamed. "A hundred and fifty-two hours!" The words roared in my helmet like thunder. I'd just noticed the clock. I'd set my helmet clock at zero when this surf began. Graven gods, I'd been trapped in this orbiting coffin for over six Earth days.

I ripped off Geraldine's old gray glove and checked my thumbnail. Sure enough, I'd missed more telomerase infusions. Without the Net, my bioNEMs couldn't receive orders to synthesize the rejuvenating enzymes. If I didn't get those treatments soon, my handsome face would pucker. Already, I could envision tiny pockets forming around my eyes and crumpling inward like deflating airbags.

Not just my skin would degrade. Without those enzymes, my internal tissues would lose elasticity as well—and at my age, it would happen fast. Once, when I was vacationing in Greenland, I accidentally went off-Net and missed four remote telomerase appointments in a row—gruesome. What if Sheeba saw me that way? We had to get home before that happened.

There was only one option. I had to space-dive outside Provendia's Net blockade and call for help. Damned Liam. Why couldn't he leave my thruster behind?

Okay, without the thruster, I could free-dive beyond the blockade, then call for help on my sat phone. But this white helmet wouldn't mate to my old gray suit. How could I use the phone in hard vacuum? Maybe I could . . .

a. rewire the advanced quantum electronics into Geraldine's ancient ratty helmet, or
b. seal my new helmet to the old gray suit with duct tape, or

c. just carry the thing into space and yell at it through my visor.

Freaking hell.

"Hi, Nass."

Sheeba waved at me from the safety hatch above. A dark olive Sheeba, regal as a queen. Her hair glistened like a skullcap of short black fringe tipped in gold, and her amazing water-colored eyes bewitched me. I dropped my helmet.

"Hi, Shee. You came back."

Her eyebrows creased. She was worried about me. At least old Nasir still occupied some small place in her heart. As she moved down the ladder, the sway of her hips in the gray uniform made my capillaries dilate. Her shining eyes brimmed with moisture. She was crying.

"Kaioko's in sick-ward. Gee found her curled on the floor. She won't speak." Sheeba squeezed beside me on the ladder, draped her arms around my neck and hung her head.

I welcomed her with kisses. "What happened? They said Kaioko was going to the garden."

Sheeba sniffled. "That's just a phrase they use."

"You mean—she has the malady?"

"Why do you call it a malady? Do you know anything about this, Nasir?"

"Not a thing, I swear." Which was entirely true, in a way. I kissed Sheeba's fingers. They tasted of antimicrobial soap. "We have to get out of here, darling. Anyone can see something's killing off these workers."

"Be one with the zone, Nass."

"That's just surfer slang. It doesn't mean dying. The war surfer's first rule is to exit the zone alive."

"I thought the rule was to live the moment. Nobody lives forever."

Ah Shee. Innocent babe in a wicked wide world. I drew her close and patted her shoulder and tried to think back to my own early decades. Had I ever been that green?

Sheeba squirmed away. "I hate those jerkwad execs who own this place. Liam won't tell me much, but I'm getting him to loosen up. Do you know these people had to teach themselves to read?"

"That's appalling," I said.

"They've had no dental care."

"Mega-inexcusable."

"And doesn't the WTO have a law against child labor?"

"You don't mean they did that, too?"

Sheeba nodded meaningfully. "Nass, I am totally blissed with how you care and want to help these people. I feel the same way."

"Ah." I simulated a smile.

"My medical knowledge is really lame, but I'll do whatever I can. With all your karmic reiterations, you—"

"Did they forget about Vlad?" I preferred not to dredge up my multiplex soul.

"No, Liam's drawing out a plan." Sheeba got up and paced, cracking her lovely knuckles with a disturbing sound. "We absolutely have to get Vlad back. He was working on the cure."

"Shee, for once be logical. That untrained prote will never find a cure. We have to evacuate."

"Liam says his people won't leave. I already asked him." She took a scrap of cloth from her pocket and blew her nose. "Anyway, the commies won't let them go."

Commies? I had to draw several hard breaths before I could respond. "Darling, that's an atrocious slur word. The local exec may have muddled his duties, but in general, Com executives are admirable managers."

"Liam says—"

"Who cares what that juvenile delinquent says? You're executive class yourself, Shee. Remember that and be proud. You're suffering some kind of Stockholm syndrome, bonding with your captors. Executives hold the light that guides our economy. These protes would be nowhere without—"

"Cut the crap, Nass."

I opened my mouth. Then closed it. Sheeba had never talked to me that way before.

She sat on the deck and picked at the frayed edge of her cutoff uniform. Her lips twisted. "I'm sorry. I didn't mean to be rude. But here in this place, well, it's not fun to pretend anymore."

"Pretend? You think—"

"Nass." Her water-colored eyes focused on me like a pair of clear, sparkling spotlights. "Playtime's over. This is real."

I stomped away to the far side of the well, savagely chewing my lip. Okay, I admit the line about the guiding light was bullshit. Once upon a time, maybe I needed to believe that buzz. It helped Sayeed and me rally volunteers to rebuild the Asian Internet. Back in those days, we all yearned for some kind of faith. Ah, Shee, how the beliefs formed in our youth cling to us. At 248, I could still spout that creed by the kilo—and often did. We visionary Com leaders dedicated our careers to keeping everyone on Earth gainfully employed. Stability, that was the law we worshipped, and after surviving the Crash, peace was our graven motto. We dreamed of leading our moribund planet back to the golden age.

But who was I kidding? We'd built another pyramid scheme, just one more feudal pecking order, where swindlers jockeyed for top place and the rewards of greed glittered. Well, didn't our ape ancestors fling feces at each other to establish alpha dominance? I stared hard at the fungal blooms in the well—had I ever believed it was right?

Then the irony almost made me laugh—a 248-year-old man still vacillating over right and wrong. The one truth age reveals is: There's no absolute good. There is only what works, and that has never changed. If my Com friends were overthrown, another elite would take our place. But how could I say that to my dewy-eyed Sheeba? She would have to live another hundred years to understand.

"So he's planning to board the gunship?" I said, getting

back to the main point. Philosophical questions aside, I still meant to escape and settle my score with that punk.

"He and Geraldine." Sheeba got up and dusted fungus off her legs. "They'll use your thruster to circle around and sneak in from behind."

Molto thin, unrealistic and massively unworkable. "That sounds great," I said, crossing to the ladder. "When do we leave?"

Sheeba pulled my hand off the rung, and her brown-blue-green eyes softened. Gilty gods, she melted me down. "You're not going, Nass. Liam doesn't want to put you at risk."

Is that what he said? Fuck that.

Mercifully, those words didn't pass through my lips. I pressed against Sheeba, and when she didn't resist, I clung to her, inhaling her herbal spice. Wetly, I mouthed her burnished cheek. Then I tore myself away and headed up the ladder.

"Let's just pop up and see if they need anything."

Shee followed me into the safety hatch. "Maybe you can make Kaioko smile. She likes you."

"Excellent thought."

We found the ringleaders of Heaven's miserable tribe gathered in the anteroom. They'd hidden all the kiddies on Deck Five. Juani slumped against the counter, while Geraldine hovered over Kaioko, who sat on the table with the glazed vacancy of catatonia. Only Liam sprang forward at our approach, fully on guard. Someone had raked the dismantled cyberdoc onto the floor, and he scooped up a heavy piece of its outer case as a weapon. But when he saw Sheeba, he lowered it.

What a pathetic little group. Despite the weak gravity, they sagged and hung their heads as if their very eyelashes weighed megatons. They couldn't hold out much longer. In the last six days, they'd had no more food or sleep than I had, and they lacked the advantage of my NEMs to rebuild their immune systems. Youth wasn't enough. They were walking wrecks. If Provendia knew the real situation, our troops would board and end this fracas without delay. That gunship captain had to be a total mushbrain.

Kaioko looked skeletal under the fluorescent strobe. The gray uniform hung on her like a sack. Her smooth wide face had gone dull, and her tiny eyes had lost their luster. I wanted to believe she was simply tired. Her scarf had slipped back off her forehead, and some of her burns were showing. She would be embarrassed if she knew, and I felt an urge to pull the cloth back in place for her. I whispered to Shee, "Kaioko needs a nap, that's all."

Geraldine threw me a ferocious scowl, and Sheeba laid her finger across my lips to shush me. When Liam turned away, I saw his untidy yellow braid dangling over my thruster. Here in Four's light gravity, the thruster weighed so little, he'd probably forgotten that he still wore it.

Geraldine shifted to turtledove mode. She flitted around Kaioko, cooing soft love notes and offering a cup of water. But Kaioko didn't respond when Geraldine pressed the cup to her lips. As the liquid dribbled down her chin, Kaioko didn't even turn her head away.

"Kai-Kai, please look at me. You need water," Geraldine pleaded.

I felt sorry for the evil wench. "What about Vlad?" I said, but no one paid attention. It was as if they'd been hypnotized.

Something had to be done to break this spell. I left the anteroom, cycled down to Three, jogged to the galley and jerked the bunny-face clock off the wall. Grumbling all the way, I climbed back up to Four, cycled through the lock again, and carried it into the anteroom, where the Heavenians still slumped and drooped and hung their heads just as pathetically as before. I held the bunny clock in front of Kaioko's eyes and moved the whiskers around with my index finger.

"Look, dear. See how the nose-hairs move. It's very cute, isn't it?"

For the briefest moment, her diminutive eyes followed the movement of the whiskers. "Time," she said.

"Correct." I glanced at Shee with a small thrill of triumph. "And what is time?"

Geraldine and the others google-eyed the bunny clock as if they'd never seen it before. Liam moved closer.

"It's space," Kaioko said with the faintest hint of animation.

"And what is a year?" I winked at Geraldine and nodded at the cup she was holding. She nodded back, and while I spun the bunny's whiskers to keep Kaioko distracted, Geraldine tried again to feed her some water.

No luck. Kaioko sensed the water at her lips and pushed it away. "Save it. You'll need it later." Her brother's very words. That echo gave me a creepy shock.

"We need Vlad," Shee said. "He was close to finding a cure."

"Of course we do." Her words got me back on track. "Vlad's on that gunship. Let's go get him, chief."

I headed for the door, beckoning Liam to follow, but he seemed in no hurry. He took the clock in his rawboned hands and studied it with almost comical intensity.

"Come on. They've got Vlad. They may be torturing him." I kept gesturing toward the door.

Geraldine finally jerked around and scrutinized me. Her neglected hair hung in tangles, and in the half-zipped white space suit, her body seemed less stout than before, as if she were losing weight. But her green eyes radiated their usual contempt. "Whadda you care about Vlad?"

Nasty wench. I had just tried to help her little wife. Was there nothing I could do to win her trust?

But Liam nodded. "Nasir's right. I gotta get Doc." He laid the clock down on the table beside Kaioko, then zipped up his (my) space suit. "Gee, I need you," he murmured.

"You want me to leave Kai-Kai?" Geraldine gripped fistfuls of Kaioko's uniform and buried her head against the girl's chest. What drama.

I tapped Liam's shoulder. "I'll go."

Liam drew on his gloves and checked his air gauge. "Too dangerous."

"Oh, and I suppose waiting here to die is as safe as baby fuzz," I said.

Juani caught hold of my arm, which I may have been waving a tad bit hysterically. His acned face conveyed a strange somberness. "We don't die, blade. We go into the garden."

"Whatever euphemism you like, I refuse to sit on my thumbs and wait for it. Liam, take me with you. I can steer the thruster."

"That's true, beau. Nasir's an expert with the thruster." Sheeba called that punk "beau" again. The private endearment used to be mine alone. I swallowed my feelings and nodded to keep her talking. She said, "Nasir used to be a plasmic athlete back on Earth."

Used to be? I let that pass, too. "You can count on me," I said.

Geraldine growled low in her throat like an animal. "Chief, you know he lies."

Wicked tart. I had to twist handfuls of my longjohn to keep from ripping her hair out. Liam chewed the ends of his mustache the way he always did when he was trying to string together a sentence. Finally, he marched toward the ladder well. "I need to think."

As if he had a brain. I started to follow him, but Sheeba touched my arm and whispered confidentially, "Nass, there's something I need to ask you."

My boots skidded to a halt. "Anything, Shee."

Three decks below, Provendia's gunfire started drumming Heaven's hull again, and everyone tensed. While we held our breaths and listened to the vibration thudding through the walls, Kaioko came alive. She clawed her ears and shrieked hysterically. Then she slid off the table like a limp doll. Theatrics, I told myself, denying the truth. I didn't want to believe Kaioko was sick. Why, only a few hours ago, we'd been debating philosophy.

Geraldine caught the girl in both arms, and Sheeba checked her pupils for dilation. "Kaioko, wake up," I found myself whispering under my breath.

"She's in shock. Juani, get a bed ready. And Gee, look at me. Look at me." Geraldine was babbling obscenities, but Sheeba grabbed her wrist and forced the wench to make eye contact. "You have to wrap Kaioko in blankets. Keep her warm. Do you hear me? Dip a clean cloth in water, and squeeze it into her mouth."

Geraldine wiped her runny nose and nodded.

"Can you carry her by yourself?"

"Yes," Geraldine said.

"Okay. Nasir, get the door."

Sheeba's grave tone brought it home to me that Kaioko was critically ill. I sprang to hold the door while Geraldine lifted her unconscious wife. As they passed into sick-ward, Sheeba moved with the cool, quick confidence of a primo war surfer, while I hung back uselessly and watched.

Geraldine lowered the girl's limp body onto the mattress, and I wanted to shout a command to turn off this picture. This wasn't the way the Reel should go. Rewind. Put it on pause.

"Nasir." Sheeba beckoned me to join her in the anteroom. She'd spread medical utensils on the counter. There were needles. Juani slipped quietly out to the ladder well and left us alone.

Shee said, "Nass, we have to try something."

I mumbled, "Will she die?" Unfamiliar chemicals washed through my brain, stirring sympathetic urges.

"Vlad thinks it's a blood disorder," Sheeba said. "Nobi and I both had Type A negative, so Vlad transfused Nobi with some of my blood, hoping the good would drive out the bad."

"What?" I replayed her words slowly through my brain. "That's idiotic. You can't cure a blood disorder that way."

"I know." She ran her fingers through her short black-and-blond hair, and for the first time, I noticed the lines of fatigue in her face. My darling Sheeba. Dead on her feet.

"Sit down and rest, dear. You're grasping at moonbeams."

"We had to try something. I know it's crazy. Half the things that heal people are crazy."

I drew her toward one of the benches in the waiting area, but she was too nervous to sit still. "Shee, this place is not a medical facility. And you, you're a wonderful therapist, but dearest, you're not a doctor. We should go back where we belong and leave this to the specialists."

She rifled through a cabinet and found some plastic tubing. "You have those nanomachines in your blood, right?"

My jaw moved, but my voice failed. Sheeba and I never mentioned my bioNEMs. It was a forbidden subject because Shee thought nanotech was "unnatural," another one of her fizzy notions, like refusing to suppress her ovaries.

"Dearest, I know you don't approve—"

"I've changed my mind, Nass. Anything's worth a try. Those nanothings may heal this ... despondency." She blew through one of the tubes to clear out the dust. "Will you give me some of your blood? It might work."

Precious child, she'd finally realized she needed NEMs to protect her health. But would my NEMs migrate to her body through a blood transfusion? Could it be that easy? A thought flurried through my brain: copyright violation, capital crime. I ignored it.

"Will you?" she said hopefully.

I cradled her face in my hands. "Dear Shee, yes. Take all you want."

First, she pricked my finger and ran a tiny scarlet drop through the nanoscope. Then she waggled her shoulders like a happy young animal. "I knew it, Nass. This is truly karmic. You have Type O blood."

"What does that mean, Shee?"

"It means," she said, throwing her head back, "you're a universal donor!"

"Sounds philanthropic," I said uneasily.

She gave a smile that warmed me to the marrow. Then she rolled up my longjohn sleeve, put a tourniquet around my biceps and slapped the inside of my elbow to make a vein stand out. Her face glowed with the war surfer's bliss, and I couldn't help but think, despite her short training and

my long experience, that we were both lost babes when it
came to medical procedures.

I tried to sound calm. "Take a big dose, dear heart.
You'll need a lot. Are you sure the NEMs will migrate this
way?"

She beamed. "Where's your faith?"

When she held the old-fashioned needle up to the light,
I winced. It looked awfully long. "Is it clean?" I asked.

Sheeba made a clownish face and plunged it into my
vein.

19

I KNOW WHO YOU ARE

**"Old age is like everything else. To make a success of
it, you've got to start young."**
—FRED ASTAIRE

The average executive body contains five liters of blood.
Sheeba assured me of this as she siphoned one of them
from my right arm into an empty plastic water sack. Why
precisely one liter? There was nothing precise about it. We
were walking on the murky waters of faith healing. Shee
had skipped her blood theory classes because the information was "too dry," she said. Vlad's quack idea that good
blood might chase out bad sprang from lunacy, ignorance
and sheer desperation. Still, there was a slim chance my
NEMs would migrate to Sheeba's body and jump-start her
immune system.

"Take more, dear. You need lots and lots." I watched the
wine of my veins slowly inflate the little plastic sack.

"Nass, I've never drawn blood before, but I think taking
too much could make you light-headed."

No problem. I didn't mind resting on this comfortable
steel table while Shee hand-fed me savory chili—until I recalled we were streaking through space in a disintegrating
fuel can. I sat up quickly, reeled with dizziness, then lay
back down.

"Very well, dear. Perhaps one liter will be just enough."

Juani came dashing through the anteroom, grinning. His
black braid swung like a pendulum. He waved a thumbs-up
sign and raced into sick-ward. "At least someone's gotten

good news," I said. Then my eyelids fluttered heavily. Sleep was dragging me under.

Sheeba said, "What's got him so blissed? He's been talking to Liam."

When she started toward the sick-ward door, I opened my eyes just in time to grasp her sleeve. "Don't go in there, dear. You haven't had your NEMs yet."

She gently released my fingers, settled my blood-tapped arm back on the table, then leaned to check the plump, crimson bag dangling below my elbow. When Juani came racing back through, he carried a white EVA suit draped over his shoulder, the one Geraldine had been wearing, and he spun the white helmet on his fingertip like a globe.

"Juani," said Sheeba, "you can't go spacewalking. You get vertigo."

The boy straightened up and stuck out his chest. "Be calm, Sheeba Zee. I going!"

Then the air went thick, and my vision wobbled. The fluorescent light illuminated Juani's teeth like a wall of pearly stones with a single black gap at the center. Dark, warm and damp, that gap opened and opened till it devoured the whole universe.

I awoke much later with a raging thirst.

My temples throbbed. I couldn't remember where I was. My teeth tasted minty fresh, but my body exuded a god-awful smell. I sat up and sniffed my armpits. Whew. My dermal hygiene NEMs were seriously off kilter. A water sack lay beside me, so I sucked it down. After several minutes, I recognized the fluorescent light. This was the anteroom to sick-ward.

"Hello. Anyone?"

No answer. I went to the sink, flipped open the faucet and cupped my hands under the thin jet of disinfectant. Then I unzipped the front of my longjohn and rubbed my pits and groin. How had I gotten so dirty? My thumbnail screen displayed a long menu of strange messages. Not only my dermal hygiene NEMs had gone off-line, other classes of NEMs had crashed, too. What's more, the Net was not responding. But why? For the life of me, I couldn't remember.

Oddly, the NEMs in charge of my false dental implants showed mega activity. With no doctors' orders, the little fiends had gone into a flossing frenzy, and my breath reeked of spearmint. But none of this made sense.

I felt my forehead for fever, but my temperature seemed normal. Then I checked the status of my mnemonic NEMs—and got a bizarre reading. Some of my implanted memory sticks had been switched to edit mode, and the NEMs were making confetti out of my short-term recall.

"Stop that." I clicked through the prompts, trying to get control, but the little buggers wouldn't respond.

Then, like a light shutting off, I forgot about them.

The door to sick-ward was closed, and no noises filtered through. Dimly, I sensed that Sheeba was in there helping someone whose name I should know. Someone who'd fallen ill. The idea needled me, but I couldn't quite visualize the person's face. I considered knocking on the door. Then something itchy tugged at my arm—a thick wad of bandage was taped inside my elbow. Seeing it triggered a spotty recollection. Sheeba had taken my blood.

Almost instantly, the recollection dissolved, leaving behind a troubled void. I reached for the water sack, hoping another drink would clear my head. But it was empty. Then I slid off the table and had to grab the counter to stabilize myself. Spots of bright color flashed across my retinas. Why did I feel so weak and thirsty?

The water sack was empty, so I set off to look for more. In the ladder well, the fungus blossomed in great bristling flower heads. When had I passed this way before? My sense of time waxed and waned like surf. A silver D gleamed from the opposite door. D for Down. But that wasn't down.

Then a recollection flickered like a splice of Reel. I saw dying employees. They lay motionless, speechless. Rows and rows of thin mattresses stretched away to an impossible distance, and I imagined wandering among them, seeking a way out, but the employees didn't notice me. Their bloodless faces held no expression, and their vacant eyes didn't blink. A taste of lychee nuts welled up in my mouth, and the faces turned in my direction. They were real. This wasn't a dream. Those dying workers were on this deck— in sick-ward.

I fled down through the safety lock and descended to Three.

The galley was deserted, but I found a full water sack and took a long, grateful drink. Something had frightened me; what was it? Already, the memory had fragmented. With a small rush of pride, I recalled how to work the can opener, located a clean bowl and heated some stew. But something kept nagging me. Wasn't there a mystery to solve?

My chili came out tepid. I took a few famished gulps, then carried it with me, eating while I walked. Juani's generator closet lay vacant. He'd stowed his toolbox away, and the empty cistern echoed when I tapped it. But who was Juani?

In the drying room, abandoned ovens gaped open. A bag of hard crackers had spilled across the floor, and my boots crunched through the crumbs.

"Anyone here?"

I took my bowl of chili down through the safety hatch to Two. In the forlorn ladder well, thick new metallic patches covered a badly damaged door. This spooked me. Was I getting Winny's mutated Alzheimer's? I touched the metal door, then pressed my ear to the steel. No whistling air loss. No thudding boots on the other side. Only the stillness of space.

I cycled down to One and roamed among the deserted crew quarters, eating stew as I went. Only my slurps broke the chilly silence. Long ago, I'd spent time here as a prisoner—had I dreamed that? The arc of wedge-shaped closets held no chairs, desks, bookcases, no Net connections. Not a single window anywhere. Only blankets scattered on the floors and graffiti etched into the walls.

Both ends of the curved corridor terminated at steel doors marked CARGO BAY. But the doors were not merely locked and welded shut, they were obstructed by towering stacks of steel bed frames, tables and straight-backed chairs, lashed together with chains. So that's what Heaven's furniture was used for—barricades. I added my empty chili bowl to one of the stacks, then climbed back up the ladder to Deck Two.

Halfway up, a thunderous noise shivered through the walls. That was gunfire. The ladder shook, and spikes of hot terror sizzled through my nerve endings. As I cycled through the lock, the hull clanked with brutal contortion.

Abruptly, the concussions ended, and I drew a relieved breath, hardly knowing why. The solar plant's vicious light forced me to shield my eyes, and I hurried through to the ops bay. Around the corner lay an airlock. Instinct drew me there. Juani had taken my white suit to go spacewalking, but why? The boy had a front tooth missing. Memories brightened and faded like cinders in a strong wind.

Then, like a bolt, I remembered. Juani went with Liam to the gunship. No, I was supposed to go with Liam.

They'd gone for Vlad, but Vlad wasn't on the gunship—I'd lied about that. My crewmates had taken him. And because of my lies, Juani would be captured and euthanized. He might already be dead.

But I was supposed to go there, not Juani! I never meant to harm Juani! How did this fiasco happen? I never used to fumble like this. All those error messages. The NEMs were screwing with my memory.

Abruptly, I forgot again.

In a stupor, I sat on the floor, where someone had left a flashlight. I picked it up and peered into its reflective cone. What had I just been thinking? Plans and intentions connected like bits of glass in a kaleidoscope. I touched my face—and felt puckered flesh. Pouches sagged under my eyes. I didn't need a calendar to tell time. My face was a clock. This slackening skin meant at least seven missed telomerase treatments. Seven days in Heaven—it sounded like the title of an old movie.

Then a new recollection glowed, clearer than the others. I wanted Liam to die. That's right, I'd tricked him to go after Vlad. And thanks to my lies, he'd taken the only two decent space suits in Heaven, the only helmet with a satellite phone, the only working thruster—the only way out.

My lies had killed Sheeba.

Curse my cunning soul. In a fevered rush, I went tearing back through the solar plant, where the dazzling light almost made me trip. I stumbled toward the ladder well as scattered memories came hurtling back. I had to *do* something. Find Sheeba. Figure another way out.

Just as I bounded into the well, Geraldine leaped off the ladder and knocked me flat. She straddled my chest and pinned my arms down. Tears and mucus dripped from her face, and she screamed, "Murdering commie!"

I threw her across the ladder well. I was, after all, a healthy adult executive, whereas she was a teenager.

On the other hand, she had a hammer. She whipped it out of her pocket and pointed the claw end toward me, circling sideways on bent legs as if she meant to lunge.

I yelled, "What the freak's got into you?"

"You murdered Kai-Kai," she blubbered.

Little Kaioko was dead? I didn't have time to think about that. Geraldine's clawhammer demanded all my attention. "People were dying on this satellite before I came here."

"I know who you are," she growled. Then she hurled her hammer end over end, and though I ducked, it caught me in the shoulder.

"Ow." I spun and slammed into the wall, then slid to the floor clutching my wound.

Geraldine was on me in a second. She grabbed my hair with both hands and slammed my head against the wall. Then she kicked me in the chest and knocked out my wind. "Killer. Killer. Killer," she chanted.

I retrieved the hammer, and when her bare foot came reeling toward my face, I smashed her anklebone. She shrieked and hopped away, holding her ankle in both hands, screeching like a baby.

"Keep away from me," I said.

"I taking you up there, commie. You gonna see what you did." She let go of her bleeding ankle and stood facing me with her brawny legs spread wide. Ripples of salty sweat crusted her gray uniform, and a sneer warped her features.

"I was going up in any case," I said, holding the hammer like a talisman to ward her off. "You wait here till I cycle through the lock."

"Don't try to hide. No place here you can hide from me."

I rolled my shoulders with dignity. "Why on Earth would I bother to hide from you, prote?"

Climbing the ladder, I kept the hammer pointed toward Geraldine to make sure she didn't follow too closely. After I cycled through the lock to Three, my plan was to disable the upper hatch so she couldn't follow. But I couldn't figure out how. When Geraldine started cycling through, I hot-footed up the ladder toward Four. She sprang out of Three's lock just as I climbed into Four's, and she sprinted up the ladder with a murderous expression. I barely managed to close the hatch in her face.

In Four's well segment, I tried to jam the hatch with a wad of fungus, but it crumbled to bits. Geraldine was already cycling through. She would be on top of me in seconds, so I bounded into the anteroom and stopped in front of the sick-ward door. I didn't want to go any farther.

The door stood open a crack. I could see the yellow light. "Sheeba?"

There was no sound. I stood rock still raising my hand to knock, hoping Shee would come outside. "Sheeba?"

Then Geraldine came barreling up and butted me head-long into sick-ward. I tripped over the sill and slid, face-first, across the septic floor. "Yaaah!" I leaped up and swatted the filth off my face with both hands. It was that fungus. Then I caught a glimpse of white beds and whipped away to shield my eyes from the sight.

But Geraldine blocked my escape and spun me back around to face sick-ward. "There," she said and pointed.

I didn't want to see. I fought her and covered my eyes. "Sheeba, help me."

"Your girlfriend ain't here," said Geraldine.

When I tried to move around her, she kneed me in the stomach and made me face the cots. Two rows of narrow white mattresses with threadbare sheets and thin gray blankets. There were fewer than I expected. They were bound to the floor with thick canvas straps—as if they might fly into the air at any moment. But the cots were empty. Except one. A small chemical light cube had been Velcroed to the wall above this one particular cot, and one wasted invalid lay under the blanket, staring straight up at the ceiling. Kaioko. Still breathing, barely.

Ye gilded gods, death was an ugly thing. She wheezed as if a ton of rock were crushing her chest. Her eyes shimmered like dull chips, vacant and calm.

As I confronted her empty eyes, all my memories rushed back in crystalline clarity, even the ones I wanted to forget. The glass man irradiated me with repressed knowledge, and Heaven's unabridged truth sheared through me like a laser. I remembered the malady.

Provendia's scientists had taken weeks to piece the data together. Two months ago they finally confirmed what was killing Heaven's inmates. That's why we shut off the surveillance cameras. We didn't want to watch anymore. The protes were committing suicide.

How stunned we were, sitting around the conference table with our brandy snifters in hand. The youngest director in the room was 157. Longevity obsessed us. The word, suicide, whispered from an alien world.

"You can't mean they're taking poison?" one of the directors said.

"It's not poison," said Robert Trencher. Oh yes, Trencher was there. He crossed one ankle over his knee and played with the genuine leather tassel on his loafer.

"It's something more subtle. They lose the will to keep themselves alive," he said. "Mostly, they die of thirst."

"Do they want higher wages?" I asked. "They haven't made any demands."

"We don't know why they're offing themselves," Trencher said. "They call it 'going to the garden.' We call it severe clinical depression complicated by satellite affect disorder." What a smug bastard.

Now I watched Kaioko's slack lips flutter with each difficult breath. Suicide? Why did it have to take so long? Why did she have to suffer? And why did human beings have to die at all?

If ever clairvoyant forces had shaped the universe, why did they weave this depraved repeating loop of bereavement into our evolution? Why death? Why not life eternal? Couldn't our race thrive much better with a small, select group of superior individuals living on year after year, collecting an ever-broader store of wisdom? Instead of the ugly painful onslaught of birth, struggle, reproduction and inevitable decay, why couldn't we have endless healthy life for one small, well-chosen group of human kind? That seemed an excellent solution to me.

Geraldine drew a threadbare sheet up to Kaioko's chin, but when she tried to embrace the girl, Kaioko's body flopped like a loose-limbed manikin. Geraldine wept into the mattress, and I watched her burly shoulderblades tremble.

Can you understand now why I had behaved like such a base coward at every approach to sick-ward? Willing surrender to death, the idea unnerved me. It undercut my belief system. What if I caught the contagion? Injury, illness, even age—these could be corrected. Damaged tissues could be replaced. But how do you repair a damaged will?

Now that my memories had resurrected, I began at once to rationalize and edit them again. I stood erect and assured myself that Kaioko's illness did not concern me. The deaths of my family and friends, of my beloved Prashka, those old griefs were long forgotten and healed over by time. Kaioko's death meant nothing. She wasn't even pretty. It was the sight of Geraldine's powerful shoulders quivering helplessly under her ragged uniform that finally made me cover my face in my hands.

"Can't you hook her to a food tube?" I murmured. "Give her an IV if she won't drink water?"

Geraldine jerked around, startled. "Kai-Kai wouldn't like that."

"What does that matter if it keeps her alive?" I walked a few paces away. "Where are all your other patients? There ought to be sixty."

"Sixty?" Geraldine's mood shifted acutely, and her eyes filled with suspicion.

I bit my lip. No point revealing what I knew. Besides, it was time to face facts. The only survivors left in this orbiting mausoleum were this handful of juvenile ring leaders and the squirming horde of little toads. All the adults were dead.

On the floor beside Kai-Kai's mattress lay a shrunken red sack, the remains of a blood transfusion. Clear plastic tubing hung from a hook above her pillow, still stained by a thin coating of scarlet. Inside the girl's elbow, Shee had taped a small white bandage the same as mine, and three bright drops of blood spotted the sheet nearby.

Sheeba had given my blood to Kai-Kai?

Slowly I sank to the floor as the full weight of this hit me. I'd shared NEMs with an employee. This was worse than a capital crime, it was . . . moral depravity. Perverse. Obscene. Wicked. Worse than vile. No executive shared NEMs with a worker. It was wrong on so many levels. What if the little buggers spread like a virus through the prote population? Longevity epidemic. That would change everything.

No, no, no, I would never have agreed to this. Those NEMs were supposed to help my darling fend off the malady. They were for Sheeba. Who would have dreamed she'd give my transfusion to Kai-Kai?

And yet, the longer I stared at the ruby stain on Kai-Kai's sheet, the less Shee's act surprised me. It was just like her to defy conventional taboos. Stubborn child. I stared at the three red drops with a grim smile. Those tiny healing machines were designed to renew the human body for decades, and now they were doomed to a short, confusing life in synthetic fabric.

Geraldine tugged her thick legs into a lotus position beside Kaioko's mattress. Her ankle was bruised and swollen where I'd hit her with the hammer, and tendrils of space fungus clumped between her bare toes. Fungal film covered the entire deck—except for one clean shiny spot under the blood sack. There, beneath the dripping tube, the steel deck gleamed almost as bright as a mirror. My blood was killing the fungus. How delightful. If somehow I managed to survive this zone, elude capital punishment, and live down my moral corruption, then I could sell my blood as floor cleaner.

Geraldine sneered. "Gimme back my space suit."

The wench's emotions shifted faster than spring tides. I never knew what to expect from her. She ogled the old gray suit but made no move to get it.

"Screw you," I said.

The wench shrugged listlessly and smoothed Kai-Kai's sheet. "She going to the garden soon. Juani there now."

Going to the garden was their euphemism for death. Had Juani died while I slept? No, it couldn't be. Heaven's inmates were disappearing too fast. Solitude was closing in like a vault. "When did he die?" I said, shivering.

Geraldine pushed her hair back. "Juani raking out the dead leaves. He making things tidy for Kai-Kai."

Ah, so he wasn't dead, he was cultivating his plants. This news brought me an unexpected charge of comfort. But Kaioko was fading. There was no hiding from the truth. She'd fallen into a slumber so profound, it could only be called a coma.

"Where's Sheeba?" I said.

"She and the Chief go sneak around that gunship,"
Geraldine said. "Sooner later, they find Vlad."

"Sh– Sheeba went to the gunship?"

Oh gods, what had I done?

20

FRUITY SWEET DARK

"It is not possible for civilization to flow backward
while there is youth in the world."
—HELEN KELLER

Sheeba Sheeba Sheeba, why did you go to that gunship?
Feel my legs buckling. See me dropping with a thud to
the sick-ward deck. "How long have they been gone?"

"Shoulda been back by now."

"How long, Geraldine?"

"One orbit," she said listlessly.

One flight around the Earth! The air supply in those
suits wouldn't last that long. They'd been captured—or
shot. I pushed up off the floor and careened toward the exit.
The troops would have taken her prisoner, yes. She would
be safe aboard the gunship. But she wore no signet, no executive ID. Would they bother to sample her DNA? No,
they would leap to conclusions, and the dear naive child
would not protest. I dashed through the anteroom and
leaped into the ladder well. I broke fake nails, tearing open
the safety hatch. Shee would hide her identity. Hadn't I
taught her that war-zone rule? She would surf the tide of
adrenaline and pretend to be an agitator.

How slowly the safety lock cycled. Liam was supposed
to die, not Sheeba! I could see her standing shoulder to
shoulder with that malevolent punk, squeezing his hand
and beaming with misplaced ardor. How beautifully her
dark golden face would glow as she joined him in the euthanasia stall.

Beloved Shee, don't do it!

The syrup of gravity thickened around my limbs as I dropped through the ladder segments from Four to Three to Two. Why had I wasted so many precious minutes talking to Geraldine? The solar plant blazed with all its nuclear fierceness as I dodged among the turbines. Juani was kneeling by the airlock, pressing his ear to the steel.

"My fault, blade. They out there 'cause of me." Dribbles of vomit stained the front of the old gray surfsuit he wore. "I tried to reach them, but I weak. I weak."

"No time," I said, shoving the boy aside.

He slumped and hid his face as I opened the airlock. I felt a qualm, treating him that way, but necessity drove me. Inside the lock, I clamped my gray helmet in place. No time to check the duct tape. No time.

I found Shee clinging to the hull among the shattered solar panels. In the blistering white heat of direct sunlight, she was gripping a broken support strut with one glove and clutching Liam's belt with the other. The punk had lost consciousness. Laser burns pocked his white body armor, and his long legs rippled away from the fast-spinning hull like a flag in a cyclone.

I lunged toward Sheeba, gripping handholds and hiding my face from the fiery sun. Solar reflections glared off her visor, so I grasped her helmet and tilted her face toward me. Her lips were turning blue.

No time. I hooked an arm around her waist and scrabbled back toward the airlock, using my one free hand to pull us along and wedging my boots into any kind of crevice to keep us from flying away from the spinning tank. No thoughts, only long seconds and labored panting. Radiation flared up from the bright pitted steel, burning through my gloves and forcing me to squint. Go go go, I chanted. The war surfer's mantra. With agonizing slowness, I grunted and slithered and hauled my precious Shee around Heaven's circumference. Finally, we passed into frigid shadow, and there was the oval rim of airlock.

I drew Sheeba inside and discovered she was still gripping Liam's belt. The three of us filled the narrow space like compacted debris, and when the compressor finished cycling, we fell through the inner hatch in a jumble. Juani lifted Liam while I twisted Sheeba's helmet free. She wasn't breathing. Though her hand continued to grip that cur's belt, her own lungs failed to draw air. I dropped to my knees and gave her mouth-to-mouth resuscitation.

How long did I blow air into her moist pink lips and watch her chest fill with my breath? When she started coughing, I sat back and wiped my spit from her blessed chin. Juani had removed Liam's helmet. I half hoped the chief had suffocated, but no, that punk still had plenty of air left. Sheeba had given him her reserve cylinder!

Oh beloved, what alternate dimension do you inhabit? Is there no point where our two separate realities overlap? I don't understand you, Sheeba. Is it because you haven't lived long enough, or because I've lived too long? Why would you sacrifice your very breath for that criminal?

"Rest, my love," I said, stroking her cheek.

Sheeba rolled on her side, gasping and coughing. Her first clear act was to reach for the unconscious punk sprawled next to her. Side by side, white and golden dark, they curled into each other like a pair of commas—as if their bodies were made to fit. Dark and light, they were poles apart. Freaking diametric opposites! They didn't belong together!

Even unconscious, Liam's gaunt body clenched like a stubborn white root dug up and left in the sun to dry. He had no education, no sense of style. Ten to one, he could barely read. His straw beard stuck out in bristly whorls. And his nose, ye idols, a hawk's beak. Whereas Sheeba, nubile olive-dark goddess, rounded and curved, see her flowing with liquid laughter and easy tears, as radiant as the starry ether of space. Feel the cool touch of her hands. Feel her maiden softness. There was no comparison between them.

"We—we couldn't find Vlad," Sheeba said and coughed.

"Don't try to speak, dear." I loosened the collar of her EVA suit.

"He wasn't—on the ship." She sat up despite my protests. Still coughing, she yanked off her gloves and checked her lover's pulse. Then she tore frantically at his surfsuit. "We snuck in through the waste chute. We looked everywhere. Help me with this zipper."

Underneath the suit, Liam wore a Provendia troop uniform with its familiar stylized logo, as meaningful as an alien rune. I helped Sheeba slip it off his shoulders.

"Why did you go there, Shee? You could've been killed."

"She went in my place." Juani lowered his head. His braid had come loose, and black hair spilled across his face. He supported the chief in his arms.

"No way. I wanted to go, Juani." Sheeba worked the zipper open. "Those commies didn't even know we were there till we tried to leave."

With extraordinary gentleness, she peeled the uniform away from Liam's chest. The laser beams had not penetrated his (my) body armor, but their impacts had raised tremendous red welts along his ribs.

Abruptly, Shee clenched her eyes shut, and her lovely features warped with heartbreaking despair. "I think Vlad's dead. They must have killed him before we got there. Oh Nass, why didn't we listen to you sooner?"

I bit my lip and watched a tear trickle down her cheek, yearning to comfort her with the truth. Vlad was never on the gunship. Our friends had captured him, and they were not killers. But after the lies I'd told before, I didn't dare confess.

"They probably incinerated him." She fussed with Liam's wrist gaskets. "He would've wanted to go to the garden."

"Be calm, Sheeba Zee." Juani touched her shoulder. "Wherever Vlad is, he'll recycle."

Sheeba nodded, wiping her nose.

I helped her strip the chief to his miserable ragged underwear. I hated Liam's twentysomething body. Dead pale, hairy, as smooth and muscular as only a young body could be. I kept thinking, what a handsome corpse you'll make. Soon, thug, you will be dead dead dead. And then Sheeba will be mine again.

"Juani, these are minor wounds." Sheeba gave the boy her cheeriest smile. "Chief's gonna be fine. Will you please go to sick-ward and get a bed ready?"

"Yes, Sheeba Zee." Juani sprinted away.

When he was gone, Sheeba's smile vanished. She'd been faking the optimism. I didn't realize what a clever actress she could be. But now the planes of her exquisite face drained of color. As she fussed over her sleeping hero, her voice shook. "Poor Juani came out to meet us in that awful old suit, and then he threw up in his helmet and had to go back. I didn't think we were going to make it, Nass. I thought—I really thought—"

Dear girl. I tried to caress her, but she was too keyed up. Zone hyper. She searched the punk's body for hidden wounds. "God, his neck's bruised."

"What about you, Shee? Are you okay? You didn't take my NEMs. That blood I gave was meant for you."

"His vertebrae don't feel broken. Oh god, I'm not sure." Her fingers searched the back of his neck

"Take my NEMs now, dear. I'll give another liter. You *need* them."

"We'll make a collar to stabilize his spine."

She rifled through the contents of the nearby utility closet and found some rags, which she rolled together and knotted around Liam's neck. All the while, she told me about the gunship. She said it was easy to sneak through the waste chute. That Provendia captain must have been molto smug not to set out a security perimeter. He didn't even post guards. What an ass. I couldn't imagine Provendia hiring such a dunderhead. In any case, his overconfidence allowed Liam and Shee to steal uniforms and search the ship without detection. But they didn't find a trace of their medic. They'd arrived too late, she said, as she grimly rebraided the punk's yellow hair.

The Provendia troops finally noticed them when they

tried to leave. They wanted to space-dive home under cover of darkness, when Heaven and the gunship passed behind Earth's shadow. But they mistimed their exit and came out in the light. That's when the gunship started firing.

"Darling. Ye graven gods." I accidentally leaned all my weight on the punk's knee and took pleasure in his unconscious groan.

"Nass, I was so scared, my fingers shook. I almost couldn't steer the thruster." Sheeba blinked at her empty hands, remembering, and her marvelous skin stretched tight across her cheekbones. Then she lifted the punk's shoulders. "Grab beau's feet. We'll move him up to sick-ward."

Instead of doing that, I put on his (my) white helmet to check the clock. Then I slowly drew it off. "Sheeba, do you realize we've been in this satellite for over eight Earth days."

"I haven't been counting, Nass. Help me carry him."

"Darling, wait. We don't belong here. We have our space suits and a working thruster. Let's leave now."

"And desert these people?" Sheeba's eyebrows furrowed. "You don't mean that. Besides, the minute you step outside, the gunship will start firing. See what they did to beau."

I clenched my teeth and struggled to hold steady. She kept calling that thug by my name.

Sheeba leaned and rested her chin on my shoulder. "You want to protect me too much, Nass. I'm a grown woman. You have to let me run my own risks." Then her voice dropped to a whisper. "Liam told me something heinous about Provendia.Com."

From her tone, I knew what was coming. "Sheeba, that punk has hidden motives. You can't believe everything he says."

"They issued a euthanasia order," she whispered. "They plan to euth' everyone here."

"Ah." I pursed my lips.

"Yeah, one of the kids found their vicious memo in the trash. They're *beasts*. I *hate* them."

"I thought these protes couldn't read," I said, stalling.

"Euthanasia, Nass." Her eyes glittered darkly.

In the boardroom, drinking brandy with my colleagues, the decision had seemed easy to justify. But now and here? Too much Reel was clouding my judgment. Nothing seemed easy anymore. "Maybe they wanted to prevent an epidemic."

"It's grievous. I can't believe it's legal."

"Well, it's one more reason why we need to get away." I took her hands. "The Agonists are waiting outside. I saw them."

"Nass, you're dreaming. C'mon, lift beau's feet and help me."

"His freaking name is not freaking beau!"

Blood rushed to my head, and I stomped away. Out of sight around the curving corridor, I leaned against the wall to calm down. Sometimes, talking to Shee was like trying to breathe vacuum.

I rubbed my jaw, felt the loose, sagging skin and stretched my neck to take up the slack. And I pondered. My space suit and thruster lay right there within reach. The cylinders were low on air. Probably the batteries could stand a recharge. Those were mere details. The phone in my helmet was still roaming, searching for the Net. All I had to do was dive outside the communications blockade and place a call.

Sheeba's arms circled my waist from behind, and she pressed her body against my back. I could feel the swell of her hard little belly. "Please, Nass. I didn't mean to hurt your feelings. You know I love you."

"You do?" Anger instantly drained from my limbs, leaving me slack and unsteady. When I turned to face her, my nose came level with her soft curving throat. She smelled of rich sweat.

"Of course, Nass. You've been like a father to me. I wouldn't even be here if not for you."

"Shee." I drew her close and buried my face against her collarbone so she couldn't see the puckers around my eyes. Like a father, she said. My lips crushed against her throat.

Gently, she loosened my grip. "Help me, okay? I can't lift him by myself. I need you."

"Okay," I said, turning my ravaged face from the light. But my brain was not engaged. Like a father. I wrapped the words in cottony silence.

Vacantly, I helped her lift the juve off the floor. Like a father. Sheeba spoke in little gasps as we hauled her thug up the ladder well. She told me how they had disguised their voices on the gunship to impersonate Provendia guards and how they nearly got caught when they lingered too long in someone's office browsing the Net. Beau had never seen the Net. She said Beau really liked it.

Like a father. I listened and moved and smiled at the right places. My brain drifted off to some distant exile where it couldn't bother me. Father, a pair of syllables. In Three's light gravity, we made fast progress, and by the time we got to Four, the chief of thugs weighed considerably less. We guided him into sick-ward and stretched him out on the mattress next to Kai-Kai. But I was nobody's father.

Geraldine still sat in her lotus position, lightly snoring, but she snorted awake when Sheeba ripped a sheet to bind Liam's ribs. The wench looked at her unconscious chief, then at Sheeba. Her eyes drooped with sleep. "Vlad?"

Sheeba shook her head. "We didn't find him."

Geraldine's chocolate cheeks bunched in furious knots. Then just as quickly, her muscles relaxed, and all energy seemed to ebb out of her face. She rocked on her haunches. Back and forth, back and forth, like clockwork. Her wife Kai-Kai remained deeply quiet, though a slight movement of her upper lip showed she was still breathing. Sheeba felt for her pulse.

Then Geraldine rested a hand on Liam's unconscious thigh. "Now there be two for the garden."

"No one's going into the garden." Sheeba ripped the sheet with her teeth. "Do you hear me? Kai-Kai and the chief are both going to recover." She spoke with force, but there was no pretense of a smile.

"Where's Juani?" I said.

Geraldine pointed at the ceiling. She meant Deck Five. She seemed enervated. Maybe it was the stuffy sick-ward air that robbed her of motive force. Sheeba shook my ankle to get my attention.

"Nasir, go check on Juani, okay? I'm worried about him."

"Okay," I said. Like a father, her words echoed. You've been like a father to me.

"He's probably tending his garden," Shee said.

"Okay," I said again. This time I moved.

Heavy blooms of fungus filled the well segment leading to Five. I had to brush them off the ladder to find a grip. Just because I had hired Shee to massage my aching joints, that didn't make me an old man. A father? The fungus felt stiff and rubbery. I held my flashlight between my teeth and ripped it loose by the handful. I was strong, passionate, open to new ideas.

Savagely, I ripped and tore, and the fibers cut my palms. Shee knew my age. I hadn't concealed it. But had anyone ever caught me drooling in my soup or taking afternoon naps? No. At the safety hatch leading to Five, I scraped the lever free with my split fingernails. My body did not feel old. My muscles rippled with steroid vigor. My sexual organ performed faithfully. Damp crumbs of fungus rained down and got in my eyes.

Fungus grew so thick inside the airlock leading to Five that I had to scoop some out before I could climb in. The spores smelled of musk and sweet burnt caffeine. Father? I was nobody's father. Slowly I hollowed out a cavity inside the lock. How long since Juani cycled through here? What kind of fungus could regenerate that fast?

I squeezed into the lock, inhaling the stuff through my teeth. Father, ha. Sheeba was deliberately mocking me. She'd fallen under the spell of that agitator, that's what. He'd corrupted her. She was no longer the dear golden goddess I used to know. Father indeed.

When the upper hatch slid open, I leaped upward into the vast echoing chamber of Deck Five, where the cen-

trifugal gravity was barely strong enough to settle me back
to the floor. Deck Five held the food vats. This was the factory proper.

Picture if you will an enormous open cylinder crammed
with an array of gleaming spherical vats, sheathed in white
insulation and linked by interconnecting pipes. No ladder
well pierces the core. No walls partition off wedge-shaped
rooms. The factory lies open from end to end, and the ster-
ile array of vats suggests a child's Tinkertoy model of a
molecule. Pristine ranks and files of white spheres reflect
against the cylinder's polished steel walls like clouds. The
food vats fill Deck Five to capacity. Do you see the gentle
steam wafting through their vents? Do you hear the soft
gurgle of fermentation? This is the Provendia food factory
you will browse in the corporate video. This is not what
awaited me in Heaven.

Oh, the vats were there, barely visible between dense
green layers of foliage. I'd arrived in a jungle. Leaves the
size of rooms, vines thicker than my body, swelling red
pulpy seedpods—I couldn't keep track of the colors and
shapes of the fruits. Exotic varieties that must have been
genetically modified to grow in fractional gravity. Melons,
squash, coconuts, avocados, ears of corn, luscious bunches
of grapes. Also flowers, exquisite blossoms saturated with
color, finer than any hothouse orchid I'd ever seen on
Earth. And running through it all like a bass note were the
fibrous black filigrees of fungus. Around the nearest spherical vat, they branched like veins. And tumbling, swinging,
soaring among the vines in every direction were juveniles.

Toddlers. Teenagers. Kids of all ages. Three boys of
about Juani's size were picking fruit and rough-housing.
An older girl cradled an infant against her breast and
scolded the fruit pickers to get on with their work. A loose
line of adolescents handed the full fruit baskets along to a
young woman, who heaped them in a dangling hoist. Their
pale bodies ranged in hue from ash white to deep caramel.
A few were as dusky as Geraldine. As the youngest ones
romped in the fractional gravity, their hair streamed in

every shade of gold, copper and jet. It was impossible to count the little demons because of the way they frolicked through the leaves.

Lensed portholes like the one in the solar plant perforated the cylinder's Up side, and sunlight slanted through in pearly parallel rays. A tapestry of mirrors swiveled the rays through the garden, illuminating fruit, faces, vines and legs, backlighting the foliage in brilliant luminous green.

One vigorous bound took me up into the canopy, where a flock of inquisitive kids leaped among the branches and converged around me, shrilling their tinny voices. Then hundreds of misters clicked on and drenched the jungle in a downpour. Rainbows shot through the leaves in vaporous hues that wavered and disappeared when the misters shut off. For an instant, droplets wobbled through the air in the surreal slow motion of reduced gravity. Then the water dripped like ringing bells, and raindrops wobbled in slow-motion off my old gray space suit. When the kids started chattering again, I leaped higher.

And here were clouds of gray-green moss, feather pillows of fern, massive knotted tree trunks wreathed in vines. Everything grew larger in the weak gravity. Overhead waved a tall swath of seeded grasses, and higher still, bean pods. Children raced and fought and squealed. They threw fruit at each other, screaming insults. They made me laugh.

And the aromas. Fruity sweet dark stinging bitter. Fanning through the air like music. Flute notes and deep sonorous drums. Every cell in my olfactory brain trembled to these perfume vibrations, brighter even than child song.

But how were these plants rooted? Did they spring to life in midair? I followed a tree trunk down to its source and found it fixed inside one of the spherical food vats. Its growth had pushed the vented hood askew. Other plants large and small sprouted from the tank as well, vying with the tree for space, and someone had wrapped layers of duct tape around and through the stems as if to tie them into the vat so they wouldn't fall out. I tore away some tape and squeezed my arm down among the roots. Warm liquid washed over my hand, and a few globules rose sluggishly into the air, then splashed in a slow dance among the leaves. The liquid had the same smell as Juani's veggie trays. Liquid nutrient. The Heavenians had "rehabbed" our food factory as a vast hydroponic rain forest.

"Blade, you some kinda tree frog."

Juani's eyelids were still puffy, but his tears had dried, and he'd rewoven his braid with colored wire. He swung hand over hand along a potato vine and landed in a crouch on the tank beside me. "This our garden. You ever see a sight like this on Earth?"

"No," I answered. "Not even close."

He picked up a little toad who'd just landed on the tank beside him, the girl with the red birthmark on her cheek. "Keesha girl," he said fondly. Then he unwound a wire bracelet from his wrist and began braiding her hair into pigtails. "Everybody love the garden. Mostly, we keep the people down on One. Chief say gravitation help their bones. But they sneak up here anyway."

"We play hide," the girl said happily.

"It's amazing," I said breathlessly.

Juani finished arranging Keesha's hair. Then he let her run off to play, and he climbed along a thick branch, motioning for me to follow. The branch dipped slightly with our weight, and its leafy end rested against a food vat crusted with green algae. Juani pulled the leaves aside and scrubbed at the algae with his fist. Soon a pattern emerged underneath. A picture was scraped into the vat's white insulation. A portrait.

Wild, tangled hair framed the old man's face. His beard forked like tree roots. Heavy lines crisscrossed his cheeks, and spots mottled his large nose. The artwork was primitive, but there was no mistaking the zeal in the man's startling, green-stained eyes.

Juani slapped the side of the vat. "This Dr. Bashevitz. He here."

"In spirit, you mean."

Juani gave me an enigmatic grin. "This the last garden. 'Xecs burned all the rest. They don't like veggies growing in the G Ring. They say our garden pose a health risk." He leaned across me and snapped off a prickly, brown pod from one of the plants, slit it open with his thumb and showed me the inside. Its inner husk gleamed like new satin, and at the center, nestling in a wisp of downy silk, were dozens of round black seeds. Juani plucked out the seeds and rolled them between his palms.

"This our future, blade. This what we gotta save."

21

JUSTMENT

"Experience is simply the name we give our mistakes."
—OSCAR WILDE

Juani and I returned to sick-ward and found Sheeba pumping Kaioko's chest with both hands. The girl's heart had stopped. Sweat gleamed on Sheeba's forehead as she performed the CPR, counting under her breath, one-two-three-four-five. Near the foot of the mattress, Geraldine sat in a trance, quietly slicing the back of her arm with a small knife. Tiny bracelets of red beads brightened in the wake of her blade.

"Nass, help me," Sheeba commanded. "When I tell you, blow two hard breaths in her mouth."

"Right."

I forgot all about hiding my puckered face. I knelt by the mattress and drew Kaioko's chin up to clear her airway. On Sheeba's signal, I puffed into her diminutive mouth and watched her narrow chest rise. War surfers train regularly in cardiopulmonary resuscitation. It's part of our safety drill. I had never kept it up two hours straight though, which is what we had to do to revive Kaioko.

Sheeba and I traded places every twenty minutes to ease our cramping muscles. Juani didn't know how to give CPR, but he blotted sweat from our faces with a rag. He didn't bother trying to rouse Geraldine. She looked scary, slumped in her lotus pose, slicing her arm.

I kept two fingers pressed against Kaioko's carotid artery, hoping for some sign. Tears of fatigue leaked from

Sheeba's eyes as she thrust downward, stiff-armed, against the girl's sternum, again and again and again. "Wish I had a cardio-stim," she muttered like a prayer.

At last, Kaioko's artery jumped. A tiny twitch. Then another. "She has a pulse," I said.

Sheeba crouched and pressed an ear to Kaioko's chest. "Yeah."

When her breaths came steadily, we collapsed on the vacant mattresses. We were completely done in. Naturally, the chief slept through it all.

"I think Liam has a concussion." Flat on her back, Sheeba spoke to the ceiling. Her voice sounded groggy and distant. "The gunfire knocked him against the hull."

I was all set to curl on my mattress and snooze, but Sheeba sat up and fished through the medical tray till she found an unused needle. With the swift efficiency of surfer adrenaline, she prepared the girl's vein and drew out a blood sample. Then, holding the crimson vial in her fist, she hurried to the anteroom.

I staggered after her, fighting fatigue. "Sheeba?"

Among the litter of parts from the eviscerated cyber-doc, she found a nanoscope. Then she swept everything else off the counter with her arm. Next she placed one bright red drop in the 'scope, wiped her hands on the front of her uniform and stooped to peer through the eyepiece.

"I see a few NEMs. Not many."

Exhaustion seamed her face, and sweat matted her short hair. Her skin was greasy from lack of bathing, and her fabulous water-colored eyes drooped at the corners. I wanted to take her in my arms forever.

"Nass, will you give more blood for Kaioko?"

I flinched.

"You did it before," she said, coaxing.

"For you, Shee." I leaned against the counter and watched her fluttering eyelids. Maybe Sheeba didn't realize what she was asking. Execs her age had dewy ideas. Maybe sharing blood with a worker didn't repulse her as it did me.

Sharing health? But when had that act changed to wickedness? And who decided those things? There was a time when I would have laughed at such a rule. Did morals come and go like fashion trends? Kaioko's blood smeared anemically under the nanoscope. And I doubted. Over how many decades had my attitudes hardened and crusted over?

Abruptly, Sheeba's eyes lost focus, and when she swayed, I caught her. The adrenaline charge wasn't powerful enough to keep her going. She needed food and water and rest.

"Juani!" I yelled. "Those provisions we hauled up here, where are they?"

The boy stuck his head through the sick-ward door. "In the 'pactor room."

I didn't ask what the 'pactor room was. "Get me some. Get enough for everyone."

Sheeba didn't want to eat. She refused water, too, pleading with me to donate more blood for Kaioko. What could I do? My darling was ready to faint from thirst. And like she said, I'd already subverted the moral code once. My depravity was a fait accompli.

"Okay, take another liter."

Sheeba smiled.

After drawing my vital fluid, she sat on the floor between her two patients, Liam and Kaioko, alternately checking their pulses and feeding herself spoonfuls of cold protein stew. Meanwhile, I rested on another mattress, feeling strangely lighter.

My illicit ruby sack hung from a peg on the wall and drained much too slowly into the girl's vein through a makeshift rig of plastic tubing and clips. Sheeba didn't complain about the light gravity or the primitive conditions of this sick-ward, but the deficiencies must have frustrated her. This clinic didn't have basic heart monitors, much less medical amenities like cardio-stims. A dismal place to get sick.

Geraldine ignored her bowl of stew, but Juani and I gulped the food in big mouthfuls, and I emptied three water sacks. This second bloodletting also made me woozier and thirstier than the first. I couldn't seem to get enough to drink, and forming complete thoughts proved a challenge. Let's see, if my body held five liters, and Sheeba took two, what percentage was that? It sounded like a lot.

When no one was looking, I peeked at my thumbscreen and clicked a few menus. Good news, my IBiS showed a steady production of new red and white cells to replace the lost ones. New plasma, too. My NEMs were working overtime to restore my vital sap. Thank the gilty gods, they hadn't bothered to wait for doctors' orders. I grabbed a water sack for another swallow, and as I leaned back to tip it into my mouth, zillions of pin-sized black spots obliterated my view of the ceiling.

"Man, you look pale," Juani said.

Sheeba held my head and made me lean forward till my nose practically touched the scummy floor. "Take deep breaths," she said. As if I wanted to snuffle up that fungus, ha. Then she made me lie flat on my back and put my feet up on a pillow while she patted my forehead with a cool damp cloth. Molto comforting. I nuzzled against her hand. If only my face hadn't developed those annoying little grooves and puckers, it would have been celestial.

But her attentions were cut short. The thug chief chose that instant to rise from the dead. He sat up groaning and wincing, making a production out of the minor bruises on his ribs. Sheeba abandoned me and rushed to his side. She wanted him to lie down again, but he refused. Too much to do. Everything depended. Blah blah blah. What an infernal superman. Sheeba mentioned that I had saved his life— again. When he noticed me lying on my mat, he lifted my arm, and—I figured I was hallucinating—he gave me the prote handshake.

"Gee was wrong about you, Nasir. You a good man."

Next, an odd thing happened. He was going through the pockets of his (my) EVA suit, looking for his flashlight, when his pulled out a small shiny bit of gilded metal. It was the good luck ankh Sheeba had hidden there for me, eons ago, when we first began this blighted war surf. As he turned it over curiously, the polished Egyptian cross reflected sick-ward's light like a mirror.

Sheeba noticed what he'd found and took it. "Silly junk." She threw it against the wall.

Liam seemed as surprised as I was. "Sheeba, what is that thing?"

She shook her head. "Just a gold-plated trinket. It reminds me how stupid I used to be."

"But it's the symbol of the life force," I said. "You gave it to me as a gift. You told me it had rejuvenating power."

"Nass, that was make-believe." Her mouth set in a hard line as she adjusted one of the clips on Kaioko's transfusion tube. "I'm done with fairy tales." Poor exhausted child.

She fed her punk stew with my spoon and gave him the rest of my water. As soon as he could stand without wobbling, he gripped my arm with manly affection—presumptuous cur. Then he whispered quiet instructions to Juani, and he set off again to go EVA and play Heaven's dogged guardian.

Sheeba followed. What did she mean, deserting her sick patients? Why, look at poor Kaioko ringing death's doorbell. And me. I felt nauseous. In fact, a moment later, I turned on my side and threw up. About a liter of bright red Chili Diablo oozed across the floor like molten lava.

"Bless a Jeez." Juani made a face and went to get a mop.

Wiping my mouth, I happened to glance at Geraldine, who was staring straight at me. No longer blank, her dark eyes shimmered with malice, and she clenched her teeth in a mega-unfriendly way. Another mood swing. I was just trying to decide if I should call for help when she sprang across the room and grabbed my throat.

Freaking hell, not again. In Four's light gravity, she literally lifted me off the mattress by my neck. I clutched at her hands and tried to get my feet underneath me, sputtering through my constricted larynx. Geraldine's muscles knotted, and her handsome, scarred face quivered with the effort of strangling me.

I started going faint. Ye gilders, I would not let this hysterical juve choke me to death. No way would Nasir Deepra meet his end at the hands of a teenager. Especially not in a vomit-stained longjohn. I went at her face with my fingernails.

Then she punched my head so hard, I lost balance and fell against the wall.

"I know who you are," she growled, touching the scratches I'd made on her cheek. "Chief won't believe me, but I know."

Her blow rang my artificial eardrums, and the noise blared like an unholy siren. Louder it grew. As shrill as the sonic lathe.

Then Juani ran in, threw down his mop and grabbed Geraldine by the shoulders. "Gee, the alarm. The alarm going off. We gotta get ready."

Geraldine stood gawking like an idiot while I cringed and tried to look harmless. Juani shook her again and repeated his announcement about the alarm. The siren was not in my head after all. What I heard was the blare of a major warning signal.

"What is it, Juani?"

"Justment," he said, still gripping Geraldine.

At the mention of that unusual word, she seemed to come to herself. She slapped Juani's hands away and said, "Help me strap Kaioko."

To my utter bafflement, they started lashing Kaioko into her mattress with thick straps of canvas. All the mattresses had these straps, but Kaioko's had been unhooked and thrown to the side. Now Juani and Geraldine cinched the straps tight around her chest, legs and forehead. The girl lay as deeply submerged in her coma as ever. Why did they suddenly feel the need to restrain her?

Next, Juani gathered up all the loose items in the room. Empty blood sacks, plastic tubing, chili bowls.

Geraldine motioned him toward the anteroom. "We gotta stow Vlad's mess. Come on."

Juani pointed to me. "What about him? Strap him in?"

Geraldine's nostrils flared as if she were sniffing something vile. "Let him bounce in his puke." Then she marched away.

Juani opened a wall bin and tossed all the loose items inside. He offered me the mop. "Hurry, go clean up your mess before Justment."

I frowned at the pool of vomit. Was he kidding? I was almost too dizzy to stand. Juani shrugged, laid the mop at my side and went into the anteroom to help Geraldine. I heard the two of them banging cabinet doors. It sounded as if they were packing up the dismantled cyberdoc in a sudden mania of spring cleaning.

My vomit smelled vile. With a sigh, I stripped the sheet off my mattress and, on hands and knees, I wiped the floor clean. Then I searched for the little ankh Sheeba had thrown away. Carefully, I polished the gold-plated charm with my fingers and zipped it inside the breast pocket of my longjohn.

"We going up to the garden, blade. Best place to be during Justment." Juani took my arm and helped me stand.

Geraldine blocked the door, fingering the hammer in her pocket. "You go, Juani. Look after the people. I take care of the houseguest."

"What you gonna do?" Juani's hesitant tone frightened me almost as much as the wench's hammer.

"Be calm. I taking loverboy to help me lock down the power plant." She nodded at the rising sound of the alarm. "We go hurry. Justment coming."

Juani nodded. Without another word, he raced for the ladder well, leaving me alone with the angel of spite.

"There's no need for violence," I said.

Geraldine ignored me. She knelt at Kaioko's bedside, kissed the sleeping girl's lips, then tightened the straps more securely. After another quiet kiss, she got up and motioned me to follow.

"Where's Sheeba? I want to be with Sheeba."

Geraldine spoke without turning. "Doll-face below."

She barely looked at me as we cycled down through the ladders and locks to Deck Two. She merely fondled the hammer in her pocket. The shallow cuts on her arm had turned dark red. I didn't dare ask her what "Justment" meant. The way Juani talked, it sounded like Armageddon. As we climbed down the ladder, I felt nauseous, and the warning siren hurt my head.

In the solar plant, we found Liam and Sheeba lashing down a pile of machine parts under a cargo net. Curiouser and curiouser.

"What's going on?" I shielded my face so Sheeba couldn't see my wrinkles.

"Justment," Liam said. "Gotta go lock everything down."

Sheeba glanced up from the magnetic bolt she was anchoring to the deck. "He means adjustment. It's nearly time for the orbit correction."

"Adjustment?" My brain still wasn't functioning clearly.

"Remember, we saw the last one from Kat's shuttle nine days ago. They send a signal from Earth."

Heaven quakes. I remembered. The guidance rockets on the satellite and its counterweight fired out of time with each other. We hadn't approved the funds to replace a burnt-out synchronizer, so every orbital adjustment shook Heaven like a whiplash. All too vividly, I remembered Juani tapping the X wall. "He old. He tremble."

"This tank will break apart!" I yelled.

Geraldine punched my shoulder. "There," she said, pointing toward ops bay. "We go get ready for Justment."

She shoved me through the door before I could react. I was still weak from the bloodletting, and Sheeba and Liam were too fully occupied securing loose items in the solar plant to notice what Geraldine was doing. As soon as we'd passed into the ops bay, she closed the door behind us and twisted the wheel to locked position. In bewilderment, I watched her wedge her hammer so no one could turn the wheel from the other side.

The desks and office supplies still lay overturned and jumbled across the floor, and nothing was tied down. I didn't see any way to secure so many loose objects. Was this how the wench meant to kill me—death by office furniture?

"Geraldine, let's talk this out."

She shoved me aside and started rummaging through a pile of phone rechargers.

"Honestly, we're sure to find some common ground if we try." I edged around her toward the door.

"Stay where you are." She hurled a fax printer against the wall and kept digging.

"You're angry. I can see that. You're going through a tough time."

Abruptly, the siren intensified to a ululating scream. The adjustment. Those heavy steel desks would rocket around the room like meteors. When I slid another centimeter toward the door, Geraldine flung an ashtray straight at my head, and the damned thing clipped my chin. Then she went back to mining the loose pile of office supplies.

"Sheeba, help!" I shouted, pounding on the locked door.

Geraldine seized something buried under a jumble of optic cable, and while she wasn't looking, I jerked her hammer free from the wheel and leaned all my weight to release the lock.

"Gee." Liam's baritone voice thundered through the door. "Come out, Gee."

He must have finally recognized the wench's intentions—murder and suicide in one.

"This," Geraldine announced triumphantly. "This what I looking for."

She waved a small opalescent cube in the air. It looked like a holographic sales brochure. So what? A piece of marketing literature. When the door fell open, Liam grabbed my forearm and yanked me through to safety. Sheeba was waiting to enfold me and soothe my nerves.

Then Liam went for Geraldine. We watched through the open door.

"Stay back, chief. I going to the garden," she warned, holding up the little cube.

Liam grabbed her waist and lifted her like a sack. She twisted and shrieked, but he carried her out of ops bay and set her on the solar plant floor. Then Sheeba slammed the ops bay door and locked it.

"Shit, Gee." Liam wiped sweat from his forehead. "You crazy?"

"Yeah, crazy." She handed him the sales brochure, then pointed at me. "He the one, chief. I told you."

Liam looked at the cube's blank facets and shrugged. "What does it mean?"

Sheeba crouched over his shoulder. "This is an advertising brochure." She touched the tiny button inset near one corner.

That button set off an avalanche. The room went wild. Walls flew against me, and I couldn't tell which side smashed my head first. The solar beam painted jagged shapes through the air like a dancing laser.

"Nass, the adjustment has started." Sheeba caught my forearm and drew me against her. "Hold this."

As the walls bucked back and forth, she closed my fingers around one of the cables anchored to the floor with magnets. We bunched together, all four of us, clinging to the cable as our bodies flipped first one way, then the other, while the room seesawed.

In the ops bay, large objects crashed. I could hear their noise through the walls. A trail of saliva or maybe vomit laced across my cheek, but I couldn't let go of the cable to wipe it. I felt like a rag that someone was shaking to get the dust out.

Gradually, the oscillations diminished, and I lolled against Sheeba for comfort. Everyone was breathing heavily.

"Hold tight. Next wave coming." Liam reached across

Sheeba to squeeze my shoulder, an act of silent reassurance. No doubt, he saw I needed it.

As the deck started rocking back and forth again, I wrapped my arms around the cable. Long ages ago, I had lounged in Kat's cozy shuttle with a drink in my hand and watched this phenomenon from a distance, idly speculating how it would feel.

Kaioko, strapped to her heaving mattress, was mercifully asleep. And Juani in his garden. What would that be like? I envisioned toads bouncing among the leafy steel food vats. And it struck me that if the newscasters ever learned about this, the scandal would lead the top of every hour for days. I made a mental note to release funds for that burnt-out synchronizer ASAP. But ASAP might not be soon enough. The walls were flying again.

The cable abraded my sweating hands. One quake followed another, with only the briefest of intermissions. At some point I lost my grip and ping-ponged among the turbines. Up and down became meaningless. The solar beam spun, and I grappled to catch hold of any surface, but the steam pipes scalded my palms, and the cargo net was full of sharp, bouncing machine parts. I let go and whirled away with bleeding knuckles. Liam grabbed my belt and drew me back to the cable.

Eventually the lulls grew longer than the quakes. I settled to the deck, caught my breath and tried to inventory my bruises. The veins on the backs of my hands stood out like knotted strings. Had my face aged that much, too? Geraldine started blubbering. That's all we needed.

"Nasir?"

I twisted around to face Sheeba, and what a look she gave me. Her water-colored eyes flashed like two northern lakes reeling in storm.

I tried to cover my wrinkles with my ugly hands. How hideous I must have looked. But no, she wasn't looking at my complexion. She was holding that sales brochure. Its active holograms danced around the cube like tiny marbling rainbows. The brochure absorbed her attention.

She didn't have time to say anything more. Another oscillation sent us flying, and Heaven's ailing tank careened from side to side. By a miracle, the hull stayed in one piece. I didn't let go of the cable this time because, even if it sliced my palms to the bone, it was still safer than bouncing against a hot steam pipe.

Behind the ops bay door, furniture bashed the walls. I visualized desks rifling through the air and shards of broken plastic flying like daggers. How on Earth did the aging hull survive such punishment? Even after the quakes began to dwindle, I couldn't stop shaking.

"First seven waves the worst," said Liam. "The rest not so bad." He let go of the cable and took the weeping Geraldine in his arms.

"Nasir," Sheeba said again. "This is a Provendia brochure."

She was still holding the little cube, staring into the depths of its holograms. I couldn't see them well from the side. They were designed for straight-on viewing. I said, "That makes sense, dear. This is a Provendia factory."

"But Nasir, look at this photograph of the chairman emeritus." She held the little brochure in her hand like a fission grenade. "Nasir, it's you."

22

FIX MY PAIN

"There is no one, no matter how wise he is, who has
not in his youth said things or done things that are so
unpleasant to recall in later life that he would expunge
them entirely from his memory if that were possible."
—MARCEL PROUST

" **D** id you sign the euthanasia order?"
    Shee's eyes blazed at me, and her lips trembled.
She was waiting to hear a reasonable explanation. Her dear
friend, Nasir Deepra, the man with the multiplex soul,
would not exterminate innocent people. She wanted me to
say the man in the photo was my rogue twin brother, my
runaway clone, my look-alike third cousin.

Believe me, I thought about saying those things. When I
hesitated, her lovely burnished cheeks went pale. I should
have lied. Instantly, glibly, I should have told her what she
wanted to hear. Despite the photo caption listing my name,
she would have believed me. But I didn't say anything.

Then her eyes changed. She handed the cube to Liam,
who took it with a bewildered frown and tilted it sideways.

Sheeba, please berate me. Scream. Punch me in the jaw.
Do anything. Only, don't look at me that way. Words
wedged in my throat, and shame burned my face. Maybe
Shee saw the wrinkles puckering around my eyes. Maybe
not. What her eyes reflected was a rotting, 248-year-old ca-
daver, clinging so tight to a fistful of wealth that he would
murder children. After a moment, she exhaled a broken

sigh. If she had broken my spine in two pieces, it would have hurt less. With that quiet breath, she annihilated me.

"Chairman Emeritus," Liam read aloud, "Nasir V. Deepra."

Another quake convulsed us, less extreme than the earlier ones. We gripped the cable in reflex until the oscillations ended. Then Geraldine edged away while Liam turned the little cube in his fingers, comparing its iridescent projections to my living face.

Geraldine growled, "You believe me now."

Her tears had long since dried. In a dead voice, she explained how she found the cube in the trash and gave it to Kaioko as a play-pretty. Her green eyes narrowed in my direction, and she laid her hammer across her knee. It was Kai-Kai who discovered how to make the pictures come out.

Quietly, Sheeba hissed, "Stop the euth' order, Nass." Then she pinched a pressure point on my wrist that drove hot daggers of pain up my arm.

Her violence shocked me. It left me speechless.

"He the one," Geraldine snarled low in her throat, pointing at me with her hammer. "He say the people have to die."

Another aftershock jolted us sideways, but no one reached for the cable this time. I could have made logical arguments, but what was the point? These youngsters wouldn't appreciate the gravity of a financial panic. Sheeba's fingers encircled my wrist, threatening another attack. Sheeba? My darling didn't give pain, she took it away.

"Can I push him outta the airlock?" Geraldine said.

Sheeba released me and closed her eyes. Her expression almost made me want to take Geraldine's offer.

"Forgive me, Sheeba."

She jerked away as if I carried a contagion worse than Heaven's malady. Her multicolored eyes flared like suns, and through clenched teeth, she said, "Call that ship, and make them stop."

I didn't know she was capable of turning on me with such fury. "My phone doesn't work," I said weakly. But it was the truth. If I could have called the board and rescinded that order, I would have. For Sheeba, yes, at that moment, I would have done it.

Geraldine sprang to her feet. "He want euth'? I show him euth'. Let me take him, chief."

Liam worried his beard and took his own time reasoning out a reply. "Nasir, you save my life twice. You give Kaioko your blood." He frowned at my photograph shimmering in the cube. "Why you come here?"

His question made my lips twitch. A lifetime ago, we planned this surf, the Agonists and I. Grimly, I recalled our motives. His question demanded an answer I couldn't give.

"We were playing a silly game," Sheeba said.

"Darling, no." I gestured for her to keep silent, but she wouldn't.

"The bullshit ends here, Nass." Angry spots darkened her olive cheeks. She threw her head back and gazed at the ceiling as if searching for explanations. "I lied, too. I've been so—so dumb. All this time. I pretended that we came seeking endarkment, but that was just crap I downloaded off the Net. It didn't mean a thing."

"Dearest, you truly believed—"

"Let me talk. It's my turn." She scooted across the deck till her back pressed against the wall. "I came here for recreation, like you, Nass. I wanted a quick spiritual high. Metaphysical head candy. I'm a murderer, as much as you are."

Liam looked from Sheeba to me, and his blue irises glinted. "You both smarter than me. You trick me very completely."

"Don't believe her." I gripped handfuls of air. "You know what she's like. She's innocent."

"Chief, I take care of this commie." Geraldine tapped my shoulder with her hammer, and I winced.

Liam nodded. "Lock him on One for now."

"Let him live? After what he done?" The wench stamped her foot.

"I said for now," the chief answered.

Geraldine spun and smashed her hammer into my elbow. Then she kicked me toward the door. "Move, 'xec."

"Yaah!" I sprawled across the floor, clutching my elbow. "Sheeba, forgive me. Please, I beg you. I'm so sorry."

But the time for forgiveness was past. Sheeba wouldn't look at me. She huddled against the wall with an expression of utter misery. Another temblor convulsed Heaven, the weakest yet. When it ended, I dodged around Geraldine and tried to embrace Shee from behind. But the evil wench punched me in the kidneys, and when I fell, she kicked my ribs. I clutched at Sheeba's legs and pressed my lips to her feet. "I love you."

"Get off me." Sheeba tore free and sprang beyond my reach. Her face, ye gods, how it twisted.

When Liam touched the nape of her neck, she flinched away from him, too. She would have fought him, but he forced her arms down and held her. Spasms shook her body. At last, she stopped resisting and buried her face against his filthy shirt.

I said, "How much to let her go? I have money."

He hit me high on the cheekbone. Geraldine's punches had been mean, but Liam's blow carried the vengeance of Heaven. It was savage, inordinate, without reserve. My false eye lost its signal. A bone snapped in my cheek, and when my dental implants fell loose against the back of my throat, I nearly gagged. It would have been a relief to lose consciousness, but that mercy wasn't granted. Geraldine dragged me into the corridor.

"Kai-Kai waiting to die. You like that?" She poked and jabbed me all the way to the ladder well. With only one eye, my depth perception was gone. She smashed my face against the safety hatch, then shoved me into the lock and stepped on my back as she climbed in beside me. "You wanna call your guards to euth' her? It be easy now. She strapped to a mattress."

Yes, Kaioko was suffering alone in sick-ward because of me. And Sheeba would die here, too. I'd lost her. My achievements, titles, wealth and possessions shriveled to ashes. What had it gained me to store up trillions of deutschdollars? Nothing I could buy would ever restore the broken pieces of Sheeba's faith.

Geraldine bounced on top of me in the safety lock. "You never ask how Kai-Kai lost her pretty hair." When she pushed me through the lower hatch, I missed the ladder and fell to the floor below. "She got splashed with hot soup during Justment."

The wench dropped down beside me and landed random kicks on my torso. I imagined Kaioko's blistered head.

"Why you couldn't fix the rockets, huh?" Geraldine yanked me to my feet and thrust me through the bulkhead door. "Why we have to shake so much?"

My mouth filled with bile, and I choked it down. That euthanasia order wasn't the first one I'd signed. And this wasn't the first war my policies had launched. Twelve billion people on Earth were too many. Someone had to make tough decisions.

"Move it." Geraldine threw me into the same wedge-shaped cell whose E, W, and A's I had memorized ad nauseum during the first hours of my incarceration. Then she spat on the deck and slammed the door. Is it necessary to add that she turned off the light?

• • •

"By dark, you mean death, Sheeba!"

I'd shouted those words a year ago. We'd been sharing one of our late-night movie fests, lounging in a mountain of pillows.

Sheeba grinned and squeezed my thigh. "Nass, you're leaping to conclusions."

"I know what you're thinking, that I've lived too long." Her stray remark about one of the actors had flipped my jealousy switch. I felt petulant. "You think I don't deserve longevity."

"Poor beau." She caressed my head against her chest and gently rocked me like a baby. "You get so defensive. Why would I think that?"

"Because I'm useless. I don't contribute anymore. All I do is consume and have fun." I nuzzled against her and inhaled her herbal scent, needing her to contradict me.

"But you serve on those boards," she said.

"Ha, we just rubber-stamp memos. No one really needs me." I prayed she would disagree.

"Didn't you have a child once?"

She threw me off track. That wasn't the argument I expected. "You mean the sperm I left on deposit? I don't know if EuroBank ever used it."

"You didn't ask?"

"They pay my interest on time. It's not my concern how they manage the assets."

Sheeba's velvet eyebrows pleated in three edgy creases. Was that the only lame reason she could think of why someone might need me—a damned offspring? Her question fanned my flaming insecurity. When she sighed and restarted the movie, I jerked away.

"You don't think I have any saving graces."

"What do you need saving from, Nass?"

• • •

What, indeed? In the dark cell, I listened to Geraldine's bare feet slap away down the corridor. My dental implants no longer fit in my battered face, so I took them out and pressed my ear against the steel to hear the sluicing and whuffing. Deck One sounded hollow. All the toads had been evacuated up to Five, and I missed their shrill voices humming through the walls. They were in the garden now, climbing through the trees, chasing rainbows. Did they know the word, "euthanasia"?

"Deepra, you sap. You're weak," I said aloud, twisting the blanket till it shredded in my hands.

Curse the bloody Reel. My action had condemned

everyone here. Even with a working phone, I couldn't reverse the euthanasia order. The board had already voted, and things had gone too far.

"Stupid, stupid, stupid." I butted my forehead against the wall. "Sheeba, forgive me."

My left thumb began throbbing too painfully to ignore, so in a kind of stupor, I checked my IBiS. Its faint glow flared in the dark like a match head. The IBiS was suffering some kind of major system overload. Way too many missed appointments. Whole categories of NEMs were going on standby till they received fresh instructions through the Net. Among others, my liver NEMs were going off-line.

But more bizarrely, NEMs that had shut down earlier were spontaneously reactivating. And not just my dental NEMs. The little sodders in my thyroid had started generating new T-cells—without doctors' orders! That was unprecedented. Against all odds, the NEMs seemed bent on their healing mission. Yet their anomalous behavior couldn't sustain my interest. Sheeba despised me.

My fingers traced the shattered line of my cheekbone, as a person prods a toothache, making it hurt. If I could have touched that euthanasia order, what would it feel like? I tugged at my sagging flesh. Soon I would have wattles. A glossy black curl came loose in my fingers. How quickly my youth was decomposing. All these decades, the mop-headed boy in my mirror had suckered me. I'd believed that was me, but he was just a tailor's dummy bought off a shelf. This withering eyesore was the real Nasir. My disguise had never fooled Sheeba.

A vignette of memory flashed, clearer than I wanted—Liam touching the nape of her neck. I huddled against the wall, remembering the natural way she turned to that punk for comfort. Ah Sheeba, how you fix my pain.

Wildly, I thought of writing her a note to explain my actions. Maybe if I told her what happened to my family . . . but of course, there was nothing to write with. Another black ringlet came loose in my hands, and what did it matter? No physical attraction of mine would have won Sheeba's love. Shee and I were born in different times.

She would never appreciate my reasons for signing that order. She didn't live through the horrors of sewage raining from the sky and shiploads of livestock dying beyond the reach of hungry people onshore. She didn't have to stitch together a new world from the moldering body parts of the old one. Guarding the status quo was not in her lexicon. That moral imperative emerged from my day and time.

I twisted the blanket till its threads unraveled. She didn't see the faces at the barred window of the warehouse in Lahore. No, scratch that. Edit that out. I don't want to re-member that part. Focus on something else. Quickly . . .

When I got to Lahore that night, there was looting, mad-ness. Prashka wasn't there. Debris blocked the streets, and ragged orange fires painted the sky. I tried to call her, but mobs had ravaged the cell towers. So I made for the old warehouse district, which by a miracle was still intact. When my Mercedes ran out of petrol, I traded its useless keys to a guard for the pass code to a deserted building. Han Tang's Golden Empress Foods. I barricaded myself inside, climbed to the roof, and set up my antique radio. All night, I listened to the ham operators broadcasting from Calcutta. I lay there weeping, wanting to die.

But at dawn, thick smoke brought me awake, and thirst drove me inside. My appetite for life proved stronger than grief. I drank the juice from a can of lychee nuts.

Then the rioters came. They broke the fences and flowed through the warehouse district like a raging tide. I set the building's security field to drive them away with electric shocks, but there were so many. They pressed thick around my walls, and the ones in back shoved forward, so the ones in front couldn't stop. Their weight broke the glass windows, and their faces crushed against the sizzling electrified bars. I hid in the men's room and drank lychee juice, pretending I couldn't hear. . . .

Two months later, when the mobs were gone, I still had

pallets of lychee nuts. Gradually, I began to trade with the other survivors, and we set about rebuilding. That's right, Shee. That's who I am. A survivor. Must I be the apologist for my entire generation? Sheeba, have you forgotten that we *rebuilt the world.*

A quiet noise vibrated through the steel. An echo of steps. Someone was walking down the corridor toward my cell. I wiped wetness from my cheeks and ducked into the far corner, blinking my one good eye and waiting as the door scraped open. There in the half-light stood Juani. No mistaking his awkward teenaged frame, though shadows hid his face. He propped the door open with his bare toe and placed a tray on the floor. Then he turned to go.

"Juani, wait. Talk to me. What did they tell you?" Without my dental implants, the sentences slurred together. Maybe I hoped to trick Juani into letting me out. Maybe I feared the loneliness.

He held the door with his hand. "Gee showed me your picture, blade. Why you want to euth' us? We living as fast as we can."

I drew the folds of the shredded blanket around me. Juani rubbed his thumb back and forth over a flange on the door. When he saw I couldn't answer, he stepped over the sill to leave.

"How's Kaioko?" I blurted. "Did she—go to the garden yet?"

Juani spoke over his shoulder. "Kaioko still breathe." Then he shut the door and left.

I threw off the blanket and pounded the steel door. Kaioko. Juani. The girl with the amoeba birthmark. "Murderer," Sheeba said.

She thought euthanasia was evil. Yet in my day . . . in my time . . .

"Emotional blocks," I said aloud to the empty darkness. "Deepra, you're the ace of war surfers. Who gives a flying fuck about a handful of teenaged protes?"

I did. I cared. There, I said it. Damn the Reel. Damn my soul to hell.

I curled on the floor and buried my head in my arms, but I could not forget the scorn in Sheeba's eyes or the taste of lychee nuts. The gunship's noisemakers started up another racket, and Heaven's rusty walls creaked. On a higher deck, something wrenched loose with a loud popping screech. It sounded as if another piece of the hull had come loose. For several seconds, the entire factory reverberated, and I held my breath. Then, silence fell.

I crawled across to Juani's tray. In the darkness, my hands closed on a water sack and a shallow dish that held something knobby and firm—broccoli. I stuck a piece in my mouth, longing for that fresh sweet taste. But I couldn't chew. I couldn't remember where I'd dropped my teeth.

And then, ye gods, I saw something few people ever get to see. I saw that my time had passed.

23

LIKE CLOCKWORK

"To everything, there is a season, and a time for every purpose under Heaven."
—ECCLESIASTES

Death is an autoimmune disease. Medical researchers have confirmed that fact finally. After learning the keys to our biocode and defeating all the antagonistic little d's of disease, disorder and decay, the physicians still can't put an end to Death. We've added centuries, but immortality remains beyond our outstretched fingertips. Perhaps our bodies finally die from a lack of distraction. With no more ailments and infections to battle, the human organism grows bored and launches an attack on itself. So the true cause of Death is boredom. This is my theory, at least.

Consider an example: I've been sitting here all this while, telling you my story, waiting in the anteroom to sick-ward. This is the last evening of my life. A few hours ago, one of Provendia's noisemakers knocked out the last functioning solar panel and blew Heaven's lights again, so my only illumination is this emergency fluorescent tube. I'm waiting for Heaven to pass out of Earth's shadow into the sun so Juani can fire up his thermionic generator and recharge our grid. As soon as that happens, I will die. You'd think I'd be making the most of my remaining time.

Picture me sitting cross-legged on the anteroom floor, listening for noises, sporadically recording this story in my implanted memory stick, and at times dreading the end. I've been trying to understand Sheeba. Yet now and here in this fleeting instant, all I can think about is that damned fluorescent tube blinking over my head. It makes my skin look green, and I can't shut it off. I'm sick of waiting. I crack my knuckles. I try yoga. In thwarted fury, I consider ramming my head against the wall to get it over with. You see what I mean about boredom?

Sheeba said we make up our past like a fairy tale. Her words inspire me to get on with this pack of lies. My life, yes.

"Murderer." Her judgment rang through the cold air of my cell on Deck One, and between alternate bouts of wretched self-loathing and total boredom, I slept. In Heaven, time has no measure. More than once, I awoke to Provendia's gunfire. The rusty hull trembled and grated, but the barrages sounded casual, almost languid. Thank the gods, they didn't use the sonic lathe again, only the noise-makers. The gunship captain was finding this war too tame. It offered no opportunity for career advancement. I dozed again.

My final round of sleep in that dark, locked cell must have lasted several hours because I awoke with a feeling of satiety. My first anguished thoughts were of Sheeba. Yet it was clear that my body had rested long and well. Not only that—my broken cheek had healed. I explored it with my tongue. Bizarre.

Then I pressed my ribs where Geraldine had kicked me—and felt no pain! The fractures had mended. And the swelling in my bloodied nose had gone down. I found my teeth and fitted them into my gums. Then I touched my face—and cried aloud. Smooth skin. Taut and springy with youthful elastins. I jumped to my feet, found the direction of spin by instinct, and bounced on my toes like a giddy adolescent. The glass man had made me whole again.

My thumb projected a stream of glowing icons, and I scanned them eagerly, learning what had happened. Incredible as this sounds, my injured false eye had regenerated. All my dormant NEMs were bringing themselves back online!

Cut off from the Net, with no access to their handlers,

their hard-coded urge to heal drove them to improvise. Whole herds of the little NEMs were teaching themselves independence and developing work-arounds. My liver enzymes had moved back to normal. My T-cells were leveling out. This old body had revived without doctors' orders.

And what about this joy I felt, this confident new hope? Where did it spring from? Sheeba still hated me, and doubtless, the juves still intended to fling me into the void. How could a few hours of sleep so completely change my wretchedness to cheery optimism? This attitude was false.

This buoyant mood had to be a product of NEM secretions in my brain. Still, they were damned good drugs, and they charged me with vigor. No more self-pity for Nasir Deepra. Time to get moving!

There was bound to be a way to break Sheeba's addiction to this war zone, and I absolutely knew I would find it. After devouring the water and sweet veggies someone had left on a tray, I checked to see if the door was locked. Yes, but the mechanism was a simple latch. My brain must have picked up IQ during the night, and I could see at once how to defeat the latch. Okay, so I needed something thin and narrow to slide through and—my hand closed on the ankh zippered in my longjohn pocket. Sheeba had given me the charm for good luck. This had to be a sign that I was destined to triumph.

The juves, the euthanasia order, my dismal insights from the night before, all those memories faded. No recollections distracted me from the present moment. I slipped the little talisman under the latch—gently, steadily—and with a click, the lock fell open.

Out in the curving corridor, I looked both ways and saw no one. Instinct told me to seek food. The NEMs had synthesized quite a variety of compounds to heal my injuries, and my organism needed replenishment. I recalled hoisting cartloads of food and water up to the 'pactor room on Deck Four, and although the memory had no context, I didn't stop to wonder why. I headed for the food.

With a stealthy, war-surfer tread, I cycled up through the

ladder segments, listening to the walls with my fingers. My
nerve endings browsed vibrations and fed back eerie tactile
images of rooms, objects, humming machinery, humans. It
was as if I could use sound waves to see through steel. A
group of juveniles conspired in the solar plant. I slipped by,
undetected.

On Deck Four, I immediately recognized the 'pactor
room. Where did that other door lead? I recalled an anteroom, but I didn't waste time thinking about it. The 'pactor
room held a row of ordinary presses that compacted pro-
glu bales into dense, hard cubes. And stacked on the floor,
on top of the machines, and in every conceivable niche
were the provisions. I tore open the first water sack within
reach and gulped.

A familiar Provendia logo branded every bag of hard
crackers and can of stew. I could have torn the cans open
with my teeth, but the glass man wanted something better
to eat than that pro-glu crap. The lid to one of the com-
pactors hung open, so I looked inside. And what I saw
made me salivate like a beast. The glass man recognized
what was in there. Seeds.

Mega-kilos of seeds from the garden. Hard round seeds.
Soft pulpy ones. Black. White. Varicolored. Silky. Winged.
Big as my thumb. Fine as sand. I plunged in, up to my elbows, scooped up great handfuls and let them slide through
my fingers. My mouth craved to taste them. I stuffed my
cheeks and crunched the delicious kernels.

See me hunching over the compactor, chomping, chewing, slobbering in ecstasy. How the glass man relished the
nutty flavors, as spicy and carnal as grains of Earth. Half-
chewed husks dribbled down my chin as I closed my eyes
and feasted. And on my tongue, the fetal DNA unreeled.

I sampled. I gorged. My belly swelled and ached, and
still, the glass man wanted more. Deep hungers drifted toward consciousness. I ate more, fueling more desire for
novel strains of DNA. As the unfamiliar compounds hit my
bloodstream, my energy surged, and there came a moment
when ideas churned and clicked into place. Mine or the

glass man's? I'm still not sure. It was as if the flavors cat-
alyzed a transmutation. A plan formed at the back of my
brain: Escape and seek resources, then return.

I pushed back from the seeds as if waking from a trance.
Did I stop to wonder about this abnormal binge? Not for a
moment. I thought with my feet and made straight for the
ladder well.

Someone's ragged old EVA suit still draped my body,
and the air gauge still read almost full. I slapped my hip
and found a collapsible helmet dangling from my belt. The
gloves were wadded in my pocket. Outside, a ship waited,
and on that ship were resources I needed to break Sheeba
free. That's all I could remember. I headed for the airlock.
No more pandering to caution or looking for thrusters. I
would space-dive to the ship and take command. One, two,
three, like clockwork.

Not for days had I experienced this level of mental clarity. Deck Two had an airlock exit, but juveniles were there,
plotting in the solar plant. How could I slip by them? Then,
like flipping a switch, I recalled a full-blown photographic
memory of the A13 schematics. The engineers had installed an airlock in the cargo bay. Of course.

I dropped down through the ladder segments to Deck
One, silent as breath, and opened the door to the cargo bay.
As soon as the door fell open, the sugary reek of pro-glu
wafted into the ladder well. I stood in the doorway, examining the bales stacked on top of the hidden airlock.

A slight vibration warned me that someone was coming
down from Two. Instantly, I stepped into the cargo bay,
pushed the door closed and listened. My hearing had
sharpened. I could sense when the person dropped down
the ladder and moved away through the opposite door.
From the light step, I knew the person was small, probably
a child gone astray. Did I waste time questioning why a
child would be here? My logic centers ticked through pos-
sibilities like a computer. Then I forgot the child and focused on the airlock.

In full Earth gravity, I shifted the bales aside—never

wondering how I could lift objects more than twice my weight. There in the sugary dust, the rim of the airlock gleamed like a jar lid. One full pallet still blocked my way, so I leaned hard and slid it across the deck.

My mind worked at light-speed, yet how could I fail to notice the blind spots? Familiar details churned like disconnected motes in a fog. Only later did I piece together the clues and understand the full scope of my transmutation. Without my doctors issuing restraining orders through the Net, my NEMs were reinventing themselves on the fly, and for the first time in their constricted little lives, they probed new healing frontiers. Though I didn't realize it then, my brain NEMs had adapted one of my own native thought patterns, a behavior long established in war surfs. The crystal bugs were editing my memories to safeguard me from the Reel.

They did a first-rate job, too. They eliminated every troubling doubt, every diversion. I felt blissfully at one with the zone. Those NEMs kept me preter-focused, and you should have seen me shoving that pallet out of the way. I performed like a superhero.

I tell you this now, but at the time, I didn't even pause to consider it. I wanted only to get outside and find help for Sheeba. The chemicals of zone rush charged through my flesh and saturated my blood. With rapid grace, I donned the old helmet and gloves, opened the airlock and jumped in. I was just about to close the hatch and start the airlock cycling, when an instinct stopped me. Something looked out of place.

My artificial eyes roved everywhere, scanning for anomalies. Aha. Someone had jimmied the compressor vent. I could almost read the oily fingerprints left on the metal grill. In one confident stroke, I ripped off the vent cover and recognized the booby trap inside. A canister of lethal gas.

It was connected to the vent's control valve through a snarl of primitive copper wire. I recalled someone saying how airlocks could be rigged as execution chambers. With

uncanny speed, I calculated how to disable the triggering
device. Then I did something inexplicable—yet it seemed
right. I took off my gloves, nicked my right index finger on
the sharp hatch rim, and squeezed a few drops of blood
onto the copper wires. At the time, this insane act didn't
faze me, but only now, after long and terrible thought, can
I explain it to you. The glass man viewed that booby trap as
a cancer, and he deployed those drops of NEM-rich blood
to "cure" it.

While I curled inside the airlock, watching my blood
seep among the wires—this may sound incredible, but I
swear it's true—I could perceive the movement of each
individual nanoelectronic machine. Not through human
eyesight, no, but through some other species of perception altogether, a sort of bond or quantum entanglement.
Somehow, I *knew* what my NEMs were doing. They were
dissolving   the   wire,   molecule   by   molecule—
safeguarding my health. And the little suckers worked
fast.

Then I heard another noise in the ladder well. A squeak-
ing door hinge. A muted footstep that only my meta-
normally enhanced hearing could pick up. That child was
coming back. After two more footsteps, I extrapolated that
the child had thin bones, narrow arches and one supinated
ankle. The door to the cargo bay wasn't completely sealed,
and through the sugary reek of product, I deciphered a fine
pungency of teenaged female sweat. I eased out of the airlock, leaving my small bloody army to do its work on the
wires, and I tiptoed toward the door.

Something about the child's gait felt familiar. I knew the
sound of that breath. For an instant, my brain went on
pause as—inconceivable as this sounds—my NEMs split
in factions and debated. The mites were trying to resolve
whether this girl would . . .

a. remind me of the Reel and therefore distract me, or
b. provide me with crucial need-to-know data.

The b's won, and I identified the child three seconds before she pushed open the cargo bay door.

"Kaioko."

She stepped over the sill, batting her tiny, bright eyes. She looked ghostly. "Hello, sir. You go spacewalk?"

At the sight of this resurrected girl, my mental concentration fell apart like a depolarized array. Suppressed memories came rioting back in one befuddling swirl. I tugged off my helmet and lowered myself to the floor.

Kaioko glanced at the open airlock, the vent cover lying askew, the bales of product scattered helter-skelter. She registered each impression with a slight nod. Then she touched my cheek where the bone was still knitting back together.

"What are you doing here?" I managed to wheeze.

She blinked her beady eyes. "Sir, I not sure. I feel—changed."

Changed was an understatement. The last time I saw Kaioko, she'd been strapped to a mattress in sick-ward, lost in a coma. Now here she was standing in the cargo bay like a spectral vision, interrupting my escape. She must have climbed all the way down the ladders without assistance. Her head scarf was gone, and a fine black fuzz of new hair covered her scalp.

"I knew you be wanting to leave, sir, so I came." She tottered a little unsteadily on her feet.

"Sit down before you fall."

"I getting well, sir."

"You don't look well." But she looked alive, and that was a miracle. None of the other stricken protes had ever recovered from Heaven's malady. Our scientists hadn't documented a single survivor. "Sit down, child." I patted a spot on the floor beside me.

Kaioko obeyed. "I not feeling afraid anymore. You made me brave, sir."

"Me? What did I do?"

"You gave me this." She grasped my nicked finger and squeezed it till a crimson bead welled up.

My blood. That's right, I'd donated a transfusion. Had my NEMs brought about her cure? Well, that was an intriguing thought.

Then, to my astonishment, Kaioko stuck my bleeding finger in her mouth. As my blood merged with her saliva, a faint sensation began to flow through my hand. Like a tingling current. A second later, it grew more insistent. Then it swelled like a brilliant explosion, jangling my senses. No, not my five human senses—those other ones that felt like quantum entanglement or maybe data-streaming. My glass man had just recognized his kin.

My NEMs flowed in Kaioko's veins, and as she held my nicked finger in her mouth, I *knew* them. They *communed* with me. Intimate knowledge vibrated through my flesh, and the crystal lattice inside me sang like a harp. But the onslaught of this new sensory information was too alien. I pulled my hand away and broke the connection.

Kaioko smiled.

"Did you feel that?" I asked.

"Feel what, sir?"

Softly, I brushed the fine new hairs covering her head like baby fuzz. Apparently, she hadn't noticed. At the time, this baffled me, but now I understand. Her NEMs had been growing only a few hours, whereas my little fiends had been reproducing for decades. Kaioko's silicon twin was a mere embryo compared to the seasoned maturity of my glass man.

"So you don't want to die anymore?" I asked.

She grinned. "I not going to the garden yet."

"Good." I tilted her face up with my fingertips to examine her pupils, the way Sheeba would have done. They looked healthy and normal. Her carotid artery pulsed like a clock, strong and steady. Her forehead felt cool. I was no doctor, but her recovery seemed genuine. The strange link we'd shared unsettled me. Meta-bizarre. I studied my nicked fingertip, hesitating.

"Kaioko, why did you want to—go to the garden?"

She scrunched up her face and toyed with her silky new

hair. The livid scars were fading. On impulse, I seized her arm and pushed back her long sleeve. The crosshatched knife wounds on her forearm had healed over.

"I want to go be useful," she said.

"You thought dying would be useful?" I looked at her quizzically. Her explanation didn't make sense.

She drew a deep breath and tried again. "Juani say, all good things go to the garden. Nobi there. Our parents, too. We recycle."

I had to replay her words in my head three times to understand. She meant they disposed of their dead in the garden. At some point, I must have read a memo about biomass recycling. Nothing's wasted on a satellite. I thought of the broccoli.

"Nobi make the air we breathe."

I nodded automatically, letting this information wash over me. My tongue curled. The seeds I'd eaten came from the garden. The water. Even the breath in my lungs flowed from the exhalations of my decomposed employees.

"I not worth much here," Kaioko continued. "Always afraid. Can't learn to count. Can't save the people." She twisted her fingers. "Juani say the garden make everything new."

"Oh child." I took her into my lap. "That's wrong. We need you alive a hell of a lot more than the garden needs fertilizer."

Kaioko grinned shyly. "I not afraid anymore."

As if to test her words, Provendia's gunship launched another round of lethargic strafing. Outside the hull, the noisemakers popped, and their compression waves thundered through the steel deck where we were sitting. Here on Deck One, their uproar shook our bones, and despite Kaioko's brave boast, she sucked her cheeks between her teeth and hid her face under my arm.

When the gunfire ended, I continued to hold her. She felt warm in my lap and—precious. Don't laugh. She felt to me like a living sack of gold. My NEMs were circulating through her body, and that idea fascinated me. We were blood relatives, in a weird synthetic sort of way, and I kept obsessing about our communion. I wanted to know how it worked. When my NEMs disconnected from the Net and started developing their own healing scenarios, something new was unleashed inside me, something robust and preter-resilient. Ye graven idols, my imagination ran rampant. Could the glass man actually come alive?

I stroked Kaioko's bony back and thought this over. A silicon life-form sharing my space? Some roommate. But he was a healing dervish. Despite all my injuries, he kept bringing me back to wellness. What if the crystal man could give me what every human being had longed for since the dawn of time? Immortality. The capital I.

When Kaioko shifted in my lap, I craned to see my thumbnail over her shoulder. More NEMs had come back online. Only a few categories were still struggling for solutions. The nanomachines were evolving fast. They'd healed my wounds in one night, and look at this child in my lap. Hours ago, she couldn't even sustain a regular heartbeat. I grasped my fingertip and squeezed another drop of blood. Reestablishing our link excited me with equal measures of curiosity and dread.

Then Kaioko sat up and grinned. "I hungry. You, too, sir?"

Before I could offer her my bloody fingertip, she hopped out of my lap and began tearing at one of the bales of product. She ripped away the dense outer layer and dug two spongy, brown masses from inside. They looked like spun sugar. She put one in her mouth and offered the other to me. "Don't eat much," she said through her mouthful. "It's been 'pactored.'"

I gazed at the pulpy mass in her hand. My Com actually sold that dreck as food?

"Let it melt before you go swallow." Kaioko opened her mouth and showed me the brown crumbs dissolving on her tongue.

I must have made a face, because she laughed and almost choked. I had to clap her on the back, and tears ran down her cheeks. But as soon as the coughing ended, she stuffed more of that product in her mouth. "I really hungry," she said, beaming.

Shouts ricocheted down the ladder well. "Kai-Kai! Where are you?"

We both turned at the sound of Geraldine's voice. Two sets of footsteps shook the ladder, and by the weight, I knew Liam was there. He and the wench were searching for Kaioko. She must have slipped out of sick-ward without telling anyone. Quickly, I glanced at the airlock, where my platoon of silicon soldiers had finally hacked through the wires and disarmed the gas canister.

"You want to leave," she said.

I didn't answer. There was no time to try our communion again. Geraldine would be here in seconds, and my glass man and I were in full agreement—we had to escape. So I jerked the battered helmet over my head, but before I could slip on the gloves, Kaioko seized my arm.

"Sir, I come to ask you, please stay."

The steps on the ladder sounded closer. "I can't. I have to go."

She grabbed my bare hand. And I *knew* the bioNEMs in her skin oil. Our sweat intermingled, exchanging data. We shared molecules full of code, and the sensation unzipped my frame of mind. We stared at each other, trying to comprehend what was happening. But this was the wrong time. My NEMs took control again, edited my memories and focused me on escape.

"Let me go." I pushed Kaioko away, and when she stumbled, my qualm of regret vanished before it registered.

Naturally, Geraldine stuck her head through the door just in time to witness Kaioko's fall. Like a judge wielding a gavel, the wench came at me with her hammer. But I wasn't the same Nasir she'd kicked down the ladder well. The glass man had grown strong. This time, her hammerblows fell on my NEM-hardened chest like kisses.

Kaioko got to her feet and tried to intervene. "Stop, Gee. He a good man."

But Geraldine's rage had its own momentum. The muscles of her face bunched in knots, and she aimed her hammer at my teeth. In reflex, I knocked the tool out of her hand.

"Augh." She bent double and cradled her wrist. This made me smile. Then Liam came through the door. He cast a confused glance at Kaioko, who stood by my side.

"He hit her." Geraldine pointed at me. "He trying to get away."

Liam laid a restraining hand on Geraldine's shoulder. "Kai-Kai, how you feeling? You look better."

He was right. Her ashy, pale complexion had softened. Pink spots glowed in her cheeks, and her lips had changed from lavender to rose. She virtually bloomed with health. How extraordinary. I wanted to explore this novel phenomenon, but before I could form a single hypothesis, I forgot! My mind darted back to the main priority: escape and seek resources. The open airlock waited.

Liam saw the direction of my gaze and moved to block me. "I can't let you go," he said quietly.

"You want to fight me? Bring it on, junior."

He widened his stance, lifted his fists and crouched, waiting for me to make the first move. Stupid kid. I wanted to take him out. Hot virile instincts flushed up my chest, and my hands automatically clenched. I wanted to wipe the floor with his insolent carcass. But this wasn't the time.

So I snorted and fumed and forced myself to calm down. "We'll finish this later, punk."

With effortless speed, I lifted him off his feet and tossed him into the pallets. Bales of product tumbled down on top of his lanky form, burying everything except for one boot. Geraldine roared curses and ran to dig him out, and while they were distracted, I dropped into the airlock.

When I tried to close the hatch, Kaioko leaned inside. "Please stay here, sir. Your blood can cure the people."

At that moment, I honestly couldn't recall the malady, or the euthanasia order, or my part in this sad little war. My focus had never been so sharply defined. I pushed Kaioko away.

Then, out of nowhere, Sheeba appeared. Her burnished face hovered above me, framed in the hatch rim like a magnificent cameo portrait. Where had Sheeba come from? I hadn't heard footsteps approaching. I'd been too focused on escape.

"Nasir, stay and help us."

"Sheeba?"

"I beg you. Stay and make amends for what you've done."

"What I've done?"

Alarms went off in my brain. Sheeba, my heart's blood. My one and only desire. I longed to pull her down into the airlock and take her away at once. But she wasn't wearing a space suit. And somewhere in my edit-censored consciousness, a thin voice warned the time wasn't right. Sheeba had too many allies here. She was sunk too deep in her zone intoxication. To wrest her free, I would need reinforcements.

"I'll come back," I whispered. "That's a promise."

Then Geraldine grabbed my sleeve. Her injured right arm hung like a broken wing, but with her left, she savagely pinched a handful of my biceps and twisted. Enraged NEM chemicals blasted through my veins and riveted my attention. I scraped her hand against the sharp metal rim of the airlock. Her cry almost made me stop, but the glass man immediately zipped, shunted and stored away my remorse, and I scraped her hand again, forcing her to let go. Sheeba pleaded, but I couldn't hear what she said. I concentrated only on exiting the zone alive.

Then Liam rose above me like a vengeful hawk. His forehead was bleeding, and his rope of blond hair had come unbraided. Bits of dried pro-glu stuck to the side of his face. I bared my teeth. "We'll settle this later, count on it."

Just as I yanked the airlock, Geraldine's clawhammer slammed down and struck my forearm. Its sharp fangs bit straight through the old gray space suit and punctured my skin. Blood spurted through the gash, and the brief pain made my eyes water.

"He can't leave now," the wench cackled. "I tore his space suit."

But it was my turn to laugh. In a split second, the hatch sealed, I jammed the manual override, and instead of waiting for the lock to decompress, I immediately opened the outer door. The escaping air blew me out of Heaven like projectile diarrhea. I barely caught the handhold, but the powerful vigor of the glass man kept me hanging on. Fluttering in the void, I grinned at my bloody arm. The NEMs had "healed" my space suit. Clever little sodders.

A heartbeat later, I spotted the Agonists lurking in Heaven's shadow, exactly where I knew they would be.

24

THE BIG I

"Keep on raging—to stop the aging."
—THE DELLTONES

"We have to go back!"

My shout detonated through Kat's shuttle. I seized Kat's helmet and twisted it off with such force that the gasket tore. We jostled together in the cabin's zero gravity

"What the hell do you think you're doing? We just saved your skinny ass." Kat wiped sweaty red hair from her eyes and pushed me away.

My heart thundered against my rib cage, and my muscles twitched with excess energy. My attention remained as centered as a collimated laser beam: Seek reinforcements and return for Sheeba.

When Kat voiced a command to ignite her rockets, I dragged her bodily out of the pilot's seat. "Do NOT move this shuttle."

"Nasir, calm down." Verinne interceded with her gravelly voice of reason. "We're running low on fuel. We'll come back later."

"There's no time." Every iota of my emotional energy centered on Sheeba's welfare—but there was also a darker motive driving me—an alien desire. The NEMs wanted to stay inside the Net blockade. They didn't want to take any more doctors' orders.

"Avoid the Net," I said aloud, not stopping to analyze my reasons.

"What did those fucking agitators do to you?" Grunze caught my shoulders and hugged me to his chest.

"Nasty Nass, did they pluck out your fingernails?" Winston giggled. "I bet fifty thousand you'd come back with exotic scars."

"Whatever they did, you're going to pay for my neck gasket." Kat picked at her damaged helmet. "We've been killing ourselves for days, hiring mercs, dealing with lawyers, paying off that slimy Captain Trencher. . . ."

Grunze released me from the hug, but continued to grip both my shoulders. "You won't believe how famous we are, sweet-pee. We're back in first place again. By the way, Chad had to sell some of your furniture."

"Yeah, your gunship captain has a cosmic appetite for gratuities," said Kat.

"Sheeba's in terrible danger. I need your help—"

When Kat drifted toward the pilot's seat again, the NEMs electrified my rage. I could not let her move us in range of the Net, where the doctors would rein in my glass man—not while Shee was still in danger. I knocked Grunze aside to get at Kat—using more force than I realized. Grunze thumped against the control housing with a vicious pulpy smack, and my sharp ears recognized exactly which of his ribs had fractured.

"Huh?" My old friend gaped at me.

"He's nuts." Kat threw her helmet at my chest.

"He's having a psychotic episode. Grab him," Verinne said coolly.

As they grappled my four limbs, we bucked and wrestled in weightlessness, butting heads, shoulders and knees against the confining oval of the cabin. But even my glassy strength could not hold out against four superannuated codgers pumped up on human growth factor. Verinne sprayed my nostrils full of Sleep-Eze. Then Kat strapped me into Winston's bunk and tied my hands with millicord.

Dreams have sounds, did you know that? Snippets of audio, recorded who knows how many decades past, they lodge in your brain like tidbits of rotting debris. In time, their meanings break apart, recompose and gather new context. I awoke hearing Prashka's voice. "We're falling," she said. "Hold me."

I opened my eyes to rosy light glimmering against a silk-upholstered ceiling. I lay nude in a sunken pool of pillows. Gentle sizz music chimed from hidden speakers, and a smell of cherries wafted through the air. It took me another groggy minute to understand what had happened. The Agonists had brought me back to my luxury hotel suite at Mira. They thought I needed rest, so they left me in the care of my Net-linked doctors while they went back for Sheeba. Sheeba, my beloved. I bolted out of bed.

And got tangled in the blankets. And fell on my chin. My limbs wobbled like Jell-O. What the heck?

When I tapped my IBiS, holographic icons gushed out of my thumb. The glass man was virtually begging me to notice what the doctors were doing. Dozens of physicians were barraging me with warnings that my NEMs had gone rogue, and they were launching programs to blunt my brainpower, dull my senses and constrain my muscles back to the flaccid condition they called "normal." And for these services, they were metering unspeakable fees.

"Screw this." I bit my thumb and got on the phone to Chad.

"Boss, you're alive! I've been trying to get through for hours. Your Fortia bonds are maturing, and it's time to roll over—"

I cut him off. "Find the Agonists. Where are they? Get me coordinates, and order a damned taxi. I need to get back there."

"I'm on it," Chad said.

I rubbed my eyes. Wasn't there something else? My memory was still way too disconnected. Something I was supposed to do . . . With a jolt, I remembered the failing hull.

"Chad. Tell Provendia to call off the gunship. No more stupido noisemakers. And put that euth' order on pause."

"But boss—"

"This is coming straight from my lips to your cyber-ears. Do it now."

"It isn't that easy. You know Provendia won't break the chain of command."

Gilty gods, Chad was right. Those geezer bureaucrats couldn't make a move without first crossing every T. The stodgy CEO would want to convene a board meeting and get everyone's input. Then someone's assistant would have to generate a memo. Every Com followed the same slug-gish rigmarole. Top-heavy command, that was the prob-lem. Too many senior execs.

I sighed and rubbed sleep from my eyes. "Okay, let the CEO chase down enough rubber stamps to cover his ass in ink. Just make sure he calls off the gunship."

"Got it, boss."

"And get me two new space suits. Make one pearly pink."

I stumbled into the bathroom, looking for my clothes, and for the first time in days, I saw myself in the mirror. Ye gold-plated statues. My body rippled with youth! Glossy black ringlets, tight manly buns—the only thing real was the haggard droop of my eyes. I deactivated the mirror and got dressed.

Then I surfed through the hotel's online gift shop and bought some things for Sheeba. A new pink-and-white smartskin, moisturizing body wash, chocolate truffles, a handheld movie viewer, a diamond tiara.

Climbing into the taxi, my spirits lifted like the fake-happy bounce of Peps. And I could guess the reason. My NEMs were blissed to be heading back toward the Net blockade, away from the meddlesome doctors. My energy centered on a different goal though. I was going to liberate Sheeba. But so many details remained fuzzy.

"Listen, crystal guy, we need an understanding," I said aloud in the speeding taxi. "The extra muscle power comes in handy, and better vision is good. The beefed-up IQ is also cool. But you can't screw with my memories. That could be dangerous to both of us."

The cybercabbie bobbed his plastic head, but the glass man didn't respond.

A shiver rifled up my spine. What was I doing, talking to myself like a lunatic? The glass man wasn't a real person. He was a whimsical fantasy I'd dreamed up. A metaphor. The NEMs were millions of separate healing machines, at least a thousand different kinds, and each one had a narrow, specialized function. Sure, they assembled into an interlocked lattice to relay health data, but that didn't mean they could think as a unit. They were medical devices, not a life-form.

"Are we clear?" I said to the empty taxi. "Hell, I'm coming unzipped."

But then, as if a floodgate had opened, my memories surged back. I recalled everything. Prashka. Lahore. The lychee nuts. Sheeba's scornful voice. "Murderer!" A dozen times, I watched her bury her face in Liam's shirt. How in hell would I convince her to come away with *me*?

My vertebrae compressed like a stack of millstones. It was worse than the Reel. All the way to the rendezvous, my neck ached. How could I redeem myself in Sheeba's eyes if she didn't trust me? I sorted through the paltry items from Mira's gift shop—silly junk. These trinkets would never induce her to leave Heaven. I needed a better gift—but what?

"Amends," she had said.

The two freighted syllables resonated like a hundred children's voices singing through steel. Memories were a curse.

I phoned the Agonists en route. Grunze answered, but he refused to talk. His ribs were still mending from where I'd smacked him, and he was doing psychotropics to ease his hurt feelings. He passed the phone to Kat.

"Are you over your fit of nerves?" Kat's teeth clicked against the phone mike. "We're going in for Sheeba."

Verinne joined the conference call. "Nasir, we're trying a soft dock on Heaven's port. Why won't the cargo doors open?"

"No, that won't work. I cleared the airlock, but the cargo doors are weighted down with product." Then I told them about the lethal gas in the airlocks.

"Well, we can't go in through the hull rip," Kat said. "That whole area's mined with tactical nukes."

"What lame bimbus would have done that?" I said.

Winston giggled. "Ask your gunship captain."

"There's something else," Verinne said. "Captain Trencher mentioned a health quarantine."

"Trencher? Robert Trencher? Fucking Robert A. Trencher is the gunship captain?" Only a few weeks ago, I'd personally demoted that asshole. How had he turned up here? Someone had been pulling strings behind my back.

"He's the one," Verinne said. "He's taking bribes to keep quiet, but he doesn't know who we are."

I paused to contemplate the vicious justice of the universe. My onetime protégé, Robert Trencher—liar, coward, incompetent numbnuts—he was the captain to whom I'd nearly surrendered? Gods, wouldn't he love to turn the tables and get me in his power.

"Life is strange," I reflected. "Just keep looking for an entrance. I'm on my way."

The taxi rendezvoused with Kat's shuttle directly over the South Pole. The big Dolphin 88 was there, too, overloaded with fans and tourists. Hovering nearby were a chartered wide-body Hedgehog and a sleek Astral yacht with Greenland.Com markings. Our live audience of fans had sextupled, and Chad informed me that millions more watched from home. A few hundred kilometers away, Heaven spun on its chain, followed by the ever-vigilant gunship. Apparently, Trencher hadn't received a recall order yet. My Provendia colleagues were still crossing their t's.

"We can't find a way in," Verinne said.

"Keep trying." I tugged my hair. We were this close, with all the right gear, plenty of money, virtually unlimited surfer resources, and we couldn't find a way into Heaven? It was almost laughable.

While Verinne and Kat pored over A13's schematics,

Grunze sat in the pilot's seat, maintaining a stern silence. He was pouting. I took the navigator seat beside him and squeezed his knee. "Okay, Grunzie, I'm sorry. I didn't mean to bust your ribs."

"You ambushed me," he said, peeved. He wasn't used to losing fights. "Are you on some kind of pills?"

"Grunzie, I was overwrought. That zone was pure hell."

Win sat Velcroed in his bunk, grinning like a mental patient. "Show us your scars, Nasty Nass."

Verinne queried for new data. "We'll settle bets later. Right now we need a tactical plan to rescue Shee."

"Shee may not want to come away with us," I admitted, shamefaced.

"Why the fuck not?" said Grunze.

Verinne stopped scrolling through her search results. "Nasir, what have you done?"

Why did everybody assume it was my fault? Hell, there was no easy way to explain without humiliating myself. "There's this guy," I began. Then I told them how a crafty young agitator had put Sheeba under a spell. He was a devil. He'd mesmerized Shee with his wicked lies. Of course, I didn't mention the malady. No point scaring my friends. As I reeled off Liam's crimes, they grew incensed. That dangerous agitator was brainwashing our darling. My friends agreed we had to get her away fast, whether she wanted to come or not. Shee was such a child, she couldn't see her own best interest.

"We'll need weapons," Grunze said.

"No prob. I packed a picnic." Kat's eyes gleamed. She sailed across the narrow cabin and flipped open a bin containing a rack of stun guns, sticky-string pumps, sleep gas and riot gear. All nonlethal of course. It wasn't considered sporting for surfers to carry deadly weapons. Kat said, "You like my yummy gadgets?"

"We still need a way in. Guess we'll have to punch another hole in the hull." Grunze laced his fingers behind his bald head and leaned back in his seat. "Where's the best place, sweet-pee?"

"Grunzie, you forgive me?" I asked.

He smiled and cuffed me across the jaw, just hard enough to bounce my skull against the headrest. It was his way of showing tenderness. "One mil says I get to Sheeba before you do. So where do we rip a new door?"

I studied the cutaway drawing, and my mind flip-flopped between the glass man's driving instincts and my own guilty memories. Deck One? Sheeba might still be there in the cargo bay, along with Liam, Geraldine and Kaioko. No, we couldn't risk a rupture on One. Deck Two? That held the solar plant and the circulating pumps. Besides, half of Two had already been blown away. Another hull breach there might shiver Heaven to pieces. Deck Three housed the thermionic generator, where Juani would be working on his CAES. Deck Four was sick-ward, and the juves needed that medical equipment.

Verinne tapped Heaven's tapering apex with her stylus. "How about Deck Five? It's the largest."

"No, that's where the toads are hiding," I said.

"Toads?" My friends gazed at me as if my teeth were in crooked. Grunze said, "What the fuck are toads?"

An image flitted across my mental screen, a dozen little kids gazing up at me as if I held the keys to secret knowledge. "I mean—Sheeba might be there. No, we certainly can't punch a hole in Five."

After that, we drifted apart and brooded, scratching our heads and glumly tugging our earlobes. Winston took a nap. Verinne continued to study A13's schematic, but no one in our crew could generate a fresh idea.

Worse, even if we found an entrance, I still had nothing to offer that would lure Sheeba away. The idea of dragging her against her will revolted me. She would never forgive that violation. But try as I might, I could think of no enticement powerful enough to win her over.

Why didn't the freaking NEMs boost my brainpower? I slapped the sides of my skull. Just when I needed him most, the crystal man went slack.

Suddenly, I remembered we hadn't crossed through the

blockade yet. We were still hovering outside its perimeter, within easy reach of the Net-linked doctors. Had my glass man succumbed to their orders? I checked my IBiS, and icons bubbled out of my thumb. Right, those quacks were still trying to wrestle my wayward NEMs into submission. A war of crossed signals raged through the Net, as deadly as any hail of laser fire. My glass man's fight for independence was absorbing all his attention. And those sadistic doctors kept ratcheting up their fees.

"Take us through the blockade!" I shouted.

"If you think that will help." Grunze powered up the shuttle and eased us forward.

"Boss, I'm losing you. What about the Fortia bonds? Should I sell . . ." Chad's voice faded from my earphone.

As soon as we crossed the blockade and lost Net access, I felt a deep liberating shift in my joints. My neck muscles relaxed, and my stomach calmed down (I hadn't noticed the stomach cramps). Soon my flesh started to tingle, not just in my thumb but everywhere. That's when a single word trumpeted through my brain like harmonic epiphany. The word was a name. And the name was Vlad.

Of course. Vlad would know a way into Heaven. And Vlad would be the perfect apology gift to offer Sheeba. If I brought back the young medic, she would soften her opinion and forgive me. Then maybe she would come away from that death trap.

I spun and faced Verinne. "You took one of the agitators. Where is he?"

Verinne's wrinkly old eyes narrowed. "That prote wouldn't tell us anything."

"It doesn't matter. We need him," I said.

"What for?"

My brain clicked through possible lies. It was too embarrassing to admit that I needed to bribe Sheeba to trust me. I said, "He may know a back door into Heaven."

Kat plowed between us. "Heaven has a secret entrance? Plasmic."

Don't ask me how this notion burst into my head, but

the more I thought about it, the more plausible the back-door idea sounded. Of course. Liam would surely have built a private entrance, and Vlad would know its location. "That agitator can show us the way in," I said.

Verinne chewed her wizened lip. "We turned him over to Trencher a couple of hours ago."

"Two hours ago!" Trencher would have slated the medic for euthanasia by now. But if they interrogated him first, he might still be alive.

Kat twisted her hair. "It'll take a megaton of deutsch to buy him back. You wouldn't believe how Trencher nickels-and-dimes us."

Then Verinne's gray eyes canted slyly. "We could steal him back."

"From a Com gunship?" Kat recoiled so violently, she bumped into Grunze and sent him spinning off at a tan-gent. "They'll terminate us."

Grunzie bounced against the cabin wall. "Kat's right. Do you want to get us laid off? I'd rather die than lose my job."

"Weenies, Verinne knows they won't fire us. We own too many shares." I blew Verinne a kiss. "Let's do it."

Grunze stuck out his chin. "Maybe you own mega-shares, Nass, but I've been running through my holdings pretty damn quick these last few years."

"Me, too," said Kat, "and we know Winny's broke. At this stage in my life, the last thing I want is to risk getting kicked downstairs. I can't live as a prote."

Verinne settled against the window and crossed her arms. "Whine all you like. I don't care what the fuckers do to me. I'm an *Agonist*."

The others gawked at her. Verinne was usually the con-servative one. And she never used the F word. Her attitude stunned them. I was the only one who knew how little Verinne had to lose. "Cara. You and I will go together."

Smile wrinkles rayed across her cheeks. The widow's peak in her pale forehead seemed to point straight through me, and grainy creases circled her desiccated throat like necklaces of sand. As I studied her dying face, I realized Verinne had no intention of coming back from this surf. This would be her grand exit. But I had to come back. I had to save Sheeba.

And to do that, I needed the others. Things could get dicey on that gunship. Verinne and I could not handle the surf alone. But how could I convince Kat and Grunze to risk losing their executive status?

Then something clicked. An idea. "Grunzie, Katherine, here's a proposition. How would you like to live forever?"

"Yeah right." Kat rolled her eyes, and Grunze merely scowled and waved me off.

I crooked my little finger at Grunze. "Immortality. We're talking the big I. It's time you knew the truth about this war zone. There's something I've been hiding."

"You think we didn't know that?" Grunze shook his head.

"Help me get the agitator, and I'll show you how to achieve perfect, enduring health forever."

Winston pulled the blanket off his head and sat up in his bunk with a yawn. "Define perfect." His question took me aback.

As Verinne drew closer, a nervous tic jerked one of her eyelids. "Nasir, this is nothing to joke about."

"It's not a joke. I'll tell you everything if you agree to help me. All of you. I want your word on it. Surfer's honor. I can't do this without you."

Kat poked my chest with her finger. "Why should we believe you?"

"Because I have evidence." I held up my left hand and, with the theatricality of a striptease artist, drew off my glove. "Check my IBiS, friends."

Kat grabbed my thumb to read the bubbling icons, and Grunze leaned over her shoulder. For long seconds, no one spoke. They browsed my health status with fierce, widening eyes.

Winston tried to free himself from his Velcro restraints. "Would perfect apply to brain cells?" His handsome old reprobate face opened with hope.

"Yes, Winny. Take a risk," I coaxed. "Where's your surfer spirit?"

To demonstrate my new powers, I rattled off a chain of prime numbers, crushed a stainless steel cocktail shaker in my fist, then lifted Grunzie one-handed and bounced him against the shuttle's low ceiling—which, of course, meant nothing given the zero gravity.

"Let me go, you pipsqueak." Grunze felt my biceps and deltoids with his meaty fingers. "You've been training."

I smiled. "Eternal youth, burly boy. Help me get this agitator, and I'll let you in on the secret."

Their artificial eyes fairly popped out of their sockets when I described all the injuries my NEMs had healed. Two small items I omitted—how my NEMs "cured" that poison gas booby trap and how they "healed" my punctured suit. For the sake of credibility, I left those parts out.

"Is it true? Immortality?" For the first time in months, a moist gleam brightened Verinne's eyes.

"Yes, cara." I waved my arms and inadvertently propelled myself up to the ceiling. "Youth everlasting. It's true."

Grunze puffed out his chest. "I'll take the bet."

Winston let out a deep, ragged breath. "I'm in."

Peer pressure triumphed, and Kat caved. "You'd better be right."

"Swear you'll go with me to the gunship," I said, "on your honor as war surfers."

Grunze gestured. "Fuck you sideways. We swear."

So we huddled together, and I cupped my hand around my mouth as if spies were listening. Then I told them the secret: Avoid doctors' orders. My NEMs evolved because they were cut off from the Net.

Verinne arched one eyebrow. "Why didn't we know this before?"

"Because the doctors were protecting their despotic patents," I said.

"No, that's not right." Winny's speech came out slurred

as usual. He leaned forward, resting his hands on his knees. "You've always been prejudiced against doctors."

I'd forgotten Win was an MD himself. "Present company excepted, Winny boy."

"Let me get this straight." Grunze rubbed his boulder-shaped head. "If we stay here inside Provendia's blockade for a couple of weeks, we'll change into superhumans?"

"You don't have to stay here. Go anywhere you like. Just surround yourself in a Net blockade. Liberate your NEMs from doctors' control, and you'll live forever." I gave Winston a friendly wink.

"No Net access?" Kat chewed her hair. "That's harsh."

"Immortality has its price," I said. "Maybe you can find some doctor-blocker wetware."

"It's the damn doctors that keep you alive." Win's outburst startled all of us. His face went red from his effort to steady his palsied muscles. He leaned forward, straining the Velcro straps in his bunk. "It was doctors that invented bioNEMs. Doctors like me." He poked his chest with his thumb. "Yeah, me. Bimbus ol' Winny. I was on that project team."

"Winston, I . . .." His words disoriented me. If Sheeba had been here, she would have hugged poor Win to soothe his feelings, but I was too flabbergasted to move. Apparently, so were the others.

"You think I like being the butt of everybody's joke? Boozing it up to cover my dementia? Pretending I don't know what's happening? I used to be a physician."

"Win." Kat sailed over and enfolded the trembling man in her arms.

Verinne hovered and stroked his elegant head, but his clear blue eyes lingered on me. I felt his reproach like a brand.

"Winston, I'm sorry. I didn't mean to insult you."

"Trust me, the medical community doesn't know about this," he continued. He was having one of his rare lucid moments. His slur almost disappeared, and his eyes showed active intelligence. "We programmed the NEMs with failsafes. Do you think we would unleash immortality? Imagine what that might lead to. We couldn't begin to predict—"

"But Win, I'm living proof." To convince them, I pulled Sheeba's ankh from my breast pocket and sliced a gash in my wrist. The wound self-sealed in under a minute.

"That shouldn't happen." Winston examined my unblemished skin, for all the world like a skeptical high-church doctor. "If what you say is true, you must have encountered some catalyst. An aberrant virus, a biocontaminant, something. This is a freak mutation."

Kat grabbed Winston's collar. "Are you saying our NEMs won't evolve like Nasir's did?"

"Not on your life. He's been exposed to some triggering agent. It's—it's—" Winny squinted from one face to another, and his elegant head quivered. "What were we saying?"

Grunze frowned, and Verinne coughed. Kat tightened her arms around Win's shoulders. "So much for your secret of youth, Nass."

"Hell, I'll give you *my* NEMs," I blurted.

Mouths dropped open. Kat blanched. Verinne said, "It's a capital crime."

"Screw the docs," I said. "If we stay off the Net, they'll never know we violated their miserly copyrights. You'll have perfect health forever, I promise."

Winston leaned forward. "Is that a good thing, Nass?"

Again, his question threw me off balance. "Immortality." I lifted my hands. "You choose."

He wrinkled his handsome nose. "Okay. But—why are we going to the gunship?"

Win's lucid moment had fizzled. It grieved me to see his blue eyes cloud over. "Because you gave your word," I said softly.

Kat sighed and kissed him. "Nass means a gambling debt."

"Oh, I get that." Win kicked his blanket to the floor. "We're doing a war surf."

I glanced from Grunze to Verinne, then to Kat and Winston. As if on cue, we grinned at each other. Then we raised our fists and howled—

"WAR SURF!"

25

YOU CAN AFFORD IT

"It's not catastrophes, murders, deaths, diseases, that
age and kill us; it's the way people look and laugh,
and run up the steps of omnibuses."
—VIRGINIA WOOLF

We planned the surf in record time because I told them
A13 might disintegrate at any moment. They'd seen
the pitted hull. They knew how precarious it was. Sheeba's
life depended on our speed. We had to get Vlad fast, then
rush back to save her.

First, we laid a false trail to hoodwink Trencher. We accelerated directly away from the gunship and swerved behind a field of Greenland.Com factories—rough-looking
old junkers with no running lights—an ideal hiding place.
Then we veered very fast toward Earth's South Pole, and
Kat's high-performance shuttle gave us a ride to remember.
From four thousand kilometers out, we zoomed straight up
under the gunship like stealth lightning. In less than an
hour, we eased into the blind spot beneath the gunship's
belly.

The ship still tracked Heaven's whirling spin around its
counterweight, and Kat set her onboard navigation computer to match it. Since we lay a considerable distance out
from the center of rotation, we circled at terrific speed.

This time, I asked Win politely if he would stay and
man the shuttle, and he graciously agreed. That last burst

of clarity had sapped his strength. As we prepared to go
EVA, I briefed the crew on the waste chute Sheeba and
Liam had used for their entry. Our scans showed Trencher
had still not deployed a security perimeter. Preter-gross incompetence. I made a mental note to have him fired—then
erased it. Trencher was just the sort of greasy slime to fer-
ret out our identities and launch a WTO investigation.

Verinne handed out short-range radios so we could talk
to each other despite Provendia's Net blockade, and as we
stepped through the airlock, the usual banter ensued. The
chitchat waned, however, when we realized how fast our
shuttle was whirling through space and how tight we had to
grip the handholds to keep from flying off. The ovoid gunship loomed above us as glossy and wet-looking as black
oil. We pinged its hull with locator fixes and set our
thrusters navigation to track its angular momentum. We
had to glide only a few dozen meters to the gunship and
grab hold, but this rushing velocity kept us tense and quiet.

Grunze went first. He banged into a scoop drive, slipped
off, then caught a vernier and clung tight. He didn't make it
look easy. Verinne went next. Waiting for my turn, I realized how different this surf felt from others in the past.
With my spanking new EVA suit and best-of-breed
thruster, I should have been mega-blissed on the delicious
sting of fear. But I wanted to get it over with. The only
thing that mattered was getting back to Sheeba.

When my turn came, I made a wild leap for the scoop
drive, missed my target, and Grunzie caught my leg. Thank
the golden gods for his weight training. With one hand, he
slung me in an arc toward the row of handholds. We made
it. See us plastered against the glassy hull, belayed to each
other by a safety line, and slithering along the surface like
four anxious flatworms.

We found the waste chute welded shut. Give Trencher
his due—no one would use that entry again. While Grunze
made asinine jokes about the ship's constipation, Verinne
and I reviewed the schematics on our heads-up display. We

had to crawl another death-defying ten meters to reach the nearest airlock.

Trust Verinne to bring the right surf accessories. She unclipped an electropick from her belt, and with one zap, she breached the airlock entry controls. As soon as the outer door slid open, I leaned in and pressed against the wall to feel for the vibrations. My crewmates must have thought I was nuts. But I felt no sirens, no buzzing alarms. Trencher, what a stiff.

We cycled through the airlock, then cautiously edged into the vacant corridor. Verinne had assured us the gunship used standard ambient magnetism to simulate one-half Earth gravity. So we weren't surprised to find ourselves traipsing along the empty corridor like acrobats. No guards anywhere.

Ambient mag gravity feels weird. It's not even close to the real thing. As you move through it, the programmable lining in your space suit automatically configures to the magnetic fields generated by the floors and walls. This permits you to walk, bend, sit, even jump up and down with a certain efficiency. But your body has no weight. You feel no familiar downward pull. Your flesh and blood bob around freely inside the restraining silken cage of your suit, and your stomach does gymnastics. It's macabre. At least ambient magnetism creates no Coriolis effect—thank the engineers for small favors.

Trencher's laxity allowed us to locate the crew quarters and steal uniforms, just as Sheeba and Liam had done. In fact, we were able to prowl through the entire ship without detection. Once my crewmates got over their initial anxiety, they couldn't stop grinning at each other. Sneaking around an active Com gunship engaged in live war—this had to be the sleekest surf they'd ever done.

We found Vlad locked in the brig. The bunk on which he lay, his tray of untouched food, and a small portable toilet were enveloped together in a transparent quarantine balloon. And perched around the balloon like a ring of creepy voyeurs were six active videocams on tripods. Vlad was sick. And Trencher was catching some Reel.

Verinne, our resident camera geek, slipped behind the videocams and set them to run instant replays for a few minutes.

Once the cams were disabled, Grunze poked the diaphanous medical balloon. "What's wrong with this guy? He looks shriveled."

True, Vlad had lost a lot of weight in his brief captivity. His eyelids looked like husks.

Kat backed away. "Don't touch him. Remember what Trencher said about the quarantine."

"His malady isn't catching." I slit the plastic balloon with my surfer knife, and Kat let out a squeal. "Hush," I said, lifting the young medic in my arms. With my NEM-boosted strength and the gunship's half gravity, he weighed almost nothing. "Let's get him suited up. Careful, mind his head."

Kat took a few deep breaths and checked her heart-rate monitor. "You'd damn well better know what you're doing, Deepra."

Verinne had brought a spare EVA suit—the pearly pink one. As we dressed Vlad, his head and limbs rolled loose, and his eyes didn't focus. I was the only one who understood his broken prote drawl. He wanted to go to the garden.

We snuck out of the brig completely unnoticed—a totally Valium Class One surf. Any Fred could have done it. Trencher had to be the most inept executive in Com annals. It galled me to think I'd been the one to hire him. What had I ever seen in that nudnik?

It was near the airlock that the Provendia guards ambushed us with a hail of paralysis darts. "What the freak?" "Look out!" "They've got us pinned!"

The nasty darts stung like wasps. I took three in the shoulder, went down on one knee, and dropped Vlad. Verinne groaned when the darts hit her back, and Kat screamed curses. As the troops closed in, Grunze put up a heroic fight, ripping handfuls of darts from his chest and kick-punching his assailants. He delayed them just long enough for Verinne and Kat to slip into the airlock.

I crawled over and sealed the hatch behind them—it was the last move I made before my legs stopped working. But the girls didn't complete their exit. The paralysis darts had already attacked their central nervous systems, and their vocal cords froze so quickly, they couldn't speak the final commands. Just as well. If they'd gone EVA in that immobilized condition, they might have drifted into eternity.

The guards opened the airlock, dragged their rigid bodies out and piled them on top of the prostrate Grunze. Then they added Vlad and me to the heap. We couldn't resist. My lock-jawed crewmates gazed at me with absolute terror.

I knew what they were thinking—job termination. Loss of executive privilege, demotion to the protean abyss. They visibly quailed, and I can only imagine what black nightmares swarmed behind their unblinking eyes. My friends. I was the one who'd brought them to this. While the guards bumped our petrified bodies along the corridor, I rapidly made up lies.

Trencher was waiting on the bridge. He looked just as I remembered, hairless and bony, with skin like a bruised lily. The man had no eyelashes, and his reptilian eyes swiveled odiously. He had narrow shoulders and wide, womanish hips. Even the padded Provendia uniform failed to lend him an air of command. The guards dumped us at his feet.

"Honorable Chairman Deepra. My mentor and guide. What an unexpected pleasure." His voice rolled smoother than synthetic honey. He snickered and wet his lips.

Thanks to my NEMs, the paralysis drug wore off quickly, and I was able to squirm and look around. Bad news. An active Net link glowed in a nearby workstation, which meant my NEMs had lost the shelter of the blockade. Soon, the doctors would launch new restraint orders. But for the moment, I still felt strong. While Trencher paraded around, gloating and nudging us with his boot, I twisted carefully to browse my thumbscreen. It was blank. No icons. No message menu. Just a pale, manicured thumbnail.

Was I dead? I didn't feel dead. I could still see and—I took an experimental breath—yes, my lungs still worked. Then I realized what had happened. The glass man had found a way to disconnect my IBiS from the Net.

"Aren't you going to fight?" Trencher goaded, swishing his hips. "You're pathetic. I expected more from the world-class surfer ace. Oh sure, I browse the Agonist Web page. I know all about you and your secret club."

Spite twisted his leathery face. He stood tapping his foot, hands on his brass-studded belt, waiting for my answer. I pretended to experiment with my vocal cords, humming and clearing my throat as if they were still frozen. Then I spoke in a fake husky whisper.

"Everything you say is being recorded."

"Are you kidding me?" The man emitted the most unnatural laugh I'd ever heard. He sounded like a screeching animal. "You're trespassing illegally, Mr. Chairman Emeritus. Playing your surfer games, shelling out your stingy bribes. You think you're king of the gods. But this time, you're a bygone."

"You have the right to remain silent," I croaked. "Everything you say will be used against you."

"What the hell?" His eyes rolled suspiciously. "What scam are you playing?"

I could move freely—the glass man had eliminated every trace of Trencher's drug from my system. But I remained on the floor, pretending to struggle against the paralysis, waiting for the right moment. "This is an unscheduled inspection, Trencher. We've been testing your security measures. I've already sent my report to the board."

"You're bluffing."

"Am I? Call your CEO."

Of course I was bluffing, but I had to brave it out. Trencher was a bimbus. Maybe I could sucker him. I snuck a peek at the workstation screen, hoping for godsends. Deep within Provendia's rust-clogged chain of command, Chad had been working through channels, getting that euthanasia order stopped and retiring this gunship back to base. The recall message should have hit Trencher's in-box by now. If only he would read it, then my bluff might work.

"The board has known about your negligence for months," I lied. "This is just a fact-gathering visit. Your termination's already stamped and dated."

"Termination? After all the crap I've fetched and toted for you? Fifty years I've walked in your buggery footsteps, eaten your leftovers, shined your bloody shoes!"

"Stow it, Trencher. Check your mail. I believe you'll find new orders." I sat up with much show of groaning and stiffness. My arms hung limp, my hands curled inward. I nodded awkwardly toward the Net screen.

He saw the direction of my gaze. "Check the incoming," he ordered the crewman. His lily skin was going damp.

"We were friends once," I said, shamming a tone of regret. "It's not my style to leave friends in the lurch."

"Hell yes, we were friends." He hung over the screen browsing the scroll of new emails. "Deepra, you can't let them fire me."

"Maybe I can get you off."

When he turned to face me, I rubbed my thumb and forefinger together, discreetly signaling a request for a bribe. At that, his hairless white scalp drew up in ripples, and the bare humps of his eyebrows turned pink. "Clear the bridge," he ordered. What a dunce. He totally fell for it.

Kat and Grunze still sprawled together on top of Vlad, exactly as they had fallen. Their movements were sluggish and weak. Beneath them, Vlad lay unconscious. Verinne pushed herself up to a sitting position, but she couldn't speak. I waited till the last guard closed the door and left us alone with Trencher.

He fidgeted at the screen, scanning every new email and rubbing his knobby head. He muttered steadily to himself.

"Yeah, security's a little lax, but who cares about this dirt-wad factory? Nobody comes here. This is a shit job. That's all I get anymore, and it's because of you, Deepra. You blackballed me. Hell, you were my role model. I used to worship you, man."

His behavior sickened me. Was this the kind of disciple I inspired? "Cut the flattery. Do you want my help or not?"

"Like I have a choice?" He sat down at the workstation and lifted the headset to transmit a query. He was calling my bluff. I sprang to my feet and batted the headset away.

"Huh?" He propelled himself backward in the rolling chair and bashed against the navigation con.

"You have two seconds to get some health care for my inspection team," I commanded.

Trencher bit his fingers and eyed me with unabashed fright. "I don't believe you." If he'd called the guards, I would have gone for his throat, but instead, he hunched over the screen and went back to browsing email. I stood above him like an executioner, ready to strike a blow to his neck if he made a wrong move. Silently, he clicked through his enormous backlog of messages. And there it was in the queue, the recall order. It had come in an hour ago.

"See." I jabbed my finger at the screen. "Now hustle."

Trencher went maximally unzipped when he saw the email. The man honestly thought we were going to fire him. It made me sad to watch him scurry around like a nervous lizard, doing my bidding. He ordered paralysis antidotes for Vlad and the Agonists, gave us his private quarters to recuperate in, and had his personal chef prepare us a nice snack. While my friends convalesced, he kept peeking in to ask what else we might need. I finally sent him off to put his résumé in order.

"Poor Trencher." I tucked his plush blanket around Vlad's shoulders.

"That schlemiel? You'd feel sorry for the WTO." Kat stuffed her cheeks with ersatz lobster roll.

Grunze licked mayo from his fingers. "Just like Sheeba. You two are a pair of bleeding hearts."

"But you spin lies like a true artist, caro." Verinne patted my hand and sipped a squeeze-bulb of champagne.

Recovering in the captain's suite, we shared the after-glow that follows a difficult surf. We told jokes, relived critical moments, devoured large quantities of food. I slipped a satin pillow under Vlad's head and tried to feed him some water.

"Why don't you buy Trencher's contract and ship him out to Uranus?" Grunze seized another sandwich. "Show him who's alpha male."

"You can afford it." Kat picked meat fiber from her teeth.

"Yeah, while you're at it, buy this whole fuckin' gun-ship." Grunzie gestured at the cabin's elegant fixtures. "It'd make a primo trophy."

"Right, I can afford it." My crewmates were always egging me to spend money. It was part of our game. Yes, I could afford the gunship. I could afford lots of things. While I dribbled water between Vlad's lips, Grunze and Kat smirked, waiting to hear how I would meet their chal-lenge. I blew kisses and almost spouted a wisecrack, but then, somewhere, the karmic scales of justice pivoted on their axes. Or possibly, the NEMs inspired me. For what-ever reason, I got a new idea.

"I know what Sheeba wants."

The Agonists stopped chewing and stared at me strangely. Perhaps it was the tremble in my voice.

"It's a stroke of genius," I went on. "Why didn't I think of this before?"

"Don't keep us guessing. What is it?" said Kat.

I smiled mysteriously and lowered Vlad's head to the pillow. Saving the medic's life might earn Shee's forgive-ness, but this brilliant new gift could actually convince her to like me again!

The medic was too sleepy to drink water, so I let him rest, and while my friends razzed me for details, I used Trencher's phone to call Chad. My cyberassistant had megatons to tell me. He'd succeeded in killing the euthanasia scheme, but the board wanted an emergency meeting to find out what was going on. He offered to go as my proxy. Chad was very talented at blowing smoke rings and spinning cover stories—but I cut him off midsentence.

"Chad, I want you to buy Heaven."

Kat dropped her crème brulée. "That's what you're giving Sheeba? That shabby old tank?"

"Buy all the worker contracts, too," I shouted jubilantly over the phone.

Verinne arched both eyebrows, and Grunze choked on his chocolate chip cookie. They acted as if I'd wobbled right over the edge. "That's too much." "It'll bankrupt you." "Nasir, think."

I grinned like a loon.

Chad went into diligence mode. Had I weighed this decision carefully? Did I realize the magnitude of the transaction? I spoke a preprogrammed code word to short-circuit his questions, and we worked out the details in minutes. When my friends objected, I cavalierly waved them away. Everything had to fall together at light-speed, with absolute secrecy, and Chad loved that kind of intrigue. He suggested that we set up a blind trust.

I covered the phone and said, "Hey, guys, will you serve as my trustees?"

"You're loco, Nass. Absolutely unzipped," said Grunze. "What's the annual salary for a trustee?"

When I named a figure, my companions displayed a unanimous change of heart. "Yeah, put my name down." "Me too." "I'm in."

"We'll serve in perpetuity, caro"—Verinne gave me a devious wink and whispered behind her hand—"once you share your immortal bioNEMs." Running the risk of a little capital punishment didn't frighten Verinne one bit.

Naturally, Chad and I were of one mind about hiring cyberstaff instead of human managers. In seconds, Chad recruited a team of AIs to control Heaven's orbit, maintain the Net blockade and file the tax returns. Oh, Sheeba was going to love this.

After further consideration, I asked Chad to make some rush purchases on the hot market. For starters, I wanted . . .

a. end-to-end hull renovations
b. new orbit synchronizers
c. a state-of-the-art medical lab
d. a gross of EVA suits
e. a complete new lighting system
f. interactive learning modules for grades K through 30
g. some windows

Despite my code word, Chad introduced another note of caution. "Boss, how are we going to pay for all this? I already cashed most of your bonds to bribe that Captain Trencher."

"Sell more. Sell my Provendia stocks."

Dumping those shares would bring an end to my cushy chairman-emeritus gig, but I didn't reflect on my future. All I wanted was to regain Sheeba's good graces, and this was bound to do it.

Vlad still lay in a daze on Trencher's bed, but the glass man would help me cure him. I rubbed my hands together, imagining Shee's delight when she saw her lop-jawed medic again. A sweet euphoria eased through my veins. Everything was going to be all right. Heaven would be safe, and Shee would come home, and our lives would get back to normal.

As soon as my friends felt well enough to travel, I asked them to carry Vlad to the shuttle and give him first aid. I would stay behind and deal with the captain.

Poor Trencher was such a wreck, I decided not to tease him any further. We kept the terms simple. Trencher agreed to return our bribe money and to remain cosmically mute about our surf. In return, I would deep-six the "report" on his lame security. As an afterthought, I told Chad to recommend the numbnuts for promotion. After so thoroughly humiliating him, it was the least I could do. Besides, he and Provendia deserved each other.

As I prepared to depart, he personally checked the self-sealed dart holes in my space suit. "Mr. Chairman, you teach me new lessons every time we meet. You're my guru, sir." Then he gave me a tearful hug. No doubt about it, Trencher was destined to rise.

26

JUST TAP

"People like you and I, though mortal of course
like everyone else, do not grow old no matter how
long we live."
—ALBERT EINSTEIN

By now you may have asked yourself—many times—
why you keep browsing this memoir. The narrator, you
will say, has no redeeming traits. He's a pint-sized, elderly
blowhard with false hair and a small lump of biomachinery
for a heart. Yet here you sit scrolling through my words,
well past the middle of my story, and you may still be wondering, just as I am—why the freaking hell is Nasir Deepra
waiting in that anteroom to die? We're coming close now.
Please keep me company. This place is lonesome.

Back in the shuttle, Vlad's thin body rested in the bunk.
We covered him with Win's blanket and Velcroed him in so
he wouldn't float free. Kat dribbled a little water into the
young man's mouth through a microgravity tube—but he
didn't swallow. He showed all the symptoms of the malady.

"Do you have a cyberdoc?" I asked.

Kat pointed aft toward the medical bin. "What kind of
drug does he need?"

"He needs blood," I said. "A couple of liters."

Picture, if you will, the alarm that glared at me from
four executive faces. Imagine how they drifted into walls,
speechless with outrage. Unfortunately, the speechless
phase didn't last long.

"Are you totally brain-dead?"

"Share executive blood with a prote?"

"You're not serious."

My friends nervously laughed and elbowed each other, assuring themselves I'd made a bad joke, but when they saw me fish through Kat's medical bin and pull out the portable cyberdoc, they moved closer and watched with suspicion. When I asked the device how to set up a blood transfusion, Kat knocked it out of my hands.

"Deepra, you're loco."

Then they all spoke at once, and I had to yell to make myself heard. "Vlad can't help us if he's dead."

My shout temporarily shut them up. I found the cyber-doc drifting under the bunk and latched it to the wall so I could study its control panel. The mechanism was about the size of an espresso machine, and it looked equally complicated. I'd never operated one before, but the screen alleged that, with its user-friendly help features, even a child could perform open-heart surgery. Again, I asked the device how to set up a blood transfusion.

"Nasir, tell us what you're doing." Verinne sounded like a psychiatrist trying to soothe a raging lunatic. The others quietly surrounded me.

"Don't try anything," I warned them. "This boy has a condition, and I can cure it with a large concentration of my NEMs. Two liters of blood will do the trick."

"Smutty talk," Kat hissed.

"But Nasir," Verinne said, "what you're suggesting's unethical."

"Plus it's obscene," Kat said with a sniff. "Mixing blood. Ick."

"Who says so, huh?" I slipped a pillow under Vlad's arm. "Who decides what's obscene and what's not?"

Grunze eased next to me. "Sweet-pee, this isn't you talking. Something's got into you.."

"Sheeba found the cure by accident," I said. "At first, we thought one liter would be enough." I tapped Vlad's arm and scrutinized his veins. His head lolled back and forth. "Look at him. He's dying of thirst, but he won't drink."

"Who cares? He's a hostile." Kat made a grab for the cyberdoc, and when I caught her wrist, she scratched me. "Why don't we just feed this guy some more Peps and interrogate him?"

I ignored her and watched the cyberdoc extrude an appendage to tap Vlad's vein. Then I rolled up my sleeve.

"Katherine asked you a question." Grunze gripped the back of my neck. "Why do we need to cure this sodder's disease?"

Glassy NEM power rippled through me, and I shook off Grunze's hand. With a look, I dared him to touch me again. "Everything I do is for Sheeba."

Figuring out how to work Kat's cyberdoc proved much easier than convincing the Agonists to let me do it. Kat's whine about obscenity was absurd. She was kowtowing to moral fashion, I saw that now. On the other hand, Verinne made logical arguments against sharing NEMs with employees. Widespread longevity would change all the equations of supply and demand, she said, and it wasn't fair to saddle unschooled workers with so many extra years.

"Yeah, think about it," said Grunze. "If protes started living as long as we do, where in hell would we put 'em all?"

"This is only one boy, and we need his help to find Sheeba," I reminded them, smoothly failing to mention the liters of blood I'd already donated to Kaioko.

It was Winston who came closest to stopping me. "Nasir, if workers get NEMs, it might cause another Crash."

Winston's words touched each of us. At a profound level, he stirred the old fear that drove all our decisions. The Crash. No one liked to speak of it. I'm not sure which memory we hated worse, the Crash or what we did to survive it. Do you imagine we wanted to face that sordid time again?

But the global climate was still degrading, and our fragile economy was growing feebler by the decade—because we senior execs were the only ones shoring it up. That's why we kept ourselves strong and vigorous—we knew what could happen. If we didn't fend off another Crash, who would? The survival of our society, our values, our culture, everything of worth depended on the lessons we'd learned from history, and no short-lived employee could appreciate our hindsight. For the good of humankind, we had to keep longevity to ourselves. I am not a wicked man. Let me confess, breaking that taboo made me shudder.

"But I don't care. Sheeba needs us."

"Well, I'm not watching." Kat put on her helmet and went EVA.

Verinne flinched when the cyberdoc tapped my vein. Grunze wouldn't make eye contact. They soon followed Kat outside and left me to perform my depravities in private. Maybe they did so out of friendship rather than repugnance. I wanted to believe that.

Winston stayed, though. I floated in free space beside Vlad's bunk during the transfusion, and Win held my foot so I didn't drift too far from the cyberdoc. I thought he'd forgotten what I was doing, but he surprised me.

"Why do you wanna save these protes, Nass?"

"It's not them. It's Sheeba."

"Slippery Nass, you've made friends with 'em."

"You're dreaming. Hand me that gauze."

An hour later, Vlad sat up and asked for water. The Agonists had returned by then, but at first Vlad didn't see them. I was still feeling woozy myself from giving so much blood, and as I drifted against the bunk, one of the metal rails barked my shin. Damn, this bloodletting gnarled me. My NEMs always took a while to recover.

As soon as Vlad understood how to suck nutrient through a microgravity straw, he downed a full liter. His color was returning, and I could swear his lopsided face was filling out with new flesh. We toasted each other with squeeze-bulbs of orangeade. Then Vlad stretched out his fingers and stared at his hand, as if he were flabbergasted to find himself still alive.

"Feeling better?" I said. "You want to go home?"

He nodded and gave a slight smile. "Thank you." When

he noticed the others, he drew back in the bunk, clinging to the straps that held him secure in the weightless cabin. No doubt, they'd given him unkind treatment earlier. "Nasir, you know these commies?"

"Don't call us that, you filthy agitator."

"Katherine, be calm," I said, waving her back.

My friends hovered in a loose knot near the console, watching with sour expressions while I floated beside the bunk shielding Vlad.

"I'll take you home if you'll show me how to get in," I said, unrolling a printout of Heaven's plan.

Vlad eyed my crew, then shook his head.

"Kaioko's sick, and she's been calling your name," I whispered.

"Everyone die sooner later," he said. But he didn't deny knowing a way in.

Since my small lie hadn't worked, I tried another tack. I showed him the cyberdoc screen that still displayed stats from our transfusion. "Look, we found the cure. You were right about good blood chasing out the bad. I gave you some of mine, and it made you well."

Vlad grasped the cyberdoc and read the stats. Then he asked the device for additional reports. He seemed well versed in its capabilities. Before this, I didn't even know he could read.

"There's something here in your blood," he said, pointing his stubby finger to an arcane line of code on the screen. "Something I don't recognize. What is it?"

"It's probably some medication I take. What does it matter? You're cured."

Vlad studied the data with an uncertain frown. Then he placed his hand in the cyberdoc's mouth and gave himself a health exam. Evidently, the results astonished him. Perusing the report, he absentmindedly polished off a second liter of orangeade.

"Will you give your blood to the others?" he asked.

"Sure," I lied, tapping the map of Heaven. "Show us how to get in."

It took time and cunning to overcome Vlad's mistrust of my crewmates. My generous blood donation and his own restored health were the strongest points in our favor. I kept feeding him squeeze-bulbs of nutrient, and finally, we bamboozled him into showing us Heaven's back door. When his finger touched the spot on the map, it seemed so obvious that, subconsciously, I must have already known it. Or maybe the glass man did.

Heaven was made from a fuel tank, and its pointy end had once been the tank's nozzle. That made a natural opening. There in that nozzle, Liam had improvised an emergency airlock out of scrap and spare parts. Surrounding this makeshift airlock like a protective fence were the six colossal couplings that linked Heaven to its tether. And shielded within this fence, the secret lock led straight into the garden.

"Heaven's blind," I told my friends. "They've lost all external sensors. Unless Liam happens to be spacewalking when we board, they won't see us coming."

"We can tap the hull to let them know," Vlad said innocently.

"Dear boy, that's brilliant." Kat snuggled under Vlad's arm.

She'd gotten very chummy with the medic since my NEMs had restored his looks. Her favorite live-action role play was Mata Hari, the exotic lady spy. So she flapped her fake eyelashes and worked her scarlet-dyed mouth into a kind of sexual grimace. She probably thought this would seduce the youth into revealing information. Or maybe the medic had caught her fancy. His physique was growing more supple with each passing minute, and the intelligent gleam had returned to his brown eyes. Even his lopsided jaw seemed more symmetrical.

Kat ran her fingernails through his wavy brown hair. "Is there a secret code we should know?"

"Nothing special. Just tap a few times." Vlad shied from her advances with a perplexed raise of eyebrows.

He recommended that we wait for Heaven to pass into

Earth's shadow. No sense exposing ourselves to solar radiation. When the time came, we suited up, all six of us. I didn't have the heart to leave Winston behind again. While Vlad wasn't looking, Kat handed out the stun guns and sticky-string pumps, and we quietly slipped the weapons into our pockets. I didn't want the medic to know we were armed. As an afterthought, I grabbed the portable cyberdoc and zipped it in my backpack, explaining that Sheeba might need first aid.

Kat positioned her shuttle as close as possible to the tether couplings, then programmed the autopilot to track Heaven's spin. We were taking a risk leaving the shuttle unattended, but everyone was stoked for the surf. We set our thrusters on low, stepped through the airlock and dove.

This close to the center of rotation, we spun with less angular momentum than we had on the gunship. Earth's night face cast a cloudy glow, but with metavision, we could see continents glistening through the smog, like hazy galaxies scattered across the dark oceans.

At first, the massive alloy couplings that attached Heaven's tether appeared to be fixed hardware. But closer, we could see the metal joints flex and buckle. The tether's thick, woven composite stretched wider than a city street, and it oscillated constantly. If there had been a medium to carry sound waves, we might have heard it singing. Those shocks created by the orbital adjustment had never completely disappeared. They'd merely died to a steady quiver, dampened by the tether's friction.

Maneuvering between the couplings proved trickier than we expected. Grunze and I miscalculated and overshot. Kat collided with a metal buckle. Vlad bounced like a newbie. Only Verinne navigated with style and touched down at the nozzle rim.

Heaven's secret airlock was small, and we had to enter one at a time. Vlad dropped through first while the rest of us clung to the couplings and waited our turns. I went next. Since we were in Earth's shadow, I expected the garden to be dark, but it wasn't. Small solar cells glimmered through the foliage like ultraviolet glowworms, backlighting the leaves and haloing every object with a silvery sheen. The effect was enchanting. By this soft luminescence, I found Vlad perched in the leafy crown of a tree. Beside him sat three little boys and a young girl with a baby.

A weight thudded onto my back, and thin arms reached around my neck. With a laugh, the child swung around in front of me. Keesha. Her birthmark blushed purple in the silvery light. She squealed and smeared my faceplate with fingerprints.

I set her on a limb and ripped off my helmet. "Tell the kids to hide. Quick, Vlad. Before my friends come." It was only too easy to imagine Grunzie scorching one of the kids with his stun gun.

Vlad didn't hesitate. He stuck a thumb and finger in his mouth and gave three shrill whistles. Like magic, Keesha and the others vanished among the leaves. Throughout the length and breadth of Deck Five, foliage trembled as kids scrambled into hiding, and I watched them disappear with relief.

Seconds later, the Agonists dropped through the airlock and gathered in the treetop. They gawked at their surroundings like tourists. The garden frankly astonished them. Nothing had prepared them for this botanical opulence limned in spectral silver light. One by one, they slipped off their helmets and inhaled the humid air.

When the misters switched on, moisture beaded our skin, and Verinne laughed like a girl. "Nasir, what *is* this place?"

Kat slid down a huge wet leaf and bounced in a web of vines. "This is plasmic!"

Grunze tore off a branch. "It's real. I've seen a few hot-houses on Earth, but nothing like this."

Verinne rolled her face against the wet leaves and caught the dripping vines in her arms. Her shoulders relaxed as if years of stress had fallen away. Winston stuffed a long green veggie down the front of his EVA suit and pranced like a clown. Kat poked a flower behind her ear.

"This greenware's worth a pile of deutsch." Grunze sniffed one of the vats. "Is it some kind of research project?"

I caught Vlad's eye and winked. "Maximal nondisclosure. None of you say a word about this."

Why did I lie to my own crew? It felt wrongheaded, and yet an instinct prodded me to shield the garden.

Kat plucked more blossoms, and Verinne squeezed the juice of a yellow fruit onto her tongue. Winny stuffed more veggies in his suit, and Grunze slid an arm down in one of the vats to check out the nutrient.

"Focus, guys. We've come for Sheeba," I reminded them.

As Vlad led us through the maze of flora down toward the ladder well, my pals tripped over vines and grabbed the trees for stability. They weren't accustomed to the Coriolis effect, but that didn't slow them down. They swung on vines and threw fruit at each other and spat seeds. Totally infantile. They would have lost themselves among the glimmering plants if I hadn't hustled them along.

The whole time, I kept my eye peeled for errant juves, but thankfully, none of them showed their faces. When we found the airlock to Deck Four, I discreetly asked Vlad to wait behind and be the last one through. I felt oddly protective of the toads.

Had I made a mistake bringing the Agonists here? What would happen when my friends met the Heavenians? I began to have serious doubts, but there was a momentum building, a sort of rising tide, and it carried me along at breakneck speed. My eyesight grew sharp, and my reactions quickened. The Agonists were resources, a voice kept telling me. The glass man flexed his (my) overtensed muscles.

No solar cells brightened the ladder well. Heaven's fickle power grid had crashed again. So with helmet lights glaring, we descended the dark ladder and gathered around the bulkhead leading into sick-ward's anteroom.

"I'll go in first and talk to them," I whispered while

Vlad was still above us in the garden. "Maybe we can get Sheeba away without violence."

"Talk? They're fuckin' *agitators*." Grunze checked the settings on his stun gun.

"Violence is what we came for," Kat said as she slotted a load of sticky-string in her pump. "One hundred says we have casualties before this is over. We'll get primo Reel."

Winston chuckled and sprayed laser beams at the wall. "Mega-sleek surf."

When Verinne unpacked her cameras, I saw disaster building. She'd brought a bag full of Bumblebees, and she clipped tiny camcorders to each of our collars. She wanted to cover every angle. "This Reel will be very special to me, Nasir. Imagine. We're actually surfing inside Heaven."

"Wait while I go first. If we swarm in there all at once, they might hurt Sheeba."

My friends accepted that reasoning. They agreed to wait in the ladder well while I went ahead. But Verinne activated the small camera in my collar. "We'll be watching, and if we see trouble, we'll come."

Warily, I touched the wall and listened for vibrations. Sheeba was in the anteroom speaking to Kaioko. Liam was there, too, along with Geraldine and Juani. With my NEM-sharpened senses, I could feel their different respiration rates. All the ringleaders were gathered on the other side of that door. Behind me in the ladder well, the Agonists fondled their weapons. Ye graven beasts, I felt caught between fire and kindling. "This is all about Sheeba," I whispered.

"Of course it is." Verinne patted my shoulder. "Settle down. We can do this."

When Vlad dropped into the well, the others hid their weapons, and I drew him aside. "You and I should go first. We don't want to start an accidental fight."

Vlad glanced at the others. "You don't trust them. I understand."

His words brought me up short—because he was right, I

didn't trust them. Or did I? Who was I conspiring with and who was I deceiving? Neither? Both? Vlad opened the bulkhead door, and with a quickening breath, I peered into the anteroom.

27

IS THIS ENOUGH?

"There's no such thing as old age, there is
only sorrow."
—EDITH WHARTON

" Beau, what happens after death?"

Sheeba asked me that question the night before we entered Heaven. It was late. We were lounging in my suite at Mira, and she was rubbing my toes with a smooth, round, polarizing magnet. Her question startled me out of a luxurious doze.

"After death? Nothing," I said. "Your mind's obliterated."

"No paradise? Rebirth to a higher plane? Lake of fire, maybe?"

"You just black out."

She squeezed lotion in her hands and rubbed my heels. "Do we go on dreaming?"

"*Nada. Nichts. Niente.* We cease to exist. End of story."

"Hm. That's a funny thing to wish for."

I jerked as if she'd pinched me. "Sheeba, why do you keep saying that? I don't wish for death."

She tickled my feet. "Cross your heart and hope to die?"

"It's no joke," I said.

"Nass, it's okay to wish for death sometimes. Everybody does."

"Not me. Not you. Not anybody we know."

Her questions were ruining our otherwise magnificent therapy session. My muscles tensed up again, so she massaged my calves and worked her thumbs along the backs of my thighs. Then she straddled my legs and kneaded my buttocks. I groaned softly, and just as I was relaxing, she said, "You look for death in these wars."

"Wrong. I am totally at one with the survival instinct."

She giggled and bounced on my legs. "And you say I'm full of fizz. Ha ha ha." Then she tickled my ribs. "You don't have the slightest inkling what happens after death."

I twisted and grabbed her hands to make her stop tickling me, but she arm-wrestled me down. The girl was strong.

"Swear it doesn't fascinate you." She laughed. "Swear."

She had me pinned. I said, "Sheeba, this isn't funny."

"You think about death all the time." She squeezed my wrists. "You fear it and hope for it, and you spend molto deutsch running away from it. That's a lot to feel about *nada*."

• • •

A lot to feel, yes. Megatons. As I peeked into the anteroom, Kat and Grunze milled restlessly behind me in the dark ladder well, fingering their concealed weapons. Verinne checked her video feeds, and Winston covertly recharged his laser pistol. I felt their menace building like voltage.

When Vlad and I slipped into the anteroom and closed the door behind us, Sheeba didn't notice at first. She was bending over the work counter, studying an image through the nanoscope. Liam stood beside her, draping his lanky arm around her shoulder. Kaioko sat on the table swinging her legs, while Juani and Geraldine leaned against the opposite counter, chewing plant stems. The scene was quiet, domestic. The fluorescent light flickered.

Only an instant elapsed before Sheeba turned and saw me. Or perhaps it was an age. In that immeasurable time, I perceived the contented way she leaned into Liam's caress, and jealousy sliced through me.

"Vlad!" Kaioko jumped off the table and ran into the medic's outstretched arms.

Juani grinned. "Blade, is that you? You found Vlad."

Geraldine hefted her hammer. While Kaioko hugged the medic, Sheeba faced me uneasily, and Liam swept up a heavy scrap of metal from the floor. He would have thrown it at me, but Sheeba touched his hand. "Put it down. He brought Vlad."

My heightened senses picked up exactly how much pressure she used and how intimately their gazes locked. Liam lowered the weapon.

I took off my backpack, drew out the portable cyberdoc and set it on the table as a peace offering. Liam eyed me warily, noticing my new suit. He kept the scrap metal handy.

Sheeba ran her fingers over the cyberdoc's controls. "You came back to make amends."

"I stopped the euthanasia order, Shee."

"He tricking us." Geraldine came toward me.

"No, wait," I said. "The gunship's gone. The war's over."

"Liar." Geraldine twirled the hammer left-handed. Her right arm hung in a sling. I'd done that when I escaped. I'd broken her wrist.

A splint shackled Liam's leg, and even in the reduced gravity, he moved with a limp as he edged around the table. I must have done that, too, when I tossed him into the bales. His face showed bruises. "Why you here?" he asked.

"Sheeba . . ." I couldn't think what else to say.

Vlad met Liam in a hasty embrace, and they exchanged quick greetings. Then Vlad gestured toward the door. "Four 'xecs waiting outside to take Sheeba Zee."

"I'm not going anywhere," Sheeba said.

Liam gripped his metal bludgeon and signaled to Juani and Geraldine to guard the door. The boy leaped to obey, but Geraldine didn't follow the chief's order. She moved behind me and hooked her hammer claws around my throat. "Let me kill him."

"He save my life," Vlad said. Rapidly, the medic told them how I'd bargained him away from the gunship and given him a transfusion. Sheeba shot me a startled smile, but Liam narrowed his eyes and chewed his mustache.

Kaioko said, "Gee, let him go. I told you he a good man."

But Gee didn't. When I tried to move, her clawhammer pressed into my Adam's apple. I could have flung her against the wall with one hand, but my goal was peace, not violence.

So I drew a deep breath. "Heaven's yours, Sheeba. I bought it for you. All these employees belong to you now. You can do whatever you like with them."

Sheeba's eyes went wide—with anger. "Say you don't mean that the way it sounds."

That wasn't the reaction I expected. This was going all wrong. I meant to make her happy. When I tried to explain, Geraldine's hammer claw bit into my neck and cut off my wind.

Sheeba took a step toward me, but Liam drew her back, and I hated him for that. He shielded her with his body—as if I would ever harm her. He said, "You bring these others to euth' us."

I pushed Geraldine's hammer away. "Stupido punk. I came for Sheeba. Do you want her to stay here and die?"

Liam's face reddened, and he raised the chunk of metal to strike me. Then, in a spasm of voiceless rage, he flung it across the deck. Its ringing clatter unsettled everyone, and the sound he made in his rich, manly baritone came out more a whimper than a roar. Words rumbled deep in his throat as if he were strangling. "Sheeba, go with him. You be better away from here."

"But we found the cure!" Shee turned to her nanoscope and bounced on her tiptoes. "Vlad, you have to see this."

The medic crossed the small room and bent to peer through the eyepiece. Sheeba jittered with excitement. "You see? It's a sample of Kaioko's blood. Those crystals are called NEMs. They made her well."

Vlad drew away with a puzzled frown. Then he lifted the cyberdoc from the table and activated its memory. "That's the same thing Nasir gave me."

"It's the cure," Kaioko whispered, almost reverently.

She stood at his elbow, bright-eyed and pink-cheeked. I think she'd grown taller.

Vlad beckoned me toward the nanoscope. "Come and look, Nasir."

Liam nodded to Geraldine, and grudgingly, the wench let me pass. I squinted through the eyepiece, and there among the pearl and ruby platelets, I saw diamonds. The faceted silicon molecules zigged and zagged in linear search patterns, sharply sculpted, transparent, methodical. As I watched, a few of them linked to form a tiny diaphanous membrane, which folded up like origami to create a multilimbed crystal. This fantastical, jagged creature rolled along in a jerky dance till it found mates and formed a six-pointed ring. As more rings adhered together, they began to shape the first trace outlines of a lattice.

Sheeba nudged my elbow. "I was hoping to use Kaioko's blood to inoculate the others, but her NEM count is still too low. She doesn't have nearly the concentration you have, Nass."

"I've been collecting the suckers for decades," I muttered, lost in wonder. Under the nanoscope, glassy NEMs circled and flashed. They glowed with internal energy. They scintillated.

"There are 114 people living here," Sheeba said, breaking my concentration. "Kaioko can never give enough blood to save them all. We need a hell of a lot more NEMs."

I let Sheeba's words sink in. That was way more toads than I'd guessed. "Dearest, I'll buy NEMs for everyone if you'll come away with me."

She sat on the counter. "You can't buy NEMs. They're a controlled substance."

Yes, I knew. NEMs were impossible to buy without an official, biometrically certified prescription. You couldn't even get them on the hot market. Believe me, I had tried. But I was desperate.

"Sheeba, I've ordered a complete medical lab with all the latest gadgets. Vlad can give everyone the best possible treatment. I'll—I'll—transfer these people to Earth if need be."

"Earth?" Juani fidgeted, guarding the door. "But we can't live there. Our bones crack."

"Nass, I'm staying to help. You can stay, too." Sheeba stooped a little so we were face-to-face. Her water-colored eyes sparkled with reflections from the strobing fluorescent light, and her pupils widened. Dear child, how blithely she wanted to throw her life away.

"What about the four 'xecs?" Geraldine moved to the door and flattened her ear against the steel. "They got those Nemmy things. Why don't we take *their* blood?"

Everyone turned to face the wench. "She's right," Vlad murmured.

"Yes!" Sheeba's face brightened. "We'll get the Agonists to donate blood."

In reflex, I covered the camera hidden in my collar, but it was too late. The Agonists had just overheard that exchange. Out in the ladder well, they were watching my surf on their wrist screens, and I could imagine their reactions all too clearly.

Sheeba bounded toward the door, glowing with enthusiasm. "They can give two liters apiece if we draw it slowly. That can save at least eight or ten more people."

"Don't say that," I whispered, dreading what my friends might do. Covertly, I gestured toward the camera clipped to my collar, but Shee didn't notice.

Liam did, though. He grabbed my collar, plucked off the Bumblebee and rolled it between his fingers. "Surveillance camera. You betray your friends? Whose side you on?"

"I'm on Sheeba's side." I knocked the camera from Liam's hand, and I would've taken possession of Shee by brute force, but at that moment, Geraldine screamed and jolted away from the door.

She landed flat on her back, and a wisp of smoke curled up from her hair. Juani yelped and leaped aside, too, just as more electric sparks crackled around the doorjamb. Then the door banged open, and Grunze stepped in, aiming his stun gun. Kat and Verinne stumbled in behind him, firing sticky-string at random, and Winston followed, blasting the ceiling with his laser pistol.

"Grunzie, stop," I implored. "There's no need for aggression."

Grunze slammed Juani against the wall, then zapped Geraldine's bare foot with his stun gun. Kaioko crept across the floor to her injured husband, and when Vlad tried defend her, Grunze tossed the medic into the stack of benches.

"No!" Sheeba and I wailed in unison.

Liam shoved past me and reached for Grunzie's gun. The two of them wrestled like gladiators, grunting and twisting, but it was clear who would win. Grunze was fresh, well fed and thoroughly buff, whereas Liam shuddered with exhaustion. With a banshee cry, Sheeba leaped onto Grunze's back and pounded his head and ears.

"This isn't necessary," I shouted again, trying to separate them.

Howling mightily, Grunze flung Sheeba off and pinned Liam to the deck. In the confusion, I helped Shee to her feet and steered her toward the ladder well, hoping to spirit her away before anyone got seriously hurt.

"Let me go." Sheeba elbowed me and tried to pull free.

I forced her toward the ladder. "You're too young to die. You hate me now, but someday you'll—"

"I'll what? Forgive you?"

Her tone distressed me. When I briefly loosened my grip, she broke away and raced back toward her lover. But just as she crossed over the sill, Kat pumped a load of sticky-string full in her face.

"Don't," I yelled.

Sheeba halted, stunned.

"I was just trying to be helpful," Kat said.

The smart string slithered around Shee's body and trapped her in a fine, mesh cage. Then it constricted, drawing her arms and legs together till she toppled over. Liam struggled and cursed, locked in Grunze's meaty arms. Winston shot bright blue laser beams through the air. "Molto plasmic!"

"Don't move, Shee. That only makes the string draw tighter." Verinne softly uncapped a sedative spray.

The defeated juves lay still, and my triumphant friends kept their weapons aimed. Grunze planted a knee on Liam's chest. While Winston waved his pistol, Kat gave me a hearty thumbs-up and reloaded her sticky-string pump.

Verinne held the sedative close to Sheeba's nostrils, but I knelt and stopped her from spraying it. Sheeba's dewy face stared through the mesh, helpless and full of scorn. With every furious breath she drew, the strings tightened across her damp bronze cheeks.

I cradled her in my arms. "Dearest, this isn't how I meant it to be."

"Sonovabitch." Grunzie winced and rubbed his head. Kaioko had popped him with Gee's hammer.

There was a scuffle. Laser beams danced, blue bolts crackled, and in the confusion, Liam hurled Grunze backward against the counter. The young man's speed astonished me. Weak as he was, he must have been mainlining adrenaline. He jumped to his feet, rushed toward me and got hold of Sheeba. He almost ripped her fettered body from my arms. Insolent prote, his audacity maddened me.

I tugged Sheeba free and circled him, holding her body under one arm like a package. I waved Grunze off. "This punk's all mine, burly boy."

My muscles went taut, and NEM-boosted power rippled through my limbs. Zone bliss fired my neurons. When the punk feinted left, I read his intentions and dodged. This was the fight I'd lived for. I hoisted Shee on one shoulder to free my hands.

Then I kicked the punk in the face. My blow could have cracked his skull if I'd wanted. As he staggered against the table, clutching his bloody nose, I almost chuckled. His splinted leg made a funny stumping sound till he found his balance. The kid was no match for me. Not even close.

When he rushed me again, I sent him spinning with an

easy backhand. My crew cheered and whistled. But he
caught the table and kept himself from falling.

"You want more?" I taunted. "Come on, juve. Take me."

As soon as he limped within reach, I kick-punched his
ribs, and he thumped against the counter and hit his head.
Sheeba squirmed, so I hoisted her to a new position.
Slowly, Liam got to his feet. He stood weaving, wiping his
nose. Then he crouched to spring again. Stupid kid.

Sheeba was still wriggling and fighting me, despite the
entangling string. I gripped her tighter, and when Liam put
his head down to charge, I laughed and sidestepped him.
More cheers from my crew. But Liam swung around and
caught hold of Sheeba's shoulders.

"Thieving brute." I held fast to Shee's hips and tried to
sling him off. He clung to her like glue.

As Sheeba twisted and scratched at me, the string cut
across her face—like *bars*. And I almost dropped her. Then
my mind narrowed to one goal: Break Sheeba free. Step by
step, I lugged her backward toward the door. Liam's boots
skidded across the deck because he wouldn't let go, and
blood streamed from his nose. What an idiot. Couldn't he
see he'd lost?

"Back off, juve. Don't make me hurt you worse."

The punk said nothing. His jaws quivered with strain as
he held on to Sheeba.

When Kaioko touched my sleeve, I brushed her off.
We'd almost reached the ladder well. Sheeba weighed
nothing in my powerful arms. She shuddered as my grip
tightened around her waist, and I jerked her hard to loosen
Liam's hands.

Vlad picked himself up and crawled toward me.
"Sheeba Zee doesn't want to go."

I ignored the medic and yanked her left and right. Incredibly, Liam still clung to her. As I took another step
backward, she moaned with a soft, throttled sound, and for
half a second, my grip slackened. Her moan almost sev-
ered my concentration.

"Be calm, blade. Let her stay," Juani said from the floor.

The boy's head was bleeding, and he couldn't seem to move. He distracted me.

"If she stays, it's certain death," I hissed through my teeth.

"Death always certain," Juani said.

Sheeba's body stretched out between Liam and me like a failing link in a chain. With my strength, I could have torn her in two. But it was my grip that broke, not Liam's embrace. My hands dropped, and he fled with her to the far side of the table. While I stood there like a fool.

Gently, he peeled the bars of sticky-string away and kissed her face. His mouth sought out each red welt, and his fingers searched through her hair, untangling the angry threads. I turned away and stared at my trembling hands— and I tried to swallow the bitter taste rising in my throat.

"Fuck this." Grunze knocked the table aside and lifted Liam off his feet. "Get her, Kat."

Kat and Verinne darted in and grabbed Sheeba, while Win painted the walls with his laser, leaving blistered swaths in the steel.

"She's ours. Major score!" Kat crowed.

"Award-winning Reel," Verinne said proudly.

"Wait," I mumbled. "I can't do this again."

Grunze raised his fist in a victorious salute. "This is what we came for. Huah! We put these agitators *down*."

"No, this is too ugly." I swallowed the rising taste of ly-chee nuts. "We're making a mistake."

"Always such a clown. Come on, girls." Grunze covered Liam with his stun gun while Kat and Verinne backed toward the ladder well, dragging Sheeba, bound and gagged.

"It's over," I said. "Our time is over."

My crewmates laughed and kept moving. They didn't understand. I barely understood myself. But I knew there could be no half measures. This was not the time for moderation. So I batted the gun from Grunze's hands.

When its barrel shattered, Grunze's wild, questioning eyes met mine. "What the shit, sweet-pee?"

Before he could react, I seized Winston's pistol and

broke it in half. Winny blinked and staggered against the doorjamb. "Did we make a new bet?"

I slammed Kat's pump against the wall, where it burst into splinters. The load of sticky-string pooled on the floor like an alien creature.

While Liam recovered Sheeba, Kat backed away. "You've gone crazy. We're your crew."

"It's all about Sheeba, isn't it?" Verinne said quietly as she handed me her sedative spray.

"This isn't meant to hurt," I answered. Then I put all the Agonists to sleep.

They fell like broken dolls, and a scent of witch hazel hung in the air when I finished. I stood among the wreckage of their bodies, clutching the half-empty canister of Sleep-Eze. My crewmates. Closing my eyes didn't help. When I opened them again, Sheeba and Liam watched me as they might watch a madman.

I dropped to the floor, understanding at last how this surf would play out. These were the resources I'd gone to seek. The Agonists. They'd been collecting NEMs as long as I had, and their blood ran thick with nanobugs. I drew Sheeba's ankh from my pocket, pushed up my sleeve and sliced a deep cut in my arm. Warm blood splashed to the floor, cleaning bright silvery circles on the steel deck. I held out my dripping arm to Sheeba.

28

RED FRUIT

"When our memories outweigh our dreams,
we have grown old."
—BILL CLINTON

Liam was the first to move. He frisked Grunze, then the others, searching for hidden weapons. Vlad and Kaioko rose groggily and tried to revive the unconscious Geraldine, while Sheeba freed herself from the last shreds of string and hurried to check Juani's head wound.

"Don't harm them," I warned Liam as he prowled among my crew.

Instead of answering, he fell to his knees and almost fainted. Sheeba made him sit down and put his head back to stop the nosebleed. While Vlad gave first aid, Kaioko made Geraldine sit still and rest—and drink a full glass of water.

Twenty minutes later, I lay on a mattress in sick-ward, watching Vlad set up the bloodletting gear. The wound I'd sliced earlier had already healed, but my NEMs flowed readily through Vlad's needle. Perhaps the little healers felt affinity for medical gear. Across from me lay eight stricken adolescents, the latest to fall sick. In the dim yellow light, Sheeba stooped over their mattresses and checked their pulses.

"How fast can he give blood?" she asked Vlad. "We'll need a lot."

The medic shook his head. "Two liters every fifty-six days. That the rule."

"Well, I'm a rule-breaker from way back," I joked.

"Nass, we'll need more." Sheeba nodded toward the anteroom where my crew still lay unconscious. Her intention was clear. She wanted to draw blood from the Agonists.

I still could have objected. Maybe I should have. But then an amusing thought struck me—I was in a weird mood. In bygone times, didn't doctors leech blood from geriatric patients to improve their health? "Two liters apiece," I answered. "No more."

So we lay there in sick-ward, the five of us, top-ranked war-surfing crew in the northern hemisphere, stretched out like a row of carcasses in a morgue. It took over an hour to complete the procedure, and every fifteen minutes, I had to give my pals another whiff of Sleep-Eze.

Vlad siphoned our crimson elixir into clear plastic water sacks, and Sheeba piled them in the anteroom like glistening red fruit. Shee moved briskly, all business, but sometimes as she passed me, her wide, stirring eyes lingered on my face.

After she balanced the last ruddy sack on top of the pile, Liam and Vlad moved my unconscious friends out of sick-ward and carried them down to my old cell on Deck One. Liam said they would feel more at home in full Earth gravity. I tottered along behind. My glass man replaced my vital juices much faster than the normal rate, so I felt only slightly nauseous as I watched them arrange my friends comfortably on the cold steel floor. Geraldine locked them in and took the key away. But I didn't need a key. I sat outside in the hall waiting for them to wake up.

"What will you tell them?" Shee leaned against the wall opposite, studying her broken fingernails and occasionally biting off the loose bits. Vlad had returned to his lab, and Liam was patrolling the hull. We were alone.

I tucked my legs together in a lotus cross. "Guess I'll extemporize. I didn't exactly write a speech."

"Nass . . ." Her skin gleamed with sweat, and exhaustion showed in every line of her slim young body. Dried tears streaked her smudged olive cheeks like veins of gold.

In the grimy uniform, she looked more beautiful than ever. "Those things I said before . . ."

"You were right."

"No I wasn't. What you did for these people—"

"For you, Shee."

"You have a sublime multiplex soul."

"Like a cinema." I smiled. Marry me, Sheeba. The words were on my lips, but I couldn't say them.

She drew my head against her collarbone, and my nose found its inevitable sanctuary under her chin, my favorite spot in the known universe. She whispered, "We found it, didn't we? The dark."

"Will you come home now?"

"This is my home," she murmured, almost too quietly to hear. Although that was the answer I expected, it fell like a death blow. Then she said, "Stay with us."

Love triangles are not healthy, Shee. Not when I'm the third heel. I didn't say that, of course. "I can give one liter an hour—that's the quickest my glass man can brew replacements. How much more blood do you need?"

"I'm not sure." She drew away, calculating. "It's all guesswork. I think we have enough for ten or twelve people so far. But you're the only one with Type-O, so we can't do straight transfusions. Vlad says we'll have to isolate the NEMs. We're going to try recycling the blood through a hydroponic vat to strip out the A and B proteins."

"You're putting their blood into the garden?"

"Just one vat. We'll recycle it as liquid nutrient and let people drink it." Abruptly, she gripped her short black-blond hair in both hands, and fresh tears leaked from her eyes. "We're working with primitive equipment, and we don't know what the hell we're doing. We'll probably screw up—"

"Shhh. You'll do fine. Vlad's smarter than he looks, and you, you're brilliant." I put my arms around her broad, square shoulders, and we rocked gently on the corridor floor. "Darling girl, you can do anything you want. I have complete faith in you."

"Really?" She bit her lower lip. "Do you think we'll ever find what caused this disease? Vlad suspects the fungus, but I think it's the shaking."

I look at her quizzically.

"You know, the orbital adjustment," she said. "Repeated hard jolts like that can cause neurological damage and mood disorders. I browsed an article once. The brain actually bounces inside the skull and gets bruised."

I wondered. Our scientists hadn't thought of that possibility.

Behind us, someone was banging on the cell door and yelling loud complaints. Sheeba grimaced. "Kat's awake."

"Time to face my demons," I said with a gloomy smile. Then I gave her shoulders a squeeze. "Are you sure—"

She laid her finger across my lips. Then she bounded to her feet and rubbed her face with the back of her hand. "See you upstairs." As she galloped around the curving hall, she turned sideways and yelled, "I love you!"

Unspoken words echoed in my heart. I will make amends, Shee. I promise.

"Fuck you, Deepra. Let us OUT."

With a deep sigh, I faced the cell door, clutching Verinne's nearly empty sedative spray and Grunzie's stun gun, just in case our discussion got out of hand. "Step back, and don't try anything. I'm armed."

Once inside, I saw that weapons would not be necessary. My friends couldn't stand up without twisting and falling. The Coriolis effect, combined with the wooziness of blood loss and Sleep-Eze, had turned the Agonists into slapstick comedians.

"Sodder," Grunze muttered, banging into the W wall.

"Beast." Kat's feet slid out from under her body.

"What is this spooky place?" Winston asked from the floor.

At length, they settled into their blankets and glared at me. While they sucked down Heaven's water and devoured cold Provendia stew, I leaned against the door gripping my gun. I didn't need the glass man's help to invent lies. Nasir

Deepra was fully capable of fictionalizing. This time, though, I stuck to the facts. I told them we'd taken their blood to help employees.

Kat's face turned purple. Verinne stared in disbelief, and Winston dribbled stew down his chest. "So I played a little trick on you," I said. "No harm done."

"Knifed us in the back." Grunze's bald scalp clenched in angry knots. He tried to get up, but spun and tripped. "After what we've been through together. I never saw this coming. Nasir, we're quits."

"You don't mean that, Grunzie boy."

"I'm confused," said Win. "Are you an employee now? Were you demoted?"

"Shoulda been." Grunze tried to ram me, but he spun sideways and stumbled.

I stuck the gun in my waistband and showed them my empty hands. "Have I done you any material damage? You'll have eternal youth, remember? I'll give you my mutant bioNEMs, and you'll be beautiful forever."

"Just another lie." Kat threw her spoon at me, and when it swerved west and trailed a loop of red dribble, Kat's eyes opened wider than they had in years.

Verinne crawled toward me, leaning into the spin. She must have memorized her research on the Coriolis. With no tears to moisten her eyes, she squinted painfully. "You've just perpetrated the foulest crime I can think of. You've betrayed our friendship in the worst way."

"Cara," I whispered.

Verinne arched one eyebrow. "You're staying here with Sheeba, aren't you?"

When I nodded, four hardened senior execs gazed at me like lost children. Their faces suffused with fright, confusion and obscure envy.

"I always knew you loved her best," said Kat.

"You're breaking up the Agonists?" Grunze tottered to his feet and grabbed my neck in his beefy hand. "You don't need her. Come with us. We'll do gnarly surfs."

For an instant, I wanted to. When had I made the decision to stay? I didn't remember exactly. Was the glass man fiddling with my thoughts again? No, that was mystical fizz. The glass man wasn't real.

Verinne's rough fingers scraped my skin. "Nasir, if this is a love offering, it's too much. Sheeba doesn't think about you that way."

"You're the only one who can't see it," Grunze said.

My spine stiffened. "I'm old enough to make up my own mind."

"You're a romantic fool, Nasir Deepra." Verinne closed her eyes.

Win bumped against me. "Can I come visit you guys? Like on weekends?"

"No, Win. We won't be back." Katherine was right. They wouldn't want to return, and the Heavenians would not welcome them.

"At least get a decorator in here." Grunze rolled his brawny shoulders and scowled at the walls. I saw him wipe tears. "This place is a fucking black hole."

A little later, Sheeba cold-packed a liter of my blood to give the Agonists. They would sneak my mutated NEMs quietly back to Nordvik and, well hidden from the copyright police, they would try to tease out the secrets of immortality. Kat thought the whole thing was a waste of time, but Verinne believed me. And Grunze wanted to. He wisecracked about trying it out on Winston first.

I used to joke with them that life was an in-flight movie to distract us from the truth—that we're sailing through thin air with no support but our own forward motion. Now I know that's wrong. Life is a war surf.

We set our clocks at zero and skip bare-assed into the zone. People die, the conflict never ends, time is always running out and we risk everything we value on foolish bets.

But sometimes we find molto amazing crewmates.

"Remember, you're my trustees," I said.

"Rest assured, Nass." "We'll take care of things." "No problem." "Can I have your movie collection?"

Shee and I escorted the Agonists up to the secret airlock on Deck Five. Juani had picked them each a bundle of fresh veggies, and Kaioko gave them fragrant dried herbs. My friends accepted the gifts with dubious side glances. Then we exchanged insults and clumsy hugs. And all too quickly, we said good-bye. The last to leave, Verinne silently mouthed three words no one else could hear. "Bless you, caro."

"Will they do it?" Sheeba asked as the airlock cycled for the last time.

I thought about her question. The Agonists. Would they find eternal youth? Beyond Heaven's strange influence, would my NEMs stay free enough to heal them forever? I hoped so, but it was too soon to tell.

That wasn't what Sheeba meant, though. She meant, could I trust the Agonists to serve as trustees and watch over Heaven's interests. Grunze, Verinne, Kat, Win, their faces passed across my mental screen. We'd romped together for a hundred years—and with a fresh jolt, I realized I would never see them again. Friends, lovers, rivals, we'd been everything together. For a while, we'd been the finest war-surfing crew in history.

A phrase came back to me, something I'd reeled off once to impress Sheeba. "It isn't death we fear. It's losing life." So there went my life. The airlock finished its cycle, and the Agonists were gone.

Sheeba sat on a nearby tree limb, waiting for me to answer her question.

I grinned. "Yeah, they love the idea of managing my money."

"So they'll take good care of Heaven?"

"Yes," I said, nodding, "they will."

Sheeba started rocking on the tree limb, throwing back her head and giggling. "Totally stellar! Nass, this is the best present I ever got!"

I loved seeing her so happy. This was my reward, and I memorized each fleeting detail. A minute later, she calmed down and said, "I'd better check on our experiment."

She had dissolved two liters of my friends' NEM-rich executive blood in the hydropod Juani used for seedlings. According to Win, their NEMs wouldn't mutate like mine had, but Sheeba told me the little mites were already replicating and evolving new features. Whatever catalyst they needed to make the leap, they seemed to be finding it here. Sheeba planned to skim off some of the recycled solution and drink it herself first, to test it. As risky as that sounded, I didn't object. The glass man and I knew it would work.

"I'll stay here for a while and play with the toads," I said.

Shee nodded. "You'll be down soon to give more blood? Every liter helps."

"Sure. I'm timing it." I tapped my new wrist-watch, a gift from Winston.

Sheeba smiled. Then we gazed at the luxuriant foliage surrounding us. Solar beams roved like sentinels, and waxy blossoms perfumed the damp air. Any minute, the misters would come on and shower us. We seemed to be alone in the garden primeval. The toads hadn't shown their faces yet. They were waiting for the all clear from Juani.

"Wish we could save more of them," Sheeba said.

I didn't answer.

She wiped her nose. "Well, a few are better than none. Thank you, Nass. You did this. You helped me find the dark." She gestured at the leafy vines, dappled in sunlight. "If it wasn't for you, I would still be a twit in skin dye, giving hand-jobs to rich old stiffs. I'll see you below." With that, she swung down through the jungle and disappeared in greenery.

I stretched out on my tree limb, clasped my hands behind my head and smiled. Out of the mouths of babes. In the light gravity, it was easy to stay balanced on the limb. Rich old stiff, she said. Well, there were worse things to be. I smiled and lay very still and waited for the toads to come out. Behind some nearby leaves, a little pink foot dangled. A few were better than none, but not good enough for my Sheeba. For her sake, I intended to save them all.

29

RE-ZERO

"What is life? It is the flash of a firefly in the night. It is
the breath of a buffalo in the wintertime. It is the little
shadow which runs across the grass and loses itself
in the sunset."
—CROWFOOT, NATIVE AMERICAN WARRIOR AND ORATOR

"Where were you born, Shee?"
We were walking together along a downtown
street in Nordvik, on one of those rare nights when I let
Sheeba draw me out of my cozy tower. She'd persuaded
me to attend a film festival. The tickets were expensive and
hard to get, molto fashionable. And Shee was bubbling
over, telling me about the actors, quoting movie reviews
verbatim. She couldn't simply walk at my side. She had to
jiggle and dance and play chase with the adversects
buzzing around us like bright laser butterflies. Her peals of
laughter rippled through the conditioned evening air.

As we walked hand in hand along the central mall, audio messages tinkled around us, and shop windows projected enticing scents. The condo towers sparkled high
above like dark, smoky crystals. Traffic was light. A few
cyclists and blade boarders. Aircars streaked overhead.
Hardly any other walkers were out. This was an executive
section, no protes allowed. As a rule, we execs preferred to
take exercise under professional supervision.

"So where, Shee? In America?"

My question changed her mood. She grew quiet and
tense. Could my Sheeba be sulking? For several meters, we

walked in silence, swinging our linked hands, and I racked
my mind trying to understand how I'd upset her. I was just
about to walk into a shop and buy her an apology gift when
she spoke again.

"I wasn't born, beau. I was gestated."

Her bitter words stopped me. She turned away and
rapped her knuckles against a plastic lamppost, again and
again, as if she meant to leave dents. What had sparked this
sudden fit of temper? Sheeba wasn't the moody type. She
was sunny, effervescent, carefree. That's what we all liked
about her.

"Execs don't bear children," she continued, punishing
the lamppost. "My parents were anonymous donors. They
probably never met. Bank of America designed my zygote
as an investment, to meet a projected shortage of physical
therapists."

"Ah."

"I'm still paying off my nurture loan. Twenty-five years
to go."

"Ah."

I tried to think of something cheerful to say. Well, it was
no secret that most executive infants came from DNA
banks these days. With our lengthening years, we execs no
longer needed heirs in the same way as before, and the nuclear family had gone out of fashion. Live childbirth was
anathema. What executive woman would submit to that in-
dignity? When well-heeled execs wanted progeny, they
consigned the gestation to a private crèche, then farmed out
the offspring to specialized training facilities. That happened rarely though. Most executive young were brought
to term by commercial banks as speculative investments,
to meet gaps in the skill pool.

Sheeba and I left the mall and wandered into an arbore-
tum. Tiny white lights winked among the artificial trees,
and animatronic birds pecked at the turf.

"I'm a replacement part. Machines could do what I do.
But senior execs like to get their rubdowns from pretty
young girls of their own class." She kicked the base of a

fountain. Then with a grimace of pain, she dropped to the sidewalk and rubbed her toe.

Before that night, I had never seen her sulky. An impish smile almost always lighted her face. But in the shadows of that park, her eyelids creased with weeping. She snuffled and rubbed her nose and made awful sounds. I stood by, unsure what to do. Her behavior left me dumbfounded. Finally, I sat beside her on the unsanitary public sidewalk and put my arm around her shoulders.

"Shhh. Everything will be all right. You're a very good physical therapist."

That made her cry even louder. Ye icons, how does a man of my years comfort a weeping young girl? In lieu of a better plan, I talked at random.

"What does it matter how you were born? You're alive, right here, right now, in the present moment. Seize it, Shee. Ride the adventure. Look at this cheesy fountain, these plastic trees, this bench with the fake birds. It's an absolute comedy. Let yourself be amused. Every instant is like gold spilling through your hands. Spend it, Shee. Forget the past. Make yourself up as you go."

Sheeba buried her face in my tunic and squeezed me so hard, my spine popped. What she said then, I forgot for a long time. Just a few words muttered indistinctly into the folds of my tunic. I put the phrase from my mind. You might say I edited the memory. But now and here on this last night of my life, Sheeba's words come back clear and full.

"Nasir, I wish you were my dad."

• • •

In the anteroom to sick-ward, the four ceiling globes are beginning to flicker. That means Heaven is rising from behind the Earth, and the first rays of sunlight are warming Juani's generator, sending a trickle of power through the grid.

So, finally, the time has come. This is my last dawn, this feeble electric burn. I would not have chosen this fetid anteroom to spend my last four hours. I wait here because

Sheeba asked me to. She's in sick-ward, caring for her patients, and she said she might need me. But I'm growing restless. Anticipation crackles through my nerves. Minutes (epochs) pass, the emergency fluorescent tube shuts off, and a blessed incandescence warms the air.

Quietly, the door to sick-ward opens, and Shee pokes her head through. "The power's back up."

"I see."

"You can still change your mind. No one will blame you."

"Shhh. It's time."

All through the night, I've been donating blood steadily, and though the glass man replaces my life-fluid at record speed, I still can't give more than one liter an hour. When Vlad channels my sanguine juice into the hydroponic vat, it merges at once with the liquid nutrient and ferments into a rich violet wine, as dark as ichor. And it literally teems with bioNEMs. Shee and Vlad have used it to immunize thirty people here.

But other youngsters are falling sick. I can't give blood fast enough to save everyone. So my inevitable solution falls into place. Yes, I'm the one who chose this, not the glass man. He's a figment, a convenient metaphor, not a reasoning soul. I feel very sure of this.

Geraldine stomps in from the ladder well. Her handsome brown face twists in a sneer, and she turns her back on me. Her right arm flops in its sling. Kaioko stands beside her, and there's a bit of anxious whispering. It's clear the young married couple has rehearsed some scene.

With a sigh, Geraldine wheels around and scowls at the wad of gauze taped inside my elbow. "You not as slimy as I thought." Then she shakes her head at Kaioko and stomps out. Her apology makes me smile. Kaioko grins and waves, then follows her husband.

As they leave, Juani squeezes through the door, kneading a ball of sticky-string between his palms. A white bandage encircles his head. "Blade, you keep cutting both sides, sooner later, you get dull."

I laugh. "Wise words."

His eyes narrow to slits, and his furry unibrow bunches over the bridge of his nose. "Can Gee go borrow your space suit? She got more leaks to patch on the hull."

"Why didn't she ask? She was just here."

Juani rubs his shoulderblades against the doorjamb, scratching some itch. I have a hunch it's not Gee who wants the EVA suit. Despite his vertigo, the boy still dreams of spacewalking.

"Sheeba," I say, "isn't there some drug to prevent spacesickness?"

"Yeah, procyclizine, but we don't have any."

"Next time you talk to Chad, tell him to send some. Charge it to petty cash."

Juani plays with his ball of sticky-string, pretending not to hear, but I notice the dimple in his cheek. Before he leaves, he gives me a jovial, palm-to-palm slap, the prote style of handshake. "Be calm, Nass. We recycle. You'll see."

"Are you ready?" Sheeba says.

"Funny, after 248 years, I still want one more minute."

Sheeba glances back into sick-ward, where her despondent young patients lie on their mattresses, refusing food and water. Indecision furrows her golden brow.

I push up from the floor and stagger against the work counter. My legs have gone to sleep, so I shake them to stop the pins and needles of returning circulation. "I'd like to go up to the garden for one last look. Is there time for that?"

"Sure." Sheeba kneels beside me and rubs my stiff legs till the pain goes away. "We'll be here when you're ready."

"How will you do it?" I gaze down at the top of her hair. Her dark roots are crowned in shining gold.

When she realizes what I'm asking, her face tilts up, and her eyes brim with moisture. "It won't hurt, I promise. Vlad will synthesize a gas like they use in the—you know—the chamber."

"The euthanasia chamber," I say.

She drops her head and continues to massage my legs. "He says it'll be like going to sleep."

"That's fine, Shee."

"I hope your bioNEMs don't resist the sedative—"

"They won't fight."

I say this with absolute certainty. The glass man desires this solution. Deep urges stir, reassuring me. For the NEMs, this will be transubstantiation. When my body is liquefied to feed the garden, the NEMs' crystal lattices will branch outward in brave new fractal veins of symbiosis. They'll multiply through every leaf and flower, every root and seed, every living cell. As long as this satellite orbits Earth, the glass man will thrive, and his silicon bloom will glow in the healthy faces of all the people here.

I know this future. My entire organism yearns for it. But—how curious—I still want one more minute, one last look around, one final chance to gather my thoughts. Because for Nasir Deepra, this is the end.

"Thank you, Shee. I can walk now."

Her arms encircle my knees, and she clings to me.

"Shhh." I loosen her fingers. "We've talked this out. You understand my reasons."

Sheeba weeps. "I'll miss you so much."

"Let go of my legs. That's right. Let go." I speak to her tenderly, a father to his daughter. Then I lift her face in my hands and absorb her image—as if, by trying hard enough, I can forge memories that will survive the obliteration of my neurons. Pushing her away feels like letting go of my last handhold. But this is no parting. I am not saying good-bye.

Deck Five is deserted. They've moved the youngsters back to Deck One, where the Earth-normal gravity will help their bodies grow strong. I knew this before, but still it saddens me not to see them playing. Juani and Gee are occupied in the solar plant. Kaioko and Vlad tend the sick. Liam stands guard on the hull. Everyone has a task to perform. Soon, I will, too.

But for now, I spring from the deck and fly through the near weightlessness, catch a tree limb and whirl in a playful arc. The mister nozzles come alive, wetting my skin, and I dance with the rainbows. In this perfumed air, I feel free and young, strong enough to live for centuries. I bound and leap through the vines and pick a waxy flower. Then I rest on a branch to gaze at the blossom's interlacing petals.

The kids should build a treehouse here. It would be fun. Yes, I should tell them about the treehouse my brother and I built in Calcutta. A private club for our friends. High above the world, we drank Coca-Cola and spied on Mrs. Vajpee next door. I should draw a sketch so they'll know how it looked. . . .

But they'll invent their own designs.

Dr. Bashevitz's portrait glimmers at me from the algae-stained sheathing of his vat. In the changing light, his mad green eyes seem to smile. He's here, Juani said. We recycle. I reach into the vat and slide my fingers among the wet roots.

Old age is not defined by physical years. It's a perspective. As long as we see choices ahead and time to correct our mistakes, we remain young. It's when our choices are complete and our mistakes beyond correction that we understand what a lifetime is. I have never felt that until now.

But there is someone raking leaves. I hold still and listen. Through the mesh of greenery, I see him cleaning one of the vats. It's for my funeral. That must be Juani performing one last duty in my honor. Should I disturb him and risk the awkwardness or quietly back away?

Loneliness urges me to push through the flora and say, "Good morning."

But it's not Juani. It's him, the chief of thugs. "Nasir, I thought that was you."

The humidity has driven him to strip out of the white EVA suit. It's hanging near the vat, and he bends to his work in a cutoff prote uniform, unzipped to his navel. A thin, pale, haggard young man with a thatch of tawny chest hair.

This isn't who I wanted to see. "I thought you were outside."

"I was," he says. "The gunship's gone. But there's another ship. The markings say *Deuteronomy*."

"That would be the repair crew." I perch on a tuft of emerald moss near the vat. "Chad hired them to fix your hull."

He nods, skimming heavy black clumps of plant debris from the vat. His untidy braid keeps falling forward, and he has to fling it behind his shoulder. A roving solar beam outlines his hawkish profile. "How long your friends keep their promises?"

"I don't know."

He nods and scowls at his work. Raised in the bitterness of Heaven, he has no trust in the future. He's still too skeptical to hope. Sheeba will change that.

I say, "You want the truth? The Agonists are fickle. They enjoy this game for now, but at some point, they'll grow bored. My assistant Chad will stick with you though. I feel pretty certain about him."

"The only thing certain is dying," Liam mutters.

"Maybe. I used to think so."

For once, he breaks out in a long speech, and his proud baritone startles the leaves. "We living here in a crumbly old tank, circling a planet we can't live on. Got no air but what we make, no water or food but this garden. Killing sun on one side, killing cold on the other. Our sensors don't work. How we have any future? We can't even see where we are."

"But that's a good sign. My friends are maintaining the Net blockade for your protection."

He doesn't like that. I can tell from the hard set of his mouth, he's growing impatient with this talk. He lifts another rakeful of leaves, and black drops fly away in the minimal gravity. His muscles strain to catch them and guide them back to the bucket at his feet. Soon, with the glass man's help, he won't have to strain over work like this. It almost makes me laugh to think what a legacy I'm leaving this twentysomething punk.

"Did you free up those cargo doors like I asked."

"Not yet. I will," he says without looking up.

"There'll be some deliveries."

"I'll take care of it."

"Don't put it off."

He doesn't answer. His labor is rhythmic and graceful, despite his impatience. I enjoy watching, but the longer he remains silent, the angrier I grow. Certain parting words would be appropriate. Haven't I given him my beloved Sheeba, all my worldly possessions and soon my very life? Ye graven gods, I've made this punk my heir. At the very least, he could show gratitude. On impulse, I almost blurt an insult, but then he raises his blond head and gives me one of those rare, thoughtful smiles.

"I'll be good to her."

The insult clogs my mouth, and I have to chew and swallow before I can answer. "If you don't, I'll haunt you from my grave."

His smile widens, and he leans on his rake. "Sheeba be happy here. She live a long time. We keep her safe." Then he gestures at the foliage surrounding us. "You be here, too."

I bark a laugh. "After you eat me and drink me, I'll be a risen god."

Liam shrugs. "We respect you."

He's trying to comfort me. I should let him. What comes after death? I don't know.

He pulls a sieve through the dark tank, stirring liquid gurgles. The smell is sour and vivid. "I love her," he says, "as much as you."

"Yes."

I watch him prepare my tomb, the glass man's cradle. Green liquid sloshes out of the white vat, and it's so droll, it belongs on the Reel. Then a new idea occurs to me, brilliant and unexpected. It flashes outward in blinding epiphany. I see the glass man as a newborn, growing, learning. Who knows how he'll mature? I imagine his sentinel NEMs migrating beyond the garden, patrolling Heaven's hull and healing breaches, the same way he healed that rip in my space suit. I see him living inside the steel, deflecting radiation and superintending the production of electricity. Someday, my strange descendant may steer a new course through the void. It's possible.

Minutes lengthen into shadows, and dappled sunbeams play through the vines as I sit beside my funeral vat watching Liam rake leaves. In my hand, Sheeba's golden ankh sparkles. I polish it with my thumb. This surf is done. The bets are closed, and it's time to re-zero the clock. I've arrived at a place without past or future, and I ride this moment with frightening agonies of hope. Now is here.

ARE YOU READY FOR THE FUTURE?

Hyperthought
by M.M. Buckner
0-441-01023-7

Nominated for the 2003 Philip K. Dick Award

The world of 2125 is extremely toxic. It is ruled by huge corporations called Coms. The workers, or Protes, are enslaved. Humanity's only hope is a neurosurgical technique that could unlock the mind's power to alter reality—or destroy it.

"ONE OF THE BEST DEBUT NOVELS I'VE READ IN A LONG TIME."
—ALLEN STEELE

And don't miss
Neorolink
0-441-01188-8

Available wherever books are sold or at penguin.com

A837